HORROR CLASSICS

VOLUME 1

THOMAS M. MALAFARINA

H. P. LOVECRAFT • W. W. JACOBS • EDGAR ALLEN POE • MARY SHELLEY

HELLBENDER BOOKS

an imprint of Sunbury Press, Inc.
Mechanicsburg, PA USA

an imprint of Sunbury Press, Inc.
Mechanicsburg, PA USA

Copyright © 2020 by Thomas M. Malafarina.
Cover Copyright © 2020 by Sunbury Press, Inc.

For information about special discounts for bulk purchases, please contact Sunbury Press Orders Dept. at (855) 338-8359 or orders@sunburypress.com.

To request one of our authors for speaking engagements or book signings, please contact Sunbury Press Publicity Dept. at publicity@sunburypress.com.

ISBN: 978-1-62006-786-4 (Trade Paperback)

Library of Congress Control Number: 2020931524

FIRST HELLBENDER BOOKS EDITION: February 2020

Product of the United States of America
0 1 1 2 3 5 8 13 21 34 55

Set in Adobe Garamond
Designed by Crystal Devine
Cover by Lawrence Knorr
Edited by Lawrence Knorr

Continue the Enlightenment!

AS WITH ALL OF MY BOOKS, this book is dedicated to my amazing wife, JoAnne. Who, despite the fact that she detests horror and thankfully does not read a single word of what I write (which is most definitely a good thing), she encourages and supports my horror fiction endeavors. She is the most amazing woman God has placed on this earth, and somehow, I was fortunate enough to have her fall in love with a lug like me. Who could ask for anything more from life?

CONTENTS

INTRODUCTION

In early 2015, shortly after the release of my short story collection called *Malformed Realities Volume 1*, my publisher Lawrence Knorr of Sunbury Press contacted me with an idea for my consideration. He told me that a number of classic horror stories by masters such as Edgar Allen Poe, H. P. Lovecraft, and many others were now part of the public domain. He had an idea for me to do a "favorites" collection, one that would highlight some of my favorite stories I have written alongside some of my favorites from the masters.

At first, it took me a bit of thought to try to wrap my head around the concept. I don't know why, but sometimes I have a blind spot for some ideas, and I have to chew on them for a bit. I liked the idea of a sort of "best of" collection of my stuff. Unfortunately, since I love all of my stories, a "best of" would be a tough call. So I decided instead to choose those which I felt fit best into this particular type of anthology. Still, I couldn't quite comprehend why we would want to add other classic public domain stories to the collection. (As JoAnne often tells me, "It's all about you, isn't it?")

Then it hit me. Chances are there are people out there who love reading horror (hopefully my horror) but have never taken the time to read these classics or quite possibly read anything at all by these masters. And to be perfectly honest, I can't blame them. The language is often flowery and so different from how we write today that they seem to be written in a foreign tongue. They are also much less in your face than we modern writers tend to be. (Who doesn't love a good gory scene?) But I believe if you put yourself in the right mood and take your time reading their works, they can still be quite enjoyable.

For example, as any regular of mine knows, I've been a life-long lover of the horror genre. I can still recall as an eight or ten-year-old finding my oldest sister's copy of the works of Edgar Allen Poe. She was in high school at the time. Needless to say, for a little horror nerd like me, what outside of a copy of Playboy could pose more of a temptation than the writings of Poe? I opened the book and looked at the table of contents. I saw something called "The Tell-Tale Heart," which is included in this collection. I sat reading it alone in our living room, and even though it was the middle of the day, this story blew me away. I recently re-read it, and unfortunately, I've become so hardened to horror that the original effect was lost. But it is still a great, masterfully written work and one I think you will enjoy.

And if there is one story which has been interpreted many, many times throughout the years, it's been "The Monkey's Paw" by W. W. Jacobs. They even did an episode of *The Simpsons* for Halloween based on this classic tale.

I also feel I should make something clear right from the start. Putting myself in the same collection with these masters is not an ego thing, nor is it to suggest in any way that I think I deserve to be in such distinguished company; because I don't and few writers, even the best of them don't either. As such, I prefer to think of myself as the opening act for a major headliner, you know, the warm-up act. It seemed like a pretty good concept. I would set the mood and whet the reader's appetite with a few of my own original favorite tales of horror, then turn the stage over to the headliner. It seemed like a workable concept to me, and worst-case scenario would be that if for whatever reason the reader couldn't get into the main act but really enjoyed my writing, they wouldn't be disappointed because this collection is chocked full of tons of my own stuff.

So you'll see this collection set up in the following manner: three of my stories followed by one from a master, usually along a similar theme. Then the sequence will repeat with my stories followed by another story by another master. And yes, I realize it has taken me several years to make this collection a reality. I've been a very busy boy, and for one reason or another, I've started and then set aside this book more times than I care to mention. I've also written more recent stories that I think would work in this book as well as those, which I've included, but I think doing that would make this much too large a volume. That being said, I hope you enjoy the following collection of short stories and take the time to read what the true masters have to offer as well.

Thomas M. Malafarina
December 2019

SPIDER MINE

By Thomas M. Malafarina

It was supposed to be a simple forty-five minute guided tour of a former working coal mine. It was supposed to be entertaining, unique, uneventful, and, most importantly, safe. However, things don't always turn out according to plan, despite the fact that the Ashton, Pennsylvania Chamber of Commerce web site touted the mine tour as one of the best on the east coast.

Stephen thought as he sat fidgeting, second-guessing his decision to take part in the tour. "Chamber of Commerce, my butt . . . chamber of horrors is more like it." Stephen Jamison had been reluctant to agree to experience Ashton's "Miner's Tunnel" tourist attraction, but his girlfriend Mattie, who was a native of the small town, had harassed him into doing so. He was a bit miffed at her for putting pressure on him to take the tour and perhaps even angrier with himself for caving in to her demands. "Caving in?" he thought to himself, "Not the best choice of words when you're about to go a mile down below the earth in a mine car."

It wasn't so much that Stephen had a fear of the dark or even was significantly claustrophobic. It was more about the assortment of creepy-crawly critters he suspected might live down there in the dank, musty environment at the bottom of the mine, skittering about among its ancient rotting timbers.

In particular, he worried about those horrible eight-legged creatures he feared more than anything else, even more than the potential for being buried alive under tons of collapsed earth and suffering a slow and suffocating death.

Perhaps it was because he understood the chances of a collapse occurring were virtually non-existent, but the odds of his meeting up with that particular breed of horrifying insect would be more than likely.

He probably should have said something to Mattie about his arachnophobia, but the idea of doing so just rubbed him the wrong way. Mattie was different from most of the other girls he had known and dated. He didn't want to say she was a tomboy or was overly masculine; that might indicate some things about himself he was in no hurry to address, but she was a bit rougher around the edges than most girls were.

He had often wondered where that edge might have come from. Now that he had visited her hometown, gotten to meet her family and friends, he wondered no more. Stephen was raised as an upper-middle-class kid from the suburbs of northern Philadelphia. He had gone to a good high school and was studying at Penn State University Park Campus, where he met Mattie. She, on the other hand, was from this tough, blue-collar, working-class town, which seemed to have a bar on every other corner.

There was a roughness also inherent in the way everyone spoke in Ashton, even the women. Not to say they were crude or vulgar but different than what he was accustomed to. These people were all decedents of nineteenth-century immigrant miners from Europe, and their accents were a mix of English, Irish, Italian, Polish, and other such European backgrounds, which also gave the pronunciation of their words an equally odd roughness to it as well. Mattie still had a slight trace of the accent even though she had been away from the area for several years at school. However, Stephen noticed as soon as they returned to Ashton, and she began speaking with friends and family, that slight trace had become a much heavier accent almost immediately.

Stephen looked over at the still unopened heavy wooden doors of the mine, knowing in just a few seconds they would be opening, and he and the rest of his companions would be transported by rail down into the bowels of the earth. He felt fairly certain all precautions had been taken to ensure the safety of the mine visitors. Likewise, he assumed there would be adequate lighting, even down in the deepest recesses of the mine.

He had convinced himself that these precautions, plus the constant flow of tourists, might frighten the tiny creatures back into the shadows. But in his heart, he suspected none of these things could do much to keep them all completely away; the worms and ants and yes the spiders. After all, the mine was their home, and they had as much if not more right to be there than the humans did.

Chances were most people didn't give such creatures a second thought. However, Stephen wasn't like most people. He had a fear—a real and crippling fear of spiders. It had plagued him since childhood, and even back then, no matter how much his mother tried to convince him about how irrational his fear was, it nonetheless persisted. It stayed with him through childhood, into adolescence, and followed him into adulthood. And it was making its horrible presence apparent at this very minute.

He sat in the open passenger car, hands folded, clasped tightly between his fidgeting knees. His feet involuntarily tapped out their own nervous rhythm as if oblivious to his frantic commands for them to be still. He was one of about fifteen other tourists in their car, including Mattie. There were four cars filled with an equal number of people, all excited for the tour to begin.

Stephen was wondering why he had agreed to such a stupid idea. What had he been thinking? Was it really that important for him to appear so brave for Mattie? If they were to have a future together, shouldn't he be completely honest with her? Then he thought again of the tough edge, which seemed to surround her, her family, and everyone in Ashton. No, he realized he had to suppress his fears, or he would likely lose Mattie for good. The mine car moved slightly with a jolt, and it took everything Stephen had not to let out an involuntary screen.

His terror must have shown on his face because Mattie asked, "You ok, Stephen? Ya looked like ya seen a ghost or sometin'."

"Um . . . no . . . no . . ." Stephen stammered, "I'm, I'm fine. It was just that sudden movement—the jostling of the mine car. You know. It was a bit startling, is all."

"Maybe dis wasn't sucha good idea," Mattie said, her excitement appearing to fade with Stephen's discomfort replaced by concern. Stephen realized for the first time just how annoying Mattie's accent was suddenly becoming to him. It seemed the longer they were in Ashton, the more she reverted to what he thought of as that strange brogue.

He momentarily fought back his own discomfort and annoyance and said, "It's ok, Mattie. Really. Besides, this is your town. Surely, you must have taken this mine tour a dozen times before. Right?"

"Well." She said hesitantly, "Actually, I never did. Growin' up, well, I wuz always too sceart ta go down in da mine. Dis is a first fer me too."

"But if you didn't want to do it, then why are we here?" He asked, confused.

Mattie looked at him shyly and explained, "Well, I always wanted ta take the tour, but I was too afraid. I figgered it might be easier if I did it wit you. You kin be here ta protect me."

Stephen looked on in astonishment not only at Mattie's revelation but at her ever-increasing change in speech pattern. She was starting to sound just like everyone else in the strange town. He realized he was going to have to rethink this whole relationship once this weekend was over. He didn't think he could seriously spend the rest of his life listening to that annoying accent, no matter how beautiful Mattie might be.

But then again, maybe it wasn't her fault. Maybe it was his. Perhaps it was just his stress, which was causing him to think so irrationally. He really liked Mattie. In fact, he was fairly sure he was falling in love with her. And this was apparently who she was. This was Mattie. He had to get a grip. It must be the fear of going into the mine, causing all of these irrational feelings.

Stephen thought to himself, "Wonderful. Now not only do I have to worry about not showing Mattie how terrified I am, but I'm supposed to be her hero as well!"

Suddenly the mine doors opened, revealing a dimly lit blackened orifice as the cars began to enter the darkness. To Stephen, it looked like the giant maw of some demonic beast swallowing the cars one by one. A cold sweat began to trickle down his back. As his car passed through the opening, he instantly felt the temperature drop. They had all been given jackets and sweaters to wear because the temperature inside the mine was around sixty-five degrees all year round.

The tour guide was dressed like a nineteenth-century coal miner and was seated at the front of the car watching his passengers. Stephen suspected with all the noise from the rattle mine cars, the guide probably had to wait until a stopping point either along the way or at the bottom to offer his monologue.

Then as if Stephen somehow had willed it, the cars stopped along the downward slope, and the tour guide stood to begin speaking. His presentation was given in a coal region accent, which was even thicker and heavier than he had heard from Mattie. Stephen was only paying half attention as the man spoke about air shafts or something like that having to do with venting mine gasses up to the surface and allowing for fresh air to come in. He was too focused on looking at the one particular vent shaft itself.

The shafts were timber-framed openings about three feet square, traveling up through the earth to the surface. Stephen noticed how the timbers along the bottom portion of the square were positioned to form a ladder, obviously, so a mineworker could crawl up to perform maintenance. The shaft he was looking in was lit with bright spotlights providing illumination for about twenty feet up along the shaft. After that, all that remained was blackness.

Stephen stared into the blackness at the far end of the shaft, and for just a moment, he thought he saw something. It was only there for a split second then it was gone.

"What was that?" He thought. Surely, it couldn't have been what he thought it was. Could it? He would have sworn he saw two glowing red eyes staring directly at him from out of the darkness.

The min cars jerked as they once again began their descent further into the mine. Stephen did his best to beat down his growing anxiety. He shook his head as if to clear his mind of the image he thought he had just seen. Surely it had only been the result of his overactive imagination. On the other hand, maybe it was just a rat or something; not that a rat would be a good thing, it would still be a better alternative to the picture, which had suddenly appeared in his mind. It was that of a giant eight-legged creature, but that was ridiculous he knew.

When they reached the bottom of the mine, the narrow tunnel seemed to widen to a large cavernous area illuminated by bright lights. The tour guide announced, "Dis heer is da bottoma da mine. Ya kin all get outta yer cars 'n look 'round while I tell ya more about da mine."

One by one, the tourists left their cars and huddled together near the back of the mine. Stephen looked around, his eyes scanning the ceiling of the mine looking for . . . he wasn't exactly sure what he was looking for. Maybe it wasn't so much what he was hoping to see but what he was hoping not to see. He was hoping not to see another one of those vent shafts.

What he did see, however, almost caused his heart to stop beating in his chest. It was a spider—a big one about an inch around. I crawled upside-down along a piece of timber, its eight legs skittering across the moist beam. Stephen held back a girlish whimper that was forming in the back of his throat, fighting to escape.

The hideous creature crawled toward a large borehole in the wood, as Stephen looked on paralyzed with fear. A second before the thing entered the blackness of the hole, it stopped and turned to look directly at Stephen. He was sure he did not imagine it. The creature was looking right at him.

What happened next was worse than any nightmare Stephen had ever experienced. In his mind, he could hear a tiny voice forming. At first, it was almost non-existent, then it began to grow steadily in volume. The voice repeated, "We've been waiting for you. We are many. Come and join us." Then the creature's tiny little face seemed to morph right before Stephen's unbelieving eyes taking on something resembling an almost human-looking appearance. Just before Stephen thought he could no longer hold in his scream, the creature turned and dove into the borehole and out of sight.

He felt a tug on his arm, and Stephen's head pivoted quickly, not sure of what he might see there. To his relief, it was Mattie, pulling him in her direction.

"Check dis out, Stephen," she said, leading him away from the crowd of tourists toward the far end of the mine. "Heer's anudder onea dem vent shafts. Da guide tolt me dis one goes a mile straight up, all da way ta da surface."

Stephen didn't want to look up into the shaft, fearful of what he might see. Or, more likely, what might see him. He nonetheless reluctantly ventured a quick glance upward only to satisfy Mattie that he had done so.

"Yeah . . ." Stephen said. "Nice."

Mattie looked at him with disappointment and said, "Come on, Stephen, you hardly looked at it."

"That's alright, Mattie." He rationalized, "Seen one air vent, you've seen them all."

Mattie said slyly, "Well dat ain't necessarily true Stephen. I tink ya should look at dis one a little closer."

Stephen noticed that none of the other tourists were facing him and Mattie. They were all listening to the guide giving his presentation. He thought he saw the guide looking their way for a second. Then his attention went back to his audience. He suddenly realized he and Mattie were alone now, off by themselves in the back of the mine. A cold chill came out of now where and ran down his spine.

"Go ahead, Stephen. Look up. What's da big deal anyway? It ain't like it's gunna kill ya fer Pete's sake."

Reluctantly, Stephen looked up into the blackness of the shaft and once again saw the same two fiery red eyes materializing out of the blackness.

"M . . . m . . . Mattie . . . ?" Stephen managed to croak out.

"Wat's wrong, Stephen?" Mattie said in a voice much too calm and collected for the situation which was unfolding. "Wat da ya see up der Stephen?"

Stephen once again found himself paralyzed with fear by the glowing eyes, which were moving closer. As they did, he noticed an enormous black hairy insectile leg enter into the light. Stephen's breath caught in his throat. Soon another leg materialized, then another. He could hear Mattie's voice in the background sounding surprisingly distant.

"I might notta been completely honest wit ya, Stephen," she said as more of the creature came into view. Stephen could now see the head; its face. Oh God in Heaven, what an impossibly hideous face!

Mattie was saying, "Ya see, well I'been in dis heer mine before. Many times. In fact, dis mine is very special to me and to my friends, da members 'a my church."

"Church?" Stephen thought, "What the hell is she talking about? Can't she see this horrid thing?"

Its face was pink, hairless, and wrinkled, looking almost human had it not been for those two huge multi-faceted glowing insect eyes. Then creature opened its wide salivating mouth, revealing rows upon rows of shark-like teeth. The beast had now made its way completely into the light just a few feet directly above Stephen's head. He looked up at it helplessly as Mattie continued speaking calmly.

"Dat's ar spiritual leader up der Stephen. He provides us wit good fortune and healt. Den once a year we haffta give 'em wat he wants."

Two of the large hairy legs reach down out of the shaft and grabbed tightly to both sides of Stephen's head. It felt as if they might crush his skull.

Mattie said, "An sometimes, well sometimes he demands a sacrifice. An fortunately fer you, Stephen, you have da honor 'a bein' his sacrifice today."

Those were the last words, Stephen would ever hear. His body lifted off the ground and went silently into the vent shaft, where it met the waiting jaws of the spider creature. As his kicking feet disappeared into the ceiling of the mine, Mattie calmly smiled and quietly slipped back into the crowd of tourists boarding the cars, ready to head back out of the mine. She caught the eye of the tour guide who nodded knowingly to her. She returned the nod and gave a sly smile.

WHAT IS A MAN?

By Thomas M. Malafarina

"The good man is the friend of all living things."
—Mahatma Gandhi

"It is not death that a man should fear, but he should fear never beginning to live." —Marcus Aurelius

"Death may be the greatest of all human blessings." —Socrates

The massive creature sat silently, hunched on the chill, damp cave floor listening to the hypnotic drip, drip, dripping of water somewhere deep in the blackness, painstaking forming stalactites, and stalagmites as it had done for millions of years before. He could hear the steady thump, thump, thumping of his own oversized heart sounding like the rhythmic beating of tribal drums echoing in his mind as the water reverberated in the near silence of the cavern.

Lining the walls surrounding him were bookshelves reaching ten feet tall, overflowing with thousands of volumes containing the greatest writings in human history. Wooden creates and skids held stacks upon stacks of even more books; classic fiction, historical accounts, religious writings, and scientific journals. He had read them all, most more than once. He had acquired them over the many years, and they were among his most prized possessions.

In the darkness of a nearby alcove, an old-fashioned gramophone complete with hand crank stood ready for use along with stacks of hundreds of classic orchestral albums. When not reading, he loved to listen to music. On any available wall space remaining in the cavern, not occupied by bookshelves, priceless works of art by some of the great masters hung for his viewing pleasure along with ancient tapestries.

Near his feet, a small collection of hot coals burned—the remnants of his former fire. He would rebuild the fire up again soon, not for heat but for light so that he might read throughout the night. Presently, his huge muscular arms rested on his knees, allowing his shovel-sized hands to dangle down over tree-trunk like legs. His bucket-sized head hung low as his chin rested on his barrel chest below massive shoulders more than five feet across. Although the cave was quite cold, the chilly temperatures never bothered him.

To an uninformed onlooker, the monstrous hulking creature might appear to have been sleeping, but he was not. He never slept because he didn't need to sleep. In fact, he hadn't slept in years, perhaps decades. This particular restive position was the closest he ever came to sleeping. It was what he thought of as his thinking pose, and although his frightening physical appearance might suggest otherwise, thinking was what he enjoyed doing most.

He suddenly sat bolt upright, his eyes glowing like the embers in his fire. He remained motionless now, silent in the shadows, carefully listening to the shuffling noise coming from the front of the cave near the entrance. He immediately recognized the familiar gate he had heard so many times before. It was another one of those wretched things; the dead ones. Somehow one of the creatures must have inadvertently found its way into his cave. Adam could feel his anger growing. How dare this abomination enter his home! He would be sure to guarantee this encounter would not end well for the intruder.

Adam wondered how many of those mindless shambling creatures still remained in the world. Hundreds of them? Perhaps thousands? Possibly millions? He suspected millions might be an accurate assumption from a national perspective, but perhaps only a few hundred locally. Mankind had done an exemplary job of eradicating the monsters over the past twelve years.

The shambling creature slowly made its way across the cave and into the minimal light cast by the dwindling fire. Adam studied the thing carefully. It appeared to have once been a male, but decomposition had taken its toll, making distinguishing its gender almost impossible. Its clothing was in tatters, and it made that same low guttural growl they all made. The vile stench coming off the unholy beast was beyond repugnant. This one had obviously been decomposing for quite some time.

Adam knew well what these undead creatures; these zombies did whenever they encountered living humans. They ripped their victims to pieces, devouring their flesh and innards. He fumed at the very notion of one of these wretched things tromping about in his home. His anger continued to grow.

The undead monster advanced, stumbling about the cave, apparently unaware of his presence. Adam stood and rose to his full height of eight feet, yet still, the creature ignored him. Then again, they always ignored him. It seemed like he was invisible to them. This, too, caused him great frustration. Perhaps for reasons all his own, he felt it was better not to consider why he felt so angry with the creatures.

He bellowed in a booming angry voice, "Do you not see me, you disgusting pile of rotting meat? Here I am standing right before you. Am I not made of human flesh and blood? Do you not wish to partake of my body, you revolting spawn of Hell?"

The zombie stood and stared, not so much at Adam as through him. It was like the zombie was confused, uncertain as to what his next move should be. Adam believed the creature could hear him shouting, but for whatever reason couldn't sense him. He had tried this experiment on the undead countless times with the same futile results, and it was becoming maddening. Who was it who had said the definition of insanity was repeating the same thing over and over but expecting different results? Adam couldn't recall, but the recollection was making him question his own sanity.

A low moan came from the zombie's throat, sounding not so much threatening as bewildered. It started to turn away. With one mighty swipe of his muscular arm, Adam severed the creature's head from its body, sending the skull flying across the cave and slamming into a wall with a sickening crack. The body thudded to the cave floor. He wasn't certain exactly why separating the head from the body, or why by simply making the brain inactive killed the creatures; he just knew it worked.

He had accidentally discovered this fact many years earlier, more out of frustration than through any scientific process. He has come upon one of the monsters in the forest. It was a huge male, not as large as himself but still quite threatening in appearance. At that time, Adam was not only unaware that these creatures we're reanimated dead bodies. He also didn't know that they paid him no mind. He thought the creature was a living, breathing man and, therefore, a potential enemy. His natural assumption was to believe he would be attacked.

After all, throughout his entire life, anyone coming upon him would attack first and ask questions later.

Reaching out, Adam had grabbed onto the thing's left arm and pulled it from the socket. To his shock, no blood spurted from the stump, only a slight trickle of some viscous, puss-like fluid leaked out. The creature didn't seem even to notice his injury. Eager to end the encounter, Adam thrust his long arm outward toward his opponent's chest, penetrating his flesh with surprising ease and pulling out what he assumed would be his attacker's still-beating heart.

To his dismay, Adam held a dead gray, bloodless thing that teamed with maggots in its advanced stage of decomposition. And still the creature stood. It looked down at the hole in its chest for a moment then let out a deep growing sound. Frustrated and unsure what to do next, Adam bent down, retrieved the severed arm, then swinging it like a war club he struck the creature's head. Its spinal column snapped with an audible crack, causing it to fall to the ground. He test-kicked the fallen mass of flesh, and it remained inanimate. He made a mental note that if he ever came upon a creature such as this again, the head, probably the brainstem would be its weak link. Little did he know he would battle many more of the beasts in the years that followed.

Now, Adam bent down, grabbing this latest zombie's foot and dragging it toward the entrance of the cave. Then like a slow-moving soccer player, he used one of his own giant feet to pass the severed head along as well. At the cave entrance, Adam kicked the head hard, sending it flying for several hundred feet out through the night and into the darkness of the forest.

Still holding the zombie's foot, he began to swing the corpse around and around gaining velocity so he could fling the disgusting thing as far away as possible. During one of the rotations, the corpse took off flying hundreds of yards out into the darkness. Adam realized the body had flown before he had let go. He looked down and saw the thing's foot with exposed ankle bones jutting from tatters of moldering flesh still in his giant hand. With revulsion, he threw the foot as far away as possible then wiped his hand on his pants.

His cave, the place Adam called home, was located high up on the side of a mountain hidden by countless pine trees. He hoped the stench which accompanied the vile creatures would not be noticeable, but he had his doubts. He recalled a time not that long ago when the entire world stank of rotting flesh. Now the creatures were few and far between. In fact, these days, humans thought of them more as a nuisance than a threat.

He sniffed the air and could smell burning wood, not the scent of a nearby campfire but something much more intense. He looked out into the distance to the place where he knew there to be a good-sized town many miles away. He could see the orange glow of a fire burning out of control. It appeared as if the entire town was engulfed in the inferno.

"I can't believe they are at it again," he thought. "When will these people ever learn?"

Even now, after having survived a plague that practically wiped out mankind, humans still felt the need to be at war constantly. It was like people could only be satisfied if they were killing. And it apparently didn't matter if they were killing zombies or one another. He recalled several years after the initial outbreak when the then newly reformed federal government began offering the general public the opportunity to collect bounty money by killing zombies. Although the program had an official name, people began referring to it as a Dead Kill bounty; the idea being that you were killing something, which was already dead. Survivors suddenly realized instead of running and hiding from these deadly monsters. They could earn a decent living by killing them. That was the beginning of the end for the undead. Soon what was once an ocean of roaming undead became a river, then a stream and finally just a trickle, a fraction of what they had once been.

It was more than ten years since the zombie apocalypse had been caused by the dreaded Zombie Virus of 2043, also known as the Z43 Virus. Yet now, years after the so-called zombie wars, man was still killing his fellow man, even though the act of doing so created more living dead. The Z43 virus still existed inside every living human, remaining dormant until the time of death when it activated. Years earlier, the government put precautionary measure s into place to properly dispose of any new deceased, so they wouldn't return. But in the case of war there was no guarantee all the dead could be accounted for and would remain dead. There was a very good chance whatever skirmish had just occurred in that city miles away. There would be new monsters rising up from the ashes.

It troubled Adam how humans still seemed to have this need to kill each other. From his observations, there were basically two facets of human survivors in existence; the so-called civilized people who lived safely behind the walls of fortified cities and those called outlanders who lived like lawless savages in the wilderness outside the cities. The outlanders had turned their backs on civilized society in favor of a life free of legal restraints. The outlander societies were set up like tribes, with the strongest members leading the groups. Without laws to control their behavior for more than a decade, these survivors had reverted to a state of savagery not seen since the dawn of man. Most had even abandoned formal language, replacing it with monosyllabic gibberish nearly unintelligible. Not only were these outlanders at constant war with the humans inside the cities, but rival tribes constantly fought among themselves.

With a heavy heart, Adam wondered how many humans of both factions might have died in this latest conflict. The world had become a much different place than the one he had once known. So much had changed since his birth in 1792, or perhaps re-birth would be a better description. It was a hard fact to comprehend now in 2055, more than two and a half centuries later.

Adam didn't know if he personally carried the Z43 virus. True he was a man, but not a man like other men. He was not only different but unique. Perhaps this made him immune to the virus. It seemed to make him uninteresting to the dead ones, so perhaps that idea might be accurate. Or perhaps it might be the circumstances of his creation that caused the walking cadavers to leave him alone. He wasn't sure, but he hoped someday to find an answer. He suddenly heard groaning noises coming from the forest far off to his right. He realized more of the undead creatures must have followed the first.

His night vision was exceptional, and the bright moon further helped him see them coming. There were ten or more of the zombies in this cluster. Adam knew if he simply stood still, they would ignore him and walk by, but that would never do. They might find their way into his cave and fill it with their revolting stink. His cave was not much, but it was his home and had been for decades. He could not allow these things to defile his home.

Adam charged headlong into the mass of rotting walking corpses using arms, legs, hands, and feet to dismantle the creatures. In a mad frenzy of savage destruction, Adam cut his way through the throng, leaving not a single one of them standing.

One of the creatures had shuffled toward Adam, appearing to try to pass through him like he wasn't there. Adam slammed his massive hands against both sides of the zombie's head in a thunderous clap, sending brains exploding out of the creature's squashed mouth and eye sockets, like someone stomping on an open tube of toothpaste.

Two others were staggering about aimlessly. Adam raced toward them, driving his fist through the face of the first monster and out the back of his head. He pulled his muscular arm back, and the head separated from the thing's body but remained stuck on his hand. Adam slammed the head into the skull of the other zombie succeeding in not only breaking that creature's neck but also cracking open the zombie skull attached to his own massive hand.

Two more zombies stumbled into view, one male and the other female. Adam walked up to them, palming their heads like an NBA all-star. He lifted them both up by their skulls more than two feet off the ground as they squirmed and struggled to get free. Then he began to close his hands squeezing ever tighter. Within seconds their skulls crushed inward, sending shards of broken bones deep into their decomposing brains. Puss and grey matter oozed onto Adam's fingers.

After finishing the remainder of the herd in a fashion equally as repulsive, Adam decided it was time to clean up. He tossed the remains into the woods to join those of the others. This was a challenging task not only because of the number of creatures he had slaughtered but because of the savage way he had dismembered them. When he found himself in the throes of a rampage, nothing less could be expected. The forest floor looked like a charnel house.

Adam stood for a moment, smelling the disgusting stench of the beasts. He looked down at his hands and clothing finding them covered in blood, puss, and bits of flesh from his savage onslaught. He needed to get clean. Walking along a path he knew well, Adam made his way through the woods to a lake where he stripped naked a waded into the shallows to rinse both himself and his clothing. His flesh, a patchwork of thousands of scars connecting flesh of varying hues, seemed iridescent in the moonlight. He examined himself for injuries but found none.

Seeing himself bared to the world made Adam think about his past and his life. He recalled as he often did about the man he thought of as his father. That man had been a scientist. No, he had been much more than a scientist, he had been a creator, a genius, and in Adam's opinion, a god. Yet he had also been a cold-hearted, unfeeling man who had rejected Adam and hated him. Adam found it more than ironic that he should possess a kinder heart and more respect for humanity than the man responsible for giving him life.

He wondered not for the first time, what exactly was humanity? What is a man? Was he, himself not a man? Surely he must be as he was made from man. His father and creator had seen to that. And was he, Adam, not a good man? He considered himself an intellectual, perhaps not at the level of genius his father had attained, but he was very intelligent with love for art, science, mathematics, music as well as literature.

He was generally kind to his fellow man. Yes, he had killed in the past, both zombies and living humans, as well. Early on, his killing had been out of frustration, rage, ignorance, and misunderstanding. Later he learned to control his impulses and kill only in self-defense.

His father had not thought of him as intelligent, just the opposite. He had even refused to give Adam a name, referring to him instead as "the monster," "the wretch," "the ogre," and other such derogatory terms. And when news of his existence became public, the townspeople had called him "an abomination," "a devil," and "a thing." They had tried unsuccessfully to destroy him on more than one occasion.

But in his heart, he believed he was a man, no he knew he was a man, despite what others said to the contrary. Yes, perhaps he was a different sort of man, unique when compared to any who had come before him, but still a man. He felt his father had slighted him greatly, and, as such, he had chosen to give himself a name.

He recalled the day his father had been screaming obscenities at him and referring to him as something which had been dredged up from the bowels of hell. In one of his first fits of anger, Adam had risen up in defiance and had shouted at his father, "I ought to be thy Adam!"

He decided right then to take the name, Adam. And in further rebellion against his heartless father, Victor, he chose to use his father's surname. He proclaimed himself Adam Frankenstein. He hoped that singular act would do more to frustrate his creator than any other torture he might have imagined. And he was correct. Since then, the story of his creation had gained legendary status. Most people now referred to him simply as Frankenstein. Despite his life of solitude, his knowing this fact seemed to make somehow it all worthwhile. His father had died in disgrace, and the world that had shunned Adam was now essentially dead as well.

Since the time he had last escaped the persecution, he had led a life of lonely isolation, knowing how people would react to the sight of him. If his height and massive size were not enough to instill terror, his thousand of scars from where his doctor/father had stitched together body parts, were enough to horrify even the most tattooed and pierced of humans. Through the centuries, people around the world had claimed to see him lurking in the shadows. However, anyone who had the misfortune of actually meeting him face to face would take that knowledge to the grave with them. Adam was not happy about killing humans, but it was something that had to be done and which he had reluctantly accepted.

Even in 2053, in a world ravaged by a zombie apocalypse where rotting remnants of humanity still feasted on the flesh of the living, he knew he would be considered a horrible monster. During the past year, he had read reports of rumors stating that the Z43 virus was now mutating in living outlander humans. Rather than waiting until death to activate, the virus was causing living humans to mutate into an assortment of strange inhuman creatures, some of which supposedly were as big as he was.

Perhaps in another few decades, things would change. Maybe the virus would continue to mutate, creating a new race of creatures so disturbing in appearance that he would not seem so frightening. Until then, he had his cave, his literature, and an unquenchable thirst for knowledge to keep him occupied.

BEYOND THE MIND'S EYE

BY THOMAS M. MALAFARINA

"Imagination Is More Important Than Knowledge"
—Albert Einstein

"Imagination is the beginning of creation. You imagine what you desire, you will what you imagine, and at last, you create what you will." —George Bernard Shaw

Everything you can imagine is real." —Pablo Picasso

"So tell me, Chad, what do you think of my little lab?" Dr. Walker Bellamy asked as he showed the young man around the large and efficient research laboratory. The place wasn't what one might think of when imagining a typical lab, however. It was located in the basement of a ram-shackled abandoned three-story former classroom building, which was obviously in need of major renovation.

That evening Chad Jefferson had met with Professor Bellamy at the side entrance to the basement, which was marked with an old 1950's fallout shelter sign. At first, Chad was a bit leery about entering the basement in fear the depilated structure could possibly collapse down on both of them. The professor had assured him since the lab was in a reinforced fallout shelter, designed to provide a safe haven during a nuclear attack, the entire building could collapse, and they would still be safe.

However, Chad wasn't quite as confident. He recalled stories his father had told him about the nuclear attack drills he had routinely experienced during his grammar school days in the early 1960s. His dad had explained how the students would all rise in unison, then get down on their knees, crawl under their desks, close their eyes, and cover their heads with their hands. The government called it "Duck and Cover," and Chad's father said all the schools went through such similar drills.

Knowing what everyone in the twenty-first century commonly knew about the power of nuclear bombs, Chad understood his father and the other children would have had no more protection from this meaningless gesture than had they been running naked in the schoolyard. He wondered if the same naiveté had been put into practice when designating these so-called safe nuclear fallout shelters. He suspected it probably had been, and he felt quite certain if this building ever did suddenly collapse, it would crash right through the basement ceiling crushing everyone inside. Yet curiosity and the potential for much-needed earnings had gotten the better of him, so he accompanied the professor inside.

The lab occupied a space about seventy-five feet wide, and one hundred feet deep with a twelve-foot high suspended-type ceiling, and the area was awash with artificial light from dozens of recessed fluorescent fixtures. Many of the ceiling panels were missing, and those that remained were yellowed and other water stained. Some of the lights flickered and flashed rapidly on an off, giving the lab a sinister science fiction movie appearance.

"It is all very interesting," Chad replied, somewhat unsure and feeling quite out of his element.

"Yes, well, don't mind the lights," the Doctor said. "We have plenty of electricity at our disposal as well as a gas-powered backup generator. It is simply that I haven't had any luck getting someone from the university maintenance staff to stop over to replace the broken ballasts in those fixtures as of yet. It won't be a problem, however, as they shouldn't pose any detriment to my research."

Chad didn't know what he might have imagined the laboratory would be like, but he was surprised to find the place so sparsely furnished. Perhaps he thought he'd find workbenches with shelves lined with beakers, test tubes, and maybe there would be circular glass piping all around the lab, flowing with various glowing, bubbling liquids, like something from a Frankenstein movie. He'd even imagined giant electronic towers, topped with shiny silver pulsating spheres and wild flashing voltage jumping in an arc from one ball to the next. However, that wasn't at all what he found.

Instead, the room looked more like an abandoned warehouse with a series of six long folding tables set up to form a rectangular u-shape, each side two tables in length. On the tables, Chad saw a number of central processing units, flat-screen monitors, recording equipment, keyboards microphones, oscillo-scopes, headphones as well as several office-style computer chairs on wheels.

At the center of the U, there was a large leather recliner. Attached to the back of the recliner was some sort of vertical metal framework with a wiring harness, which contained thousands of wires, all of which appeared linked to the various computers and monitors. From atop the framework was suspended a device resembling an upside-down colander with wire's attached to it, appar-ently some type of apparatus to be worn on the head.

Off in the shadows toward the back right corner of the room were two larger pieces of equipment, which Chad couldn't quite identify from where he stood. One was a tall rectangular device with a glass or plexiglass access door in the front and was about six feet tall by two feet square. The other was much larger and looked like a vertical storage box, which stood about eight feet high and six feet wide with a transparent set of double doors. Chad had the image of a large portable shower of some sort, although it was clear there were no water lines or plumbing attached to it. Instead, Chad noticed more clusters of wires running from the computer servers back to both of the large boxes.

In the left rear corner of the room, Chad noticed what looked like a storage room about eight feet high with a single access door, and an open mezzanine above it. On top of the room was a collection of ductwork and ventilation tubes leading to the outside wall. Next to the front door were several metal gas cans. Chad assumed this room housed the gas-powered backup generator Doctor Bellamy had men-tioned. This was further verified when Chad realized the ductwork was for venting the gas fumes outside. Another separate harness of wires ran from the generator structure to the area where the computers were located. Chad assumed this was the main power source. In Chad's less than technical opinion, it was quite an impressive collection of electronic equipment.

Dr. Bellamy said, "I realize I've only given you a cursory overview of my research, but I'm telling you, this is a win-win situation for both of us. You'll receive the cash you so desperately need to help pay for your education. It'll be more money than you currently earn at your other part-time jobs combined. You'll only have to give up two evenings per week and spend just a few hours each of those nights here in the lab. Just think how much time that'll free up for your studies, not to mention how it'll allow you to some additional time for fun and extracurricular activities on your campus as well."

Chad Jefferson was not a student at the same technological university where Dr. Walker Bellamy was a professor, that particular school was reserved for the brightest of the bright, students who excelled in math and science. Instead, he attended a nearby, much smaller liberal arts college when his major remained currently undeclared. He still hadn't made up his mind which direction he should go, career-wise, his being equally proficient in art, music, and writing.

Chad asked, "But I still don't understand why you want to use me in your research. I mean. Just look around you. This campus is crawling with students much smarter than I am, who'd probably kill for the chance to work with you and would likely be willing to work free. I guess I don't understand why you'd come to a school like mine for an assistant, and then specifically ask for me. Heck, I was barely able to pass high school algebra. I guess I don't get it."

"Not to worry, Chad, my boy," the professor explained, "The nature of my work requires I avoid the very types of students we have here on campus. I don't need someone with great academic and analytical skills. That sort of left-brain thought process is exactly the opposite of what I require. What I need is a right-brained creative thinker with an incredible imagination. And you fit that requirement perfectly. You see, I contacted all of the top English, Art, and Music professors at your college and asked them to point me in the direction of the most creative, most imaginative and most talented student they had, and hands down, every one of them recommended you without a moment's hesitation."

This caught Chad somewhat by surprise. He had no idea his instructors all thought so highly of him. Chad knew he had a natural affinity for the arts, but never thought too much about it. In his opinion, it was something that came easy to him, and something he would enjoy spending his life doing, so he chose to pursue the college of liberal arts. He didn't yet know if he would become a commercial artist, a musician, a writer, or perhaps a combination of the three, but he knew somewhere within these three fields was where his future would lie.

Professor Bellamy asked, "Chad. Have you ever heard the expression 'The Mind's Eye'?"

Chad thought for a moment before answering, "No. I haven't. But I'd guess it means being able to see with your mind rather than just your eyes, or something like that."

"Yes, very good," Bellamy said. "When I personally refer to the mind's eye, I think of it in terms of imagination. Of course, the human mind can interpret things it sees physically through our own eyes, which is, unfortunately, the sole purpose it serves for a good many people. But for those very few, extremely creative, and imaginative individuals such as you, the mind can see things, which don't exist yet in physical form. This ability to imagine and to see with one's mind is exactly what comes into play when a musician composes a musical work, or an artist creates a painting, or a writer authors a book. Think about it, Chad. When you set out to create something, you generally start with a clean sheet of paper or canvas, isn't that correct?"

"Well, yes," Chad replied, "the same thing is true whether it is a work of art, a story, or a song. I generally start with nothing and then just start imagining what I want to do next."

The Professor slapped his knee with excitement. "Precisely! That's exactly what I'm talking about. Do you have any idea how many people look at a blank sheet and see nothing but a blank sheet of paper? They don't have any idea how even to begin the process of creating something from nothing. That's what imagination and creativity are all about, creating something where there was previously nothing."

Chad looked somewhat confused. "Well, yeah, I suppose you're right. But that's not really a big deal. I have been able to do that my whole life. I guess I sort of thought everybody could do it."

"And for the most part, you are correct. Just about, everyone is born with the ability to imagine, but some are born with a much higher degree of ability than others are. In addition, as we grow into adulthood and have to face the reality of getting an education, earning an income, and surviving in the daily rat race, gradually, this ability tends to diminish. Most people stop using the imaginative portion of their brains, and instead, they develop the analytical and logical sides because that's how we make money in this country. Those smart students you spoke of earlier, the ones who excel at this university in math, science, and business, often fall into that category. People like you, however, are of a rare breed that, for whatever reason, refuse to give up their creative side and instead work to develop those talents further and keep using them. That's specifically why I chose you, Chad. My research, my experiments are directly tied to taking a creative imagination, the mind's eye, so to speak, and magnifying that ability. The idea of my experiments is to find a way to harness the power of the creative imagination then increase that power by a hundredfold to go beyond the mind's eye. To focus that imagination and use it to better mankind."

"OK, I suppose," Chad replied, "It all sounds very interesting, and the money certainly is great. When would you like me to start?"

The doctor looked around the room and said, "Well. I suppose if you're ready, we can start on the first session immediately."

"Right now?" Chad asked, surprised to find the professor so eager to get underway.

"No time like the present. I have a lot of initial benchmark data to acquire and must go through numerous detailed calibrations of all of the equipment by synchronizing the computer program parameters with your own brain biorhythms."

"Ok," Chad replied, not having the slightest idea what the doctor was talking about but anxious, nonetheless, to begin earning his newfound income. "What would you like me to do?"

The professor replied, "Simply sit over there and relax in that recliner, while I begin the calibration process and record some initial data."

As Chad walked toward the chair, he asked about the two large devices in the back of the room. "What are those two things back there?"

"Oh, yes," Bellamy replied, "those are two units which I hope to use later in our research. It may be weeks or months until we can consider using them, however, depending upon the progress we make. The smaller of the two machines is called a rapid prototype machine, and the larger is a holographic imaging chamber."

"I know what a rapid prototype machine is," Chad said, understanding, "We learned about them in my CAD, you know, Computer-Aided Design class. And I know a little bit about holographic projections. I've seen some holographic art."

"Yes. Well, as I said, it'll be a long time until we are ready for those. In fact, for the first several weeks, you may find it very boring to be here and will likely spend most of your time simply sitting relaxed in that chair with very little else to do. I suspect you will be glad you are well paid for such uninteresting work."

"Will I be allowed to bring along my laptop or cell phone while sitting in the chair, you know, to play some video games or something to help pass the time?" Chad asked.

Bellamy looked at him as if he were about to deliver some unfortunate news, which he, in fact, was and said, "Sadly, no, that won't be acceptable, as it violates the very essence of my studies. However, you are welcome to bring a book or perhaps an audiobook if you would like for at least during the beginning sessions, as both of those items can help to stimulate the imagination. Later once our work gets into full swing, I'll be asking you to leave those at home as well, and I'll want you to do all of your own creative thinking without outside influences."

Chad thought about it for a moment, "I see what you mean. It makes little sense for me to sit like a zombie staring at the TV when you are studying creativity. My dad always called television 'the idiot box.' He said television would eventually turn all of us into unimaginative robots who have to rely on someone else to entertain us."

"Sadly, your father was quite correct," Dr. Bellamy replied. "Many of our youth have lost their ability to imagine, and at what I consider a much too young an age. That's one of the main reasons I chose to begin my research; first, to understand how the creative mind functions, then to take that ability and enhance it dramatically."

For the next several hours, Chad sat quietly on the recliner with the strange electronic "colander" helmet on his head. He closed his eyes, and he allowed his mind to wander, thinking of various unrelated ideas as the doctor had instructed him to do.

Finally, when he thought he might fall asleep, the doctor said, "Well, Chad. That should do just nicely. I think we'll stop there for the night."

As Chad arose from his chair in preparation to leave, he hesitated for a moment, watching the doctor prattle about his various computers. When Bellamy realized Chad was still behind him, he looked up and said, "Oh yes, your pay. Sorry about that, my boy, sometimes I am so absent-minded." The professor handed the young man a fifty-dollar bill, thanked him, and Chad left the basement laboratory, got into his car, and headed home.

The next several weeks were as uneventful as the first night had been. Most sessions consisted of Chad sitting in the recliner, reading, and allowing his imagination to take the words and create mental images. Sometimes he'd reach for a blank sheet of paper and do a quick sketch of whatever image he happened to be thinking at the time. As far as he was concerned, the experiment could continue like this indefinitely.

Chad felt the doctor had paid him well for not doing much of anything. He'd been able to quit his other three part-time jobs thanks to his newfound income and was able to spend the extra available time on his own very special project. He was combining his artistic and writing skills in the development of his own graphic novel. He had the idea brewing in his mind for many years, and now he was slowly making it a reality.

The novel was a ghastly horror story with over-the-top scenes of violence and some of the most horrid creatures he could imagine. His goal was to complete it by the end of the school year, and if he was lucky, find a publisher shortly after that. He dreamed someday the novel would become popular and would make him rich and famous, or at least earn him enough to pay for his growing student loan debt.

As Chad sat in his chair sketching, Bellamy, who had temporarily left the lab, returned and looked over the various data streaming across the computer monitors. He nodded his head happily, apparently satisfied with the results.

"I think the equipment is finally calibrated to your own unique brain wave signature. I'd like to try something, Chad," Bellamy said. "I see you have a sketch pad there with you." Bellamy reached into his lunch bag, which sat next to the computer and retrieved a bright shiny apple, "How are you with drawing still lifes?" he asked.

"Pretty good," Chad replied, "my art instructor said I have a great natural talent for rendering things realistically."

Dr. Bellamy said, "Excellent. Here is what I would like you to do. I'm going to place this apple on the table, and I want you to draw it as realistically as you can."

"That should be easy, Dr. Bellamy. But I only have a drawing pencil, so it'll have to be in black and white."

"Not a problem Chad. It doesn't really matter what colors you use to draw it. What does matter is how you envision it in your mind while you're drawing it. If you can envision the apple exactly as it appears to your physical eyes, colors, shading, and all, in your mind's eye, we could be well on the way to having some great success tonight."

Chad didn't fully understand what the doctor was looking for, but he did know how to draw and had no problem imagining, so he immediately began studying the apple, looking for subtleties of color, light, reflection, and shading and began sketching what turned out to be an incredible likeness. When he was finished, he turned to hand the sketch to the professor and was astounded to see what looked like an almost exact duplicate of the apple from the table now displayed prominently on the computer screen.

"Wow!" Chad exclaimed, "How did that get there?"

The doctor laughed exuberantly and proclaimed, "You put it there. Isn't that completely amazing, Chad? That image on the computer screen is the digitized rendering of what you imagined in your mind while you were sketching the apple."

Upon closer examination, Chad noticed it wasn't actually a duplicate of the apple but something very close. The colors were a bit too vibrant, the reflections too shiny, the size a bit abnormal, but it was nonetheless a good representation.

The doctor pressed a few keys, and the smaller machine at the back of the laboratory sprang to life with a whirring noise

"What is that for?" Chad asked.

The doctor explained. "There is a slight difference between what one imagines and what one sees. For example, you probably noticed the color and gloss differences between the apple on the table and the one on the screen, not to mention the size difference. This is caused by your imagination."

"I'm not sure I understand," Chad said, confused.

"Well, think of it this way," Dr. Bellamy said, "Reality is one thing, and imagination is something else entirely. Imagination is, by nature, fluid and not traditionally capable of focusing. Therefore, with study, we can very well analyze, determine, and quantify that difference in an individual subject such as you. That's where the computers come into play. Through a series of detailed experiments just like the one we did tonight, we can determine just how far your imaginative mind's eye varies from what your physical eyes really see. Then we can allow the computers to compensate for the difference and force a more exact image to be displayed on the screen."

Chad said, "So we have the apple on the table and the apple in my mind. The apple on the computer represents what I saw in my mind. Now by comparing the differences, the computer will be able to take the image from my mind and before displaying it, will modify the image based on the measured differences and someday produce an exact replica of the apple on the table on the computer monitor. Is that right?"

"Precisely," Dr. Bellamy said with pleasure, "that is exactly what I am trying to do. You're very astute, Chad, my boy."

"I'm sorry, Dr. Bellamy. But I don't see why this would be any different than simply taking a picture of the apple and displaying it on the computer. I know there are cameras out there capable of photographing enough views of the apple to generate a solid 3-D image of the apple on any solid-modeling Computer-Aided Design system. I've used solid modeling in many of my graphic art classes. I know it can be done. Why take the extra step of going through my imagination?"

"Well," the doctor said with some hesitation, "maybe it's time to let you in on the ultimate goal of my experiments. You see, what we're doing here is just the most elementary steps in a process that someday, perhaps in your lifetime, will be available to anyone and which will end all world hunger, crime, as well as wars and hopefully, will usher in a new dawn of enlightenment for all of mankind."

Chad looked at the professor as if he were out of his mind. He couldn't quite figure out how his getting an apple to appear on a computer screen could do anything to help mankind.

Dr. Bellamy walked over to the rapid prototype machine, which had just stopped running. He reached inside and took out an exact physical replica of the apple as it had appeared on the computer screen. Of course, it didn't have the color of the displayed image as was constructed of a dusty material used in the solid modeling process. However, it was the exact size of the apple, as depicted in the 3-D solid modeling computer program displayed on the computer monitor.

"Just imagine, Chad," the doctor said with excitement. "Just think if instead of this fiber-based model, I held a real, delicious, juicy apple in my hands. Now, what if instead of an apple, it was a turkey, or steak or maybe a much-needed medicine or a cure for some fatal disease. What if we were able to hook ourselves up to a machine like this and a few seconds later, the cure for any illness would come out of a device such as the one back there, although of course, a much more sophisticated version, but a similar device none the less. Do you see where I am going with this? What if we could have anything we imagined?"

Chad thought for a moment. "I suppose that would be pretty good," he said, unaware of how insignificant he made the accomplishment sound.

"Pretty good?" The doctor asked, stunned by the understatement, "Chad, my boy, it would be much better than pretty good. It would be revolutionary. Remember on the old Star Trek TV shows how the crew had those machines they called "Replicators." Whenever one of the crew wanted something, all he had to do was ask the machine, and the item appeared? If we could do that, no one would ever go hungry again. There'd be no need for money or greed or any such trappings. Everyone would instantly have everything required right at his or her fingertips. There'd be no reason to steal, hurt, or kill anymore. Crime and war would become outdated. Mankind would be free to pursue intellectual endeavors like the sciences all day long, not to mention art, music, literature, and philosophy. You name it. Initially, the system might just contain a few essential items, but eventually, the database would grow exponentially in size, making more and more items available. In addition, these devices will become more sophisticated and able to handle larger and more complex items. When that becomes a reality, there would literally be no limit to what could be instantly produced."

"Wow!" Chad exclaimed, "You really think all of that could someday come from the work we're doing right here, today?"

The professor looked at him knowingly and said, "Absolutely. We're pioneering a new frontier, Chad. Whatever progress you and I make here in the project's infancy, will forge a trail for others to follow. And with the mind and imagination I believe you possess, we could actually see many amazing advances happen very quickly in our work as well. I only wish I could find more wealthy backers to help finance my work. If so, I honestly believe I could buy the necessary equipment to cut decades off of my research."

"Yeah. Too bad, I can't simply imagine money and make it appear," Chad said innocently. "That sure would solve both of our financial problems."

The doctor looked at Chad with amazement as if the boy had just suggested something so ridiculously simple, yet so incredibly on target, that he wondered why he hadn't thought of it himself. If he could find a way to fine-tune his equipment so the products generated by Chad's mind could become exact replications, he could very possibly use the boy to help him take the experiment to the next level and thereby become his own financial backer. He decided not to let the boy know of his excitement or of his plans. Bellamy needed Chad's mind to be clear and free of any distractions if he were ever going to take the experiment to the final step, that step being a journey beyond the mind's eye. He decided instead to tuck away the idea until he succeeded with a few additional experiments then, perhaps he could find a way to test it out without making Chad aware of what he was doing.

"Um, ah, yes," the doctor stammered, trying to act as if Chad had said something irrelevant. "If it were only that easy, my boy. Anyway, I think your work here is done for the night, Chad. I just have to take some measurements of the apple model and make some additional adjustments before heading home. So I'll see you again next Tuesday night. Is that correct?" He handed Chad two fifty-dollar bills.

"You bet," Chad said, noticing the increase in pay. "Uh, yeah. See you then."

Dr. Bellamy worked until very late in the night, adjusting and readjusting his machinery. Just before dawn, he started up the holographic imaging chamber and sent the apple image from the computer to the chamber. However, the truth was, that particular chamber was not simply an imaging chamber as he had told Chad but was a very special piece of machinery of his own design which, he had been developing for many years. When he walked over and opened up the front door of the machine, not just a holographic image of an apple was inside, but a full-size physical replica of the apple. Bellamy reached down and picked up the apple, staring at it as if contemplating whether he should risk taking a bite or not. After a moment's hesitation, he bit into the apple, and his eyes lit up with joy at the incredible taste the apple produced. It was like an apple, but so much more. It was the single most scrumptious piece of fruit he had ever eaten in his life. He had never even imagined such an incredibly delicious taste, but then again, he hadn't imagined this one either. Chad had.

Over the course of the next several weeks, Bellamy worked on fine-tuning the equipment. He had set it so precisely that all Chad had to do was look at any object, imagine it in his mind for just a second, and it would instantly appear on the computer graphics screen in the exact, proportioned size, shape, and color with absolutely no deviation from the original. Dr. Bellamy made a point of never turning on his holographic machine while Chad was in the lab. The most he would do was occasionally do a rapid prototype of the object for measurement and calibration, but he would never activate the other machine.

One night the doctor said to Chad, with a slight but noticeable hesitation, "I would like to take our experiments a step further if possible. Up until now, we've only been experimenting with simple solid objects. I'd like to try something new, something more complex and involved. I've equipped the computer with a specially designed animation/rendering program. I want to see what happens if you imagine a living, moving object."

"Wow!" Chad said with excitement, "That sounds really cool!"

For the remainder of the evening, Chad sat watching a lab rat running around in its cage as the doctor adjusted the equipment. Chad tried his best to imagine the small creature in all of its detail and to include every nuance of its movements, every twitch, every wrinkle of its nose, the blinking of its eyes everything.

"Excellent!" the doctor suddenly announced. "Very good, Chad! Why don't you take a little break and come over here and see what you have created."

Chad removed his colander hat, as he now thought of it, and walked over to the computer screen where the professor was sitting staring in amazement. On the screen before him was a rat, not exactly like the rat from the cage, perhaps a bit larger but every bit as detailed as the real thing. It was running happily about the screen. "Unreal! That is so cool," Chad said. "When this is perfected, you could literally change the entire cartoon animation industry."

The professor stifled a laugh at how naive the young boy was. He had absolutely no interest in animated films or any other such nonsense. His goals were much higher than that. He cared nothing about cartoons, animation, anime, or whatever it was the young people called it nowadays. So as before, he dismissed Chad early for the evening and moved on to the next phase of his experiments. Chad was happy because it meant he could spend the evening's remaining time developing his horrifying new graphic novel.

Of late, Chad found he had been actually having trouble focusing on his lab responsibilities as well as his schoolwork. His mind kept drifting back to his graphic novel. In the past, he'd often found he had such trouble reining in his creative imagination. But lately, it seemed to be even more difficult to do so. It was almost as if Dr. Bellamy's experiments had produced an unplanned side effect. It was as if his ability to imagine and create was beginning to grow exponentially as well, opening all sorts of new and previously unavailable avenues of inspiration.

Most people who weren't artistic by nature didn't realize just how much of a double-edged sword being creative was. In one sense, it was a blessing when one needed to come up with new and original ideas quickly. However, it was also a curse because often, when a creative idea chose to manifest itself, it simply had to come out, and there was very little the person could do to keep it from doing so. An extremely persistent idea would often completely preoccupy Chad's mind until he finally found an outlet for the inspiration, a way to make it concrete. Lately, that need seemed to be constant, more persistent, more demanding, and more uncontrollable than ever before.

Alone in the laboratory, Dr. Bellamy again turned on the holographic chamber in the back of the lab and began downloading the lab rat data from the computer to the chamber. Within seconds, he was astounded to see a small furry living version of the animated lab rat running about the inside of the chamber.

"Absolutely amazing!" The doctor shouted with astonishment. "I've created a living creature from the mind's eye of that incredibly gifted young man. This level of success so early in my experimentation is, well, it's beyond my wildest expectations." Bellamy took a small cage and placed it on the floor next to the chamber door. When he carefully opened the door, the rat scurried out of the chamber and right into the cage, which Bellamy quickly secured.

The doctor stared closely at the rat through the bars and noticed something very odd about the creature. It seemed to possess an almost human-like intelligence in its black eyes, but also something, more than that, something which might be considered a dark and almost sinister look, lurking just below the surface.

One of his fingers accidentally slipped through the bars of the cage and too close to the rat. Instantly, without a second of hesitation, the creature bit down hard on the man's finger, shredding off a large chunk of flesh and bits of a shattered fingernail. It held the torn flesh between its forepaws and began feasting on it as blood ran down between its razor-sharp teeth, over its lip, and down onto the bottom of the cage.

Bellamy screamed with pain and revulsion, dropping the cage to the floor. He was fortunate the enclosure door didn't spring open, or he would have found himself trapped in the lab with the horrid beast. He grabbed a paper towel and wrapped his wounded finger to slow down the bleeding until he could attend to it better later.

Then with his good hand, he picked up the cage by its carrying handle and walked it over to the far corner of the lab near the generator room. He clumsily took one of the gas containers and doused the animal with gasoline. The rat looked directly at Bellamy, their eyes meeting, the unspoken knowledge of a mysterious unexplainable intelligence passing between them, as the rat's eyes told Bellamy, it understood what the doctor's murderous plan was. At first, Bellamy was taken aback by the strange understanding, and then as the pain in his finger throbbed, he disregarded the momentary feeling and continued with his plan.

When the cage was a safe distance from the rest of the stored fuel, he lit a match and dropped it in, watching the rat slowly and agonizingly burn to death, screaming and howling in its flaming torture. He smelled the acrid stench of burning hair and cooking meat as the creature rolled, kicked and writhed in its final dance of death. Just before the hideous roasting thing finally succumbed, Bellamy thought he heard it speak. Unbelievable, he was certain he had heard it say, "No. Please. Don' kill me." The high-pitched plea sent a cold chill down the doctor's spine, but he could only hope it was just his imagination, and for the sake of his own soul, he hadn't actually heard what he thought he had heard.

Early the next week, when Chad showed up for his scheduled session, he asked Dr. Bellamy if they would be doing more of the animation type experiments similar to those they had done the previous week. This caught the doctor off guard, and for a moment, he appeared very uncomfortable by the very suggestion.

He gingerly rubbed his bandaged finger, trying his best to sound confident and said, "Uh, no. No Chad, not this week. We may do more of that at another time, but tonight we'll focus on more stationary objects again."

Chad was a bit disappointed because he knew to stare at nonmoving objects, and imagining them was extremely boring as was the final product when compared to the fun they had animating the lab rat on the computer screen. Before he could think about it further, the professor asked him, "Chad? I have what might seem like an odd question for you." Then after a moment's pause, he asked, "Have you ever been hypnotized before?"

The boy thought for a moment and said, "Nope. Never. I considered it one time at one of our high school assemblies where there was this hypnotist, but I was never lucky enough to be picked to be a volunteer."

"Well," the doctor said, "I'd like to try something to help you focus your concentration more acutely and to assist in more quickly getting usable images from inside your mind to the computer. Would you be all right with that? I assure you it'll be perfectly safe."

Chad hesitated for a moment then said, "Well. Sure. I suppose it'd be alright."

Then Bellamy assured him, "Just in case you were wondering, while you're under hypnosis, you'll still have full control of your faculties and can't ever be made to do anything you wouldn't be willing to do while fully awake."

With Chad's agreement, the doctor placed him into a hypnotic state using a simple pen, which he waved back and forth in front of the boy's eyes. When Chad was completely under hypnosis and resting slack-jawed comfortably in the recliner in a deep trance, Dr. Bellamy reached into his wallet and withdrew a crisp brand new fifty-dollar bill.

"Chad?" the doctor said in a calm and reassuring voice. "I want you to study this bill very carefully. It's a similar bill to the ones I have been giving you each week. In fact, I will be giving you this bill at the end of the night as payment. What I want you to do is look at the front and the back, making sure you get every single detail into your mind, you don't have to worry about memorizing the nuances because your subconscious will automatically do that for you. Your subconscious mind will catalog the most minuscule of details of the paper and thread weaves as well as the shades and hues of the ink. I just want you to study the bill itself, and concentrate with all of your might. Can you see the bill clearly in your mind's eye?"

"Yes, I can see the bill," Chad replied in a sleepy, almost robotic voice. The doctor looked over at the computer monitor and was thrilled to see the replica displayed on the screen, rotating slowly, showing the exact details on both the front and back of the bill. Ulysses S. Grant repeatedly came into view then passed by as the bill rotated in circles. With a few quick keyboard strokes, the professor saved the image to the computer's hard drive.

"Good. Very good," the doctor prompted. "Now Chad. I want you to imagine a stack of almost identical fifty-dollar bills, one hundred bills thick, and imagine each serial number on each bill as being random, non-repeating, and non-sequential. And I want you to imagine a paper band tightly surrounding the stack of bills with the number five thousand stamped on it. Can you do that for me?"

"Yes, I can do that for you," Chad once again said as, on the computer monitor, a rotating stack of fifties appeared on the screen, just as the doctor described. He was beyond elated and once again saved the file immediately.

The doctor suggested, "I'd like you to do one more thing for me. Can you imagine a cube, three feet wide by three feet deep by eight feet high made up completely of similar stacks of fifty-dollar bills like the ones you just imagined? And can you picture a wheeled wooden dolly positioned underneath the cube of wrapped bills with a convenient handle for pulling? Is that something you think you can do, Chad?"

Chad's closed eyes squinted with extreme concentration; sweat beginning to bead on his forehead, as he did what the doctor asked. On the computer screen, an image of the cube on the cart appeared as a full three-dimensional rendering. Bellamy couldn't believe his eyes. This young man had just created a small fortune in fifty-dollar bills. Without a moment's hesitation, Bellamy raced over to his computer and again saved the final image file to the computer.

If the next part of his experiment was successful, he'd have a never-ending supply of cash and would be able to leave the university, purchase his own lab equipped with state of the art equipment, and would never need to go begging for money again. He quickly downloaded the file from the computer to the holographic chamber. Within seconds, right before the doctor's bulging eyes, an incredible rectangular cube-shaped stack of money appeared inside the chamber complete with cart and handle as he had requested.

Although the money was technically counterfeit, Bellamy instinctively knew the fake money would be completely undetectable by any known means the authorities had of scanning, as the bills would be identically in every way to real money, even down to the smallest fiber of the woven paper.

He quickly opened the door to the unbelievable box, grabbed the handle of the cart, and pulled the money cube out onto the lab floor. As he did, the stack toppled and fell to the floor, creating a mountain of neatly bound stacks of money. Elated beyond comprehension, Bellamy dove into the pile of money-grabbing stacks, ripping off their paper bands, and throwing the money all around madly like the cartoon character Scrooge McDuck. He was so enthralled with his instant riches that he completely forgot about closing the door to the chamber, as well as the fact that Chad was still sitting in the recliner hypnotized and hooked up to the computer equipment.

Chad's eyes began to flitter beneath his closed lids as his ever-active imagination continued working. Without the doctor's verbal direction and suggestions, he was once again free to relax, allowing his busy mind to run wild with whatever it chose to imagine. And since Chad had been so preoccupied of late with his horribly violent graphic novel, it was the first thing to pop into his subconscious.

As he lay quietly in his recliner, Chad wasn't even aware of the hideous and monstrous images his mind was generating; scenes of mayhem with horrible, ungodly creatures rising up from the bowels of Hell to maim and devour their innocent victims. His mind's eye imagined deformed repugnant beings with protruding eyeballs, whose very touch could cause flesh to boil and objects to burst into flames.

Within seconds, the horrible images moved from his mind to the computer screen, then directly to the still connected, still active holographic imaging chamber. Bellamy was busy caressing his newfound wealth and had his back to the doorway of the holographic closet when the first creature materialized.

The doctor suddenly heard heavy breathing behind him and a low guttural growl as he turned slowly to come face to face with something his analytical mind couldn't have possibly imagined. The creature was about four feet high, naked, and had shining leathery-like flesh with large eyes, bulging so far from their sockets as to almost look comical. Perhaps he could have found some humor in their appearance had it not been for the wide-open mouth filled with long, curved razor-sharp fangs.

At that very moment, the realization hit him. He remembered Chad, the computers, the chamber, and the fact that everything was still online, connected, and functioning. Then he had an epiphany regarding the duality of a mind rich with creativity and imagination. He had always been able to appreciate the positive aspects of such a gift, but he hadn't considered the notion that such a blessing might also be a curse.

A mind gifted with such genius of extreme imagination was not something one could simply turn off and on. Inspiration stimulated creativity. Once this often-unforeseen stimulus put the imagination in motion, it was like a runaway train, needing to run its course, unable to stop until it either exhausted itself or crashed violently at the end of the line. Trying to hold it at bay, to prevent it from expressing itself was like trying to hold back the ocean; it simply couldn't be done. Now Bellamy saw that a tsunami of deadly inhuman creatures was heading right for him.

Behind the first horrible creature was another even more hideous thing. It appeared to be female, although barely so. Its body was that of a gorgeous voluptuous woman, clad in a black evening dress, with ample cleavage and flawless skin. But that is where the similarity to anything beautiful or even human ended.

Its face was a horrid mass of twisted, distorted rotting flesh with the right side of the face and nose missing, revealing a bone-white skull. The facial remnants were encircled by strips of filthy brown cloth bandages from its chin to the top of its head as if this were the only thing preventing the accumulation of rotting flesh from sliding off of its skull and splattering to the floor. At the top of its head, just beyond the bandages, a large portion of is cranium cap was missing, and its brain bulged from the opening like a horrid bowl of pulsating grey gelatin.

The two creatures moved slowly from the chamber as another unearthly thing began to take shape inside. It looked like some twisted version of Frankenstein's monster, yet somehow, it was frighteningly much more horrifying and deformed. Flames shot from the fingertips of its outstretched reaching hands.

Some of the flames shot past the other creatures like miniature flying balls of fire. Several struck the pile of money, while others flew off toward the area where the gasoline cans were stored. Unfortunately, the previous week, when Bellamy had doused the rat's cage with gas, he neglected to clean up the mess, and several rags still saturated and still slightly damp with gasoline laid around the burned cage. These discarded rags quickly caught fire, and soon the basement lab became engulfed in flames.

One of the flaming fingertip projectiles struck Bellamy directly in the chest, knocking him backward onto the burning pile of bills. As his clothing caught fire, the first two creatures jumped upon him and began systematically dismembering him, ripping him apart limb by limb, devouring his toasting remains with a ferocity born of Chad's imaginative graphic novel. Although their own leathery skin was blistering and burning, they appeared unable to ease their savage feeding frenzy, even to save themselves.

As Chad lay in a trance on the recliner he was startled to semi-consciousness by the commotion, not enough to realize what was happening but to a sufficient degree that his own subconscious self-preservation response kicked in and he was able to get up and slowly walk toward the front door of the lab. Without realizing what he was doing, the young man opened the door, walked out into the cool evening, and closed the door tightly behind him. When he got about a block from the building, the basement lab exploded, and the entire multi-storied structure collapsed downward in a massive heap. Apparently, the professor had been wrong about the reinforced fallout shelter.

Chad suddenly awoke to find he was standing in the street as fire sirens began to sound in the distance signaling their approach. The last thing he recalled was his relaxing on the recliner as Dr. Bellamy was beginning to hypnotize him. Yet now he was a block from the former lab with no knowledge of how he had gotten here or what had happened.

Sometime later, authorities conducted a meticulous arson and criminal investigation. Everything in the lab burned beyond recognition, leaving no trace of any notes, equipment, or the professor himself. Also missing were any signs of the money or the creatures, which had come from the holographic chamber. Chad didn't volunteer to come forward to tell authorities of his involvement in the experiments as only he and the professor knew of their activities. He decided if any of the teachers from his college were to question him, he'd simply tell them Bellamy wanted him to do a drawing for him or else he would make up some other such lie. Chad didn't know why he had decided to be so secretive about his involvement with Bellamy but instinctively seemed to think it would be for the best.

In the end, no one, including Chad, would ever know the extent of Bellamy's experiments. Nor would they know how close the man had come to fulfilling his lifelong dream. Ironically, because of Bellamy's own natural human greed, the very type of behavior he sought to eliminate from the world had been responsible for turning his dream into a tragic fatal nightmare.

HERBERT WEST REANIMATOR – "A"

By H. P. Lovecraft

• PART I

Of Herbert West, who was my friend in college and in after life, I can speak only with extreme terror. This terror is not due altogether to the sinister manner of his recent disappearance but was engendered by the whole nature of his life-work, and first gained its acute form more than seventeen years ago, when we were in the third year of our course at the Miskatonic University Medical School in Arkham. While he was with me, the wonder and diabolism of his experiments fascinated me utterly, and I was his closest companion. Now that he is gone and the spell is broken, the actual fear is greater. Memories and possibilities are ever more hideous than realities.

The first horrible incident of our acquaintance was the greatest shock I ever experienced, and it is only with reluctance that I repeat it. As I have said, it happened when we were in the medical school where West had already made himself notorious through his wild theories on the nature of death and the possibility of overcoming it artificially. His views, which were widely ridiculed by the faculty and by his fellow-students, hinged on the essentially mechanistic nature of life; and concerned means for operating the organic machinery of mankind by calculated chemical action after the failure of natural processes. In his experiments with various animating solutions, he had killed and treated immense numbers of rabbits, guinea-pigs, cats, dogs, and monkeys, until he had become the prime nuisance of the college. Several times he had actually obtained signs of life in animals supposedly dead; in many cases, violent signs, but he soon saw that the perfection of his process, if indeed possible, would necessarily involve a lifetime of research. It likewise became clear that, since the same solution never worked alike on different organic species, he would require human subjects for further and more specialized progress. It was here that he first came into conflict with the college authorities, and was debarred from future experiments by no less a dignitary than the dean of the medical school himself—the learned and benevolent Dr. Allan Halsey, whose work in behalf of the stricken is recalled by every old resident of Arkham.

I had always been exceptionally tolerant of West's pursuits, and we frequently discussed his theories, whose ramifications and corollaries were almost infinite. Holding with Haeckel that all life is a chemical and physical process and that the so-called "soul" is a myth, my friend believed that artificial reanimation of the dead can depend only on the condition of the tissues; and that unless actual decomposition has set in, a corpse fully equipped with organs may with suitable measures be set going again in the peculiar fashion known as life. That the psychic or intellectual life might be impaired by the slight deterioration of sensitive brain-cells which even a short period of death would be apt to cause, West fully realized. It had at first been his hope to find a reagent that would restore vitality before the actual advent of death, and only repeated failures on animals had shown him that the natural and artificial life-motions were incompatible. He then sought extreme freshness in his specimens, injecting his solutions into the blood immediately after the extinction of life. It was this circumstance which made the professors so carelessly skeptical, for they felt that true death had not occurred in any case. They did not stop to view the matter closely and reasoningly.

It was not long after the faculty had interdicted his work that West confided to me his resolution to get fresh human bodies in some manner and continue in secret the experiments he could no longer perform openly. To hear him discussing ways and means was rather ghastly, for, at the college, we had never procured anatomical specimens ourselves. Whenever the morgue proved inadequate, two local negroes attended to this matter, and they were seldom questioned. West was then a small, slender, spectacled youth with delicate features, yellow hair, pale blue eyes, and a soft voice, and it was uncanny to hear him dwelling on the relative merits of Christchurch Cemetery and the potter's field. We finally decided on the potter's field, because practically every body in Christchurch was embalmed; a thing, of course, ruinous to West's researches.

I was by this time his active and enthralled assistant and helped him make all his decisions, not only concerning the source of bodies but concerning a suitable place for our loathsome work. It was I who thought of the deserted Chapman farmhouse beyond Meadow Hill, where we fitted up on the ground floor an operating room and a laboratory, each with dark curtains to conceal our midnight doings. The place was far from any road, and in sight of no other house, yet precautions were none the less necessary; since rumors of strange lights, started by chance nocturnal roamers, would soon bring disaster on our enterprise. It was agreed to call the whole thing a chemical laboratory if discovery should occur. Gradually we equipped our sinister haunt of science with materials either purchased in Boston or quietly borrowed from the college—materials carefully made unrecognizable save to expert eyes—and provided spades and picks for the many burials we should have to make in the cellar. At the college, we used an incinerator, but the apparatus was too costly for our unauthorized laboratory. Bodies were always a nuisance—even the small guinea-pig bodies from the slight clandestine experiments in West's room at the boarding-house.

We followed the local death-notices like ghouls, for our specimens demanded particular qualities. What we wanted were corpses interred soon after death and without artificial preservation, preferably free from malforming disease, and certainly with all organs present. Accident victims were our best hope. Not for many weeks did we hear of anything suitable, though we talked with morgue and hospital authorities, ostensibly in the college's interest, as often as we could without exciting suspicion. We found that the college had first choice in every case so that it might be necessary to remain in Arkham during the summer when only the limited summer-school classes were held. In the end, though, luck favored us; for one day, we heard of an almost ideal case in the potter's field; a brawny young workman drowned only the morning before in Summer's Pond and buried at the town's expense without delay or embalming. That afternoon we found the new grave and determined to begin work soon after midnight.

It was a repulsive task that we undertook in the black small hours, even though we lacked at that time the special horror of graveyards which later experiences brought to us. We carried spades and oil dark lanterns, for although electric torches were then manufactured, they were not as satisfactory as the tungsten contrivances of today. The process of unearthing was slow and sordid—it might have been gruesomely poetical if we had been artists instead of scientists—and we were glad when our spades struck wood. When the pine box was fully uncovered, West scrambled down and removed the lid, dragging out and propping up the contents. I reached down and hauled the contents out of the grave, and then both toiled hard to restore the spot to its former appearance. The affair made us rather nervous, especially the stiff form and vacant face of our first trophy, but we managed to remove all traces of our visit. When we had patted down the last shovelful of earth, we put the specimen in a canvas sack and set out for the old Chapman place beyond Meadow Hill.

On an improvised dissecting-table in the old farmhouse, by the light of a powerful acetylene lamp, the specimen was not very spectral looking. It had been a sturdy and apparently unimaginative youth of wholesome plebeian type—large-framed, grey-eyed, and brown-haired—a sound animal without psychological subtleties, and probably having vital processes of the simplest and healthiest sort. Now, with the eyes closed, it looked more asleep than dead, though the expert test of my friend soon left no doubt on that score. We had at last what West had always longed for—a real dead man of the ideal kind, ready for the solution as prepared according to the most careful calculations and theories for human use. The tension on our part became very great. We knew that there was scarcely a chance for anything like complete success, and could not avoid hideous fears at possible grotesque results of partial animation. Especially were we apprehensive concerning the mind and impulses of the creature, since in the space following death, some of the more delicate cerebral cells might well have suffered deterioration. I, myself, still held some curious notions about the traditional "soul" of man and felt an awe at the secrets that might be told by one returning from the dead. I wondered what sights this placid youth might have seen in inaccessible spheres, and what he could relate if fully restored to life. But my wonder was not overwhelming since, for the most part, I shared the materialism of my friend. He was calmer than I as he forced a large quantity of his fluid into a vein of the body's arm, immediately binding the incision securely.

The waiting was gruesome, but West never faltered. Every now and then, he applied his stethoscope to the specimen and bore the negative results philosophically. After about three-quarters of an hour without the least sign of life, he disappointedly pronounced the solution inadequate but determined to make the most of his opportunity and try one change in the formula before disposing of his ghastly prize. We had that afternoon dug a grave in the cellar, and would have to fill it by dawn—for although we had fixed a lock on the house, we wished to shun even the remotest risk of a ghoulish discovery. Besides, the body would not be even approximately fresh the next night. So taking the solitary acetylene lamp into the adjacent laboratory, we left our silent guest on the slab in the dark and bent every energy to the mixing of a new solution; the weighing and measuring supervised by West with almost fanatical care.

The awful event was very sudden and wholly unexpected. I was pouring something from one test-tube to another, and West was busy over the alcohol blast-lamp which had to answer for a Bunsen burner in this gasless edifice when from the pitch-black room we had left there burst the most appalling and dae-moniac succession of cries that either of us had ever heard. Not more unutterable could have been the chaos of hellish sound if the pit itself had opened to release the agony of the damned, for in one inconceivable cacophony was centered all the supernal terror and unnatural despair of animate nature. Human it could not have been—it is not in man to make such sounds—and without a thought of our late employment or its possible discovery, both West and I leaped to the nearest window like stricken animals; overturning tubes, lamp, and retorts, and vaulting madly into the starred abyss of the rural night. I think we screamed ourselves as we stumbled frantically toward the town, though as we reached the outskirts, we put on a semblance of restraint—just enough to seem like belated revelers staggering home from a debauch.

We did not separate but managed to get to West's room, where we whis-pered with the gas up until dawn. By then, we had calmed ourselves a little with rational theories and plans for investigation so that we could sleep through the day—classes being disregarded. But that evening, two items in the paper, wholly unrelated, made it again impossible for us to sleep. The old deserted Chapman house had inexplicably burned to an amorphous heap of ashes; that we could understand because of the upset lamp. Also, an attempt had been made to disturb a new grave in the potter's field, as if by futile and spadeless clawing at the earth. That we could not understand, for we had patted down the mold very carefully.

And for seventeen years after that West would frequently look over his shoul-der, and complain of fancied footsteps behind him. Now he has disappeared.

• PART II

I shall never forget that hideous summer sixteen years ago when like a noxious afrite from the halls of Eblis typhoid stalked leeringly through Arkham. It is by that satanic scourge that most recall the year, for truly terror brooded with bat-wings over the piles of coffins in the tombs of Christchurch Cemetery; yet for me, there is a greater horror in that time—a horror known to me alone now that Herbert West has disappeared.

West and I were doing post-graduate work in summer classes at the medical school of Miskatonic University, and my friend had attained a wide notoriety because of his experiments leading toward the revivification of the dead. After the scientific slaughter of uncounted small animals the freakish work had ostensibly stopped by order of our skeptical dean, Dr. Allan Halsey; though West had continued to perform certain secret tests in his dingy boarding-house room, and had on one terrible and unforgettable occasion taken a human body from its grave in the potter's field to a deserted farmhouse beyond Meadow Hill.

I was with him on that odious occasion and saw him inject into the still veins the elixir, which he thought would, to some extent, restore life's chemical and physical processes. It had ended horribly—in a delirium of fear which we gradually came to attribute to our own overwrought nerves—and West had never afterward been able to shake off a maddening sensation of being haunted and hunted. The body had not been quite fresh enough; it is obvious that to restore normal mental attributes, a body must be very fresh indeed, and the burning of the old house had prevented us from burying the thing. It would have been better if we could have known it was underground.

After that experience, West had dropped his researches for some time, but as the zeal of the born scientist slowly returned, he again became importunate with the college faculty, pleading for the use of the dissecting-room and of fresh human specimens for the work he regarded as so overwhelmingly important. His pleas, however, were wholly in vain, for the decision of Dr. Halsey was inflexible, and the other professors all endorsed the verdict of their leader. In the radical theory of reanimation they saw nothing but the immature vagaries of a youthful enthusiast whose slight form, yellow hair, spectacled blue eyes, and soft voice gave no hint of the supernormal—almost diabolical—power of the cold brain within. I can see him now as he was then—and I shiver. He grew sterner of face, but never elderly. And now Sefton Asylum has had the mishap and West has vanished.

West clashed disagreeably with Dr. Halsey near the end of our last undergraduate term in a wordy dispute that did less credit to him than to the kindly dean in point of courtesy. He felt that he was needlessly and irrationally retarded in a supremely great work, a work which he could, of course, conduct to suit himself in later years, but which he wished to begin while still possessed of the exceptional facilities of the university. That the tradition-bound elders should ignore his singular results on animals, and persist in their denial of the possibility of reanimation, was inexpressibly disgusting and almost incomprehensible to a youth of West's logical temperament. Only greater maturity could help him understand the chronic mental limitations of the "professor-doctor" type—the product of generations of pathetic Puritanism; kindly, conscientious, and sometimes gentle and amiable, yet always narrow, intolerant, custom-ridden, and lacking in perspective. Age has more charity for these incomplete yet high-souled characters, whose worst real vice is timidity, and who are ultimately punished by general ridicule for their intellectual sins—sins like Ptolemaism, Calvinism, anti-Darwinism, anti-Nietzscheism, and every sort of Sabbatarianism and sumptuary legislation. West, young despite his marvelous scientific acquirements, had scant patience with good Dr. Halsey and his erudite colleagues; and nursed an increasing resentment, coupled with a desire to prove his theories to these obtuse worthies in some striking and dramatic fashion. Like most youths, he indulged in elaborate daydreams of revenge, triumph, and final magnanimous forgiveness.

And then had come the scourge, grinning and lethal, from the nightmare caverns of Tartarus. West and I had graduated about the time of its beginning but had remained for additional work at the summer school so that we were in Arkham when it broke with full daemoniac fury upon the town. Though not as yet licensed physicians, we now had our degrees and were pressed frantically into public service as the numbers of the stricken grew. The situation was almost past management, and deaths ensued too frequently for the local undertakers fully to handle. Burials without embalming were made in rapid succession, and even the Christchurch Cemetery receiving tomb was crammed with coffins of the unembalmed dead. This circumstance was not without effect on West, who often thought of the irony of the situation—so many fresh specimens, yet none for his persecuted researches! We were frightfully overworked, and the terrific mental and nervous strain made my friend brood morbidly.

But West's gentle enemies were no less harassed with prostrating duties. College had all but closed, and every doctor of the medical faculty was helping to fight the typhoid plague. Dr. Halsey, in particular, had distinguished himself in sacrificing service, applying his extreme skill with whole-hearted energy to cases which many others shunned because of danger or apparent hopelessness. Before a month was over, the fearless dean had become a popular hero, though he seemed unconscious of his fame as he struggled to keep from collapsing with physical fatigue and nervous exhaustion. West could not withhold admiration for the fortitude of his foe, but because of this was even more determined to prove to him the truth of his amazing doctrines. Taking advantage of the disorganization of both college work and municipal health regulations, he managed to get a recently deceased body smuggled into the university dissecting-room one night, and in my presence, injected a new modification of his solution. The thing actually opened its eyes, but only stared at the ceiling with a look of soul-petrifying horror before collapsing into an inertness from which nothing could rouse it. West said it was not fresh enough—the hot summer air does not favor corpses. That time we were almost caught before we incinerated the thing and West doubted the advisability of repeating his daring misuse of the college laboratory.

The peak of the epidemic was reached in August. West and I were almost dead, and Dr. Halsey did die on the 14th. The students all attended the hasty funeral on the 15th, and bought an impressive wreath, though the latter was quite overshadowed by the tributes sent by wealthy Arkham citizens and by the municipality itself. It was almost a public affair, for the dean had surely been a public benefactor. After the entombment, we were all somewhat depressed and spent the afternoon at the bar of the Commercial House, where West, though shaken by the death of his chief opponent, chilled the rest of us with references to his notorious theories. Most of the students went home or to various duties as the evening advanced, but West persuaded me to aid him in "making a night of it." West's landlady saw us arrive at his room about two in the morning, with a third man between us, and told her husband that we had all evidently dined and wined rather well.

Apparently, this acidulous matron was right; for about 3 A.M. the whole house was aroused by cries coming from West's room, where when they broke down the door, they found the two of us unconscious on the blood-stained carpet, beaten, scratched, and mauled, and with the broken remnants of West's bottles and instruments around us. Only an open window told what had become of our assailant, and many wondered how he himself had fared after the terrific leap from the second story to the lawn, which he must have made. There were some strange garments in the room, but West, upon regaining consciousness, said they did not belong to the stranger but were specimens collected for bacteriological analysis in the course of investigations on the transmission of germ diseases. He ordered them burnt as soon as possible in the capacious fireplace. To the police, we both declared ignorance of our late companion's identity. He was, West nervously said, a congenial stranger whom we had met at some downtown bar of uncertain location. We had all been rather jovial, and West and I did not wish to have our pugnacious companion hunted down.

That same night saw the beginning of the second Arkham horror—the horror that, to me, eclipsed the plague itself. Christchurch Cemetery was the scene of a terrible killing, a watchman having been clawed to death in a manner not only too hideous for description but raising a doubt as to the human agency of the deed. The victim had been seen alive considerably after midnight—the dawn revealed the unutterable thing. The manager of a circus at the neighboring town of Bolton was questioned, but he swore that no beast had at any time escaped from its cage. Those who found the body noted a trail of blood leading to the receiving tomb, where a small pool of red lay on the concrete just outside the gate. A fainter trail led away toward the woods, but it soon gave out.

The next night devils danced on the roofs of Arkham, and unnatural madness howled in the wind. Through the fevered town had crept a curse which some said was greater than the plague, and which some whispered was the embodied daemon-soul of the plague itself. Eight houses were entered by a nameless thing which strewed red death in its wake—in all, seventeen maimed, and shapeless remnants of bodies were left behind by the voiceless, sadistic monster that crept abroad. A few persons had half seen it in the dark and said it was white and like a malformed ape or anthropomorphic fiend. It had not left behind quite all that it had attacked, for sometimes it had been hungry. The number it had killed was fourteen; three of the bodies had been in stricken homes and had not been alive.

On the third night, frantic bands of searchers, led by the police, captured it in a house on Crane Street near the Miskatonic campus. They had organized the quest with care, keeping in touch by means of volunteer telephone stations, and when someone in the college district had reported hearing a scratching at a shuttered window, the net was quickly spread. On account of the general alarm and precautions, there were only two more victims, and the capture was effected without major casualties. The thing was finally stopped by a bullet, though not a fatal one, and was rushed to the local hospital amidst universal excitement and loathing.

For it had been a man. This much was clear despite the nauseous eyes, the voiceless simianism, and the daemoniac savagery. They dressed its wound and carted it to the asylum at Sefton, where it beat its head against the walls of a padded cell for sixteen years—until the recent mishap when it escaped under circumstances that few like to mention. What had most disgusted the searchers of Arkham was the thing they noticed when the monster's face was cleaned—the mocking, unbelievable resemblance to a learned and self-sacrificing martyr who had been entombed but three days before—the late Dr. Allan Halsey, public benefactor and dean of the medical school of Miskatonic University.

To the vanished Herbert West and to me, the disgust and horror were supreme. I shudder tonight as I think of it; shudder even more than I did that morning when West muttered through his bandages, "Damn it, it wasn't quite fresh enough!"

• PART III

It is uncommon to fire all six shots of a revolver with great suddenness when one would probably be sufficient, but many things in the life of Herbert West were uncommon. It is, for instance, not often that a young physician leaving college is obliged to conceal the principles which guide his selection of a home and office, yet that was the case with Herbert West. When he and I obtained our degrees at the medical school of Miskatonic University and sought to relieve our poverty by setting up as general practitioners, we took great care not to say that we chose our house because it was fairly well isolated, and as near as possible to the potter's field.

Reticence such as this is seldom without a cause, nor indeed was ours, for our requirements were those resulting from a life-work distinctly unpopular. Outwardly we were doctors only, but beneath the surface were aims of far greater and more terrible moment—for the essence of Herbert West's existence was a quest amid black and forbidden realms of the unknown, in which he hoped to uncover the secret of life and restore to perpetual animation the graveyard's cold clay. Such a quest demands strange materials, among them fresh human bodies, and in order to keep supplied with these indispensable things, one must live quietly and not far from a place of informal interment.

West and I had met in college, and I had been the only one to sympathize with his hideous experiments. Gradually I had come to be his inseparable assistant, and now that we were out of college, we had to keep together. It was not easy to find a good opening for two doctors in company, but finally, the influence of the university secured us a practice in Bolton—a factory town near Arkham, the seat of the college. The Bolton Worsted Mills are the largest in the Miskatonic Valley, and their polyglot employees are never popular as patients with the local physicians. We chose our house with care, seizing at last on a rather run-down cottage near the end of Pond Street; five numbers from the closest neighbor, and separated from the local potter's field by only a stretch of meadowland, bisected by a narrow neck of the rather dense forest which lies to the north. The distance was greater than we wished, but we could get no nearer house without going on the other side of the field, wholly out of the factory district. We were not much displeased, however, since there were no people between us and our sinister source of supplies. The walk was a trifle long, but we could haul our silent specimens undisturbed.

Our practice was surprisingly large from the very first—large enough to please most young doctors, and large enough to prove a bore and a burden to students whose real interest lay elsewhere. The mill-hands were of somewhat turbulent inclinations, and besides their many natural needs, their frequent clashes and stabbing affrays gave us plenty to do. But what actually absorbed our minds was the secret laboratory we had fitted up in the cellar—the laboratory with the long table under the electric lights, where in the small hours of the morning we often injected West's various solutions into the veins of the things we dragged from the potter's field. West was experimenting madly to find something which would start man's vital motions anew after they had been stopped by the thing we call death but had encountered the most ghastly obstacles. The solution had to be differently compounded for different types—what would serve for guinea-pigs would not serve for human beings, and different human specimens required large modifications.

The bodies had to be exceedingly fresh, or the slight decomposition of brain tissue would render perfect reanimation impossible. Indeed, the greatest problem was to get them fresh enough—West had had horrible experiences during his secret college researches with corpses of doubtful vintage. The results of partial or imperfect animation were much more hideous than were the total failures, and we both held fearsome recollections of such things. Ever since our first daemoniac session in the deserted farmhouse on Meadow Hill in Arkham, we had felt a brooding menace; and West, though a calm, blond, blue-eyed scientific automaton in most respects, often confessed to a shuddering sensation of stealthy pursuit. He half felt that he was followed—a psychological delusion of shaken nerves, enhanced by the undeniably disturbing fact that at least one of our reanimated specimens was still alive—a frightful carnivorous thing in a padded cell at Sefton. Then there was another—our first—whose exact fate we had never learned.

We had fair luck with specimens in Bolton—much better than in Arkham. We had not been settled a week before we got an accident victim on the very night of burial, and made it open its eyes with an amazingly rational expression before the solution failed. It had lost an arm—if it had been a perfect body, we might have succeeded better. Between then and the next January, we secured three more; one total failure, one case of marked muscular motion, and one rather shivery thing—it rose of itself and uttered a sound. Then came a period when luck was poor; interments fell off, and those that did occur were of specimens either too diseased or too maimed for use. We kept track of all the deaths and their circumstances with systematic care.

One March night, however, we unexpectedly obtained a specimen that did not come from the potter's field. In Bolton, the prevailing spirit of Puritanism had outlawed the sport of boxing—with the usual result. Surreptitious and ill-conducted bouts among the mill-workers were common, and occasionally professional talent of low grade was imported. This late winter night, there had been such a match, evidently with disastrous results, since two timorous Poles had come to us with incoherently whispered entreaties to attend to a very secret and desperate case. We followed them to an abandoned barn, where the remnants of a crowd of frightened foreigners were watching a silent black form on the floor.

The match had been between Kid O'Brien—a lubberly and now quaking youth with a most un-Hibernian hooked nose—and Buck Robinson, "The Harlem Smoke." The negro had been knocked out, and a moment's examination shewed us that he would permanently remain so. He was a loathsome, gorilla-like thing, with abnormally long arms which I could not help calling forelegs, and a face that conjured up thoughts of unspeakable Congo secrets and tom-tom poundings under an eerie moon. The body must have looked even worse in life—but the world holds many ugly things. Fear was upon the whole pitiful crowd, for they did not know what the law would exact of them if the affair were not hushed up; and they were grateful when West, in spite of my involuntary shudders, offered to get rid of the thing quietly—for a purpose I knew too well.

There was bright moonlight over the snowless landscape, but we dressed the thing and carried it home between us through the deserted streets and meadows, as we had carried a similar thing one horrible night in Arkham. We approached the house from the field in the rear, took the specimen in the back door and down the cellar stairs, and prepared it for the usual experiment. Our fear of the police was absurdly great, though we had timed our trip to avoid the solitary patrolman of that section.

The result was wearily anticlimactic. Ghastly, as our prize appeared, it was wholly unresponsive to every solution we injected in its black arm, solutions prepared from experience with white specimens only. So as the hour grew dangerously near to dawn, we did as we had done with the others—dragged the thing across the meadows to the neck of the woods near the potter's field, and buried it there in the best sort of grave the frozen ground would furnish. The grave was not very deep, but fully as good as that of the previous specimen—the thing which had risen of itself and uttered a sound. In the light of our dark lanterns, we carefully covered it with leaves and dead vines, fairly certain that the police would never find it in a forest so dim and dense.

The next day I was increasingly apprehensive about the police, for a patient brought rumors of a suspected fight and death. West had still another source of worry, for he had been called in the afternoon to a case which ended very threateningly. An Italian woman had become hysterical over her missing child—a lad of five who had strayed off early in the morning and failed to appear for dinner—and had developed symptoms highly alarming in view of an always weak heart. It was a very foolish hysteria, for the boy had often run away before, but Italian peasants are exceedingly superstitious, and this woman seemed as much harassed by omens as by facts. About seven o'clock in the evening, she had died, and her frantic husband had made a frightful scene in his efforts to kill West, whom he wildly blamed for not saving her life. Friends had held him when he drew a stiletto, but West departed amidst his inhuman shrieks, curses, and oaths of vengeance. In his latest affliction, the fellow seemed to have forgotten his child, who was still missing as the night advanced. There was some talk of searching the woods, but most of the family's friends were busy with the dead woman and the screaming man. Altogether, the nervous strain upon West must have been tremendous. Thoughts of the police and of the mad Italian both weighed heavily.

We retired about eleven, but I did not sleep well. Bolton had a surprisingly good police force for so small a town, and I could not help fearing the mess which would ensue if the affair of the night before were ever tracked down. It might mean the end of all our local work—and perhaps prison for both West and me. I did not like those rumors of a fight that were floating about. After the clock had struck three, the moon shone in my eyes, but I turned over without rising to pull down the shade. Then came the steady rattling at the back door.

I lay still and somewhat dazed, but before long heard West's rap on my door. He was clad in dressing-gown and slippers and had in his hands a revolver and an electric flashlight. From the revolver I knew that he was thinking more of the crazed Italian than of the police.

"We'd better both go," he whispered. "It wouldn't do not to answer it anyway, and it may be a patient—it would be like one of those fools to try the back door."

So we both went down the stairs on tiptoe, with a fear partly justified and partly that which comes only from the soul of the weird small hours. The rattling continued, growing somewhat louder. When we reached the door, I cautiously unbolted it and threw it open, and as the moon streamed revealingly down on the form silhouetted there, West did a peculiar thing. Despite the obvious danger of attracting notice and bringing down on our heads the dreaded police investigation—a thing which, after all, was mercifully averted by the relative isolation of our cottage—my friend suddenly, excitedly, and unnecessarily emptied all six chambers of his revolver into the nocturnal visitor.

For that visitor was neither Italian nor policeman. Looming hideously against the spectral moon was a gigantic misshapen thing not to be imagined save in nightmares—a glassy-eyed, ink-black apparition nearly on all fours, covered with bits of mold, leaves, and vines, foul with caked blood, and having between its glistening teeth a snow-white, terrible, cylindrical object terminating in a tiny hand.

• PART IV

The scream of a dead man gave to me that acute and added horror of Dr. Herbert West, which harassed the latter years of our companionship. It is natural that such a thing as a dead man's scream should give horror, for it is obviously, not a pleasing or ordinary occurrence, but I was used to similar experiences, hence suffered on this occasion only because of a particular circumstance. And, as I have implied, it was not of the dead man himself that I became afraid.

Herbert West, whose associate and assistant I was, possessed scientific interests far beyond the usual routine of a village physician. That was why, when establishing his practice in Bolton, he had chosen an isolated house near the potter's field. Briefly and brutally stated, West's sole absorbing interest was a secret study of the phenomena of life and its cessation, leading toward the reanimation of the dead through injections of an excitant solution. For this ghastly experimenting, it was necessary to have a constant supply of very fresh human bodies; very fresh because even the least decay hopelessly damaged the brain structure and human because we found that the solution had to be compounded differently for different types of organisms. Scores of rabbits and guinea-pigs had been killed and treated, but their trail was a blind one. West had never fully succeeded because he had never been able to secure a corpse sufficiently fresh. What he wanted were bodies from which vitality had only just departed; bodies with every cell intact and capable of receiving again the impulse toward that mode of motion called life. There was hope that this second and artificial life might be made perpetual by repetitions of the injection, but we had learned that an ordinary natural life would not respond to the action. To establish the artificial motion, natural life must be extinct—the specimens must be very fresh, but genuinely dead.

The awesome quest had begun when West and I were students at the Miskatonic University Medical School in Arkham, vividly conscious for the first time of the thoroughly mechanical nature of life. That was seven years before, but West looked scarcely a day older now—he was small, blond, clean-shaven, soft-voiced, and spectacled, with only an occasional flash of a cold blue eye to tell of the hardening and growing fanaticism of his character under the pressure of his terrible investigations. Our experiences had often been hideous in the extreme; the results of defective reanimation, when lumps of graveyard clay had been galvanized into morbid, unnatural, and brainless motion by various modifications of the vital solution.

One thing had uttered a nerve-shattering scream; another had risen violently, beaten us both to unconsciousness, and run amuck in a shocking way before it could be placed behind asylum bars; still another, a loathsome African monstrosity, had clawed out of its shallow grave and done a deed—West had had to shoot that object. We could not get bodies fresh enough to shew any trace of reason when reanimated, so had perforce created nameless horrors. It was disturbing to think that one, perhaps two, of our monsters still lived—that thought haunted us shadowingly, till finally, West disappeared under frightful circumstances. But at the time of the scream in the cellar laboratory of the isolated Bolton cottage, our fears were subordinate to our anxiety for extremely fresh specimens. West was more avid than I so that it almost seemed to me that he looked half-covetously at any very healthy living physique.

It was in July 1910 that the bad luck regarding specimens began to turn. I had been on a long visit to my parents in Illinois, and upon my return found West in a state of singular elation. He had, he told me excitedly, in all likelihood solved the problem of freshness through an approach from an entirely new angle—that of artificial preservation. I had known that he was working on a new and highly unusual embalming compound, and was not surprised that it had turned out well; but until he explained the details, I was rather puzzled as to how such a compound could help in our work since the objectionable staleness of the specimens was largely due to delay occurring before we secured them. This, I now saw, West had clearly recognized; creating his embalming compound for future rather than immediate use, and trusting to fate to supply again some very recent and unburied corpse, as it had years before when we obtained the negro killed in the Bolton prize-fight. At last, fate had been kind, so that on this occasion there lay in the secret cellar laboratory a corpse whose decay could not by any possibility have begun. What would happen on reanimation, and whether we could hope for a revival of mind and reason, West did not venture to predict. The experiment would be a landmark in our studies, and he had saved the new body for my return so that both might share the spectacle in accustomed fashion.

West told me how he had obtained the specimen. It had been a vigorous man, a well-dressed stranger just off the train on his way to transact some business with the Bolton Worsted Mills. The walk through the town had been long, and by the time the traveler paused at our cottage to ask the way to the factories, his heart had become greatly overtaxed. He had refused a stimulant and had suddenly dropped dead only a moment later. The body, as might be expected, seemed to West a heaven-sent gift. In his brief conversation, the stranger had made it clear that he was unknown in Bolton, and a search of his pockets subsequently revealed him to be one Robert Leavitt of St. Louis, apparently without a family to make instant inquiries about his disappearance. If this man could not be restored to life, no one would know of our experiment. We buried our materials in a dense strip of woods between the house and the potter's field. If, on the other hand, he could be restored, our fame would be brilliantly and perpetually established. So without delay, West had injected into the body's wrist the compound which would hold it fresh for use after my arrival. The matter of the presumably weak heart, which to my mind imperiled the success of our experiment, did not appear to trouble West extensively. He hoped, at last, to obtain what he had never obtained before—a rekindled spark of reason and perhaps a normal, living creature.

So on the night of July 18, 1910, Herbert West and I stood in the cellar laboratory and gazed at a white, silent figure beneath the dazzling arc-light. The embalming compound had worked uncannily well, for as I stared fascinatedly at the sturdy frame which had lain two weeks without stiffening, I was moved to seek West's assurance that the thing was really dead. This assurance he gave readily enough, reminding me that the reanimating solution was never used without careful tests as to life since it could have no effect if any of the original vitality were present. As West proceeded to take preliminary steps, I was impressed by the vast intricacy of the new experiment; an intricacy so vast that he could trust no hand less delicate than his own. Forbidding me to touch the body, he first injected a drug in the wrist just beside the place his needle had punctured when injecting the embalming compound. This, he said, was to neutralize the compound and release the system to a normal relaxation so that the reanimating solution might freely work when injected. Slightly later, when a change and a gentle tremor seemed to affect the dead limbs, West stuffed a pillow-like object violently over the twitching face, not withdrawing it until the corpse appeared quiet and ready for our attempt at reanimation. The pale enthusiast now applied some last perfunctory tests for absolute lifelessness, withdrew satisfied, and finally injected into the left arm an accurately measured amount of the vital elixir, prepared during the afternoon with greater care than we had used since college days when our feats were new and groping. I cannot express the wild, breathless suspense with which we waited for results on this first really fresh specimen—the first we could reasonably expect to open its lips in rational speech, perhaps to tell of what it had seen beyond the unfathomable abyss.

West was a materialist, believing in no soul and attributing all the working of consciousness to bodily phenomena; consequently, he looked for no revelation of hideous secrets from gulfs and caverns beyond death's barrier. I did not wholly disagree with him theoretically, yet held vague instinctive remnants of the primitive faith of my forefathers; so that I could not help eyeing the corpse with a certain amount of awe and terrible expectation. Besides—I could not extract from my memory that hideous, inhuman shriek we heard on the night we tried our first experiment in the deserted farmhouse at Arkham.

Very little time had elapsed before I saw the attempt was not to be a total failure. A touch of color came to cheeks hitherto chalk-white and spread out under the curiously ample stubble of sandy beard. West, who had his hand on the pulse of the left wrist, suddenly nodded significantly; and almost simultaneously, a mist appeared on the mirror inclined above the body's mouth. There followed a few spasmodic muscular motions, and then an audible breathing and visible motion of the chest. I looked at the closed eyelids and thought I detected a quivering. Then the lids opened, shewing eyes which were grey, calm, and alive, but still unintelligent and not even curious.

In a moment of fantastic whim, I whispered questions to the reddening ears, questions of other worlds of which the memory might still be present. Subsequent terror drove them from my mind, but I think the last one, which I repeated, was: "Where have you been?" I do not yet know whether I was answered or not, for no sound came from the well-shaped mouth; but I do know that at that moment I firmly thought the thin lips moved silently, forming syllables which I would have vocalized as "only now" if that phrase had possessed any sense or relevancy. At that moment, as I say, I was elated with the conviction that the one great goal had been attained; and that for the first time, a reanimated corpse had uttered distinct words impelled by actual reason. In the next moment, there was no doubt about the triumph; no doubt that the solution had truly accomplished, at least temporarily, its full mission of restoring rational and articulate life to the dead. But in that triumph, there came to me the greatest of all horrors—not horror of the thing that spoke, but of the deed that I had witnessed and of the man with whom my professional fortunes were joined.

For that very fresh body, at last writhing into full and terrifying consciousness with eyes dilated at the memory of its last scene on earth, threw out its frantic hands in a life and death struggle with the air, and suddenly collapsing into a second and final dissolution from which there could be no return, screamed out the cry that will ring eternally in my aching brain:

"Help! Keep off, you cursed little tow-head fiend—keep that damned needle away from me!"

• PART V

Many men have related hideous things, not mentioned in print, which happened on the battlefields of the Great War. Some of these things have made me faint, others have convulsed me with devastating nausea, while still others have made me tremble and look behind me in the dark; yet despite the worst of them I believe I can myself relate the most hideous thing of all—the shocking, the unnatural, the unbelievable horror from the shadows.

In 1915 I was a physician with the rank of First Lieutenant in a Canadian regiment in Flanders, one of many Americans to precede the government itself into the gigantic struggle. I had not entered the army on my own initiative, but rather as a natural result of the enlistment of the man whose indispensable assistant I was—the celebrated Boston surgical specialist, Dr. Herbert West. Dr. West had been avid for a chance to serve as a surgeon in a great war, and when the chance had come, he carried me with him almost against my will. There were reasons why I could have been glad to let the war separate us; reasons why I found the practice of medicine and the companionship of West more and more irritating; but when he had gone to Ottawa and through a colleague's influence secured a medical commission as Major, I could not resist the imperious persuasion of one determined that I should accompany him in my usual capacity.

When I say that Dr. West was avid to serve in battle, I do not mean to imply that he was either naturally warlike or anxious for the safety of civilization. Always an ice-cold intellectual machine; slight, blond, blue-eyed, and spectacled; I think he secretly sneered at my occasional martial enthusiasms and censures of supine neutrality. There was, however, something he wanted in embattled Flanders; and in order to secure it had had to assume a military exterior. What he wanted was not a thing which many persons want, but something connected with the peculiar branch of medical science which he had chosen quite clandestinely to follow, and in which he had achieved amazing and occasionally hideous results. It was, in fact, nothing more or less than an abundant supply of freshly killed men in every stage of dismemberment.

Herbert West needed fresh bodies because his life-work was the reanimation of the dead. This work was not known to the fashionable clientele who had so swiftly built up his fame after his arrival in Boston; but was only too well known to me, who had been his closest friend and sole assistant since the old days in Miskatonic University Medical School at Arkham. It was in those college days that he had begun his terrible experiments, first on small animals and then on human bodies shockingly obtained. There was a solution which he injected into the veins of dead things, and if they were fresh enough, they responded in strange ways. He had had much trouble in discovering the proper formula, for each type of organism was found to need a stimulus especially adapted to it. Terror stalked him when he reflected on his partial failures, nameless things resulting from imperfect solutions or from bodies insufficiently fresh. A certain number of these failures had remained alive—one was in an asylum while others had vanished—and as he thought of conceivable yet virtually impossible eventualities, he often shivered beneath his usual stolidity.

West had soon learned that absolute freshness was the prime requisite for useful specimens, and had accordingly resorted to frightful and unnatural expedients in body-snatching. In college, and during our early practice together in the factory town of Bolton, my attitude toward him had been largely one of fascinated admiration; but as his boldness in methods grew, I began to develop a gnawing fear. I did not like the way he looked at healthy living bodies, and then there came a nightmarish session in the cellar laboratory when I learned that a certain specimen had been a living body when he secured it. That was the first time he had ever been able to revive the quality of rational thought in a corpse, and his success, obtained at such a loathsome cost, had completely hardened him.

Of his methods in the intervening five years, I dare not speak. I was held to him by sheer force of fear and witnessed sights that no human tongue could repeat. Gradually I came to find Herbert West himself more horrible than anything he did—that was when it dawned on me that his once normal scientific zeal for prolonging life had subtly degenerated into a mere morbid and ghoulish curiosity and secret sense of charnel picturesqueness. His interest became a hellish and perverse addiction to the repellently and fiendishly abnormal; he gloated calmly over artificial monstrosities which would make most healthy men drop dead from fright and disgust; he became, behind his pallid intellectuality, a fastidious Baudelaire of physical experiment—a languid Elagabalus of the tombs.

Dangers he met unflinchingly; crimes he committed unmoved. I think the climax came when he had proved his point that rational life could be restored and had sought new worlds to conquer by experimenting on the reanimation of detached parts of bodies. He had wild and original ideas on the independent vital properties of organic cells and nerve-tissue separated from natural physiological systems; and achieved some hideous preliminary results in the form of never-dying, artificially nourished tissue obtained from the nearly hatched eggs of an indescribable tropical reptile. Two biological points he was exceedingly anxious to settle—first, whether any amount of consciousness and rational action be possible without the brain, proceeding from the spinal cord and various nerve-centers; and second, whether any kind of ethereal, intangible relation distinct from the material cells may exist to link the surgically separated parts of what has previously been a single living organism. All this research work required a prodigious supply of freshly slaughtered human flesh—and that was why Herbert West had entered the Great War.

The phantasmal, unmentionable thing occurred one midnight late in March 1915, in a field hospital behind the lines of St. Eloi. I wonder even now if it could have been other than a daemoniac dream of delirium. West had a private laboratory in an east room of the barn-like temporary edifice, assigned him on his plea that he was devising new and radical methods for the treatment of hitherto hopeless cases of maiming. There he worked as a butcher in the midst of his gory wares—I could never get used to the levity with which he handled and classified certain things. At times he actually did perform marvels of surgery for the soldiers, but his chief delights were of a less public and philanthropic kind, requiring many explanations of sounds which seemed peculiar even amidst that babel of the damned. Among these sounds were frequent revolver-shots—surely not uncommon on a battlefield, but distinctly uncommon in a hospital. Dr. West's reanimated specimens were not meant for long existence or a large audience. Besides human tissue, West employed much of the reptile embryo tissue, which he had cultivated with such singular results. It was better than human material for maintaining life in organless fragments, and that was now my friend's chief activity. In a dark corner of the laboratory, over a queer incubating burner, he kept a large covered vat full of this reptilian cell-matter, which multiplied and grew puffily and hideously.

On the night of which I speak, we had a splendid new specimen—a man at once physically powerful and of such high mentality that a sensitive nervous system was assured. It was rather ironic, for he was the officer who had helped West to his commission, and who was now to have been our associate. Moreover, he had in the past secretly studied the theory of reanimation to some extent under West. Major Sir Eric Moreland Clapham-Lee, D.S.O., was the greatest surgeon in our division and had been hastily assigned to the St. Eloi sector when news of the heavy fighting reached headquarters. He had come in an airplane piloted by the intrepid Lieut. Ronald Hill, only to be shot down when directly over his destination. The fall had been spectacular and awful; Hill was unrecognizable afterward, but the wreck yielded up the great surgeon in a nearly decapitated but otherwise intact condition. West had greedily seized the lifeless thing which had once been his friend and fellow-scholar, and I shuddered when he finished severing the head, placed it in his hellish vat of pulpy reptile-tissue to preserve it for future experiments, and proceeded to treat the decapitated body on the operating table. He injected new blood, joined certain veins, arteries, and nerves at the headless neck, and closed the ghastly aperture with engrafted skin from an unidentified specimen which had borne an officer's uniform. I knew what he wanted—to see if this highly organized body could exhibit, without its head, any of the signs of mental life which had distinguished Sir Eric Moreland Clapham-Lee. Once a student of reanimation, this silent trunk was now gruesomely called upon to exemplify it.

I can still see Herbert West under the sinister electric light as he injected his reanimating solution into the arm of the headless body. The scene I cannot describe—I should faint if I tried it, for there is madness in a room full of classified charnel things, with blood and lesser human debris almost ankle-deep on the slimy floor, and with hideous reptilian abnormalities sprouting, bubbling, and baking over a winking bluish-green specter of dim flame in a far corner of black shadows.

The specimen, as West repeatedly observed, had a splendid nervous system. Much was expected of it, and as a few twitching motions began to appear, I could see the feverish interest on West's face. He was ready, I think, to see proof of his increasingly strong opinion that consciousness, reason, and personality can exist independently of the brain—that man has no central connective spirit, but is merely a machine of nervous matter, each section more or less complete in itself. In one triumphant demonstration, West was about to relegate the mystery of life to the category of myth. The body now twitched more vigorously, and beneath our avid eyes commenced to heave in a frightful way. The arms stirred disquietingly, the legs drew up, and various muscles contracted in a repulsive kind of writhing. Then the headless thing threw out its arms in a gesture which was unmistakably one of desperation—an intelligent desperation apparently sufficient to prove every theory of Herbert West. Certainly, the nerves were recalling the man's last act in life; the struggle to get free of the falling airplane.

What followed, I shall never positively know. It may have been wholly a hallucination from the shock caused at that instant by the sudden and complete destruction of the building in a cataclysm of German shell-fire—who can gainsay it since West and I were the only proved survivors? West liked to think that before his recent disappearance, but there were times when he could not, for it was queer that we both had the same hallucination. The hideous occurrence itself was very simple, notable only for what it implied.

The body on the table had risen with a blind and terrible groping, and we had heard a sound. I should not call that sound a voice, for it was too awful. And yet its timbre was not the most awful thing about it. Neither was its message—it had merely screamed, "Jump, Ronald, for God's sake, jump!" The awful thing was its source.

For it had come from the large covered vat in that ghoulish corner of crawling black shadows.

• PART VI

When Dr. Herbert West disappeared a year ago, the Boston police questioned me closely. They suspected that I was holding something back, and perhaps suspected graver things, but I could not tell them the truth because they would not have believed it. They knew, indeed, that West had been connected with activities beyond the credence of ordinary men; for his hideous experiments in the reanimation of dead bodies had long been too extensive to admit of perfect secrecy, but the final soul-shattering catastrophe held elements of daemoniac phantasy which make even me doubt the reality of what I saw.

I was West's closest friend and only confidential assistant. We had met years before, in medical school, and from the first, I had shared his terrible researches. He had slowly tried to perfect a solution which, injected into the veins of the newly deceased, would restore life; a labor demanding an abundance of fresh corpses and therefore involving the most unnatural actions. Still more shocking were the products of some of the experiments—grisly masses of flesh that had been dead, but that West waked to a blind, brainless, nauseous animation. These were the usual results, for, in order to reawaken the mind, it was necessary to have specimens so absolutely fresh that no decay could possibly affect the delicate brain-cells.

This need for very fresh corpses had been West's moral undoing. They were hard to get, and one awful day he had secured his specimen while it was still alive and vigorous. A struggle, a needle, and a powerful alkaloid had transformed it to a very fresh corpse, and the experiment had succeeded for a brief and memorable moment, but West had emerged with a soul calloused and seared, and a hardened eye which sometimes glanced with a kind of hideous and calculating appraisal at men of especially sensitive brain and especially vigorous physique. Toward the last, I became acutely afraid of West, for he began to look at me that way. People did not seem to notice his glances, but they noticed my fear; and after his disappearance used that as a basis for some absurd suspicions.

West, in reality, was more afraid than I, for his abominable pursuits entailed a life of furtiveness and dread of every shadow. Partly it was the police he feared, but sometimes his nervousness was deeper and more nebulous, touching on certain indescribable things into which he had injected a morbid life, and from which he had not seen that life depart. He usually finished his experiments with a revolver, but a few times, he had not been quick enough. There was that first specimen on whose rifled grave marks of clawing were later seen. There was also that Arkham professor's body that had done cannibal things before it had been captured and thrust unidentified into a madhouse cell at Sefton, where it beat the walls for sixteen years. Most of the other possibly surviving results were things less easy to speak of—for in later years West's scientific zeal had degenerated to an unhealthy and fantastic mania, and he had spent his chief skill in vitalizing not entire human bodies, but isolated parts of bodies or parts joined to organic matter other than human. It had become fiendishly disgusting by the time he disappeared; many of the experiments could not even be hinted at in print. The Great War, through which both of us served as surgeons, had intensified this side of West.

In saying that West's fear of his specimens was nebulous, I have in mind particularly its complex nature. Part of it came merely from knowing of the existence of such nameless monsters, while another part arose from the apprehension of the bodily harm they might under certain circumstances do him. Their disappearance added horror to the situation—of them all, West knew the whereabouts of only one, the pitiful asylum thing. Then there was a more subtle fear—a very fantastic sensation resulting from a curious experiment in the Canadian army in 1915. West, in the midst of a severe battle, had reanimated Major Sir Eric Moreland Clapham-Lee, D.S.O., a fellow-physician who knew about his experiments and could have duplicated them. The head had been removed so that the possibilities of quasi-intelligent life in the trunk might be investigated. Just as the building was wiped out by a German shell, there had been a success. The trunk had moved intelligently, and, unbelievable to relate, we were both sickeningly sure that articulate sounds had come from the detached head as it lay in a shadowy corner of the laboratory. The shell had been merciful, in a way—but West could never feel as certain as he wished, that we two were the only survivors. He used to make shuddering conjectures about the possible actions of a headless physician with the power of reanimating the dead.

West's last quarters were in a venerable house of much elegance, overlooking one of the oldest burying-grounds in Boston. He had chosen the place for purely symbolic and fantastically aesthetic reasons since most of the interments were of the colonial period and, therefore, of little use to a scientist seeking very fresh bodies. The laboratory was in a sub-cellar secretly constructed by imported workmen, and contained a huge incinerator for the quiet and complete disposal of such bodies, or fragments and synthetic mockeries of bodies, as might remain from the morbid experiments and unhallowed amusements of the owner. During the excavation of this cellar, the workmen had struck some exceedingly ancient masonry, undoubtedly connected with the old burying-ground, yet far too deep to correspond with any known sepulcher therein. After a number of calculations West decided that it represented some secret chamber beneath the tomb of the Averills, where the last interment had been made in 1768. I was with him when he studied the nitrous, dripping walls laid bare by the spades and mattocks of the men and was prepared for the gruesome thrill which would attend the uncovering of centuried grave-secrets, but for the first time West's new timidity conquered his natural curiosity, and he betrayed his degenerating fiber by ordering the masonry left intact and plastered over. Thus it remained till that final hellish night, part of the walls of the secret laboratory. I speak of West's decadence but must add that it was a purely mental and intangible thing. Outwardly he was the same to the last—calm, cold, slight, and yellow-haired, with spectacled blue eyes and a general aspect of youth which years and fears seemed never to change. He seemed calm even when he thought of that clawed grave and looked over his shoulder, even when he thought of the carnivorous thing that gnawed and pawed at Sefton bars.

The end of Herbert West began one evening in our joint study when he was dividing his curious glance between the newspaper and me. A strange headline item had struck at him from the crumpled pages, and a nameless titan claw had seemed to reach down through sixteen years. Something fearsome and incredible had happened at Sefton Asylum fifty miles away, stunning the neighborhood and baffling the police. In the small hours of the morning, a body of silent men had entered the grounds, and their leader had aroused the attendants. He was a menacing military figure who talked without moving his lips and whose voice seemed almost ventriloquially connected with an immense black case he carried. His expressionless face was handsome to the point of radiant beauty but had shocked the superintendent when the hall light fell on it—for it was a wax face with eyes of painted glass. Some nameless accident had befallen this man. A larger man guided his steps, a repellent hulk whose bluish face seemed half eaten away by some unknown malady. The speaker had asked for the custody of the cannibal monster committed from Arkham sixteen years before, and upon being refused, gave a signal which precipitated a shocking riot. The fiends had beaten, trampled, and bitten every attendant who did not flee, killing four and finally succeeding in the liberation of the monster. Those victims who could recall the event without hysteria swore that the creatures had acted less like men than like unthinkable automata guided by the wax-faced leader. By the time help could be summoned, every trace of the men and of their mad charge had vanished.

From the hour of reading this item until midnight, West sat almost paralyzed. At midnight the doorbell rang, startling him fearfully. All the servants were asleep in the attic, so I answered the bell. As I have told the police, there was no wagon in the street, but only a group of strange-looking figures bearing a large square box which they deposited in the hallway after one of them had grunted in a highly unnatural voice, "Express—prepaid." They filed out of the house with a jerky tread, and as I watched them go, I had an odd idea that they were turning toward the ancient cemetery on which the back of the house abutted. When I slammed the door after them, West came downstairs and looked at the box. It was about two feet square and bore West's correct name and present address. It also bore the inscription, "From Eric Moreland Clapham-Lee, St. Eloi, Flanders." Six years before, in Flanders, a shelled hospital had fallen upon the headless reanimated trunk of Dr. Clapham-Lee, and upon the detached head which—perhaps—had uttered articulate sounds.

West was not even excited now. His condition was more ghastly. Quickly he said, "It's the finish—but let's incinerate—this." We carried the thing down to the laboratory—listening. I do not remember many particulars—you can imagine my state of mind—but it is a vicious lie to say it was Herbert West's body, which I put into the incinerator. We both inserted the whole unopened wooden box, closed the door, and started the electricity. Nor did any sound come from the box, after all.

It was West who first noticed the falling plaster on that part of the wall where the ancient tomb masonry had been covered up. I was going to run, but he stopped me. Then I saw a small black aperture, felt a ghoulish wind of ice, and smelled the charnel bowels of a putrescent earth. There was no sound, but just then, the electric lights went out, and I saw outlined against some phosphorescence of the nether world a horde of silent toiling things which only insanity—or worse—could create. Their outlines were human, semi-human, fractionally human, and not human at all—the horde was grotesquely heterogeneous. They were removing the stones quietly, one by one, from the centuried wall. And then, as the breach became large enough, they came out into the laboratory in single file, led by a talking thing with a beautiful head made of wax. A sort of mad-eyed monstrosity behind the leader seized on Herbert West. West did not resist or utter a sound. Then they all sprang at him and tore him to pieces before my eyes, bearing the fragments away into that subterranean vault of fabulous abominations. West's head was carried off by the wax-headed leader, who wore a Canadian officer's uniform. As it disappeared, I saw that the blue eyes behind the spectacles were hideously blazing with their first touch of frantic, visible emotion.

Servants found me unconscious in the morning. West was gone. The incinerator contained only unidentifiable ashes. Detectives have questioned me, but what can I say? The Sefton tragedy they will not connect with West, not that, nor the men with the box, whose existence they deny. I told them of the vault, and they pointed to the unbroken plaster wall and laughed. So I told them no more. They imply that I am either a madman or a murderer—probably, I am mad. But I might not be mad if those accursed tomb-legions had not been so silent.

WHEN THEY COME FOR YOU

By Thomas M. Malafarina

Darkness surrounded him. Not the pitch-black sort of darkness where nothing at all could be seen, but more of a gloomy semi-darkness. He was having trouble focusing, unsure of where he was. He could determine he was lying on his back with his head either propped up with pillows or elevated in some other fashion, perhaps by some sort of adjustable bed. He felt a dull burning pain, which seemed to radiate out from the center of his chest in all directions. As bad as his chest might feel, the disorientation and dreamlike quality of his surroundings was even more disturbing.

He could hear the beeping and humming of electronic machinery all around him, but he couldn't recall where he was or why he was lying in this strange gloomy place accompanied only by the sounds of machines. In fact, he couldn't quite even remember his own name. His mind was clouded, feeling as though he'd been given some sort of mind-altering drug.

Then he slowly began to remember; drugs. Yes, that's exactly what it was; drugs for the pain. He'd been given drugs, large doses of drugs. Morphine was one of the drugs and was being dripped into his body to help with the pain. It was all gradually starting to come back to him in disjointed fragments of lost memories. At last, he finally recalled who he was, then sadly where he was and why. He realized he probably would have been better off not remembering after all. His name was Salvador, Salvador Monroe, known to his friends as Sal or Sallie. He was in bed in a hospital, no not a hospital but a hospice center. And he was dying.

Through the drug-induced fog, which he recognized was barely doing any-thing to dampen the searing agony in his cancer-riddled lungs, Sal understood one thing clearer than anything else; his remaining time was short, very short. He sensed he was extremely weak now, too weak to even raise his head, but he could still manage to slowly move his eyes about to take in most of the room. He could see he was all alone. Where was his wife? Where was Charlotte? She promised she wouldn't leave him, said she was staying with him till the very end. But where was she now?

Sal suddenly began to panic. He had known he was dying for months, but now he had a feeling, an unmistakable intuition that the end was close by, and yet here he was, alone. He didn't want to die alone. He wouldn't allow himself to die alone. He was determined to hang on for as long as possible despite the pain. He wanted to wait for his beloved wife to return. Where was Charlotte? He couldn't cross over without saying one last goodbye to his wife.

Across the room, beyond his ability to focus within the gloom, Sal saw something, the slightest of movements, almost imperceptible but enough motion to capture his attention. What was that moving over there? Was it his wife sitting quietly in the darkness? Lord, he hoped so. He tried to speak, tried to form the words, and call out her name but found he was unable to do so. His throat and lips were parched. He wanted something to drink or perhaps some ice chips to chew on, anything to quench the thirst. And God help him, he needed more morphine to dull his ever-increasing pain.

Looking closer, Sal realized what he was seeing wasn't Charlotte. It was someone, no something else entirely. A faint glow seemed to be emitting from that darkest corner of the room. It was pulsating and appeared to be of no definite form; its shape changing continuously. At first, Sal had no idea what to make of the strange phenomena. He was almost certain it was some sort of illusion or hallucination brought on by the drugs, yet he could see it so clearly.

Then Sal experienced an awareness, a knowing of sorts. Even though his eyes were seeing nothing more than an effervescent shapeless mass floating mid-air, his mind was experiencing a completely different picture entirely. He saw his long-dead father. Sal's dad had passed away some thirty years earlier, following a sudden, massive heart attack when Sal was about twenty-nine. Yet now his father appeared before him, smiling at him from across the room with a peaceful and content expression the likes of which Sal had never quite seen cross the man's face in life. He appeared as he had when he was still tall, strong, and handsome with coal-black hair only just beginning to show hints of silver.

"Popa," Sal said without speaking as his lips silently formed the words. The specter across the room neither replied nor moved; it just stood and stared with that strange, peaceful smile.

Sal had always loved and respected his father in life and mourned his passing for what seemed like years. Since then, barely a day passed by without some recollection of his father popping into his mind. He often laughed at the way he noticed things about himself as he got older, which mirrored memories of his late Popa. Sal felt tears welling up in the corners of his eyes and didn't bother trying to stop them as they overflowed and trickled down his cheeks. God, how he missed his father! He had apparently forgotten just how much.

Then he saw two more glowing objects forming on both sides of the first. Soon these illusions took shape in his mind as well, and Sal immediately recognized one as his mother, who had passed on fifteen years after his father, and the other was his older brother, Anthony who had been killed in the jungles of Vietnam when Sal was entering his first year of high school, way back on September 17, 1969. It was a date Sal would never forget.

The countenance of his mother was as he remembered her from back when he was a young boy. He loved his mother with all of his heart and thought she was the most beautiful woman ever to walk the earth. And now she stood to one side of her husband, his father, looking more radiant than Sal's finest memory could possibly recall. And on the opposite side of his father stood Anthony, who was still wearing his trademark mischievous grin, the one that always drove the girls in his high school wild.

Sal lay helpless in his bed, unable to determine what this vision, hallucination, or whatever-it-was might mean, yet at the same time, he was enjoying the feeling of seeing his departed family members once again. A realization suddenly hit him, and Sal instantly understood why they were here; they had come for him. Sal had heard stories through the years of family members near death who had claimed that long lost relatives had come to guide them across to the afterlife.

About twenty years earlier, when his father's brother, Sal's Uncle Mike, had passed away, his aunt Gertrude had told him that in her husband's final moments of life, she heard him speaking to someone across the room who she couldn't see. Gert and told Sal he had identified the invisible being as his brother, Sal's father. She was certain he had come to guide Mike to the other side. She told young Sal that when his time came, he should be sure to do what his spirit guide instructed. She said, "Sallie, when they come for you, that means it's your time to go, and you should not resist."

She told him she had no idea what might happen if someone refused to go with them, but it couldn't possibly be good. "You don't mess with such things, Sallie," she had said. "They come for a reason, maybe to protect you from something, something else. I don't know. But what I do know is when the time comes, you just must let go." And several years later, that was exactly what she had done when it was her time to pass on.

Sal had always thought his aunt Gert might have been a little bit "off," but now all these many years later, he understood she had been right, and that was why his family was here; to help him crossover to whatever awaited him in the afterlife. And in his heart, Sal knew he should go with them; it was his time. They were his family, and he missed them all so much.

He understood all he had to do was let go, and he'd be free to cross over to a better place to be with his loved ones. At that moment, Sal wanted to go with them more than anything else he could imagine. But then he suddenly experienced a brief pang of doubt and realized he couldn't go with them, at least not yet. He knew the choice to leave or stay was still his to make. And yet as much as he wanted to follow them, he owed it to his loving wife to stay if just for another day or even for another few more hours or minutes. He had unfinished business on this side. He wanted to tell Charlotte how much he loved her, how grateful he had been for how she had taken care of him during his prolonged illness, and, most importantly, he wanted to say goodbye. Was that too much to ask? She deserved at least that much, and he wouldn't leave the planet until he had done so.

Across the room, his father, mother, and brother's peaceful smiling expressions began to darken, replaced by the looks of distress and disappointment. They somehow had sensed his intentions. They looked as though they wanted to try and persuade him but were helpless to do anything but stare at him despondently. Finally, his father, who appeared to be straining with all of his strength, slowly lifted one of his arms and extended his hand, palm up in one last pleading gesture for Sal to come with them.

As tears streamed down his face, Sal sent a thought across the room, between the two worlds. That thought was of how much he loved and missed them, but he couldn't go with them. Then the three images began to dissolve and fade away along with the glowing lights from which they had appeared.

It was only then Sal realized that during the time the spirits had been present, all of the pain from his cancer had disappeared. Now, however, it was returning with a vengeance. His chest seared with agony as the disease which had been eating him alive from the inside out resumed its deadly feast.

He also experienced something else, not something tangible or anything he could accurately explain except that it was a feeling of total loss, a sense of being left behind. He had images passing through his mind of a lone man standing in the dark at a railway station as a train pulled away. He somehow understood he had just refused what was literally a once-in-a-lifetime opportunity.

Tears still coursed down his face uncontrollably, but they were no longer tears of joy over seeing his family but were now tears of mourning for the emptiness he felt inside now they were gone. It was like his family had just died all over again. But somehow it was worse than that. Previously he at least had some hope he might see them again someday, but now there was a real fear he was lost to them forever.

Through his glistening tears, Sal saw something else across the room, another glowing shapeless mass. For a moment, he felt his heart begin to race with excitement at the possibility his family might have sensed his distress and returned for him. If so, he knew he'd go with them now despite not having said goodbye to Charlotte. He was ready. However, he noticed this glow seemed different from the previous one. It was not as bright and was actually yellow and crimson in color.

The image which gradually appeared in his mind when he looked into the light was not his father, his mother, or his brother. The visage was that of a young woman. She was rail-thin, with long scraggly filthy and unkempt hair. She was dressed in a pair of filthy soiled white pajamas that appeared saturated with some type of gelatinous fluid and were practically see-through. There was nothing alluring about the vision, however, as the woman was gaunt, and her minimal breasts hung down like shriveled prunes. Her sallow cheeks were enhanced by the sunken dark-ringed eyes, which seemed to bug out of her skull. Something about the woman seemed distantly familiar, but Sal couldn't quite place her.

Her mouth hung slack-jawed and was a reddish-black hole. Her lips on the left side of the deformed opening were gone, revealing a staggered row of sporadically missing and chipped teeth. It appeared as if her face had been through some sort of explosion. As if to further solidify this impression, several wisps of black smoke seeped out of the malformed orifice, making it appear like some horribly ghastly flesh-covered chimney.

The woman turned her head slowly to the left as if to display something, something on her right side which Sal sensed she wanted him to see and which he instinctively knew he wouldn't want to see. Sadly he was correct. The entire right side of her skull was gone. In its place were an enormous gaping hole oozing a mixture of blood, fragments of flesh, and a gooey gray substance, which Sal believed must have once been brain matter. Swarms of some sort of buzzing insects, perhaps flies, flew about the opening while more wisps of smoke leaked from the dripping gash.

At first, Sal was still uncertain who the woman might be or why she had appeared to him, but then the shock of recognition hit him like a club to the side of his skull. "Meghan?" he thought questioningly. The specter across the room nodded slightly in acknowledgment of his realization. "Oh my sweet God in Heaven! Sal thought, "Oh no. Please no! Not this! Don't let it be her. Not Meghan!"

There had been very few things in Sal's life for which he could honestly say he was sorry and for which he felt guilty or ashamed. But what had happened to Meghan and his part in the horrible incident was something which had haunted him his entire life. And now the memories flooded back as if they were happening all over again.

Some thirty years earlier, Sal had been dating a beautiful young woman named Meghan Reilly. She was a widow with two young pre-school children. Her husband had tragically died when struck by a drunk driver. During Sal's time with Meghan, her two little ones had become very attached to him. Since they could barely remember their late father, Sal had become something of a surrogate dad to them.

The affair had been going strong for close to a year. There was an apparent unspoken understanding, at least on Meghan's part, that their relationship would eventually result in marriage. But then something began to change for Sal. He noticed many instances over the previous six months where Meghan had acted in a very strange, unpredictable way, leading him to believe that she might be bipolar or maybe there was just something a bit unstable about the woman.

The last thing he wanted at his young age was to spend the rest of his life with a woman whose emotions had become so unpredictable. He also couldn't see himself committing to taking on her two children as his own. Thinking about the potential problems was becoming overwhelming for him.

As a result, he became distant, unwilling to face the inevitable, and perhaps hoping she'd grow tired of him and break off the relationship. But she didn't. He then realized at some point in time he was going to have to be the one to end things. Sal, however, wasn't good at confrontation and so he subtly tried to cut the emotional ties with Meghan further, spending less time with her going out at night alone to local bars. But it seemed the more he tried to pull away from her; the more Meghan attempted to draw him closer. Eventually, he had no other option; decided he had to break up with her. One night while sitting at home alone, contemplating his dilemma and after a few glasses of liquid courage, he called Meghan, and ended their relationship over the phone; an act Sal later would come to see as avoidance, bordering on cowardice.

Meghan was devastated and heartbroken. For her, the emotional pain became unbearable. Only having been widowed for a few years, the wound was still too fresh, and Sal's leaving her was like she had lost her husband all over again. Then one night after drinking herself into a stupor, she called Sal, cursing him for what he had done to her and her children. She was screaming and sobbing using profanities he had never heard her use before. He could hear her kids crying in the background over the phone.

She said she couldn't stand living with the pain he had caused and that she was going first to kill her children then herself. Then he'd be sorry for what he had done, and her suffering would be over. Sal was fairly certain her threats were nothing more than her way of trying to get him to come over to her place to discuss the situation face to face. Be he had no intention of doing that.

He had made up his mind, and as far as he was concerned, they were finished. However, Sal still did his best to try to reason with her but found it very difficult because of her drunken state, deteriorated mental condition, and the incessant noise of her children crying in the background. Megan screamed at the top of her lungs for the kids to be quiet, but the wailing continued and even louder than before. That was until Sal heard two quick shots, and the crying ceased.

Sal felt his stomach clench at the realization of what Meghan had just done. He was in shock and couldn't believe what he had heard. He hoped to God he was mistaken, and Meghan had maybe just shot into the air. Then perhaps the children had fled from the room. But deep in his heart, he knew this was all just

wishful thinking. Meghan came back on the line screaming even more hysterically than ever, "This is all your fault, Sal. You did this. YOU DID THIS! You
killed my babies, and now you're going to kill me too. But I swear I'll be back
for you, Sal. You can bet your worthless life. I will." Then Sal heard the final
gunshot. He stood in shock for a moment before absently placing the receiver
back on its cradle.

A few minutes later, after composing himself, Sal contacted the local police,
telling them the whole story, including the part about his breakup with Meghan.
He gave them her address and said he hadn't left his home and would wait there
to speak to them if necessary. The deaths were eventually a ruled murder-suicide
committed by a despondent woman who had experienced a psychotic break.
But Sal knew he was the catalyst that drove her over the edge.

A few months later, when things quieted down, Sal chose to move away
and start a new life far from his unpleasant past in a part of the country where
no one knew him. And although time past and most local people had all but
forgotten about the incident, Sal was never able to completely come to terms
with the role he played in Meghan's death. It had haunted him for the rest of
his life.

And now, all these years later, Meghan was back just as she had promised,
standing in spirit, ruined and broken across the room from his deathbed while
he lay helplessly suffering in his final agony. The hideous specter didn't speak
but smiled knowingly at Sal with what remained of her shattered mouth. Sal
wanted to scream for help or to cry out to anyone who might come and make
this foul hell-spawned creature leave him to die in peace, but he couldn't.

A moment later, as if in answer to an unspoken prayer, he heard the door
to his room open, and his wife Charlotte slowly entered. He could see the
illumination from the hall corridor backlighting her and making Charlotte
look almost angelic. As the door closed and the light receded, Charlotte made
her way across the room to Sal's bedside, where she grabbed a tissue from the
nightstand and gently dabbed the tears from his glistening cheeks. Sal could
still see the Meghan creature lurking in the shadows as if waiting patiently in
anticipation of something, perhaps waiting for him.

As Charlotte patted Sal's cheek, one of her fingers gently brushed against
his skin. The moment her flesh met his, Sal's mind became flooded with a montage of unbelievable images. He saw numerous scenes simultaneously played
out like a collection of movies, each of which featured Charlotte in a variety of
beds with many of his closest friends naked, sweating and grunting like rutting

beasts. How could this possibly be? How could his beloved Charlotte have done such a thing to him? And why would she do so while he laid dying in his hospital bed with unspeakable pain and beeping machines serving as his only companions?

Sal's eyes grew large with shock, and his mouth flew open as he was astounded by what he had just witnessed. He wanted to believe none of what he saw was true, but he knew with certainty the images were far more than simple illusions or hallucinations brought on by the drugs. They were actually a montage of the truth of what his deceitful wife had been doing behind his back, while she was pretending to care for him. He glanced across the room and saw the hideous specter of Meghan staring back at him, grinning madly with what remained of her mangled face. She knew what he had just seen, and now she was basking the pleasure of the pain it was causing him.

"Sal?" He heard a voice say from his right. "It's time Sal," Charlotte said. "It ok. You can let go now." She reached over and placed her hand on his in a consolatory gesture. Once again, the moment their flesh met, his mind was flooded with images of Charlotte and those men, and he understood why she wanted him to let go.

What a ridiculous fool he had been. Sal had loved that woman with all his heart, but she apparently hadn't loved him for some time. Charlotte had been much younger than Sal when they had married. Then his cancer had caused him to become a burden to her. She had found comfort in the beds of other men. And now she was ready for him to die and get it over with so she could get on with her new life. The horrible and degrading sex scenes were the final images Sal had in his mind as a living human being when his body gave out its final gasp allowing his spirit to move on. But where would it move on to? His family was gone, and all that remained was that hideous specter of Meghan.

A moment later, Sal was standing across the room, looking back at his death bed. Charlotte was standing by his bedside, pretending to be in mourning while taking furtive glances down at her watch as if determining how long she might have to stand next to his body playing the dutiful wife before she could call for help and eventually leave. When the nurses who were monitoring Sal's machinery from their central station came into the room, Charlotte quickly turned on the waterworks crying as if she had just lost the love of her life.

Sal felt an icy chill settle upon his shoulder as he slowly turned and looked into the mutilated face of his one-time lover Meghan. She opened her mouth sensuously, and a disgusting odor of rotting meat came leaching out like the stench of garbage fermenting in a can for weeks. Sal saw her gray slime-covered tongue flitting about the cavernous orifice and noticed several worm-like creatures squirming in and out of open weeping soars on her glistening face. The hideous thing which had once been his beautiful lover reached up and entwined her bony fingers into the hair on the back of his head, drawing him closer. He tried with all of his might to resist her pull, but her strength was much greater than his, and she pulled his lips down to meet hers.

He could smell the foul reek of her as he struggled hopelessly to keep his lips away from hers. But no matter how much he fought, his mouth soon became pressed tightly against the crumbling maggot-infested flesh of her gaping maw. His stomach revolted as he felt her cold, slimy tongue sliding first across his lips and then diving deep into his mouth, where it flitted from side to side as if it had a mind of its own.

The Meghan thing next grabbed his hand and forced it onto one of her withered breasts as she slowly pulled her snake-like tongue out of his mouth. Sal spat some sort of foul-tasting crawling things behind her as Meghan laid her right cheek against his. From his position, Sal could clearly see what remained of her demolished brain, which appeared to be undulating impossibly as dozens of white maggot-like worms skated across its slimy covered surface in a hideous ballet of revulsion. Some of the larvae would occasionally stop to bore deep into the spongy meat and creep below the outer surface of the decaying brain tissue.

The Meghan specter whispered something into Sal's ear, "I came back for you as I promised so many years ago, my love, and now we'll finally be joined together in our own special lover's embrace in Hell for all of eternity." Sal heard a loud maniacal ear-splitting scream reverberating throughout the room and realized with horror it was coming from himself.

I WAITED FOR YOU

By Thomas M. Malafarina

Based on a work of art of the same title by Niall Parkinson

"Guilt is cancer. Guilt will confine you, torture you, destroy you as an artist. It's a black wall. It's a thief." —Dave Grohl

"Guilt is perhaps the most painful companion of death."
                                                —Coco Chanel

He awoke with a start, hearing his smartphone vibrating on the nightstand. In one clumsy motion, Robert swung his feet out from under the covers, sat upright, and looked at the phone's display for a millisecond before pressing the 'ACCEPT' icon and answering with a gruff, sleepy "Hello?" The name displayed had been Sunny Rest.

"Mr. Nelson?" The professional sounding voice on the other end of the line said. Robert felt the bed move slightly as the woman lying next to him tossed, mumbled something unintelligible, farted, then apparently fell back to sleep.

Robert rolled his eyes in disgust and replied into the phone, "Yes. This is Robert Nelson. Is everything all right?"

The voice on the other end simply said, "It's time, Mr. Nelson. You had better get over here as quickly as possible. She said she is waiting for you, but I'm afraid she has little time left."

"I'll be right there," Robert said quickly, springing to life, as he disconnected the call while gathering his various articles of clothing, strewn all about the floor. As he bent to pick up his underwear, he felt a whiskey induced belch rising in his throat and suppressed it feeling it might actually be vomit. He could taste the previous night's alcohol churning inside him, and he preferred to keep in down if at all humanly possible.

He staggered over to a doorway in the unfamiliar bedroom, which he hoped would lead to a hallway, and which in turn might get him to a bathroom. He found the bathroom and stumbled in still naked, and dropped his clothes in a heap on the worn linoleum floor. Under even the best of conditions, that phone call would have devastated him, but right now, he physically felt like crap, which was a perfect match to how he felt emotionally.

Robert splashed some cold water onto his face then used some more to wet his hair. He made a feeble attempt to finger comb the unruly mess since he was unable to find a comb or brush. The bathroom was filthy and looked as if no one had cleaned it in months. A variety of women's clothing was scattered about, and undergarments seemed to hang from almost every possible place available. He managed to dig under some random supplies and found a tube of toothpaste but no brush. So again making good use of his digits, he did his best to finger-brush his teeth.

He knew the strong tasting toothpaste would do little to mask his morning breath, which was pungent with remnants of the previous night's binge, but he had no time; he had to get moving. He had finally gotten 'the call,' and that meant there was no time to waste. Robert hurriedly threw on his underwear, then his pants and shirt, doing his best to make himself look presentable. He could only find one sock, so he threw it on the floor and slipped his shoes over bare feet the hurried back out into the hall.

"Hey! Where the hell are you sneaking off to?" A slurred, husky voice said from down the hall. It was, it was his bedmate from the previous night, whatever her name might be. He wasn't surprised to realize he had absolutely no idea. She was standing naked in the hallway, leaning on the bedroom doorframe smoking a cigarette. The woman looked a lot older, a lot less attractive and a lot more haggard than she had appeared the night before. The saying 'road hard and put away wet' flashed through his mind.

"Gotta go," Robert said, continuing toward the stairs. "Family emergency."

"Call me," the woman called after him.

"I will," he replied, knowing that would never happen. He seldom called any of these women back, even on those rare occasions when he did happen to remember their names.

He rushed out the front door of the row house, not having the slightest idea where he was. He looked around and found his car parked near the curb halfway up the block. He realized he was somewhere in the city, and no matter where that might be, he had to get to Sunny Rest as soon as he possibly could.

As he drove out of the unfamiliar city neighborhood, Robert saw signs for the bypass. Once there, he'd be able to find his way easily. Heading out of the city, he thought briefly about the woman whose bed he had just fled. How many had there been in the last month or so? He couldn't recall and didn't really want to. There was no joy to be gained from such recollections, no pleasant memories of sexual conquests, only gut-wrenching guilt.

His mind was swimming with a myriad of disjointed thoughts. He was still hungover, and now he was heading to Sunny Rest, likely for the last time. There had been many false alarms in the past, but somehow deep inside, Robert knew this was the real deal. The guilt he felt about the place he had just left was directly related to where he was now heading. He was going to see Cindy, his wife of more than thirty years, and the one true love of his life.

Cindy was in Sunny Rest Hospice Center, and she was dying. She had been dying for the past year. Despite his actions, Robert truly loved his wife, and their marriage had been one of the few successful ones. It all seemed so unfair. Most of their friends were divorced, separated, or were staying together in rotten marriages for the sake of the children. But his and Cindy's had been one for the record books, at least until cancer struck.

Her decline had been quick, and only two months earlier, Cindy had been permanently hospitalized, needing round the clock care. Then several weeks earlier, Robert was told the end was near, and Cindy would have to go into Sunny Rest Hospice Center. The hospitalization devastated Robert. During the past year, they had both known she was terminal, and they did all they could to get her affairs in order. They'd even sold their large home and moved into a small apartment and got Robert ready for his life alone after she passed. In fact, one of the things that Robert found so distressing was how they had spent far too much of her last year alive preparing for her imminent death.

Robert had tried his best to hold it together after Cindy was hospitalized but after several nights of barely sleeping and wandering aimlessly throughout the lifeless apartment, he went to his employer and requested a leave of absence. His boss agreed since Robert was obviously not able to focus on his duties any longer, and the man agreed he should be spending what time remained with Cindy.

During the first few weeks in the hospital before hospice, Robert and Cindy spent their days holding hands and reliving events of their past life together. But as Cindy's pain increased, so did the number of medicines required to suppress it. Soon Cindy was spending most of their time together sleeping. Robert stayed by her side as she continued to lose weight and wither away to nothing right before his eyes. These weeks caused Robert to plunge into a deep unbearable depression, the likes of which he had never experienced in his life.

Robert knew he had to do something, anything to distract his thoughts from Cindy's worsening condition, or he surely would go mad. However, no matter what he tried, it just didn't seem to help. Finally, one night after spending the day watching his frail wife sleep almost nonstop, Robert stopped by a local bar on his way home. He simply couldn't stand the thought of facing the empty apartment again. He wasn't normally a drinking man but occasionally would have one with dinner back when he and Cindy were able to go still out to eat. But that night he drank, and he drank and damn if it didn't feel good. Several hours later, he wasn't thinking about Cindy or his problems any longer. In fact, he was barely capable of thinking at all.

Thus began a ritual, which he practiced religiously night after night. He would awaken late in the morning and freshen up before going to the hospital. Not that it mattered since Cindy was, for the most part, unresponsive. But he always took care to eliminate any tell-tale odors for those few lucid moments his wife had each day. He would spend his time with Cindy then afterward would stop by a bar, drink until he was plastered, then go home, sleep it off and start all over the next morning. Robert knew this was dangerous as well as bad for his health, but he simply didn't care any longer. All he wanted was to be completely numb.

Then after about a week or two of this routine, something unexpected and disturbing happened and unknown to Robert at that time. It would be the first of many such occurrences. Following yet another night of binge drinking, Robert had awoken in a strange bed, naked and with an equally strange woman. He had no memory of how he had gotten there or what they had done. But regardless, he was riddled with guilt. He had never been unfaithful to his wife during their entire marriage and would have never even considered doing such a thing. Then it happened again and then again.

Soon it too became as much a part of his nightly ritual as the drinking had been. The closer his wife got to death, the more guilty he felt about it. Moreover, the worse he felt, the more he drank. It was no longer just a vicious cycle but had become a downward spiral at an ever-increasing speed. Now it seemed like every morning he woke up in some new bed with some new woman, and he had no idea how he had gotten there.

Now driving down the bypass, Robert saw the exit, which he knew would take him to Sunny Rest. Only a few minutes had passed, but to Robert, it seemed like it had been a lifetime. He felt as if he had aged ten years in the past ten minutes. He haphazardly parked his car, raced to the entrance, then down the hall to the room where he knew Cindy awaited him for what would probably be the last time. His stomach was sick with grief as he walked into her dimly lit quiet bedroom. As he approached the bed, a nurse walked by him and gave him a disapproving look. He felt taken aback, wondering why this woman thought she had the right to judge him.

He looked over to his wife's deathbed and saw her emaciated form lying there looking at him with eyes that seemed much too large for their sunken sockets. She was a living skeleton. Robert could tell she was aware the time of her passing was upon them, and all he wanted to do was vomit. He couldn't come to grips with the fact that in just a few moments, his once beautiful wife would be dead. She weakly lifted her right arm and crooked a boney finger indicating that he could come to her. She tried to raise her arms to hug him as he approached but was too weak, so he wrapped his arms gently about her skeletal frame.

Cindy's pale lips touched his ear, and he heard her say, "I waited for you." Robert understood she was ready to pass on but wanted to say one last goodbye to him first, to tell him she loved him and to make sure he would be all right without her. But as Robert softly held her, he felt her body tense and become rigid. That was when he suddenly realized his tragic mistake.

In the past, Robert had always managed to shower, shave, and properly brush his teeth before visiting Cindy, and most of those times, they rarely had the opportunity to be this close. But in his haste and stupor, Robert had forgotten to do so, and now Cindy held him closely, taking in all of the odors surrounding him; the foul stench of stale cigarettes, booze, sweat, cheap perfume, and sex. She knew instantly what he had done.

Cindy released Robert and slid weakly back down to the pillow. He stood, staring lamely down into those once beautiful eyes. Cindy's face bore a look, which seemed to encompass many emotions simultaneously; shock, disappointment, sorrow, grief, anger, and even hatred. Here bulging eyes seemed to bore a hole right through Robert. They silently screamed, "How could you?" inside his brain. Her pale lips began to tremble, and in a raspy voice, she said, "I waited for YOU!" Then, a moment later, she died, her eyes losing focus but never breaking contact with Roberts.

Robert was heartsick, realizing not only that his wife was gone but that instead of the peaceful passing they had always hoped for, the last living realization she had was that her husband was a lying cheating drunken whore monger. His memory of their last moment together would be that he had been out carousing with women while she lay dying, thinking only of him. Robert fell to his knees next to his wife's deathbed and wept uncontrollably.

———•———

Sitting on a chair in his tiny apartment, which now seemed even bigger than before, Robert sipped his whiskey on the rocks already half-drunk at two in the afternoon, having just come back from burying his wife. The funeral had been a small, private affair with only a few friends and relatives in attendance. Robert and Cindy had no children, but a few nieces and nephews had stopped by to offer their condolences.

Robert wished it had been he who died and not Cindy. He could feel his guilt eating away at his insides as cancer had devoured his wife. Worst of all, he was happy with the feeling. As far as he was concerned, there wasn't a death painful enough to make him suffer for what he had done to her. In the past, the alcohol had always managed to numb him and block out all of his thoughts, but now it seemed to have the opposite effect. Now all he could think about was Cindy and how what he had done to her was beyond unforgivable.

He clumsily lifted his glass to polish off the last of his whiskey when he noticed something strange on the wall across the room. It appeared to be a solitary black dot forming on the surface of the wall. Robert had no idea what might have been causing the stain, but he staggered over to the wall and sat down on the floor to get a closer look. By the time he arrived at the wall, a second dot had appeared. He stared at them, not having a clue what they might be.

Within a few seconds, there were ten dots evenly spaced in two semi-circles. Then beneath the dots, two shapes began to form appearing like the palms of two hands. They reminded Robert of when two hands are placed on the surface of a heavily fogged mirror, and the area around the image even seemed to be liquid-like and trickled downward.

"What the hell!" Robert exclaimed. Then the image on the wall continued to grow. Above what now looked like two black blood-dripping handprints, a haggard bloody face began to appear. At first, Robert couldn't tell if the image was that of a man or a woman as its features weren't recognizable. Then it became much clearer. He could see the hate-filled eyes bulging from sunken skeletal orbs, and he knew instantly it was his dead wife, Cindy, returned to take her vengeance.

Deep inside his mind, he heard hear dying raspy voice crying, "I waited for YOU" repeatedly as it increased in volume with each horrifying repetition. Then the wall seemed to become fluid, and the image began to stretch out coming ever closer to him. He was paralyzed with terror and the horrifying sight before him.

"I'm so sorry, Cindy," Robert began to wail as the wall stretched out toward him, the blackened image reaching for him. Then he felt the icy cold tips of the fingers touch the sides of his face, and the inside of his brain screamed with the words, "I waited for YOU!" He felt a stabbing pressure in his chest and pain shooting down his left arm just seconds before he collapsed in a heap onto the apartment floor.

——◆——

The police investigator and EMT stood outside the apartment, discussing what they had found inside.

"God! That smell was unbearable," the police officer said. "How long do you think he was dead?

The EMT thought about it for a few moments and said. "That's hard to say. The medical examiner will have to make that final determination, but to be honest with you, I'd guess it had to be a few weeks, especially based on the decomposed condition of the body."

"Yeah. That was pretty bad. So what do you think?"

"You mean the cause of death?" The EMT said, "Not sure, but my guess would be either a stroke or heart attack. From what the neighbors said, he and his wife only moved into the place a few months ago, and apparently, she died a few weeks ago. Maybe the stress of losing her was just too much."

The policeman said, "I've heard stories of couples dying within and few days of each other when the surviving spouse simply can't live without his mate. They often call it dying of a broken heart."

"Well, I don't know about that," The EMT said, "but he definitely died of something. It looked to me like he might have been sitting on the floor looking at that water stain on the wall."

The police officer said, "Could be. I checked with the super, and he told me with all the rain we've been having; lately, there've been leaks in a number of the apartment units. Apparently, the roof needs to be repaired, and the water's leaking down between the walls and has caused the stains."

"Not surprising," the EMT said. "This is an old building. But did you notice anything unusual, you know, about the stain?"

"No, not really," the police officer said. "It just looks like a big old stain to me."

The EMT said. "You're probably right. But to me, if you look at it a certain way, it resembles the backs of two people's heads walking away. You know, like a man and a woman."

The police officer looked at the image closer, then he scratched his head and said, "I don't know. I don't see it. Oh well, I guess with a spot like this, anyone might be able to see just about anything they wanted or needed to see."

"You're probably right," the EMT said. "Well, we'd best be getting the remains out of here."

BE CAREFUL WHAT YOU WISH FOR

By Thomas M. Malafarina

"Be careful what you wish for because you just might get it."
—Unknown

"The only suitable gift for the man who has everything is your deepest sympathy." —Imogene Fey

"Protect me from what I want." —Jenny Holzer

It had been yet another in a seemingly endless series of monotonous days, a day just like every other boring day of late, and Stephen had become frustrated beyond his ability to reason. He had had enough of walking about aimlessly with no destination, no plan. Was this truly to be how he would spend the rest of his natural life? He felt as if he might lose his mind and scream with insanity just thinking about how miserable his life had become, how it consisted of the same old tiring routines day after day, week after week for low these many years.

This was all the more frustrating because Stephen knew he had enough money to be in complete control of every aspect of his life—much more so than most people. Nonetheless, he continued to trudge along with the same mundane daily routine without deviation. And although he hated his life, he did nothing to try to change it because he knew it was of his own making, and emotionally, he no longer had the ability to change anything. An outside observer might say he had everything, but Stephen knew, in reality, he had nothing, at least nothing that really mattered to him any longer.

Stephen had fallen into an exceptionally deep pit of depression, having no idea how he might possibly go about digging himself out and no longer caring if he ever did. He had been depressed before, several times over the years, but this time, it seemed much worse than ever. The creeping bouts of malaise had slowly begun several years earlier shortly after it had all happened; after his pitifully bad luck had done an abrupt about-face; that is to say, at least from an economic standpoint.

Stephen had the kind of financial good fortune most people only dreamed of. He had never even imagined having such vast amounts of money. However, he knew if he could be granted just one wish, that is to say, one more wish, it would be for everything to return to the way it had once been, and all of what he now possessed would simply go away. But Stephen knew there would be no more wishes for him; those days were long gone. If he were going to find a way out of this miserable pit of despair, he would have to do so of his own volition.

What Stephen did understand, however, was he had to come up with some means by which to put some sort of distraction or excitement into his life, something new, something to stimulate him, even if that something was something out of his control and potentially dangerous. He needed to find some activity that might possibly represent some sort of alteration to his normal mind-numbing practices, any sort of change whatsoever.

Stephen no longer worried about death or injury; his luck was much too good to allow something as trivial as physical injury to occur. He had tried all of the most hazardous activities he could think of, from mountain climbing to sky diving to bungee jumping to walking down a dark alley with one hundred dollar bills hanging out of his pockets, but he realized his good luck would not allow him to be hurt.

At one point during one of his past bouts of depression, he had actually considered trying to commit suicide, but he instinctively knew no matter how hard he tried, he would never succeed; his good fortune simply would not permit it. He was destined to live a long and healthy life of great wealth, a life he no longer wanted.

As he stepped onto the elaborate brick and stone porch of his enormous mansion, Stephen thought about all he had acquired, about all he had lost and about how foolish and naïve he had been. God, he missed his wife and daughter so much, and no matter how much money or good fortune came his way, it would never even begin to make up for their loss.

He inserted his key into the lock on the finely handcrafted front door, and with a click, he walked into the darkened hallway. He switched on the overhead hall light, which simultaneously turned on a small lamp on the oak hall table. He knew he should have put the table lamp on a timer, but Stephen had no interest in taking the time to bother with such things. The dense mist of apathy that had taken over his psyche like a creeping fog of malaise was most likely responsible. It could also have been that he simply found technology to be more of an annoyance than a benefit. This was also the reason why he was able to enter the home without hearing the blaring of an alarm system in desperate need of resetting. He just didn't feel like dealing with the hassles of owning such devices. Besides, he knew he had nothing to worry about from any living being.

Stephen casually approached the hall table and placed the large grocery bag he was carrying on top of the table, then reached into his coat pocket and pulled out a wrinkled lottery ticket and laid it next to the bag. He took off his coat and hung it in the hall closet, deciding to walk down the hall past the living room and out to his kitchen. Perhaps he could make himself something exciting for dinner. He wasn't much of a cook, but maybe the distraction would be a good thing. He knew he could simply select any one of hundreds of phone numbers in his smart phone, and he would be able to order whatever he wanted from wherever he chose any time day or night. If he so desired, he could hop on a plane and fly to France or Italy or even China simply for the purpose of having an interesting meal.

"I think that's about far enough," Stephen heard a gruff voice say from inside the living room as he attempted to pass by the wide arched opening. He looked up and saw a trace of shadowed movement from deep within the darkness. A few seconds later, he caught a glimpse of two dark eyes reflected in the light from the hall, along with a flash of something metallic located approximately waist-high.

A gun, Stephen thought. There's an intruder in my home, and he has a gun. Yet he remained surprisingly calm as if the sight of a weapon pointed in his direction was a daily occurrence, which of course, it wasn't.

It was just that Stephen realized the intruder, who, although intent on something nefarious, might actually prove to be exactly what he was looking for, the answer to his own unending plight. He tried to see back into the gloom to determine what the prowler might look like but could only see the man's pale extended hand, the one holding a very menacing looking pistol.

"You know," the mysterious stranger said, "owning a house like this and not bothering to install a security system is pretty damn stupid, in my opinion."

Stephen didn't reply but stood staring into the darkness. The intruder continued, "I could have simply come up behind you and slit your fool throat if I was so inclined. You're either extremely naïve or very stupid. If you hadn't come home just now, I had every intention of robbing you blind. Oh, and for the record, I still plan to do just that."

The robber was caught off guard when instead of appearing terrified Stephen shrugged his shoulders as if he didn't care one way or the other. Stephen stood quietly for a few more moments before shaking his head as if disbelieving the strange situation he now found himself in. Then to make matters worse, Stephen chuckled aloud, unable to control himself.

"I don't see what you find so funny," the stranger said with rising indignation and a significant amount of confusion. "In case you haven't noticed, I have a gun here, Einstein. And that means I hold your life in my hands and can end it at any time I choose with the simple pull of this trigger."

Stephen was perfectly aware of the severity of his situation, but what the intruder didn't realize was that it was the entire situation, which Stephen found so oddly amusing.

After a few more moments of silence, Stephen finally decided to speak up and said with surprising calm, "Yes, I see your gun. And, yes, I also can see it's pointed directly at me. But I think I need to let you in on a little secret. If you truly believe you hold my life in your hands, then you are sadly mistaken, my friend, because you don't. However, if it makes you happy to believe in such fairy tales, then, by all means, go right ahead and shoot." Then Stephen waited for a beat expecting to hear the crack of gunfire, feigning nonchalance while all the time hoping against hope that his amazing luck would suddenly fail him, and he would be shot and finally reunited with his family. But there was no gunshot.

Although Stephen couldn't see the man's face, he was quite certain he must have worn an expression of utter astonishment at this last audacious statement. After all, what sort of madman would so boldly suggest to someone pointing a gun at him that the attacker should pull the trigger? But Stephen knew things, many things that the intruder didn't. And even without that knowledge, Stephen was fairly certain the man wasn't even an experienced burglar and certain by the man's actions so far he wasn't a murderer by nature. Had the intruder been so inclined, he could have simply knocked Stephen unconscious or killed him already rather than stopping him, and issuing what Stephen was certain was an idle threat.

"No, I didn't think so. I don't believe you're a killer, my new mysterious friend," Stephen said, now standing in a surprisingly relaxed pose as if nothing was out of the ordinary.

"Look, buddy," The man replied nervously, growing obviously more so, "I'm not your friggin' friend. And maybe you're right. Maybe I'm not a killer; at least I may not have been a killer when I walked in here, but that don't mean I can't become one." Although the man was still hidden in the shadows, Stephen could see by the way the gun was fidgeting in the reflective light that the man was getting anxious and uncomfortable. "Look, I'm a very desperate man, and desperate men do things they might not normally consider, especially if they're pushed too far. And for your information, you're beginning to push me too far."

Stephen said, "Although you may not believe it, I honestly do know where you're coming from, and I understand your situation completely."

The man waved his gun in a menacing manner and replied with frustration, "Understand? Understand? How in the hell could you possibly understand what I'm going through? Look at this place. It's a mansion, a friggin' palace. You're obviously filthy rich, and you want for nothing, while every day for me is a struggle just to try to survive."

Stephen insisted, "Look, despite outward appearances, I understand more than you realize. I can empathize with you. Please, allow me to help you. Just tell me what happened to you to drive you to this. And considering that you plan on robbing me anyway and have already threatened my life once, I think you owe me that much. Wouldn't you agree?"

"What? Agree? Are you insane? I don't owe you a damned thing," the man shouted. "I'm here to take your money, and that's all you need to know. That and the fact that if you don't tell me where you have hidden your cash, I'm gonna splatter your guts all over the wall." He lifted the gun shakily and shouted, "And don't think for one second that I won't do it either!"

Stephen tried again to reason with the man using a calm voice. "Easy now, my friend. I have every intention of giving you everything you want and possibly even more than you anticipated. All right? For starters, why don't you come over here and look in this grocery bag? You can have everything inside if you want it. Go ahead. Take a look. It's all yours."

"What? Groceries?" The man screamed. "I'm not here to beg for food, you idiot, and I'm not looking for your charity either. I am here to rob you—R-O-B—rob! So give me your money. NOW!"

"Well then," Stephen replied, still sounding strangely calm. Then take a look inside the bag, and I promise you won't be disappointed.

Furiously, the man waved his gun, ordering Stephen to step aside. Then forgetting himself, the robber stepped out from the shadows, and for the first time, Stephen got a good look at him. He was a tall, thin, relatively good-looking man with dark hair and surprisingly intelligent eyes. Stephen had expected a thug or perhaps at the very least some sort of street-smart tough guy. However, what he saw before him was someone who was very much like he had once been. The man was obviously inexperienced in his new chosen profession. Stephen was suddenly filled with excitement at the potential the man offered him. This man really could be the answer to all of his prayers.

Keeping the gun trained on Stephen, the robber slowly approached the large paper sack and quickly peeked inside, turning his attention immediately back to Stephen. Then he did a double-take, looked back into the bag, and momentarily froze with amazement, his eyes growing wide with disbelief. The hand holding the gun began to tremble slightly, and for a moment, Stephen worried it might accidentally go off. Then realizing the absurdity of his worry, he brushed the thought aside.

"What the hell!" The man shouted. "What is all this? Some kind of joke? The bag is full of money. There must be several thousand bucks in cash in here."

"Yeah. I know," Stephen replied. "Based on past experience, I would say maybe twenty or thirty grand give or take a few."

The burglar, whose real name was Thomas Stewart, stared at Stephen for a moment with an expression of perplexity, and then a light of recognition appeared on his face. He thought to himself, Oh yeah. Now I think I get what's going on here. This guy isn't just some rich a-hole who inherited a ton of money. He's a thief, a crook just like me. Then just as quickly, Thomas realized that if his would-be victim was a robber, he was obviously much more successful at the trade than Thomas had been so far. The house was incredible, so there must be more to the man than he originally assumed.

Keeping his gun trained on Stephen Thomas asked, "So what did you do, rob a bank or what?"

Stephen realized the intruder had misunderstood him and apparently had mistaken him for a fellow criminal. He laughed, "I didn't rob anyone. I just found the bag out along the highway, just as you see it there."

Thomas wasn't going to fall for such a preposterous lie, "Yeah. Right. You mean to try to tell me that you were walking down the street and found a grocery bag full of cash? Just like that?" Thomas snapped his fingers to accentuate his statement. "What do you take me for, some kind of idiot? Nobody has that kind of good luck."

"I do," Stephen replied matter-of-factly. "I have that sort of amazing financial luck all the time. In fact, do you see that lottery ticket I found?"

Thomas looked down at the crumpled ticket. "Yeah, I see it. What about it?"

Stephen replied, "Well, I also found that while I was out walking. And although you interrupted me before I had time to check the website, I'd be willing to bet it's a winner, and not just a winner but a really big winner."

"Uh-huh!" Thomas replied with disbelief. "You must take me for a real chump, expecting me to believe this load of crap you're shoveling. Do you have any idea what the odds are of anyone winning big on the lottery, let alone winning with some wrinkled up old discarded ticket you found along the road?"

"The odds are probably astronomical," Stephen admitted. "But nonetheless, I guarantee the ticket will be a major winner. That's just the way things work for me. Look. I don't know exactly what your story is, my friend, but you said you were a desperate man. Once I, too, was an equally desperate man. Now I have all of this. But I'm going to venture a guess at your current situation. I am thinking that once you were a fairly successful upper-middle-class professional earning a good living. Then the economy went bad, you lost your job, and you've either lost your home or are about to lose it. How am I doing so far?"

Thomas looked at Stephen with shocked surprise, wondering how this stranger could have possibly gotten his story so correct. He had never met the man before, but somehow, he knew about his job loss and the fact that the bank was about to foreclose on his home. Thomas was unable to reply, so he just stood staring, slack-jawed at Stephen, and slowly nodded his head in agreement.

"I would also speculate that you have a wife and family, and although your wife has stood by you so far, things are getting rough on the home front," Stephen said. "And you're afraid if you do actually lose your home, then your wife will leave you and most likely take the kids with her."

This was all so bizarre. Thomas had no idea how this man, with his oddly confident manner, could know so much about his life.

Stephen continued. "Yep. I think I nailed your situation down perfectly. And although I know you may find this hard to believe, just a few years ago, I was in the same boat as you were, or perhaps sinking ship might be a better description, then everything changed for me, overnight."

Finally, Thomas found his voice and asked, "Overnight? Not possible! What do you expect me to believe? That you found a magic lamp with a genie, who granted you three wishes? What sort of fool do you take me for?"

"Well. It was not exactly like that but something along those lines," Stephen said. "I was like you. I had a wife and daughter, but I had lost my job and couldn't find another. The bill collectors were banging on my door and ringing my phone off the hook. The bank was about to take me home."

"All right," Thomas said. "Suppose I buy into your cockamamie story. Where did all of this come from?" Thomas waved his arm to indicate the opulent surroundings of Stephen's home.

Stephen replied, "Someone offered me the opportunity to change my financial luck, and I took it. This was the result. And if you think you'd like to have what I have and more, I can arrange that for you as well."

"And why in the hell would you want to do that for someone like me who came here to rob you?" Thomas asked suspiciously. "What is this, some kind of con? Is it some ridiculous get-rich pyramid scheme? Look, buddy, I've been approached by all these types before, and I'm not about to fall for such crap and head down that particular road to ruin."

"I assure you," Stephen said. "It's not a scheme or business. And although it may seem like I'm doing you a favor, I guarantee you my reasons are purely selfish; I am doing this only for myself. You probably won't believe me, but the truth is that I am tired of all of this. When I was in trouble as you are, I thought money would bring me happiness, but it hasn't. All it has brought me is sorrow. You and everyone else might think I should be the happiest man alive, but I'm far from it. So the only way for me to truly change my life is to get someone else, such as yourself, to voluntarily take my place."

Thomas asked, "Take your place? What is that supposed to mean?"

Stephen explained, "All this amazing good fortune can only belong to one person at a time. Before me, it belonged to another man, and before him, someone else. I have no idea how far back in time it goes, but I suspect centuries. The important thing is that I have it now and am offering it to you."

Thomas once again looked perplexed and said, "This is insane. But just assume for a minute that I'm desperate enough to be willing to play along with you. How in the hell do you propose to make this supposed transfer of good luck happen?"

"It's quite simple, really," Stephen said. "All you have to do is ask me. If you just tell me you wish you could have all the luck, I currently possess and all the money you could ever need and I agree, then it will be yours. What'll happen is the good fortune will leave my body and go into yours. From that moment on, you'll never want for money again. But you have to be sure this is really what you want. And I have to warn you to be very careful what you wish for because you just might get it, as I did."

Thomas was sure this stranger was out of his mind; some kind of rich eccentric wacko. And what was that last cryptic statement supposed to mean? "Be careful what you wish for?" What was that all about? The guy was obviously some kind of nut job, Thomas was certain. As he, himself, had said earlier that he was a desperate man and desperate men tend to do things they normally would never previously have considered. So he decided to play along with the lunatic. The worst-case scenario was he might get some cash out of the deal. "Not that it really matters to me, but what is supposed to happen to you if I make this wish and take away all of your good fortune? What will become of you?"

Stephen said, "That's a good question. Here's how it works. When you make your wish, all of my luck will become yours. When the transfer is complete, this house and everything in it will be yours. I'll simply leave, and you will never see me again."

"Wait a minute! Hold your horses! I get this now," Thomas said distrustfully. "You're trying to con me into letting you go. Then as soon as you walk out that door, you'll go around the corner and call the cops. A few minutes later, they'll bust in here and haul my sorry butt off the jail. Well, fat chance, buddy! If you honestly think I'm going to let you walk out the front door like that, then you're crazier than I thought." Thomas raised the gun and pointed it straight at Stephen's chest.

Stephen never flinched or showed the slightest sign of fear. Instead, he said, "Then I suppose I have to prove it to you. I have to convince you that what I am saying is true. What do you suppose the odds are of a bullet missing me from your current distance?"

"What?" Thomas asked once again, caught off guard, "What the hell are you saying? From this distance, a blind man wouldn't miss. Are you telling me you want me to shoot you from this point-blank range? Are you suicidal or what?"

"No, not really," Stephen said. "I have to admit at one time I was but no longer. I also believe even at this close proximity, if you shot at me, you wouldn't hit me. You have no idea how powerful all of this is. Look, I realize you don't consider yourself the murdering kind, but I assure you if you pull that trigger, you won't harm me."

Thomas said, "OK. Wait a minute here. Maybe you're just out of your friggin' mind or something. I don't know. I have no intention of killing you unless I have no other choice. So I'm not about to pull this trigger just because you say so, OK? How's about this, why don't I just take this bag of money and leave?" Things were getting way too weird for Thomas, and his gut was telling him to leave immediately.

Stephen retorted, "If you think that will satisfy you, then please just take the bag and go. And feel free to take the lottery ticket as well. But I don't think that will be enough for you; I suspect you want more. And if you do really want more, so much more, then I have a better idea. All you have to do is tell me that you wish you had all of my luck, and I was left with none of it. If you do, then all the riches you ever imagined will be yours. But the key is, you can't just say the words, you really have to mean them."

For a moment, Thomas stood silently, staring at Stephen as if studying his expression for signs of deception. There were none. Thomas thought, this guy really believes everything he is saying. In his mind, he thinks he's telling me the truth. Then Thomas suddenly realized that it didn't really matter whether he believed in wishes or good luck himself because the man standing in front of him most certainly did. And what that meant to Thomas was, if he could convince this strange man he really did believe what he was saying and that he would accept Steven's proposition, then the madman really might be crazy enough to actually sign over his house and all of his money to him. Thomas decided to do his best to gain the man's confidence.

"What's your name?" Thomas asked Stephen, figuring that was as good of a place as any to start.

"Stephen," he replied. "Stephen Albright is my name. And yours? If I may ask."

Thomas hesitated for a moment then decided to be honest with Stephen. If he was going to pull this off, he had to be truthful. He said, "My name is Thomas Stewart."

Stephen said, "Very well, Thomas Stewart. May I assume you're considering taking me up on my offer? Are you ready to assume my place and claim your own financial fortune?"

"I am," Thomas replied, but still somewhat warily. He had never dealt with a crazy person before, and he had no idea what might happen next. There was also something so very odd about the way this Stephen character was in such a hurry to give away his fortune that, for the first time, Thomas actually began to feel apprehensive about everything. Although he wasn't prone to superstition, something felt not quite right about all of this. He thought of something his father had once told him: "Tommy, if something sounds too good to be true, it probably is."

But Thomas needed to believe Stephen was nothing more than an eccentric crackpot. And since Thomas still held the gun and had it pointed directly at Stephen, there was little the man could do to harm him. Yet he felt something was still very wrong with the entire situation. All sorts of internal alarms went off at once, as if warning Thomas to grab the bag of money and flee. But Thomas was convinced that these feelings were unfounded, and he decided, why should he settle for a bag of money when he could have it all? This crazy man was offering him a new lease on life.

"OK," Thomas acknowledged. Then he asked, "What should I do? I mean, how do I make all of this happen?" He didn't want to screw up what could be a very sweet deal.

Stephen explained, "Just say aloud that you wish you had all of the luck I currently have and that I would no longer have any of it. It's as simple as that. But once again, I have to warn you to make sure you really mean what you're saying and that deep down in the very pit of your soul, this is really what you want."

Thomas realized such a declaration wouldn't be a problem for him because he and his family had been struggling just to stay afloat for so many years. Things had gotten about as bad as he felt they could ever get, so bad that he had stooped so low as to try to rob Stephen's home. He even realized that if it had become necessary, he really could have murdered the man; shot him in cold blood. That was exactly how bad things had become. Thomas loved his wife and family, and as such, would do anything in his power to help them. He would have done anything if it meant helping his family. So as unbelievable as it might be, what Stephen was offering could be his last chance he had to save his family.

"Yes," Thomas said. "I'll do it." He braced himself for what he was certain would prove to be a major letdown, took a deep breath, and said, "I want what you have. I want all of the luck you possess to leave your body and come into mine. I want your riches. I want your good fortune. And I want you to have none of it any longer."

For a second or so, nothing seemed to happen. Then slowly at first, Thomas noticed a sparkling white vapor begin to seep from Stephen's body as if every pore of his flesh was emitting the haze. Soon a cloud-like fog hovered above

Stephen's head, and he swooned a bit on his feet as if the strength had been sucked out of him and looked as if he might pass out.

Then the sparkling mist slowly traveled across the space between the men and surrounded Thomas's body. He felt his skin tingle and the hair on his arms seemed to stand on end as if he were in the middle of an atmosphere charged with electromagnetic energy. Next, the vapors entered his own body through his pores, and he was filled with a strange, sort of satisfying warmth.

Thomas could see Stephen standing across the room watching him, watching the whole spectacle with calm reservation and what appeared to be a look of relief as if he had been somehow freed from some horrible curse rather than having just given away a fortune. Once again, Thomas began to sense a deep discomfort as if all of this perceived good luck might suddenly go very bad.

After a few moments, the tingling of his flesh stopped, as did the deep heat he felt inside. Those sensations were replaced with a sudden feeling of euphoria, the likes of which Thomas had never experienced before. His previous thoughts of concern vanished amid all of his happiness. Thomas realized he had never felt so strong, so positive, and so self-assured in his entire life. He believed he could do no wrong as if anything he ever attempted would be successful as if every thought he would ever have would end up being deemed pure genius. Thomas couldn't comprehend why Stephen would have ever become tired of such feelings or why he would have willingly given up the incredible sensations.

"Open the top drawer of the hall table," Stephen said, still sounding a bit weak from the ordeal. "There are some documents in there for you."

Thomas, still under the positive influence of his new-found euphoria, didn't even question why there might be anything in this house specifically meant for him. Instead, he opened the drawer and withdrew what appeared to be a large legal document as well as several smaller documents.

Stephen said, "That top document is a deed to this house and the surrounding land. There are also copies of all of my active financial accounts and investments, or should I say, your investments now."

Still stunned, Thomas opened the top document as was astonished to see the name on the cover sheet change right before his eyes. Stephen Albright began to fade and was simultaneously overwritten with his own name, Thomas Stewart. As he leafed through the remaining documents, the same thing happened to each of them. His name was now on every single financial certificate. He saw numbers totaling in the millions flashing by as he skimmed the papers.

"You mean to say it's really true? All of this? Everything? It's all mine?" Thomas asked with utter disbelief.

"Yes," Stephen replied. "Everything; all of the wealth and riches you could ever imagine will be yours for the rest of your life. That is to say unless you choose to offer it to someone else, as I have done with you."

Thomas looked aghast. "And why would I ever want to do that? Just because you were stupid enough to give it all away, doesn't mean I'm equally as crazy. This is everything I've ever dreamed about all of my life. It's more wealth than I could spend in several lifetimes. What amazing luck! I'd never give away such an incredible gift. All of my troubles are officially over. My wife, my kids, and I will have everything we ever dreamed of. She won't believe me when I tell her. Speaking of which, I have to call her right now and tell her the good news."

Stephen said nothing. He just looked knowingly with pity as Thomas tucked his gun behind his back and pulled out a cell phone. Thomas's face filled with so much joy at the thought of telling his family of his new-found fortune. But Stephen stood silently, knowing what was about to happen next.

There were laws that governed the universe, some known by man, others unknown. There were physical laws as well as spiritual and economic laws. One such law, which Stephen knew far too well, stated that there was only so much of everything available, and for everything you chose to get, you must give up something else. If you, for example, had two hours of spare time available and had to decide between going to dinner or to a movie; if you choose one, you must sacrifice the other. This rule was one Thomas was sadly about to learn.

"Jenny? It's me," Thomas said into the phone. Then after a bit of hesitation, he said. "Excuse me? Who is this? Where's my wife, and what are you doing with her cell phone?" Then a dark shadow passed across Thomas's face, and he replied to the voice on the other end of the line. "Oh, my God! Which hospital? Saint Luke's, you say? I'll be right there."

Stephen didn't ask what the problem was because it really didn't matter what the particular set of circumstances might be—he understood the result would be the same. He already knew Thomas's wife and family were dead and that the policeman simply hadn't wanted to break the news to Thomas over the phone. It was a similar scenario to that which he, himself, had been through several years ago when his own wife and daughter had been killed within a few seconds of his taking ownership of the very same gift.

"That—that was, I mean he said he was a police officer," Thomas stammered. "He said there was, was an accident. My wife and kids were injured," his voice caught in his throat, "and they're on their way to the hospital by ambulance. I had better get right over there."

"If you feel you must," Stephen said.

"Of course, I must!" Thomas shouted. "It's my family for Christ's sake. They've been injured. They need me."

Stephen said, "You mean they needed you. And you weren't there, because you were here claiming what was really the most important in your life; money."

Thomas said, "How dare you! Screw you, Stephen. You know that's not true. I was only here trying to take care of my family's future."

"And it appears you did just that. Now your family has no future," Stephen said. "I might as well tell you there's no need to hurry to the hospital. It won't do any good. By the time you get there, they'll all be dead; that is if they aren't dead already."

Thomas looked confused and furious, "What? How, how can you pretend to know that? What the hell are you talking about?"

Stephen said, "Remember, I warned you to be careful what you wished for. But apparently, you were so busy thinking about all of the money you'd have that you didn't think things through. I understand completely, because as I said, I, too, was once as desperate as you."

"But this, this thing was supposed to bring me good fortune," Thomas pleaded. "And now you tell me my family is dead. What kind of good luck is that?"

Stephen said, "A simple law of the universe is that you can't have everything. For each thing you choose to have, you either voluntarily or involuntarily choose to give up something else. And you have made your choice."

Thomas asked tearfully, "Are you trying to tell me I caused this to happen to my family by choosing to make one stupid wish?"

Stephen said, "I promised you that you'd have more money than you could ever spend, and you'd never have to worry about being injured and killed for all of your natural life. I said you'd live a long and healthy life and someday die of natural causes as a very old, very wealthy man. That's what this particular good fortune is about. And now you have all of those things."

"But my wife and my children! How can they be dead?" Thomas shouted as best as his sobbing voice would permit. "What good is all the money in the world if everyone I love is dead?"

"That might have been a good question to ask earlier. I tried to warn you to be careful," Stephen repeated. "But you didn't. And now, what was mine is yours." Then Stephen slowly turned to leave.

Thomas shouted, "Where the hell do you think you're going?" He reached around his back and once more brought out the pistol, pointing it menacingly at Stephen.

Stephen replied, "I told you before I was going to leave, and so now I'm going to do just that. You have what you came here for, and now I'm going to try and start a new life. Maybe if I am truly lucky, I will find some semblance of true happiness before I die."

"You bastard! You knew this would happen!" Thomas said accusingly. "You said you had a family once. They probably also died because of this horrible wish; this curse. You tricked me into this devil's bargain, and now I'm all alone in the world." He sobbed uncontrollably. "It's all your fault! Don't you dare move another step closer to that door or so help me God I will shoot you!"

"I'm truly sorry about your family," Stephen said, "As I was sorry about my own. In fact, I've hated myself every day of my life since I made the same bargain you just made, and I'm quite certain you too will be wallowing in misery for many years to come. But that's no longer my problem. It's yours. So if you will excuse me, I'll be leaving. Unless you're truly prepared to shoot me, I suggest you just accept your good fortune and make the best of it."

Thomas shouted with insane rage, "Die, you bastard!" Then he pulled the trigger, and the room echoed with the deafening blast from his handgun. Stephen was slammed against the wall as a bullet entered his stomach. He involuntarily reached down to the place where he had been shot, and his hands came away covered with the blood pouring from his wound.

To Thomas's shock, Stephen didn't cry out or look as if he were in any pain whatsoever. In fact, it looked to Thomas as if the man was happy he had just been mortally wounded, evident by the expression of satisfaction Stephen had on his dying face.

"You, you wanted me to shoot you," Thomas said. "That was your plan all along. Oh my God, you actually wanted to die and got me to kill you. You played me the whole time."

Stephen seemed to be staring out into space as if seeing and smiling at something or someone who was invisible to Thomas. Then he slid down the wall landing on his backside on the floor, still sitting and staring joyfully at the same seemingly empty space.

Thomas dropped the gun to the floor, then fell to his knees and buried his face in his hands, allowing the tears to flow freely. He had been desperate, greedy, and had not listened to the warnings his own subconscious had been giving him. He had been a fool. He now had all the money he could ever imagine, yet like Stephen, he had nothing. He stared at the bloody corpse of Stephen Albright and mumbled, "Be careful what you wish for . . . you just might get it."

THE MONKEY'S PAW

BY W. W. JACOBS

Without, the night was cold and wet, but in the small parlor of Laburnam Villa, the blinds were drawn, and the fire burned brightly. Father and son were at chess, the former, who possessed ideas about the game involving radical changes, putting his king into such sharp and unnecessary perils that it even provoked comment from the white-haired old lady knitting placidly by the fire.

"Hark at the wind," said Mr. White, who, having seen a fatal mistake after it was too late, was amiably desirous of preventing his son from seeing it.

"I'm listening," said the latter, grimly surveying the board as he stretched out his hand. "Check."

"I should hardly think that he'd come to-night," said his father, with his hand poised over the board.

"Mate," replied the son.

"That's the worst of living so far out," bawled Mr. White, with sudden and unlooked-for violence; "of all the beastly, slushy, out-of-the-way places to live in, this is the worst. Pathway's a bog, and the road's a torrent. I don't know what people are thinking about. I suppose because only two houses on the road are let, they think it doesn't matter."

"Never mind, dear," said his wife soothingly, "perhaps you'll win the next one."

Mr. White looked up sharply, just in time to intercept a knowing glance between mother and son. The words died away on his lips, and he hid a guilty grin in his thin grey beard.

"There he is," said Herbert White, as the gate banged to loudly and heavy footsteps came toward the door.

The old man rose with hospitable haste, and opening the door, was heard condoling with the new arrival. The new arrival also condoled with himself, so that Mrs. White said, "Tut, tut!" and coughed gently as her husband entered the room, followed by a tall, burly man, beady of eye and rubicund of visage.

"Sergeant-Major Morris," he said, introducing him.

The sergeant-major shook hands, and taking the proffered seat by the fire, watched contentedly while his host got out whiskey and tumblers and stood a small copper kettle on the fire.

At the third glass, his eyes got brighter, and he began to talk, the little family circle regarding with eager interest this visitor from distant parts, as he squared his broad shoulders in the chair and spoke of strange scenes and doughty deeds; of wars and plagues and strange peoples.

"Twenty-one years of it," said Mr. White, nodding at his wife and son. "When he went away, he was a slip of a youth in the warehouse. Now, look at him."

"He don't look to have taken much harm," said Mrs. White, politely.

"I'd like to go to India myself," said the old man, "just to look round a bit, you know."

"Better where you are," said the sergeant-major, shaking his head. He put down the empty glass, and sighing softly, shook it again.

"I should like to see those old temples and fakirs and jugglers," said the old man. "What was that you started telling me the other day about a monkey's paw or something, Morris?"

"Nothing," said the soldier hastily. "Leastways, nothing worth hearing."

"Monkey's paw?" said Mrs. White curiously.

"Well, it's just a bit of what you might call magic, perhaps," said the sergeant-major off-handedly.

His three listeners leaned forward eagerly. The visitor absentmindedly put his empty glass to his lips and then set it down again. His host filled it for him.

"To look at," said the sergeant-major, fumbling in his pocket, "it's just an ordinary little paw, dried to a mummy."

He took something out of his pocket and proffered it. Mrs. White drew back with a grimace, but her son, taking it, examined it curiously.

"And what is there special about it?" inquired Mr. White as he took it from his son and, having examined it, placed it upon the table.

"It had a spell put on it by an old fakir," said the sergeant-major, "a very holy man. He wanted to show that fate ruled people's lives and that those who interfered with it did so to their sorrow. He put a spell on it so that three separate men could each have three wishes from it."

His manner was so impressive that his hearers were conscious that their light laughter jarred somewhat.

"Well, why don't you have three, sir?" said Herbert White cleverly.

The soldier regarded him in the way that middle age is wont to regard presumptuous youth. "I have," he said quietly, and his blotchy face whitened.

"And did you really have the three wishes granted?" asked Mrs. White.

"I did," said the sergeant-major, and his glass tapped against his strong teeth.

"And has anybody else wished?" inquired the old lady.

"The first man had his three wishes, yes," was the reply. "I don't know what the first two were, but the third was for death. That's how I got the paw."

His tones were so grave that a hush fell upon the group.

"If you've had your three wishes, it's no good to you now, then, Morris," said the old man at last. "What do you keep it for?"

The soldier shook his head. "Fancy, I suppose," he said slowly.

"If you could have another three wishes," said the old man, eyeing him keenly, "would you have them?"

"I don't know," said the other. "I don't know."

He took the paw, and dangling it between his front finger and thumb, suddenly threw it upon the fire. White, with a slight cry, stooped down and snatched it off.

"Better let it burn," said the soldier solemnly.

"If you don't want it, Morris," said the old man, "give it to me."

"I won't," said his friend doggedly. "I threw it on the fire. If you keep it, don't blame me for what happens. Pitch it on the fire again, like a sensible man."

The other shook his head and examined his new possession closely. "How do you do it?" he inquired.

"Hold it up in your right hand and wish aloud,' said the sergeant-major, "but I warn you of the consequences."

"Sounds like the Arabian Nights," said Mrs. White, as she rose and began to set the supper. "Don't you think you might wish for four pairs of hands for me?"

Her husband drew the talisman from his pocket, and then all three burst into laughter as the sergeant-major, with a look of alarm on his face, caught him by the arm.

"If you must wish," he said gruffly, "wish for something sensible."

Mr. White dropped it back into his pocket, and placing chairs, motioned his friend to the table. In the business of supper, the talisman was partly forgotten, and afterward, the three sat listening in an enthralled fashion to a second installment of the soldier's adventures in India.

"If the tale about the monkey paw is not more truthful than those he has been telling us," said Herbert, as the door closed behind their guest, just in time for him to catch the last train, "we shan't make much out of it."

"Did you give him anything for it, father?" inquired Mrs. White, regarding her husband closely.

"A trifle," said he, coloring slightly. "He didn't want it, but I made him take it. And he pressed me again to throw it away."

"Likely," said Herbert, with pretended horror. "Why, we're going to be rich and famous, and happy. Wish to be an emperor, father, to begin with; then you can't be henpecked."

He darted around the table, pursued by the maligned Mrs. White armed with an antimacassar.

Mr. White took the paw from his pocket and eyed it dubiously. "I don't know what to wish for, and that's a fact," he said slowly. "It seems to me I've got all I want."

"If you only cleared the house, you'd be quite happy, wouldn't you?" said Herbert, with his hand on his shoulder. "Well, wish for two hundred pounds, then; that'll just do it."

His father, smiling shamefacedly at his own credulity, held up the talisman, as his son, with a solemn face somewhat marred by a wink at his mother, sat down at the piano and struck a few impressive chords.

"I wish for two hundred pounds," said the old man distinctly.

A fine crash from the piano greeted the words, interrupted by a shuddering cry from the old man. His wife and son ran toward him.

"It moved, he cried, with a glance of disgust at the object as it lay on the floor. "As I wished, it twisted in my hands like a snake."

"Well, I don't see the money," said his son, as he picked it up and placed it on the table, "and I bet I never shall."

"It must have been your fancy, father," said his wife, regarding him anxiously.

He shook his head. "Never mind, though; there's no harm done, but it gave me a shock all the same."

They sat down by the fire again while the two men finished their pipes. Outside, the wind was higher than ever, and the old man started nervously at the sound of a door banging upstairs. A silence unusual and depressing settled upon all three, which lasted until the old couple rose to retire for the night.

"I expect you'll find the cash tied up in a big bag in the middle of your bed," said Herbert, as he bade them good-night, "and something horrible squatting up on top of the wardrobe watching you as you pocket your ill-gotten gains."

He sat alone in the darkness, gazing at the dying fire, and seeing faces in it. The last face was so horrible and so simian that he gazed at it in amazement. It got so vivid that, with a little uneasy laugh, he felt on the table for a glass containing a little water to throw over it. His hand grasped the monkey's paw, and with a little shiver, he wiped his hand on his coat and went up to bed.

In the brightness of the wintry sun, next morning, as it streamed over the breakfast table, Herbert laughed at his fears. There was an air of prosaic wholesomeness about the room which it had lacked on the previous night, and the dirty, shriveled little paw was pitched on the sideboard with a carelessness which betokened no great belief in its virtues.

"I suppose all old soldiers are the same," said Mrs. White. "The idea of our listening to such nonsense! How could wishes be granted in these days? And if they could, how could two hundred pounds hurt you, father?"

"Might drop on his head from the sky," said the frivolous Herbert.

"Morris said the things happened so naturally," said his father, "that you might if you so wished attribute it to coincidence."

"Well, don't break into the money before I come back," said Herbert, as he rose from the table. "I'm afraid it'll turn you into a mean, avaricious man, and we shall have to disown you."

His mother laughed, and following him to the door, watched him down the road, and returning to the breakfast table, was very happy at the expense of her husband's credulity. All of which did not prevent her from scurrying to the door at the postman's knock, nor prevent her from referring somewhat shortly to retired sergeant-majors of bibulous habits when she found that the post brought a tailor's bill.

"Herbert will have some more of his funny remarks, I expect, when he comes home," she said, as they sat at dinner.

"I dare say," said Mr. White, pouring himself out some beer, "but for all that, the thing moved in my hand; that I'll swear to."

"You thought it did," said the old lady soothingly.

"I say it did," replied the other. "There was no thought about it; I had just—What's the matter?"

His wife made no reply. She was watching the mysterious movements of a man outside, who, peering in an undecided fashion at the house, appeared to be trying to make up his mind to enter. In mental connection with the two hundred pounds, she noticed that the stranger was well dressed and wore a silk hat of glossy newness. Three times he paused at the gate and then walked on again. The fourth time he stood with his hand upon it, and then with sudden resolution flung it open and walked up the path. Mrs. White, at the same moment, placed her hands behind her and hurriedly unfastening the strings of her apron, put that useful article of apparel beneath the cushion of her chair.

She brought the stranger, who seemed ill at ease, into the room. He gazed at her furtively and listened in a preoccupied fashion as the old lady apologized for the appearance of the room, and her husband's coat, a garment which he usually reserved for the garden. She then waited as patiently as her sex would permit, for him to broach his business, but he was at first strangely silent.

"I—was asked to call," he said at last, and stooped and picked a piece of cotton from his trousers. "I come from Maw and Meggins."

The old lady started. "Is anything the matter?" she asked breathlessly. "Has anything happened to Herbert? What is it? What is it?"

Her husband interposed. "There, there, mother," he said hastily. "Sit down, and don't jump to conclusions. You've not brought bad news, I'm sure, sir," and he eyed the other wistfully.

"I'm sorry—," began the visitor.

"Is he hurt?" demanded the mother.

The visitor bowed in assent. "Badly hurt," he said quietly, "but he is not in any pain."

"Oh, thank God!" said the old woman, clasping her hands. "Thank God for that! Thank—"

She broke off suddenly as the sinister meaning of the assurance dawned upon her, and she saw the awful confirmation of her fears in the other's averted face. She caught her breath, and turning to her slower-witted husband, laid her trembling old hand upon his. There was a long silence.

"He was caught in the machinery," said the visitor at length, in a low voice.

"Caught in the machinery," repeated Mr. White, in a dazed fashion, "yes."

He sat staring blankly out at the window, and taking his wife's hand between his own, pressed it as he had been wont to do in their old courting days nearly forty years before.

"He was the only one left to us," he said, turning gently to the visitor. "It is hard."

The other coughed, and rising, walked slowly to the window. "The firm wished me to convey their sincere sympathy with you in your great loss," he said, without looking round. "I beg that you will understand I am only their servant and merely obeying orders."

There was no reply; the old woman's face was white, her eyes staring, and her breath inaudible; on the husband's face was a look such as his friend the sergeant might have carried into his first action.

"I was to say that Maw and Meggins disclaim all responsibility," continued the other. "They admit no liability at all, but in consideration of your son's services, they wish to present you with a certain sum as compensation."

Mr. White dropped his wife's hand, and rising to his feet, gazed with a look of horror at his visitor. His dry lips shaped the words, "How much?"

"Two hundred pounds" was the answer.

Unconscious of his wife's shriek, the old man smiled faintly, put out his hands like a sightless man, and dropped, a senseless heap, to the floor.

In the huge new cemetery, some two miles distant, the old people buried their dead and came back to a house steeped in shadow and silence. It was all over so quickly that at first, they could hardly realize it, and remained in a state of expectation as though of something else to happen—something else which was to lighten this load, too heavy for old hearts to bear.

But the days passed, and expectation gave place to resignation—the hopeless resignation of the old, sometimes miscalled, apathy. Sometimes they hardly exchanged a word, for now, they had nothing to talk about, and their days were long to weariness.

It was about a week after that that the old man, waking suddenly in the night, stretched out his hand and found himself alone. The room was in darkness, and the sound of subdued weeping came from the window. He raised himself in bed and listened.

"Come back," he said tenderly. "You will be cold."

"It is colder for my son," said the old woman, and wept afresh.

The sound of her sobs died away on his ears. The bed was warm, and his eyes heavy with sleep. He dozed fitfully and then slept until a sudden wild cry from his wife awoke him with a start.

"The paw!" she cried wildly. "The monkey's paw!"

He started up in alarm. "Where? Where is it? What's the matter?"

She came stumbling across the room toward him. "I want it," she said quietly. "You've not destroyed it?"

"It's in the parlor, on the bracket," he replied, marveling. "Why?"

She cried and laughed together, and bending over, kissed his cheek.

"I only just thought of it," she said hysterically. "Why didn't I think of it before? Why didn't you think of it?"

"Think of what?" he questioned.

"The other two wishes," she replied rapidly. "We've only had one."

"Was not that enough?" he demanded fiercely.

"No," she cried, triumphantly; "we'll have one more. Go down and get it quickly, and wish our boy alive again."

The man sat up in bed and flung the bedclothes from his quaking limbs. "Good God, you are mad!" he cried aghast.

"Get it," she panted; "get it quickly, and wish—Oh, my boy, my boy!"

Her husband struck a match and lit the candle. "Get back to bed," he said unsteadily. "You don't know what you are saying."

"We had the first wish granted," said the old woman, feverishly, "why not the second."

"A coincidence," stammered the old man.

"Go and get it and wish," cried the old woman, quivering with excitement.

The old man turned and regarded her, and his voice shook. "He has been dead ten days, and besides, he—I would not tell you else, but—I could only recognize him by his clothing. If he was too terrible for you to see, then, how now?"

"Bring him back," cried the old woman and dragged him toward the door. "Do you think I fear the child I have nursed?"

He went down in the darkness, and felt his way to the parlor, and then to the mantelpiece. The talisman was in its place, and a horrible fear that the unspoken wish might bring his mutilated son before him ere he could escape from the room seized upon him, and he caught his breath as he found that he had lost the direction of the door. His brow cold with sweat, he felt his way around the table and groped along the wall until he found himself in the small passage with the unwholesome thing in his hand.

Even his wife's face seemed changed as he entered the room. It was white and expectant, and to his fears seemed to have an unnatural look upon it. He was afraid of her.

"Wish!" she cried, in a strong voice.

"It is foolish and wicked," he faltered.

"Wish!" repeated his wife.

He raised his hand. "I wish my son alive again."

The talisman fell to the floor, and he regarded it fearfully. Then he sank trembling into a chair as the old woman, with burning eyes, walked to the window and raised the blind.

He sat until he was chilled with the cold, occasionally glancing at the figure of the old woman peering through the window. The candle end, which had burnt below the rim of the china candlestick, was throwing pulsating shadows on the ceiling and walls, until, with a flicker larger than the rest, it expired. The old man, with an unspeakable sense of relief at the failure of the talisman, crept back to his bed, and a minute or two afterward, the old woman came silently and apathetically beside him.

Neither spoke, but both lay silently listening to the ticking of the clock. A stair creaked, and a squeaky mouse scurried noisily through the wall. The darkness was oppressive, and after lying for some time screwing up his courage, the husband took the box of matches, and striking one, went downstairs for a candle.

At the foot of the stairs, the match went out, and he paused to strike another, and at the same moment, a knock, so quiet and stealthy as to be scarcely audible, sounded on the front door.

The matches fell from his hand. He stood motionless; his breath suspended until the knock was repeated. Then he turned and fled swiftly back to his room and closed the door behind him. A third knock sounded through the house.

"What's that?" cried the old woman, starting up.

"A rat," said the old man, in shaking tones—"a rat. It passed me on the stairs."

His wife sat up in bed, listening. A loud knock resounded through the house.

"It's Herbert!" she screamed. "It's Herbert!"

She ran to the door, but her husband was before her, and catching her by the arm, held her tightly.

"What are you going to do?" he whispered hoarsely.

"It's my boy; it's Herbert!" she cried, struggling mechanically. "I forgot it was two miles away. What are you holding me for? Let go. I must open the door."

"For God's sake, don't let it in," cried the old man trembling.

"You're afraid of your own son," she cried, struggling. "Let me go. I'm coming, Herbert; I'm coming."

There was another knock and another. The old woman with a sudden wrench broke free and ran from the room. Her husband followed to the landing and called after her appealingly as she hurried downstairs. He heard the chain rattle back, and the bottom bolt drawn slowly and stiffly from the socket. Then the old woman's voice strained and panting.

"The bolt," she cried loudly. "Come down. I can't reach it."

But her husband was on his hands and knees groping wildly on the floor in search of the paw. If he could only find it before the thing outside got in. A perfect fusillade of knocks reverberated through the house, and he heard the scraping of a chair as his wife put it down in the passage against the door. He heard the creaking of the bolt as it came slowly back, and at the same moment, he found the monkey's paw and frantically breathed his third and last wish.

The knocking ceased suddenly, although the echoes of it were still in the house. He heard the chair drawn back, and the door opened. A cold wind rushed up the staircase, and a long, loud wail of disappointment and misery from his wife gave him the courage to run down to her side, and then to the gate beyond. The flickering streetlamp opposite shone on a quiet and deserted road.

MEMORIAL DAY

By Thomas M. Malafarina

"**R**ow-zann! Row-zann!" the ghostly nagging voice still called from a past more than ten years removed. It sometimes came when she least expected it, like the haunting howl of a chilling wind blowing between the tombstones in a graveyard on a dark night. Although the voice was no longer a thing of actual sound or substance, when it arrived in her mind, it nonetheless was as chilling in its haunting resonance as if it were real. It would be wrong to say the voice actually haunted her. It had become more like one of those memories similar to a particularly annoying pop song, which for some reason occasionally pried itself loose from the recesses of her memory and which would take a major distraction to forget.

It had been more than a decade since Rosanne had last heard her mother's voice calling to her in that crow-like caw, insisting that Rosanne do this for her or fetch that for her. It wasn't that Rosanne hadn't loved her mother or didn't want to do everything she could to help. It was just that her mother, then in the final stages of Alzheimer's, was so downright mean to Rosanne at every opportunity.

Even before the disease, her mother hadn't been the most pleasant person in the world, projecting an air of superiority, condescension, and criticism toward Rosanne as well as Rosanne's husband and son. But despite it all, the old woman was still Rosanne's mother and she loved her. It ate at Rosanne to see her mother deteriorating before her eyes as the dreaded disease took more of her each day.

Rosanne recalled how her mother's doctor had made excuses for the old woman's behavior by saying it wasn't her speaking, but it was the effects of the disease. He explained that her mother was sinking further and further into a dream world and wasn't only losing her memory but losing touch with reality as well. He said she was confused, disoriented, and no longer able to function on her own or take care of even her simplest of needs.

Rosanne had known her mother a lot longer than the doctor, however, and she knew the Alzheimer's hadn't so much changed her mother as it had seemed to magnify those negative traits, which Rosanne had done her best to ignore throughout the years. Because her mother had always been so verbally abusive of others, she had had in fact, driven away most of her own family throughout the years. Soon the only relatives left to tolerate her were Rosanne, her husband Tony, and their son Albert. Rosanne's father had passed away several years before the disease struck her mother, so the burden of the woman's care fell to Rosanne.

She soon learned her mother needed more care than she could provide, and as such, Rosanne had no choice but to sell her mother's home and put the woman into an elderly care facility. She hated to do this, but her mother had become incontinent and needed constant care and monitoring.

Rosanne visited her mother as often as possible, and each time her mother's verbal abuse became more intense. She accused Rosanne of stealing her home and money and forcing her into a "hell-hole" and "prison," which was how she described the facility. Rosanne had researched the rest home before placing her mother in their care, and its reputation was exemplary. In addition, she constantly checked on her mother's care to the point where she was considered quite annoying by the competent and professional rest home staff.

Yet still, her mother persisted and unceasingly bombarded her with insults and threats every time she visited. "You did this to me, Row-Zanne!" The old woman would cackle. "You put me in here. You stole my money. You sold my house. Someday I'll get you for this Row-Zann!" Most times, after visiting her mother, Rosanne left in tears. She knew what the doctors said was probably true, and it was the Alzheimer's talking, but the words still came from her own mother's mouth, and they cut her like a knife.

Then one day, the disease took its final toll, and Rosanne's mother passed away. Rosanne and her family arranged for her mother's burial at a local cemetery next to Rosanne's father, grandmother, and grandfather. There were also several aunts and uncles buried in the family plot. Rosanne, Tony, and ten-year-old Albert said their goodbyes during a small, almost private ceremony. Most of her mother's former friends were either already dead or had been driven away by the woman's abrasive personality. As the family left the cemetery, Rosanne knew it was very possible if not probable, she would never return.

—— •◦• ——

Rosanne breathed a sigh of relief as she drove home from a very busy day at work. It was always this way right before a busy holiday weekend, and this Memorial Day weekend would be no exception. She felt stressed by trying to get all of her work completed before she left for the day and yet was excited about the next few days to come.

Tony had the long weekend free as well, and her son Albert, now twenty years old, was coming home from college for a visit. She hadn't seen her son since the Easter holiday break and was eager to see him again. She was feeling especially nostalgic this year for some reason recalling a time when she was a little girl, and every Memorial Day, she, her mother, and father would visit the family plot and place flowers on the graves of their loved ones. Maybe that was why she had been thinking about her mother that morning.

During the last several years of her mother's life, Rosanne had let that particular holiday tradition go by the wayside. She was too busy raising her family, working fulltime, and dealing with her mother's illness to worry about such matters. Now, however, she was starting to feel guilty about it. Rosanne supposed it was because she was thinking about Albert coming home from college for the weekend. They hadn't been back to her mother's grave in over ten years and realized they probably would have difficulty locating the family plot. That just seemed wrong to her. Albert was a young man now, and it only seemed proper that he at least know where his ancestors were buried.

Despite her misgivings, Rosanne decided that early Memorial Day morning, she, Tony, and Albert would pay a visit to the cemetery and see the place where her family rested.

—— •◦• ——

The three of them walked over toward the cluster of headstones, some of which were quite old and worn. As they passed by each marker, Rosanne explained who each occupant was and what their particular relation was to Albert.

"That one is your great-grandfather, and over there is your great-uncle," she said, trying to keep things interesting. She could tell Albert really didn't want to be there, but being a good son, he was doing his best to make his mother happy.

She thought of how often she had conceded to her own mother's requests with the hopes of gaining her favor and keeping her satisfied. She hoped, not for the first time that she wasn't becoming as controlling as her mother had been. Her whole life, Rosanne strived not to be like her mother, yet sometimes she still worried about it.

"Where is Grandma buried?" Albert asked, surprising Rosanne and bringing her out of her private thoughts.

She hesitated for a moment and said, "Um, somewhere around here." She looked about for the location. As she did, she asked, "Do you remember Grandma very well, Albert?"

"No, not really," he replied. "I mean, at least I can't remember how she was, you know, before she got sick and got all weird in the head and stuff."

"Albert!" Tony snapped. "That's not very respectful."

Albert said contritely, "Yeah. I guess you're right. Sorry about that, Mom. It's just . . ."

"I know, Honey. That's all right," Rosanne said compassionately. "The truth was, well, your grandmother always had been tough to live with, and after she got sick, she hadn't been herself for a very long time."

"You know what the bad part is, Mom?" Albert said.

"No, sweetie. Tell me."

He said, "The worst part is I can't remember her before, the way she might have been. Instead, sometimes I can still hear her calling you to come and do something for her in that horrible voice, Row-zanne! Row-zanne! Man, that always gave me the creeps."

Rosanne suddenly felt cold chills run down her spine at Albert's recollection, especially when she remembered how she had been thinking of the same terrible voice earlier that weekend.

"God!" She thought to herself, "That woman has been dead for over ten years. Won't she ever just get out of my head and leave me alone?"

Then Rosanne realized she wanted nothing better than to find her mother's grave, show it to Albert and get the hell out of there. The place was really starting to freak her out. A strange surrealistic sensation had begun to creep into Rosanne's mind as if the entire cemetery had become a dream-like landscape. Her legs started to feel heavy as if she was trying to walk around in a thick, deep bog full of mud.

She took a few steps backward, trying to read the headstones despite the unwelcome feeling, looking desperately for her mother's grave. Rosanne recalled the stone they had chosen was not too large and sat low to the ground. She looked over at Albert and Tony, seeing them as if through dense fog or frosted glass. She tried to speak and at first had some difficulty. She felt as is her tongue had grown thick, and her throat might be closing. What in the world was happening to her? Feeling a bit dazed, she somehow managed to force out the words, "It's right around here somewhere."

The statement cut off suddenly as the heel of Rosanne's shoes clumsily bumped against a low grave marker, and she lost her balance teetering over. She managed to take two stumble-steps backward and fell hard to the ground. On the way down, her head slammed against the corner of a nearby tombstone. The marble was unforgiving, and its edge sharp and polished surface acted like a blade slicing through her flesh with ease. A trickle of blood, along with part of Rosanne's hair and scalp, clung to the glimmering knife-edge of the stone.

Rosanne was now barely hanging onto consciousness as she lay on the ground, her own blood pooling beneath her head. Her vision was fading in and out of the blackness. The pain she felt in her skull was excruciating, and her vision was rapidly failing. Through her fog, she was able to see the name on the headstone, the one that had been responsible for tripping her. It was her mother's headstone.

Then Rosanne was certain she must be hallucinating because otherwise, what she thought she was seeing was impossible. In front of her mother's grave marker, she saw what appeared to be the shape of a translucent wriggling aged hand with withered gnarled fingers and long split nails appearing to have risen right up out of the ground. There were worms slithering between the horrifying appendage's fingers, which were caked with moist filthy dirt. Rosanne saw a wedding ring on the hand and recognized it immediately. Her mother's wedding ring.

Tony rushed to her side now and was calling her name repeatedly, trying to keep her conscious while at the same time Albert was desperately dialing 911 on his cell phone. However, Rosanne didn't hear Tony's concerned and loving voice. Instead, all she could hear was her mother's angry witch-like cackle screaming, "Row-zann! Row-zann!" as her own life faded away to blackness on the cold cemetery ground.

THIS TRAIN

By Thomas M. Malafarina

The man in black sprawled in his seat in the empty Pullman passenger car. He panted, practically out of breath. His long, lean legs stretched out far in front of him. His feet, which were clad in worn snakeskin boots, rested comfortably in the aisle. Sweat beaded on the passenger's forehead and dripped down the back of his neck. He took off his dusty black Stetson, placed it on the seat next to him, and removed his kerchief to mop his brow.

How in Sam Hill could he have been so lucky as to have gotten away? The deck had been stacked against him. Yet here he was, alive and escaping on this train. He thanked his lucky stars for whatever fortune had befallen him.

The man's real name was Jefferson Lincoln Carson, but he went by the moniker "The Carson City Kid," a name he had picked up somewhere along the line, which was strange since he had never been to Carson City. Carson stretched out his arms, expecting them to be sore or stiff from injuries he might have received during his escape but was surprised to find not even the slightest of muscle aches.

He looked around at his luxuriant surroundings. The seats were covered with plush red velvet. The brass and oak interior was polished to a shimmering luster. He had never seen anything quite like it before.

Carson thought again about his narrow escape and tried to figure out just how he had managed to find his way onto this locomotive. He had robbed the First National Bank and then fled the scene. He recalled throwing the sacks of loot over his getaway horse, as he thought he was galloping safely out of town. That was just before that damned Sheriff Walter Cobb and his posse of better than twenty men were suddenly bearing down on him at full bore, guns a'blazin.

He had been certain he was a dead man. His stomach lurched with terror, and his heart lodged in his throat as guns roared, as bullets whizzed past his head. Frantic, Carson whipped his horse mercilessly and dug his spurs into its flanks as he urged the beast onward. He pushed the horse to its limits as if the devil himself was after him.

Just when he thought he was out of range, one of the low-down polecats shot his horse right out from under him. He recalled falling to the ground and lying with his left leg pinned under the nag. Carson imagined himself being captured by the posse and strung up over the nearest tree. He would dangle by his neck, legs kicking, gasping for air until he finally breathed his last. His body would be left hanging for weeks until the crows and other scavengers slowly picked his flesh. Soon all that remained would be a maggot-infested half-eaten carcass.

He heard the thundering hooves of the approaching posse and somehow managed to wriggle free, get to his feet, and limp away. He had thought his leg would be broken or at least aching, but so far, his luck had held. Carson had tried to retrieve the money sacks. But to his dismay, he had to abandon them in a hail of bullets which came raining down on him from the posse. He had fled for his life down into a canyon running along the side of a stream. Then just when he thought the posse was going to get him, a heavy fog rolled in off the water and filled the valley, blocking his pursuers' vision.

They continued to shoot wildly into the fog, but he somehow miraculously managed to elude them. As soon as he cleared the fog bank, he saw the train just getting ready to pull out from the station. He couldn't recall there being any train station in the valley or tracks for that matter, but he knew better than to look a gift horse in the mouth, especially since his own horse was now dead. He managed to jump onto the moving passenger car just in time to escape.

As he rested, Carson saw a sickly-looking, pale-skinned stranger dressed in a black suit enter at the far end of the car. The man wore a rather expensive looking Stetson similar to Carson's, but in much better condition. Carson nodded briefly at the stranger. He suddenly realized how much he might like to steal that fancy new Stetson. The stranger didn't nod back. He just sat staring through dark, deep-set eyes.

An unexplainable cold chill ran down his spine. The man's actions seemed to be a might un-neighborly. Such a lack of common courtesy riled Carson perhaps more than it should have. He got to thinking that in a different set of surroundings like in the saloon, this stranger might have found himself with a belly full of lead. God knows Carson had killed many men for less. He had made up his mind that the stranger's fancy hat would be his before this trip was over, and mayhaps the stranger would come up missing from this train as well.

Before Carson could think any more on the subject, the door at the far end of the car opened again, and another man slunk in to take a seat across the aisle from the first. This man likewise stared silently at Carson. This one wore dirty range clothing and was clearly a cowpoke or perhaps a farmhand. Then the door opened again, and another man entered, followed by yet another and then another.

They sat silently, staring at Carson. He had a strange suspicion that perhaps all of these characters knew each other. They might all be in cahoots, possibly planning some sort of move against him. Even though he had no real reason to feel this way, Carson had always been a man who lived by his gut. And right now, his gut was screaming at him to be on his guard. He reached down slowly with both hands and placed them on the walnut handle grippers of his trusty six-shooters. He didn't know what these characters had in mind, but he would be ready for whatever it might be.

Those guns had gotten him out of a passel of trouble throughout the years. They had also brought down more than their share of varmints of both the four-legged and two-legged varieties. If this bunch of tenderfeet thought they could take him, they were about to see the error of their ways. Carson sat perfectly still watching the staring strangers and waiting for the right moment to make his move.

The door opened yet again, and several more men entered, each taking available seats and sitting quietly. All of their haunting eyes seemed to bore holes in Carson. Finally, the door opened one last time, and a woman entered. She wore a tight red frilly dancehall gal dress, and her hair was pinned way up high, just the way Carson liked it. Her skin was pale as a china doll. He found it disturbing how her palled flesh made her ruby lips appear much too red. She wore a blood-red silken scarf around her neck.

As she stood in the aisle, her eyes never left Carson. She reached up and began slowly removing the scarf from her neck. As she did so, she revealed a set of black, gruesome-looking handprint bruises encircling her long, thin porcelain neck. When Carson looked up into her dark, sunken eyes, his breath caught in his throat. Those eyes bore the dead, stark emptiness of a corpse. They seemed completely void of emotion. He recognized that look immediately as the same dead stare his own soulless eyes reflected back at him from a looking glass. But there was something else. Her eyes spurred another sudden recognition within him. He sat up straight and shouted, "No! No! That can't be!"

He knew he couldn't possibly be seeing what he was seeing. It was Belle, his Belle. She had been his lover many years earlier. She had deceived him by sharing her bed with another man, and Carson had strangled her for the betrayal.

Carson had known she was a dance hall girl, a whore, but he had fallen for her anyway. He had been fool enough to believe there might be more than lusty good times between them. He had believed her when she told him she loved him and especially loved his eyes. Carson had even considered giving up his outlaw ways and taking Belle far away from her life of sin. However, he soon learned she couldn't change her ways. When she did him wrong, she not only tore his heart from his chest but also made him insane with rage.

That was why he had wrapped his hands around her thin, frail neck squeezing ever tighter until her eyes bugged from their sockets, and she finally stopped breathing. Those bruises he now saw on the throat of this unholy creature before him were the same ones he had put there. But how could Belle be here on this train standing in this passenger car?

Then with horror, he realized something that had previously escaped him. These were not strangers as he had originally thought. The one over there in the business suit was Jacob Whitman. He had been a card shark, and Carson had murdered him more than six years earlier. And that Stetson he was wearing wasn't just nicer than his, but he realized it actually was his as it had appeared the day Carson had taken it from Whitman's cooling corpse.

And that cowpoke across the aisle from Whitman wasn't that? Yes, it most certainly was Pecos Bill. Yet, Carson had shot Pecos through the heart more than two years ago after quarreling. Carson slowly looked more carefully at each of the remaining silent passengers and to his horror; he recognized them and realized he had killed every one of them. How could this be?

It was as if the air around him was suddenly becoming thick and heavy. He felt like he did whenever he had a nightmare about facing down a rival in the street. In those dreams, when he tried to draw his guns, his lightning speed was gone, replaced by a slow and heavy useless motion. He knew during those nightmares he was about to die, and that same feeling coursed through his body now. The hair on his arms and the back of his neck rose, and his gut tightened. Beads of sweat returned to his brow.

One by one, the ashen-faced passengers rose from their seats. Carson suspected what they might have in mind. He had not survived in his line of work for so long, not knowing how to read a man's intentions. He pulled his guns out of his holsters only to find his hands empty, pointing absolutely nothing at the crowd as they shambled slowly up the aisle toward him.

Carson's muscles tensed, and his heart beat frantically in his chest. What the hell was going on? Where were his trusty six-shooters? He looked down at his empty hands, then out at the approaching crowd, and knew this was not a bad dream. It was something much, much worse than a nightmare. This was real.

And now he was trapped on this train; this Godforsaken train to who-knows-where with a carload of what? Ghosts? Devils? Carson tried to get out of his seat with the hopes of fleeing the mass of horrifying creatures but discovered he couldn't move.

Soon he was surrounded by the hoard. They simultaneously opened their mouths, revealing giant black caverns full of long dagger-sharp fangs. They raised their hands, and Carson saw claws the likes of those he had seen on many a mountain lion.

Soon the lumbering throng fell upon him and pulled on his arms and legs, scratched his flesh, and tore his hair. He screamed in agony as they ripped and pulled his limbs out of their sockets. They slashed the innards from his body as though they were gutting a hog. The last thing he saw before he died was the face of Belle looking down at him, smiling with her blood-dripping fang-filled mouth. That horrible mouth came ever closer. He knew what she wanted. She wanted his eyes.

DUELERS ALLEY

By Thomas M. Malafarina

"We shall not grow wiser before we learn that much that we have done was very foolish." —Friedrich August von Hayek

"There is no refuge from memory and remorse in this world. The spirits of our foolish deeds haunt us, with or without repentance." —Gilbert Parker

She was simultaneously filled with both exhilaration and terror as she stood on the moist cobblestones in the chilly dawn air, her lips quivering and her teeth chattering. But this physical reaction wasn't simply from the cold morning mist coming off of the Atlantic Ocean at the port of Charleston on that day in 1785. It was more likely from the dreaded anticipation of what was about to occur in just a few moments. She was at a crossroads in her life, and she knew whatever happened in the next few minutes would drastically change the course of her life forever.

How had she been so foolish to allow things to go so far? Her mother had warned her about such folly. "No good respectable young lady would encourage such a thing," she had insisted.

Emily knew her mother was right, yet still, she couldn't help herself. Emily was a very pretty young woman and knew it. She was also a bit of a flirt. For her, the idea of two handsome and wealthy eligible young men both vying for her affection was a thrill she couldn't help but enjoy, not to mention encourage.

John, the son of an affluent shipping merchant, had courted her for months, showering her with affection in the form of lavish gifts and sonnets of love he had composed especially for her. Andrew was a young physician whose practice was growing rapidly and had a very good future in Charleston had likewise been courting Emily and proclaiming his unending love for her.

She should have stopped it. She could have easily chosen one of the men, and the other would have ceased his advances. It was as her mother said, "the thing a good and respectable young lady" would do. Her mother had been lecturing her about this for several months now.

"Ladies, do not lead gentlemen on," she had insisted. But that was exactly what Emily had done. And it wasn't simply because she enjoyed the attention, which she most certainly did. It was because she just couldn't bring herself to decide, to choose one over the other. She truly did believe she loved both of her suitors equally, although she understood in her heart of hearts that such a concept was impossible. Her mother argued that a girl as young as Emily had no idea of the real meaning of love anyway.

Regardless, the situation came to a head the previous evening as such things often do, when the two men had clashed at a local pub. Andrew had accused John of being the spoiled child of a rich, unsavory smuggler and swindler. John had called Andrew a quack, saying that several of his patients had died because of his ineptitude. Neither of their accusations was true, and their slanderous insults had nothing to do with the actual reason for their mutual hatred. Emily, of course, was that reason. She was the real catalyst for their inevitable confrontation, as was the fact that they both loved her so desperately knowing only one of them could have her. Neither man could live with the knowledge that the other might win Emily's affection while he had not.

As such, the confrontation at the local pub over too much ale had occurred. Then after the ridiculous accusations had been made, there was little choice remaining but for each man to demand satisfaction in the form of a duel to defend their mutual honor.

The three now stood as the early morning mist crept along the bricks and cobblestones in the alley, Dueler's Alley, as it was known. This was to be the place where fate would decide what she had been unable to do. She stood in front of one of the stone walls on both sides of the long shadowy corridor. Dueler's Alley had gotten its name because this was the location where most of the duels in Charleston had been fought. Whether by knife, sword, or gun,

Dueler's Alley was the place where men went to shed blood. And shed blood they did; by the gallons. The lifeblood of hundreds of men was now soaked deep into the soil beneath the bricks in this place of death.

The alley was lined on both sides with stone buildings and brick walls, making it the perfect place for guns to be fired without much worry of stray bullets striking innocent townspeople. In the courtyards on both sides of the alley, tall oak and maple trees grew shading the lane, giving it a dark and eerie appearance. One might expect to see the ghosts of past duelers walking among the living, and many townspeople of Charleston would swear to the Almighty that they actually had witnessed such ghastly specters.

John and Andrew now stood back to back in the distance down the shaded alley, their pistols raised, muzzles pointed skyward. Both were dressed in black dress pants, high boots, and their finest white linen shirts. Their faces were stern with anticipation. Standing next to them were two young men Emily knew to be their close friends, apparently there to act as their seconds. It was the responsibility of these men to assure the duel was conducted in accordance with the rules established by the government for such activities.

Emily was permitted to watch from the end of the alley at the intersection with Cumberland Street but was not allowed to stand any closer. Neither Andrew nor John showed the slightest trace of fear or apprehension. For Emily, the exhilaration she felt was overwhelming. Here were two men, both of who had professed to love her, and they were just moments away from trying to kill each other over her. She would be bound to marry the survivor no matter which one it was.

But then she had a horrible thought. What if both men died? What would she do then? She would have no man to marry. She would be known around Charleston high society as the foolish young girl who had two men desiring her and now had none. If that happened, would another suitor step forward? She wasn't getting any younger. She was almost nineteen, practically a spinster.

Suddenly she wanted to scream, "No! Stop!" to try to call off this whole ridiculous duel, but she knew it would be a futile gesture. The seconds had already begun the count, and the two men were starting to walk away from each other. She could do nothing to stop it. Women had no say in such matters of honor. Men felt they simply couldn't understand. Yet, where was there any honor in taking the life of another man? Surely if anything, such an act should bring dishonor to the winner and a curse on his immortal soul.

Andrew was walking down the narrow alley toward her, his face a stony mask of concentration. Likewise, John was walking at the same measured pace, but in the opposite direction. How many paces had they walked so far? Emily didn't know.

"Eight," she heard one of the seconds counting off, followed by "nine." She knew the rules; she had heard stories of past duels. Twenty-one was the final count, the point at which the men would turn and fire. So many men had died in this alley. She imagined a giant crimson pool lurking beneath the alley; a reservoir comprised of the collective blood of hundreds of now-dead men. She envisioned it as a bubbling cesspool of stinking, rotten fermenting gore, a lake of the damned. A cold chill raced down her spine, and she shuddered involuntarily.

"Thirteen," the seconds called in unison as the men continued to walk further apart. "Fourteen."

In seven more paces, the men, her men, would turn and fire. Then for better or worse, it would all be over, and she would know who had lived and who had died. Would it be Andrew? He was a successful physician, a man of medicine who knew the human body better than most men. He would know where the best place would be to aim his bullet for maximum lethal effect. However, although not a doctor, John was an outstanding marksman, and his father's money had bought him one of the best and most accurate guns available. Would that be enough to tip the scales his way? She didn't know. God, this waiting was unbearable.

"Nineteen," the seconds counted.

Two more paces and it would all be over. She wanted to hide her eyes to shield them from the horror which was about to unfold. She wanted to turn and run, but her feet felt as if they had turned to lead.

Then she heard the final call, "twenty one" and time seemed to come practically to a halt as things around her began to move a thousand times slower than they should have.

She saw everything in all of its painful clarity. Andrew began to pivot on his heel, turning while simultaneously dropping the barrel of his gun into firing position. At the other end of the alley, forty-two paces away John was doing the same. As Andrew pivoted, his eyes met Emily's for just a fraction of a second, but in that brief moment, she saw confidence, which told her Andrew was most definitely going to win this; he was going to kill John.

Her heart seemed to rise up into her throat, blocking her ability to catch a breath. "Oh God no!" she screamed silently in her mind, but it was to no avail. A moment later, she heard two almost simultaneously reports as both guns exploded, one just a second later than the other. In the distance, she saw John stagger backward as a patch of crimson began to spread on his crisp white shirt around his heart. His face showed an expression which was a combination of shock, pain, and realization that he was about to die. She also saw Andrew fly backward, obviously struck high on the left side of his body.

Then she felt something she had not expected. It was a burning, searing pain in her throat. She pulled up her hands reflexively to her neck and felt the sticky warmth of her own blood flowing hot between her fingers. John was now obviously dead, his body lying still on the ground. Andrew was likewise on the ground writhing in pain but didn't seem to be mortally wounded. He was clutching his left shoulder, which appeared to have been broken by the impact of the bullet, and he was looking up at Emily in horror. His mouth seemed to be screaming something. It was the word, "No!"

Emily suddenly realized what had happened. That split-second Andrew had taken to look into her eyes was enough for his body to become positioned at such an angle that John's bullet careened off Andrew's shoulder bone. But where had it gone?

She then understood exactly where the bullet had gone. It had ricocheted off Andrew's shoulder and had found its way into her throat. She understood now she too had been mortally wounded. As the last light of life began to fade from her dimming eyes, she thought about what her mother had told her about respectable young ladies. She had not chosen to do the right thing as her mother had urged her. Now, sinking to her knees, Emily realized that fate had made its own decision. The last thought Emily had was of asking forgiveness for her foolishness from John, from Andrew, from her mother, from God, and lastly from herself.

THE TELL-TALE HEART

BY EDGAR ALLEN POE, 1843

TRUE! nervous, very, very dreadfully nervous I had been and am; but why WILL you say that I am mad? The disease had sharpened my senses, not destroyed, not dulled them. Above all was the sense of hearing acute. I heard all things in the heaven and in the earth. I heard many things in hell. How then am I mad? Hearken! and observe how healthily, how calmly, I can tell you the whole story.

It is impossible to say how first the idea entered my brain, but, once conceived, it haunted me day and night. Object there was none. Passion, there was none. I loved the old man. He had never wronged me. He had never given me an insult. For his gold, I had no desire. I think it was his eye! Yes, it was this! One of his eyes resembled that of a vulture—a pale blue eye with a film over it. Whenever it fell upon me my blood ran cold, and so by degrees, very gradually, I made up my mind to take the life of the old man, and thus rid myself of the eye forever.

Now, this is the point. You fancy me mad. Madmen know nothing. But you should have seen me. You should have seen how wisely I proceeded—with what caution—with what foresight, with what dissimulation, I went to work! I was never kinder to the old man than during the whole week before I killed him. And every night about midnight, I turned the latch of his door and opened it oh, so gently! And then, when I had made an opening sufficient for my head, I put in a dark lantern all closed, closed so that no light shone out, and then I thrust in my head. Oh, you would have laughed to see how cunningly I thrust it in! I moved it slowly, very, very slowly, so that I might not disturb the old man's sleep. It took me an hour to place my whole head within the opening so far that I could see him as he lay upon his bed. Ha! would a madman have been so wise as this? And then when my head was well in the room, I undid the lantern cautiously—oh, so cautiously—cautiously (for the hinges creaked), I undid it just so much that a single thin ray fell upon the vulture eye. And this I did for seven long nights, every night just at midnight, but I found the eye always closed, and so it was impossible to do the work, for it was not the old man who vexed me but his Evil Eye. And every morning, when the day broke, I went boldly into the chamber and spoke courageously to him, calling him by name in a hearty tone, and inquiring how he had passed the night. So you see, he would have been a very profound old man, indeed, to suspect that every night, just at twelve, I looked in upon him while he slept.

Upon the eighth night, I was more than usually cautious in opening the door. A watch's minute hand moves more quickly than did mine. Never before that night had I felt the extent of my own powers, of my sagacity. I could scarcely contain my feelings of triumph. To think that there I was opening the door little by little, and he not even to dream of my secret deeds or thoughts. I fairly chuckled at the idea, and perhaps he heard me, for he moved on the bed suddenly as if startled. Now you may think that I drew back—but no. His room was as black as pitch with the thick darkness (for the shutters were close fastened through fear of robbers), and so I knew that he could not see the opening of the door, and I kept pushing it on steadily, steadily.

I had my head in and was about to open the lantern when my thumb slipped upon the tin fastening , and the old man sprang up in the bed, crying out, "Who's there?"

I kept quite still and said nothing. For a whole hour, I did not move a muscle, and in the meantime, I did not hear him lie down. He was still sitting up in the bed, listening, just as I have done night after night hearkening to the death watches in the wall.

Presently, I heard a slight groan, and I knew it was the groan of mortal ter-ror. It was not a groan of pain or of grief—oh, no! It was the low stifled sound that arises from the bottom of the soul when overcharged with awe. I knew the sound well. Many a night, just at midnight, when all the world slept, it has welled up from my own bosom, deepening, with its dreadful echo, the terrors that distracted me. I say I knew it well. I knew what the old man felt, and pitied him although I chuckled at heart. I knew that he had been lying awake ever since the first slight noise when he had turned in the bed. His fears had been ever since growing upon him. He had been trying to fancy them causeless, but could not. He had been saying to himself, "It is nothing but the wind in the chimney, it is only a mouse crossing the floor," or, "It is merely a cricket which has made a single chirp." Yes, he has been trying to comfort himself with these suppositions, but he had found all in vain. ALL IN VAIN, because Death in approaching him had stalked with his black shadow before him and enveloped the victim. And it was the mournful influence of the unperceived shadow that caused him to feel, although he neither saw nor heard, to feel the presence of my head within the room.

When I had waited a long time very patiently without hearing him lie down, I resolved to open a little—a very, very little crevice in the lantern. So I opened it—you cannot imagine how stealthily, stealthily—until at length a single dim ray like the thread of the spider shot out from the crevice and fell upon the vulture eye.

It was open, wide, wide open, and I grew furious as I gazed upon it. I saw it with perfect distinctness—all a dull blue with a hideous veil over it that chilled the very marrow in my bones, but I could see nothing else of the old man's face or person, for I had directed the ray as if by instinct precisely upon the damned spot.

And now have I not told you that what you mistake for madness is but over-acuteness of the senses? now, I say, there came to my ears a low, dull, quick sound, such as a watch makes when enveloped in cotton. I knew that sound well too. It was the beating of the old man's heart. It increased my fury as the beating of a drum stimulates the soldier into courage.

But even yet, I refrained and kept still. I scarcely breathed. I held the lantern motionless. I tried how steadily I could maintain the ray upon the eye. Meantime the hellish tattoo of the heart increased. It grew quicker and quicker, and louder and louder, every instant. The old man's terror must have been extreme! It grew louder, I say, louder every moment!—do you mark me well? I have told you that I am nervous: so I am. And now at the dead hour of the night, amid the dreadful silence of that old house, so strange a noise as this excited me to uncontrollable terror. Yet, for some minutes longer, I refrained and stood still. But the beating grew louder, louder! I thought the heart must burst. And now a new anxiety seized me—the sound would be heard by a neighbor! The old man's hour had come! With a loud yell, I threw open the lantern and leaped into the room. He shrieked once—once only. In an instant,

I dragged him to the floor and pulled the heavy bed over him. I then smiled gaily, to find the deed so far done. But for many minutes, the heartbeat on with a muffled sound. This, however, did not vex me; it would not be heard through the wall. At length, it ceased. The old man was dead. I removed the bed and examined the corpse. Yes, he was stone, stone dead. I placed my hand upon the heart and held it there many minutes. There was no pulsation. He was stone dead. His eye would trouble me no more.

If still, you think me mad, you will think so no longer when I describe the wise precautions I took for the concealment of the body. The night waned, and I worked hastily, but in silence.

I took up three planks from the flooring of the chamber and deposited all between the scantlings. I then replaced the boards so cleverly so cunningly, that no human eye—not even his—could have detected anything wrong. There was nothing to wash out—no stain of any kind—no blood-spot whatever. I had been too wary for that.

When I had made an end of these labors, it was four o'clock—still dark as midnight. As the bell sounded the hour, there came a knocking at the street door. I went down to open it with a light heart,—for what had I now to fear? There entered three men, who introduced themselves, with perfect suavity, as officers of the police. A shriek had been heard by a neighbor during the night; suspicion of foul play had been aroused; information had been lodged at the police office, and they (the officers) had been deputed to search the premises.

I smiled,—for what had I to fear? I bade the gentlemen welcome. The shriek, I said, was my own in a dream. The old man, I mentioned, was absent in the country. I took my visitors all over the house. I bade them search—search well. I led them, at length, to his chamber. I showed them his treasures, secure, undisturbed. In the enthusiasm of my confidence, I brought chairs into the room and desired them here to rest from their fatigues, while I myself, in the wild audacity of my perfect triumph, placed my own seat upon the very spot beneath which reposed the corpse of the victim.

The officers were satisfied. My MANNER had convinced them. I was singularly at ease. They sat, and while I answered cheerily, they chatted of familiar things. But, ere long, I felt myself getting pale and wished them gone. My head ached, and I fancied a ringing in my ears, but still, they sat and still chatted. The ringing became more distinct : I talked more freely to get rid of the feeling: but it continued and gained definitiveness—until, at length, I found that the noise was NOT within my ears.

No doubt I now grew VERY pale; but I talked more fluently, and with a heightened voice. Yet the sound increased—and what could I do? It was A LOW, DULL, QUICK SOUND—MUCH SUCH A SOUND AS A WATCH MAKES WHEN ENVELOPED IN COTTON. I gasped for breath, and yet the officers heard it not. I talked more quickly, more vehemently, but the noise steadily increased. I arose and argued about trifles, in a high key, and with violent gesticulations; but the noise steadily increased. Why WOULD they not be gone? I paced the floor to and fro with heavy strides, as if excited to fury by the observations of the men, but the noise steadily increased. O God! what COULD I do? I foamed—I raved—I swore! I swung the chair upon which I had been sitting and grated it upon the boards, but the noise arose over all and continually increased. It grew louder—louder—louder! And still, the men chatted pleasantly and smiled. Was it possible they heard not? Almighty God!—no, no? They heard!—they suspected!—they KNEW!—they were making a mockery of my horror!—this I thought, and this, I think. But anything was better than this agony! Anything was more tolerable than this derision! I could bear those hypocritical smiles no longer! I felt that I must scream or die!—and now—again—hark! louder! louder! louder! LOUDER!—

"Villains!" I shrieked, "dissemble no more! I admit the deed!—tear up the planks!—here, here!—it is the beating of his hideous heart!"

RING-RING

By Thomas M. Malafarina

The hands on the wall clock seemed to crawl at a pace slower than that of a one-legged snail. Christina stared at the minute hand, which mocked her in what appeared to be its deliberate reluctance to obey the laws of space and time. The clock was one of those old white-faced office wall clocks with large black numbers and equally dark hands. She was thankful it didn't have a bright red second hand because she was certain watching that arm slowly dragging its way around the clock face might have caused her ever-greater consternation. It wasn't that she was bored with her job or that she didn't like it, but she most certainly was in a hurry to get home.

"Home," she thought wistfully to herself. "My home. Our home."

Christina was happier at that moment than she had ever been in her life, perhaps happier than she ever imagined she could be. She and her long-time boyfriend had not only recently gotten married, but they had also just settled on and moved into a new home. They were almost finished furnishing and decorating the place, and in her opinion, it was perfect. In fact, her entire life couldn't be any better.

Even though she and David had lived together for several years, there was something very special about this final commitment; and their new home just helped to solidify their relationship. She extended her left hand and examined her lovely engagement ring and matching wedding band. She could hardly believe the day had finally come. It was something she had dreamt about her entire life. She was quite certain nothing could make her happier. Christina almost felt guilty for being so elated by her good fortune.

Then suddenly, an unwelcomed thought crossed her mind. It was something she remembered hearing her wizened old great-uncle Edward say when she was just a little girl. Edward had been the official sad sack and self-appointed naysayer of the family. It seemed no matter what happy occasion might be taking place, Edward always found something negative to add to the conversation and, more often than not, bring any level of merriment to a screeching halt. For some reason, there was one expression she now remembered him saying most often.

Even though Edward had been dead for better than twenty years, Christina could still hear his voice in her head saying in own especially rough manner, "You got to watch out for life, 'cause just when everything seems to be going just right, life is waiting around the corner to jump out and kick you right in the balls."

Despite her youthful displeasure with his choice of vernacular, not to mention the fact that she lacked the male physical accouterments of which he spoke, Christina understood very well the lesson he was attempting to convey. He obviously had lived a very long time and understood that when things were going exceptionally well, we as humans tend to take for granted that life will continue in that direction. But life, being what it is, tends to be fraught with a variety of unwanted obstacles that can appear in our path as impediments to the continued happiness we desire. Moreover, sometimes, those obstructions can take the form of an extreme tragedy such as terminal illness or death of a loved one. And now for some strange reason, she was thinking about how incredibly happy she was until Edward's words had returned to remind her of her vulnerability.

Although she knew this level of extreme joy might not last forever, she wanted to be at least able to enjoy it without feeling guilty for doing so. She certainly didn't need to think about Edward and his infernal bellyaching. Despite her desire to the contrary, she couldn't get his words out of her mind. Now she was beginning to fear what exactly it might be that life was waiting to dish out to ruin her happiness. She suddenly thought of her husband, David. Was he all right? Had something happened to him? Was there some sort of awful, malignant tumor growing inside his brain. Or perhaps there was an aneurysm just waiting for the opportunity to explode and make her a widow? For a moment, she considered calling him just to hear his voice and know all was well.

"Stop it," Christina said aloud. She had been feeling so happy just moments earlier, but now these thoughts of Edward and his stupid folk logic were coming dangerously close to ruining her day. She realized it was fortunate she had been working alone in the computer server room today. The last thing she'd want was for one of her co-workers to hear her yelling at herself like some sort of crazy woman. Christina would be the first to admit at times she tended to be a bit quirky as did most of her peers, but still, she was certain shouting aloud might be considered somewhat beyond the realm of mere quirkiosity.

The computer room was small, only about fifteen by twenty feet with a single glass-paneled door for both entry and exit. Gaining access to the room was by key-card only. Most of the available space was occupied by large, heavy black metal racks, which held her company's many servers. The only furniture in the room was an old metal surplus office desk and a well-worn swivel chair. Littering the top of the desk was a variety of computer keyboards and monitors used to access and maintain the numerous programs running on the company's network. There was also an old-style telephone on the desktop. It was there to make outgoing calls only. There was no number associated with the extension, so no one could call in. This was to assure privacy for the person manning the computer terminals, yet still, allow them outside access to contact necessary office personnel and for emergencies.

Christina knew this because, after several months or so on the job, she realized the only calls she ever received were on her private cell phone. The old-fashioned black plastic desk phone never rang. When she had inquired, she learned about its non-accessible status. As such, she used it to call other office extensions as required and basically never thought about it again. That had been over three years earlier, and during that entire time, the phone remained silent.

Now she sat silently staring down at her wedding ring, doing all she could to try to bring back the happy feelings she had been experiencing earlier and block out those terrible thoughts of her great uncle "Doom and Gloom" Edward. Of course, she couldn't. It was like trying to tell yourself not to think of some annoying song, which happens to be repeating in your mind or telling yourself not to think of a particular number.

She knew the only way to get past both the negative feelings as well as the fact that time was dragging on was for her to get busy. If she lost herself in her work, she could solve both problems at the same time. So she dug back into her work, yet the uneasy feeling still seemed to remain, although it felt a bit less severe than earlier. Before long, she was completely engrossed in her duties and oblivious to the world around her. Then she heard it, a distinct sound. It was the desk phone ringing.

"What the hell?" Christina thought. "That phone never rings."

And what was with that ring? It didn't sound like any of the melodious ringtones all of the other office phones had, but rather it was a simple, old-style telephone ring. She wondered why the ringtone chosen for that phone was such an old and creepy sort of thing. It reminded her of something out of the old Twilight Zone TV series. A cold chill raced down her spine. Hesitantly, she reached down and picked up the receiver. That earlier feeling of unease returned even stronger.

"Hello?" She said apprehensively into the receiver. To her surprise, all she heard was a dial tone. However, that wasn't completely true. There was something else Christina thought she heard, just underneath the humming dial tone, something strange. There was a buzzing like that caused by a swarm of insects. For the briefest of moments, Christina imagined the corpse of her great uncle Edward rotting in his grave as scores of insects slowly devoured him, laying their maggoty eggs beneath his decomposing flesh and hatching more generations of vile flesh-eating insects.

She thought, "To Hell with that," and she slammed down the receiver staring at the phone as if waiting for it to ring again. Then Christina rationalized that most likely, some random number generating telemarketing program somehow stumbled onto the right combination, which connected it to the extension of this phone. She assumed even though there was no published number associated with the phone, somewhere in the computer system, there had to be some number tied to it, or else she wouldn't have been able to make outgoing calls.

Christina was surprised at how something as simple as that stupid ringing phone could put her on edge. That, she recalled, combined with her thoughts of old Edward and managed to take her previously wonderful mood and darken it substantially. She looked up at the clock on the wall and saw to her surprise that several hours had passed. It was only an hour or so until it was time for her to go home to her wonderful husband, David. Then the phone rang again.

She stared at the phone for several rings, not certain if she should pick it up or not. Finally, she saw her hand slowly reaching over to grab the receiver from its cradle. It was as if she were watching her hand moving in some sort of surrealistic nightmare. It was like she couldn't control her hand from doing what it somehow knew it had to do. A moment later, she found the phone pressed against her ear with the same eerie dial tone humming. She could also once again hear that insectile buzzing, running just beneath the dial tone. She didn't speak a word but waited helplessly as the buzzing seemed to increase in volume until it was louder than the dial tone, which had somehow faded into the background. The buzzing continued to get louder until it reached a point where it began to hurt her ears. She wanted to put down the receiver, wanted to cry out in pain but was somehow helpless to do anything.

Then just when she thought she couldn't stand it any longer, both the incessant bussing and the dial tone stopped, and the line went almost completely silent. But there was something else there on the line, something distant and almost indiscernible. It was a slow, wheezing, hissing sound like someone struggling to breathe. Or perhaps a better description might be "pretending to breathe." Christina once again thought of Edward moldering in his grave. With sudden realization, she knew it was he at the other end of the line, years dead yet somehow there pretending to breathe like a living human being rather than a mere shadow of what he had once been.

Suddenly the phone erupted with a ghastly scream that sent chills reverberating throughout Christina's now trembling body. A raspy voice came howled over the receiver, shouting, "Right in the balls!"

Then the line went dead. With quivering hands, Christina placed the receiver once again back in the cradle. She had immediately recognized that horrible voice. Even after two decades in the grave, the voice of her great uncle Edward was as clear as if he were standing right in front of her. Then she knew something was very wrong. "David!" she suddenly thought.

Christina picked up her smartphone and quickly dialed her husband's number. It rang several times, then went to voicemail. Her concern now rising to panic level, Christina disconnected the call and pressed redial. After three rings, a man's unfamiliar voice answered, saying "Hello? Who is this?"

"David?" Christina asked, knowing the voice she had heard was not that of her husband. Nonetheless, she asked again, "David? It's Christina. Is that you, David?" Her voice was fraught with obvious concern.

Instead of hearing her husband's voice, she heard the voice of the same stranger saying, "This is State Police Sergeant Jason Martin. Can you please identify yourself, Ma'am?

"What?" Christina said. "I don't understand. This is Christina Willington. I'm calling my husband David's phone. Who is, I mean, where's David? Where's my husband?"

"Ma'am? Are you the wife of David Willington, who resides at 1874 Woodglenn Road in the town of Yuengsville, PA?"

"Yes, yes, that's me," Christina insisted. "Please put David on the phone. I need to speak to David." Bet even as she spoke the words Christina somehow knew in her heart that David would not be answering the phone, not now, not ever again.

The policeman's voice was speaking to her from somewhere very far away. Christina's mind only partially heard the words she already knew he would say. "Ma'am? I'm so very sorry to have to tell you, well, there's been an automobile accident involving your husband. I'm so sorry, Ma'am, but your husband has been killed."

Christina could hear someone screaming, a woman's voice wailing and sobbing, "No. No. Please, God, no." It took a few seconds for her to comprehend it was her own pleading voice she was hearing. Somewhere in the back of her mind, she heard the horrible cackling laughter of her long-dead Great Uncle Edward.

DOUBLE YELLOW

By Thomas M. Malafarina

"It must be, I thought, one of the race's most persistent and comforting hallucinations to trust that "it can't happen here"— that one's own time and place is beyond cataclysm."

—John Wyndahm, *The Day of the Triffids*

Wyatt drove robotically along the winding country two-lane road. It was the same road; he had traveled daily for almost thirty years during his long commute to and from work. Little had changed with that particular stretch of highway during those many years save for the occasional resurfacing project, followed by the repainting of the white lines along the shoulders of the road as well as the solid double yellow lines down the center.

This was Wyatt's first day returning to work as a purchasing agent for a major corporation after being absent the entire previous week, suffering from a particularly nasty strain of some sort of flu bug that had apparently been making its rounds. He had started feeling poorly the previous Saturday morning, and by evening, he was sicker than he had been in a very long time, exploding from both ends as it were. Wyatt could imagine little that might be worse as he had sat on the toilet with a bucket on the floor in front of him, just waiting for the next wave of sickness to strike, which it often did simultaneously.

By Sunday night, the worst of his illness was over, but he was feeling very weak, so Wyatt decided to take off Monday to rest and recover before making any attempt at returning to work. But when he discovered he felt no better Tuesday morning, he once again stayed home and slept most of that day as well.

Late Tuesday night, he tried eating some clear soup broth, which his wife had made for him, hoping to feel well enough to return Wednesday. However, as things turned out, he didn't make it on Wednesday either. After trying to do a few things around the house in a feeble attempt to get himself back to normal, he began to feel worse once again. So he took off Thursday and Friday as well.

He had decided it might be better to wait and start fresh on Monday. The weekend had gone fairly well, and by Monday, he was feeling about as good as he could be expected to feel after such an ordeal. Wyatt's wife suggested that what he really needed now was to get back into his daily routine and put the illness behind him. He was still a bit foggy in the brain, but he guessed that was to be expected after being down for so long.

As he drove along the road in the early dawn darkness, Wyatt noticed the highway appeared somehow different than it had looked a week earlier. Something about it had changed. He couldn't quite determine what the difference was, however. At first, he wondered if, perhaps, the state workers had resurfaced the two-lane while he was off, but he could see in the light from his high beams that the road had the same worn surface as previously. He always left for work before sunrise and arrived home after dark, so he was accustomed to the way the road looked in his headlights. Yet still, something definitely seemed different. He wondered what it might be. Then, he realized what it was: it was the lines.

That was it. Apparently, someone must have repainted the traffic lines during his time away. The single white lines along the shoulders were much whiter, and the solid double yellow lines down the center glowed with a sort of phosphorescence the likes of which Wyatt hadn't noticed before.

He wondered why anyone would have bothered to repaint the markings on a road that was in such dire need of resurfacing. It made no fiscal sense, and the contrast between the lines and the worn highway surface was almost disturbing. Then Wyatt looked more closely at the lines and suspected he might have been incorrect, and perhaps they hadn't been repainted after all. Yet the lines still did seem to stand out from the rest of the roadway for some unexplainable reason.

Maybe it was the result of some strange convergence of atmospheric conditions; the darkness of the predawn; the position of the moon and stars combined with the absence of clouds. Perhaps he was viewing the lines through a magnifying morning mist. Who knew? For whatever reason, the lines seemed to glow with an incredible iridescence. Then Wyatt noticed something else about the lines that he couldn't begin to explain—they suddenly made him feel very uncomfortable.

For the first time in all of his years of traveling along the same road, Wyatt felt as if he was a prisoner, held captive by the lines. Although he understood such a thought was illogical as well as completely irrational, he couldn't seem to shake the sensation, which was beginning to feel almost claustrophobic. Perhaps he was still feeling the effects of his illness of the previous week, and it was playing tricks with his mind. Whatever the reason, the feeling was extremely intense.

In his heart, Wyatt understood the lines were there for public safety. In fact, both sets of lines were accompanied by rumble strip grooves cut into the highway beneath them, so if a driver started to doze at the wheel and his car began to cross the lines, he would be awakened by the sound and feel of his tires on the grooves. This might prevent him from hurting himself or others. Like the lines themselves, the rumble strips were there to protect motorists and to help enforce traffic control regulations.

"Control," Wyatt thought suddenly. Yes, wasn't that their real purpose? Wasn't that the true reason for the lines? To control the flow of traffic? To control the actions of the motorists? Or perhaps their purpose was much more sinister than that.

He began to question if just maybe the double yellow lines were one more method the government used to manipulate him and his fellow motorists; to force them to adhere to yet another ridiculous bureaucratic regulation. Control simply for the sake of control.

"What if there were no lines?" he thought to himself. Then he wondered if he suddenly found himself on a blank roadway with no lines in sight, would he stupidly veer over into the opposite lane, into the path of oncoming traffic and be involved in a collision? On the other hand, would he go off the roadway to the right and smash into a tree or maybe drive over an embankment? He was quite certain he wouldn't. The very thought was ridiculous. Then again, if it were really dark, foggy, raining, or snowing heavily, without the benefit of the brightly painted lines, he might inadvertently do just that.

He reluctantly accepted that the true purpose for the lines was nothing sinister, but that they were simply there for his own welfare. In fact, he was beginning to question the rationale of his own earlier thoughts and was wondering why he was becoming so foolishly fixated on something as mundane and trivial as double yellow highway lines in the first place. The lines kept him driving safely on his side of the road the oncoming traffic on their side. Then Wyatt began to wonder if the lines really did do their required job of keeping people on their respective sides of the roadway after all.

Now Wyatt's heart seemed to skip a beat when he realized the naivety of his last series of thoughts. The lines were just that; simply painted markings. They had no mystic or magical powers. In fact, they weren't a real barrier in any true sense of the word. Even with the warning rumble strips cut into the road beneath the lines, they could do nothing to prevent someone from crossing over and slamming headlong into his car. Wyatt had read countless newspaper stories about drivers who had passed out or had heart attacks while driving, then had crossed the double yellow lines, crashing into the oncoming vehicles.

And how many accounts had he read of drunk drivers doing the same thing? Wyatt realized as if for the first time, the lines did absolutely nothing to protect him from the potential madness of the drivers in the oncoming lane. He was starting to realize what a game of Russian roulette it was to drive down the highway on a daily basis. Any driver he might encounter at any moment could be the bullet, the one destined to cross the lines, crash into him and take him out.

Then as if horribly on cue, a set of overly bright headlights appeared in the distance coming toward Wyatt in the opposite lane. At least he hoped the lights were still in the opposite lane. From his distance, he couldn't tell. The lights could just as easily have been in his own lane, heading straight for him. This could be it, he thought, the one potential fatality fate had chosen to attach his name to. Wyatt broke out in a cold sweat, thinking about how the only thing standing between him, the oncoming car, and imminent death was a double yellow line painted on the road surface. His hands began to tremble, as the headlights got closer.

He imagined a deadly scenario in which the driver of the oncoming car might have been depressed over some personal tragedy, perhaps an unfaithful wife or girlfriend or perhaps the upsetting death of a loved one. If the driver were despondent enough, he might very easily decide to drive insanely into Wyatt's car in a sudden suicidal impulse. If that were to happen, there would be no way Wyatt could get out of the vehicle's path in time.

As the car got closer, Wyatt saw it was still on its proper side of the road, but he didn't feel in any way assured it would stay there. When the car got even closer, Wyatt's hands became wet with sweat, and he could feel rivulets of perspiration trickling down the center of his back. Then a moment later, it was over. The car had passed by, and its taillights were a mere shrinking memory in his rearview mirror.

Wyatt began to wonder what he would have done if the person in the other car actually had come over into his lane. He looked over to the right of the roadway and saw about a two feet wide shoulder, which dropped off into a deep culvert for water drainage. A few feet beyond that was a row of telephone poles. There was absolutely nowhere for him to go in that direction safely.

Then he looked to his left, thinking that if a car came most of the way over into his lane, he might be able to squeeze through on that side, but he saw another short shoulder and an even steeper drop off, behind which was a slight embankment thick with trees. Perhaps if he made it to the culvert on that side, his car might be totaled, but at least he had a chance of surviving. Then the strange stream of thoughts once again raced through his mind; he truly was trapped between the lines on the highway like a prisoner with no means of escape.

"What in the hell is wrong with me?" Wyatt asked aloud, suddenly realizing the potential problems that would be brought on by implications the unfortunate series of emotions he had just experienced. "Wyatt, you idiot. You have got to get a grip."

He had no idea what was going on with his head or why the weird luminescent double-yellow lines had brought on such feelings of discomfort, if not almost crippling terror. But whatever it might have been, he had to make it stop and quickly. Wyatt still had to drive an hour to work each way every day, and unless he could find some method to suppress the horrified emotional state he suddenly found himself in, he wouldn't be able to return to his job. Wyatt knew that no job meant no money.

For a moment, he seriously considered turning around and heading home, realizing perhaps he wasn't as well as he originally assumed. "Maybe if I stay home for another day or two, things will work themselves out, and then I'll be back to normal." He had only traveled about ten of his fifty-minute commute, so he still had the majority of his trip ahead of him. He knew the idea of turning around was impractical. What would he say to his wife? The terror he felt deep in the pit of his stomach was irrational; he was certain. He knew he felt fine physically, however, his brain that for some reason, seemed to be giving him all the trouble; that and those strange glowing double yellow lines.

As he cleared, the top of a hill Wyatt could see the interstate out in the distance, not more than three or four miles away. He realized if he could make it to that major four-lane roadway with its guardrails and large grass-planted median strips separating the oncoming lanes, he'd be fine.

It can't be more than five minutes away. Wyatt thought. If I can just avoid other cars for the next few miles, I'll be home safe. That was when he saw a new set of headlights in the distance coming toward him.

"Oh my God, no!" Wyatt said. "Not another one." Once again, he immediately broke out in an icy sweat. First, his upper lip and forehead began to bead with moisture lightly. The other car was getting closer now, its headlights growing in size. Wyatt was certain that the car was slightly veering over toward his side of the road.

The beads of sweat had now formed rivulets running down his face as well as the center of his back. Wyatt could feel his heart start to beat faster in his chest. He involuntarily gripped the steering wheel tighter although his palms were so wet he could barely maintain his hold.

Then he saw the car was definitely crossing over into his lane; Wyatt was certain of it. He could hear the steady thumping in his brain as his blood pulsed rapidly though his body. It grew louder by the second, sounding like the foot pedal of a heavy-metal drummer, high on some illegal substance, manically slamming against a bass drum.

Wyatt felt a sudden pressure in the middle of his chest as if someone twice his size had just sat on top of him, trying to crush the very life out of him. He felt a sharp pain coursing down his left arm. The world around him started to fade and grow darker. He could scarcely hear the thudding of the rumble strips over the pounding of his heart. The last thing Wyatt saw were the headlights of the suicidal maniac's oncoming car heading straight for him.

—— • ——

"Damn shame," the township patrolman said to the state trooper in frustration.

"What do you suppose happened?" The trooper inquired.

The patrolman explained, pointing to the woman standing outside of a minivan, which was halfway off the opposite side of the highway and wedged down in the culvert.

"That woman over there said she was on her way to town to get a coffee before taking her two kids to daycare. The two kids are OK as well, thanks to their car seats."

"Anyway, she said she was driving along when suddenly that car crossed the double yellow lines into her lane, heading right for her. Luckily, at the last minute, she managed to turn sharply to her left and just miss getting hit. The driver of that sedan went off the road, down into the culvert, rolled over once, and slammed into a tree. It appears the driver was killed instantly."

The trooper asked, "So what are you thinking? Heart attack?"

"Most likely," the patrolman replied. "He is the right age, overweight, and his skin appears to be dusky in color, likely from lack of oxygen."

"Well," the trooper replied. "I suppose that lady and her two kids are lucky she was able to get out of the way at the last minute. Otherwise, we'd have a real mess to clean up. This is bad enough."

The patrolman said, "Yeah. Every time something like this happens, I realize just how vulnerable we are when the only thing separating us from disaster is a painted double-yellow line."

"I agree." The trooper replied. "Kind of makes you not want to leave home in the morning."

THE AGE OF MAN

By Thomas M. Malafarina

"The world is beautiful, but has a disease called man"
—Friedrich Nietzsche

"If people are good only because they fear punishment, and hope for reward, then we are a sorry lot indeed."
—Albert Einstein

"Man is the cruelest animal." —Friedrich Nietzsche

The man known only as Peter sat quietly in the guest chair, waiting for his automotive service to be completed. He was participating in a ritual the humans of this world referred to as "getting the oil changed." His vehicle was visible through the large glass show windows, which opened onto the "Speedy Service" area of the Mega Lube Quick Oil Change garage where a team of young men dressed in oil-stained coveralls worked like an army of ants to change the oil and do a sixteen-point inspection, whatever that was, on his compact automobile.

Peter didn't know if the vehicle actually needed to have its oil changed and suspected it might not, but he understood this was another good opportunity to observe them, to see how they interacted with each other. Unfortunately, Peter had arrived a bit early on this Saturday morning and was one of the first customers at the facility, so he sat quietly, alone, looking around the empty waiting area.

It was a fairly small room, perhaps ten feet square, the periphery of which was surrounded with many comfortable metal and faux leather-covered guest chairs, identical to the one in which he sat. To Peter's left was a break in the chairs where a door stood closed, displaying the sign reading "Rest Room" with universal symbols for both male and female creatures. Peter understood these illustrations meant the room was considered "unisex," which to the best of his comprehension didn't mean it was for humans equipped with both types of genitalia, male and female, but that it had facilities capable of handling the needs of both human sexes. From his months of living as one of these beings, he knew the purpose of such a room was to be a place where they went to "relieve themselves" as they called it; to empty their bowels and drain their bladders of waste material. He quickly did a mental check of his body to see if it required any such evacuation and determined he wasn't in need at the moment.

There was a square black wrought iron decorative coffee table with a transparent glass top situated between the u-shaped row of chairs leaving very little legroom, upon which sat a large low, rectangular box bearing the logo and name of some eating establishment called Dunkin Donuts. Peter stared at the box curiously for a few seconds noting its pleasant design. He determined, whoever Mr. Dunkin might be, he really knew how to market his product.

"Help yourself," a kind-sounding voice said from across the room. Peter observed over on the far side of the small room was an area reserved for employees, equipped with machines, which he knew were called cash registers. In the background, behind the service counter were some additional windows and doors leading out to a larger shop that he determined was used for more time-consuming repairs, as opposed to the "quickie oil change," which was conducted in the area where his vehicle was currently being serviced.

The price for the "quickie" oil change was $39.99 and also included their checking all essential fluids, checking tire pressure, the mysterious sixteen-point inspection, and also a complete vacuuming of the interior of the vehicle. The smiling man who was addressing Peter appeared to be the proprietor of the establishment, or perhaps the manager. Whoever he was, Peter understood him to be the male human in charge of the entire operation.

"Excuse me?" Peter said with something of a confused look on his face.

"The donuts," the man explained. "Help yourself to a donut while you wait. There's also a pot of coffee brewing, which should be ready by now." The man pointed to a pot of coffee across from the service desk against the far wall.

"Thank you. That's very kind of you," Peter replied, determining it was the appropriate response to such an offer.

"You're most certainly welcome," the man predictably said. Peter had become quite familiar with the proper comments and responses uttered in the various service industries he had been observing. He suspected when his business transaction was completed, the man would suggest he either "have a nice day," or perhaps indicated he should "have a good one," whatever that meant. He never understood that particular phrase. Peter wasn't even sure he had "one" of whatever it was they were speaking, let alone whether he had a "good one" or perhaps one which might be deemed less desirable. Then the man said, "It's just one more way we try to provide the best service possible for my customers."

Peter cataloged this reply for further consideration and analyzed the phrase "best service for our customers." Although the man seemed cordial enough and the gesture of providing complimentary food and beverages appeared to be quite generous, Peter assessed from the man's comments, the purpose of the kind act was derived from the perspective of increasing business revenue, rather than simply being an act of kindness. He couldn't comprehend how offering him a bit of food would do anything to increase the quality of the oil change service he was about to receive, however.

Then Peter finally understood; the proprietor was hoping by providing such free enticements while some of his competitors might choose not to do so, he'd be able to steal those customers away from those competitors. The donuts and coffee were not so much an act of generosity as some sort of bait to lure customers into a trap; that trap being the subliminal planting of a motivator to get them to offer him their return business. Peter suspected if he took the time to check out the various competitors' prices, he might find the costs at this particular establishment to be perhaps a dollar currency unit or perhaps two higher than the rest.

He quickly did the calculation and determined if his assessment were true, and assuming the business did fifty oil changes during a typical Saturday morning at two dollars more than his competitor did, the business would earn an extra one hundred dollars for an investment of about ten dollars. Peter believed that to be what was known as a substantial profit for a minimal investment. In addition, if the customers were pleased with the service and remembered the additional snacks, they'd perhaps pass the information on to their friends. This would result in not only return business but in additional business as well. Peter had read somewhere during his research, "word-of-mouth" was the best form of advertising in a capitalistic society. The more analysis he did, the less generous the gesture seemed. "Interesting," he thought.

He reached into the box, retrieved an item he knew to be a Boston Cream donut, and began to eat it. He didn't know what the city of Boston, which he understood was in a state called Massachusetts, had to do with the donut he was currently eating in Pennsylvania, but he enjoyed it nonetheless. He chose to pass on the offer of coffee, as he had never been able to acquire a taste for it. In fact, he couldn't understand how humans could possibly frequent any of the high-end coffee shops and agree to pay exorbitant fees for a simple cup of something that he smelled and tasted so foul. This phenomenon always perplexed Peter.

He sat enjoying the delicious creamy center and the chocolate topping of his donut, watching the big-screen television, suspended from the ceiling, and playing some twenty-four-hour network news broadcast. As he did so, he heard a one-way conversation coming from behind and off to the right of him. He determined someone was entering the waiting room through the outside door and was speaking on a cellular telephone. Peter never ceased to be amazed at how, when some humans were conversing on a cell phone, the rest of their surroundings seemed to disappear from their field of vision. They often spoke about the most intimate of topics right in front of a room of total strangers as if no one could hear their conversations.

"Yeah. I fixed her but good," the voice said as a large overweight man about six-foot-three inches tall with a head of uncombed hair dressed in blue jogging pants and a gray stained sweatshirt walked right past Peter as if he wasn't there. The man flopped into a chair along the wall to the left of Peter and continued his conversation.

Peter did a quick analysis of the man. He was perhaps forty years old, appeared to have been once athletic, perhaps a high school or college football player, whose muscle had gone to fat many years ago. His face was somewhat bloated and red; his nose showing the signs of veining Peter understood came from drinking too much of the substance known as alcohol. Peter determined based on his quick assessment, the man would likely be dead of a heart attack or stroke within five or ten years if he kept up his current lifestyle, which Peter had no doubt he certainly would.

He also determined that the man was much wealthier than his outward disheveled appearance, by the confidence the man exuded in both his posture and mannerisms. The man was obviously an alpha-male type in a very high-paying, perhaps stressful position, who was used to getting what he wanted when he wanted it.

The man had probably just gotten out of bed, thrown on some previously worn clothing, and rushed right out to have his oil changed. This was another fact, which always astonished Peter. He couldn't understand how some humans thought nothing of showing up in certain department stores and places of business such as this with total disregard for their personal appearance. It was as if they felt the people providing the service were so insignificant that they, the customers, had no need to care about how they looked or smelled for that matter. Peter felt if he were one of the employees working in such an establishment, he might feel slighted by this lack of respect. Then again, neither did the employees seem to take much pride in their own personal appearance.

"I figured it was her own damned fault," the man said, continuing with his conversation. "She's the one who had the wreck. She tore the door off her freaking forty thousand dollar Lexus luxury SUV. Let her suffer." There was a hesitation while his friend, on the other end of the conversation, responded. Peter liked how he had been obviously correct in his assessment of the man's affluence; as such, a vehicle was beyond the reach of most common workingmen.

The man resumed his side of the conversation, "Yeah, the insurance company gave her a loaner, a piece of crap KIA. Oh my God, I laughed my ass off." Peter found it quite disturbing how the man used the name of his God and creator in the same sentence with a word commonly used as a term of profanity for one's posterior. It appeared some humans showed as little respect for their chosen deity as they did to the people around them.

"She asked me how she was supposed to take the kids to school and show up in a KIA. Haha. Dude! It was hilarious. Can you imagine a car like that parked on my street? All of the neighborhood women were like feeling sorry for her because of her having an accident, while all the husbands were thinking how stupid she was. The dumb bitch."

Peter found this also incredibly offensive. How could the man demean the woman whom likely only a few years earlier, during one of the human's most sacred marriage ceremonies he had sworn to love, honor and cherish for the rest of his life? Yet here, the man was joking with another male friend at his so-called life-mate's expense.

Peter had observed many males such as this during the time of his research and often wondered if these men who acted with so much of what was known as machismo or behaved in a fashion, which could be determined to be perhaps a little too masculine, were actually covering up for homosexual tendencies. He understood what homosexuality was and as an outside observer, found the practice quite curious. He had no moral stand on the practice, just a natural inquisitiveness. It appeared to Peter, this man enjoyed being with his "buds" as such men called their male friends, much more than he enjoyed the company of the woman he had chosen for his partner in life. Although he wasn't judgmental, he found the entire state of affairs very odd indeed. There was another pause while the man listened to his friend respond over the cellular phone.

Just then, a serviceman walked in with a piece of paper, showing two drops of some viscous fluid. The customer told his friend on the phone to hold on for a moment while he spoke with the attendant.

"Sir," the worker said, "on the right is what your transmission fluid should look like, and as you can see, yours on the left is much darker. It indicates its time to flush and replace your transmission fluid."

"How much?" The large man asked curtly, cutting right to the chase, as humans were fond of saying.

The serviceman replied confidently, "Only ninety-nine ninety-five, and we can have it done in about half an hour."

The large man looked at the attendant as if he were insane and said, "No. Don't bother." The serviceman walked away, obviously unhappy that he missed the opportunity for a sale, and the man resumed talking to his friend.

"Dude! This guy from out in the garage just tried to rip me off. He wanted to charge me like a hundred bucks to change my transmission fluid. Screw him, dude. You know Vinny? Yeah, yeah, that Vinny. He's got a bunch of illegals working for him at his garage, and I know I can get it done there for like half that price. This dude here was trying to screw me over."

"Anyway, where was I?" He asked, "Oh yeah. Well, last night we went out for our sixth-anniversary dinner, and I told her we were going in the KIA. I even made her drive it, as a punishment. We showed up at a top-shelf mucho-expensive restaurant driving a piece of crap. It was wild! No, no, I told you, I wouldn't let her take my Lexus. Screw her. I made her take the KIA. Dude! It was great! She cried her freakin' eyes out."

Again, what Peter heard trouble him. This human was actually taking enjoyment from making his so-called "true love" suffer what she'd perceived as obvious humiliation on the celebratory anniversary of the couple's taking their wedding vows. Peter found himself becoming enraged. He assumed the feelings were a side effect of his being stuck in the human body for a prolonged time.

"Ford Focus?" The man behind the counter called jarring Peter from his angry thoughts. That was the make and model of the vehicle Peter was driving, which meant his service was completed. Peter looked out the windows and saw his car outside the garage, waiting for him. He walked to the service counter and paid for his service with cash, all the while listening to the man's conversation and determining his next action.

When he finished his transaction, the man behind the counter smiled and said jovially, "Have a good one." There was that strange expression again.

"Thank you very much, and the same to you," Peter said, issuing what he determined to be the appropriate response. Once again, he wondered silently, "What is this mysterious "one," which this man hopes will be good for me? Strange, very strange indeed."

As he walked away from the service counter, he heard the man on the cellular telephone tell his friend, "Sorry, man; I gotta go. My Lexus is finished." Peter walked outside and got into his car, preparing to drive away when he heard the door to the shop opening as the large man walked out onto the pavement. He looked down at Peter in his small compact Ford, as if actually seeing Peter for the first time, giving him a disgusted look similar to the expression one might make if he stepped in something nasty a dog might have left on a sidewalk.

Peter slowly nodded in the direction of the large man appearing to offer a greeting, and the man's face immediately turned to one of complete shock as he involuntarily reached up, grabbing his chest as if experiencing incredible pain. His face became ashen, and foam dribbled from the corners of the large man's mouth as his tongue began to swell, extending over his lips, which had turned blue. He shook and convulsed, obviously having difficulty breathing. A moment later, the big man collapsed in a heap on the ground.

Peter turned his car to the right, heading away from the service center. Looking in his rearview mirror, he saw the main door burst open as several workers rushed out to come to the man's aid. Peter knew the men were wasting their time trying to revive the big man, as he had been dead before his body had hit the ground.

Turning out onto the busy highway, Peter followed the flow of automobiles to the next traffic light, where he stopped behind a sub-compact automobile adorned with three bumper stickers that he found very interesting. Peter was fascinated with the humans' use of bumper stickers, and he loved to read them, as they told him a lot about the person who was driving the vehicle.

He was amazed at how no matter how grand the vehicle was or what the person behind the wheel might look like upon the first inspection, their real innermost feelings and passions, their heart and soul always became known in their choice of bumper stickers. He recalled the words to a song he had heard once on the radio, saying, "I saw a Dead Head sticker on a Cadillac." He didn't know who the performer, a human named Don Henley was, but the man certainly was accurate in his lyrical assessment. He knew about the counterculture band from the 1960s called the Grateful Dead and understood the irony of the juxtaposition of a fan of the band now driving a luxury vehicle. Peter noticed the vehicle in front of him was being driven by a young girl.

The far-right sticker showed a globe-shaped illustration of the earth with the slogan, "You only have one mother." After a few moments of contemplation, Peter realized the slogan was a positive one suggesting other humans should respect "Mother Earth." He thought that was rather clever.

The center sticker was lettered in pink and read, "Save the Ta Tas." This one confused Peter for a moment until he recalled the expression "Ta Tas" was a slang term for female breasts. Then he understood this meant to make people aware of the driver's support of breast cancer awareness. He believed anything, which supported raising funds to help medical researchers battle such a scourge, was a good cause as well. He believed this young girl had many good ideals.

The final sticker on the far left side of the bumper expressed the exact sentiments Peter was feeling. The bumper sticker read "Mean People Suck." Peter knew when a human said something "sucked," it meant it was a bad thing, and this bumper sticker was saying mean people were not good. He couldn't find any flaw with that concept, either. Peter supposed mean people certainly did suck.

He thought about the big man he had just terminated. He recalled how one of the man's final physical actions was sucking desperately for air, which would never come. This caused him to chuckle at the unplanned bit of ironic humor. He was quite relieved to see the young girl's noble philosophies displayed for the all to see. Peter knew it was a rare occurrence in this badly troubled world.

During his short time of observation, Peter was amazed at just how mean-spirited the entire world had become. It was as if everywhere he went, everyone he met was immediately looking for an argument or a fight. This even occurred with people they claimed to love. It was an international epidemic; no one seemed to have kind words for anyone else as if meanness was the normal mode of operation, and kindness was non-existent.

Peter felt a rumble in his stomach and realized his body needed nourishment. He pulled into one of his favorite fast-food establishments and decided to skip the drive-through and dine inside. It would also give him another chance to do some additional last-minute observations, as his time was now short. He recalled this would be one of his last opportunities because he had to make his final report very soon.

The lines were long inside and the restaurant crowded, but he didn't mind the wait, as it gave him another occasion to study the people around him. While waiting, he noticed a woman in the line next to him with two unruly pre-school age children. Peter loved studying the children most of all. They were so young, so innocent and still, for the most part, untainted, although he saw many examples of that innocence shattered at much too early an age. He believed if there was any hope whatsoever for humanity, it was in its children. The two children were obviously bored with waiting, and the older child, a male, was picking on his younger sister, who was whining to her mother.

Peter knew it was the nature of children to behave as such, and whether they chose to admit it or not, humans were simply higher-level animals who needed to be properly trained in regards to appropriate behaviors. It was up to the parents of such children to supply that training and discipline, no matter how arduous a task it might seem, but Peter's experience had been that few parents were actually willing to provide the necessary guidance.

It was true that humans were at the top of the food chain thanks to their highly developed brains, but they still had to be taught right from wrong, acceptable behavior from unacceptable. Perhaps that was a major part of the problems he had observed over the past several months. Perhaps lack of parental guidance was what allowed the meanness to grow, then flourish, then become the societal norm.

Peter understood if humans didn't have their brainpower and had to rely on their physical strength, alone, they'd be much further down the food chain indeed. Homo sapiens, thinking men, toolmakers were only in their place of superiority because of their brains and their ability to form a cohesive, function- ing civilization.

Mankind tended to take this civilization and civilized behavior in general for granted when, in reality, it was as fragile as a porcelain figurine. Peter knew under the wrong circumstances, civilization could break down into anarchy within a day. So-called civilized man could revert to a savage practically over- night. Unfortunately, most humans didn't believe such a thing was possible.

"Sit still, you little bastard," Peter heard the woman say to her son. His heart sank once again with despair. How could this woman, a mother, say such a profane and despicable thing to her own child? This was the fruit of her womb, what most humans once considered the greatest gift of all. Yet this was how she treated the child. The older boy looked at his mother with a level of anger and hatred Peter couldn't believe, even from a human. He knew he once again had been accurate. This was where the meanness, distrust, and anger began. The younger girl watched the encounter said nothing, but Peter knew she was learning from what she saw, and someday she'd likely treat her own children with the same level of disrespect.

Up at the front of the line, an obviously frazzled cashier, a teenage girl, stood behind the counter while an angry woman shouted at her relentlessly.

"What is wrong with this place?" The woman ranted, "Do they go out of their way to hire retards to work here?"

"I'm very sorry, Ma'am," the girl implored. "I'll be happy to get you another burger. It'll just be a minute."

"I don't have a minute, you moronic fool," the woman screamed as her face reddened with rage. "I don't want your stinking food, and I don't have time to wait. This place disgusts me!"

With that, the angry woman took her tray of food and threw it at the terrified girl behind the counter. French fries and soda covered the girl's uniform, and the corner of the plastic tray struck her on the side of the forehead, making a slight cut as she cried out in pain. The woman stormed past Peter toward the door in a rage.

"Such outrageous anger over nothing," Peter thought.

Peter looked sternly at the woman as her hand touched the door to leave, nodding his head imperceptibly. She stopped in her tracks, her hand still on the handle, and then she slowly turned around to face the staring crowd. The anger had left her face, replaced by a look of extreme horror as she stood, mouth agape, unable to utter a sound. She began to quake all over as if having some sort of seizure, her eyes rolling back into her head as foam began to flow from her mouth, her swollen tongue lolling out over her lips. Suddenly her mouth clamped down hard, and the crowd of onlookers gasped as the convulsing woman's teeth bit through her tongue, drenching her blouse with blood as the severed tongue fell to the floor with a sickening splat. After several more spastic tremors, the woman collapsed like a rag door to the floor.

The people in the restaurant looked at each other for a moment, unsure of what to do. Peter wouldn't have been surprised if they suddenly broke out into applause based on the mean-spirited behaviors he had observed in the past. Instead, they did something almost as bizarre. They turned to resume waiting for their food as if nothing had happened. The workers went back to their tasks as well; no one attempting to offer aid, although Peter knew it was much too late for such actions anyway; this woman was dead.

Still, despite the woman's rude and unacceptable behavior, she was a fellow human being, and Peter thought someone might at least attempt to offer some form of assistance. The manager of the restaurant halfheartedly dialed 911, Peter believed not so much out of concern, rather to avoid a possible lawsuit. Then business went on as usual as the people waited for the arrival of the ambulance and their lunches. Peter thought perhaps the break down in civilization actually was already occurring, but at a slower pace than had, some global catastrophe had occurred.

Peter turned away in revulsion at the behavior of the humans; his body no longer feeling hunger. He considered eradicating everyone in the restaurant, and he could have done so with ease, but instead, he chose to leave. He walked from the restaurant via the opposite door, got into his car, and headed toward his apartment, hearing the whine of the approaching ambulance in the distance.

As he drove, he thought about all he had observed during his time among the humans, and about the report, which he'd have to make very soon. The age of man had been one of great and meteoritic advances in science, medicine, and technology but simultaneously seemed to have declined equally as fast when it came to the simple act of respecting one's fellow human. It sickened him to have to do what he knew he had to do, but it was his responsibility to report the facts as he observed them.

He thought about the meanness, which permeated the world. He recalled the various television "action" programs showing countless acts of violence committed by one human on another, not to mention the evening news, which he considered much worse because it was reality and not fiction. Even the television situation comedies, which were the most successful touted mean lead characters, who portrayed antisocial despicable beings, albeit in a manner that was humorous and entertaining, making such behavior almost seem acceptable to the viewers.

Some of the actors in such programs were often idolized like Gods for their real-life off-screen despicable behaviors as well. It was as if the entire world had forgotten about the importance of what the humans once called the "Golden Rule," the idea of doing onto others, as you would have them do unto you. Instead, it seemed to have been replaced by a new rule; "Do unto others, before they do onto you." The finality of the realization caused a sinking feeling to enter the stomach of the body, which Peter inhabited.

Peter walked head down into his apartment, knowing what awaited him and the weight of what he had to say. He staggered into his bathroom, stripped, and took a long hot shower. He hoped the cleansing water could symbolically wash away the filth and grime he felt his encounters with the human had left on his body this day. Although he knew he wouldn't have this human body for much longer, he felt it should be in pristine condition when he made presented his final findings.

After his shower, he walked naked out into his bedroom and stood before the double doors leading to his walk-in closet. He looked across the room at the clock radio on his night table, seeing the time was 11:59. He waited until the clock read exactly 12:00 noon, then he opened the doors to his closet. Peter was immediately bathed in a wash of incredible white light, brighter than anything ever witnessed on earth. With is humanoid eyes practically closed to shield them from blindness, Peter entered the closet and walked directly into the light, which enveloped him in its warm, reassuring glow.

A booming voice he knew very well spoke to him inside of his mind. "Peter. The time has come for you to tell us what you have observed."

Peter's head hung down in humble acquiescence. "What I have to report makes me sick in my heart. What I've observed is wanton hatred, distrust, corruption, greed, promiscuity, disrespect, and ingratitude for what all creatures should perceive as the greatest gift of all, the gift of life."

"Are they all without hope, Peter? Is there not one among them who can be salvaged?" The voice asked again. Peter stood trembling with tears flowing from his eyes, saying, "I don't know. Their only hope is with the children unless they, too, are likewise already on an irrevocable course of corruption. I suppose somewhere among these creatures, there might be a few who are worthy, but as you know, determining who they might be is beyond my capabilities. Most of them, I believe, are beyond redemption. While some may be basically good people, they too have become tainted and morally corrupted by trying to exist in their fetid environment."

"In a sewer teeming with a thousand rats, there are bound to be one or two basically pure of heart, but when forced to survive among the worst of the worst, they too can become contaminated and become something less than pure."

The voice spoke again. "Yes, Peter, I know of what you speak. If the majority of the creatures are corrupt than eventually, the good ones will likewise become damaged as well. The question is, should we eliminate the bad in favor of the good, or eliminate them all and begin again."

Peter asked uncertainly, "Would you do such a thing? Would you destroy them all and start over?"

"Not all but most. It wouldn't be the first time we have had to do so, and I suppose it may not be the last. Mankind has incredible potential if properly focused, and we believe in that potential, but it always seems like just when man is on the verge of achieving his predetermined greatness, he falls prey to his darker animal side, and we must intercede. It has been a long time since we have had to take such action against man, but perhaps the time has once again come. What say you, Peter?"

Peter raised his head, and as tears rolled down his human face, he said, "Yes, I'm afraid it's time. The age of man is over, and mankind must be made to start again."

The loud voice said in resignation. "So be it. As before, we will allow a few to survive to begin again, without their technology or medical and scientific advances. They'll be as they were in the beginning, innocent, and they'll survive, or they'll perish. They'll either advance down the road to enlightenment, or they'll repeat the mistakes of their past. We'll return again someday and see which direction mankind has taken and once again decide their fate."

Peter felt lifted out of his human form and drawn upward toward the incredibly bright light as behind him, the body, which had served as his host, collapsed to the floor of the closet.

BEYOND THE WALL OF SLEEP

BY H.P. LOVECRAFT

I have often wondered if the majority of mankind ever pause to reflect upon the occasionally titanic significance of dreams, and of the obscure world to which they belong. Whilst the greater number of our nocturnal visions are perhaps no more than faint and fantastic reflections of our waking experiences—Freud to the contrary with his puerile symbolism—there are still a certain remainder whose immundane and ethereal character permit of no ordinary interpretation, and whose vaguely exciting and disquieting effect suggests possible minute glimpses into a sphere of mental existence no less important than physical life, yet separated from that life by an all but impassable barrier. From my experience, I cannot doubt, but that man, when lost to terrestrial consciousness, is indeed sojourning in another and uncorporeal life of far different nature from the life we know, and of which only the slightest and most indistinct memories linger after waking. From those blurred and fragmentary memories, we may infer much, yet prove little. We may guess that in dreams, life, matter, and vitality, as the earth knows such things, are not necessarily constant, and that time and space do not exist as our waking selves comprehend them. Sometimes I believe that this less material life is our truer life and that our vain presence on the terraqueous globe is itself the secondary or merely virtual phenomenon.

It was from a youthful revery filled with speculations of this sort that I arose one afternoon in the winter of 1900-01, when to the state psychopathic institution in which I served as an intern was brought the man whose case has ever since haunted me so unceasingly. His name, as given on the records, was

Joe Slater, or Slaader, and his appearance was that of the typical denizen of the Catskill Mountain region; one of those strange, repellent scions of a primitive Colonial peasant stock whose isolation for nearly three centuries in the hilly fastnesses of a little-traveled countryside has caused them to sink to a kind of barbaric degeneracy, rather than advance with their more fortunately placed brethren of the thickly settled districts. Among these odd folk, who correspond exactly to the decadent element of "white trash" in the South, law and morals are non-existent; and their general mental status is probably below that of any other section of native American people.

Joe Slater, who came to the institution in the vigilant custody of four state policemen, and who was described as a highly dangerous character, certainly presented no evidence of his perilous disposition when I first beheld him. Though well above the middle stature, and of somewhat brawny frame, he was given an absurd appearance of harmless stupidity by the pale, sleepy blueness of his small watery eyes, the scantiness of his neglected and never-shaven growth of yellow beard, and the listless drooping of his heavy nether lip. His age was unknown since, among his kind, neither family records nor permanent family ties exist, but from the baldness of his head in front, and from the decayed condition of his teeth, the head surgeon wrote him down as a man of about forty.

From the medical and court documents, we learned all that could be gathered of his case: this man, a vagabond, hunter, and trapper, had always been strange in the eyes of his primitive associates. He had habitually slept at night beyond the ordinary time, and upon waking, would often talk of unknown things in a manner so bizarre as to inspire fear even in the hearts of an unimaginative populace. Not that his form of language was at all unusual, for he never spoke save in the debased patois of his environment; but the tone and tenor of his utterances were of such mysterious wildness, that none might listen without apprehension. He himself was generally as terrified and baffled as his auditors, and within an hour after awakening would forget all that he had said, or at least all that had caused him to say what he did, relapsing into a bovine, hall-amiable normality like that of the other hill dwellers.

As Slater grew older, it appeared, his matutinal aberrations had gradually increased in frequency and violence; till about a month before his arrival at the institution had occurred the shocking tragedy which caused his arrest by the authorities. One day near noon, after a profound sleep begun in a whiskey debauch at about five of the previous afternoon, the man had roused himself most suddenly, with ululations so horrible and unearthly that they brought several neighbors to his cabin—a filthy sty where he dwelt with a family as indescribable as himself. Rushing out into the snow, he had flung his arms aloft and commenced a series of leaps directly upward in the air, the while shouting his determination to reach some "big, big cabin with brightness in the roof and walls and floor and the loud queer music far away." As two men of moderate size sought to restrain him, he had struggled with maniacal force and fury, screaming of his desire and need to find and kill a certain "thing that shines and shakes and laughs." At length, after temporarily felling one of his detainers with a sudden blow, he had flung himself upon the other in a demoniac ecstasy of blood-thirstiness, shrieking fiendishly that he would "jump high in the air and burn his way through anything that stopped him."

Family and neighbors had now fled in a panic, and when the more courageous of them returned, Slater was gone, leaving behind an unrecognizable pulp-like thing that had been a living man but an hour before. None of the mountaineers had dared to pursue him, and it is likely that they would have welcomed his death from the cold, but when several mornings later they heard his screams from a distant ravine they realized that he had somehow managed to survive and that his removal in one way or another would be necessary. Then had followed an armed searching-party, whose purpose (whatever it may have been originally) became that of a sheriff's posse after one of the seldom popular state troopers had by accident observed, then questioned, and finally joined the seekers.

On the third day, Slater was found unconscious in the hollow of a tree and taken to the nearest jail, where alienists from Albany examined him as soon as his senses returned. To them, he told a simple story. He had, he said, gone to sleep one afternoon about sundown after drinking much liquor. He had awakened to find himself standing bloody-handed in the snow before his cabin, the mangled corpse of his neighbor Peter Slader at his feet. Horrified, he had taken to the woods in a vague effort to escape from the scene of what must have been his crime. Beyond these things, he seemed to know nothing, nor could the expert questioning of his interrogators bring out a single additional fact.

That night Slater slept quietly, and the next morning he awakened with no singular feature save a certain alteration of expression. Doctor Barnard, who had been watching the patient, thought he noticed in the pale blue eyes a certain gleam of peculiar quality and in the flaccid lips an all but imperceptible tightening, as if of intelligent determination. But when questioned, Slater relapsed into the habitual vacancy of the mountaineer, and only reiterated what he had said on the preceding day.

On the third morning occurred the first of the man's mental attacks. After some show of uneasiness in sleep, he burst forth into a frenzy so powerful that the combined efforts of four men were needed to bind him in a straightjacket. The alienists listened with keen attention to his words since their curiosity had been aroused to a high pitch by the suggestive yet mostly conflicting and incoherent stories of his family and neighbors. Slater raved for upward of fifteen minutes, babbling in his backwoods dialect of green edifices of light, oceans of space, strange music, and shadowy mountains and valleys. But most of all, did he dwell upon some mysterious blazing entity that shook and laughed and mocked at him. This vast, vague personality seemed to have done him a terrible wrong, and to kill it in triumphant revenge was his paramount desire. In order to reach it, he said, he would soar through abysses of emptiness, burning every obstacle that stood in his way. Thus ran his discourse, until with the greatest suddenness he ceased. The fire of madness died from his eyes, and in dull wonder, he looked at his questioners and asked why he was bound. Dr. Barnard unbuckled the leather harness and did not restore it till night, when he succeeded in persuading Slater to don it of his own volition, for his own good. The man had now admitted that he sometimes talked queerly, though he knew not why.

Within a week, two more attacks appeared, but from them, the doctors learned little. On the source of Slater's visions, they speculated at length, for since he could neither read nor write and had apparently never heard a legend or fairy-tale, his gorgeous imagery was quite inexplicable. That it could not come from any known myth or romance was made especially clear by the fact that the unfortunate lunatic expressed himself only in his own simple manner. He raved of things he did not understand and could not interpret; things which he claimed to have experienced, but which he could not have learned through any normal or connected narration. The alienists soon agreed that abnormal dreams were the foundation of the trouble; dreams whose vividness could for a time completely dominate the waking mind of this basically inferior man. With due formality Slater was tried for murder, acquitted on the ground of insanity, and committed to the institution wherein I held so humble a post.

I have said that I am a constant speculator concerning dream-life, and from this, you may judge of the eagerness with which I applied myself to the study of the new patient as soon as I had fully ascertained the facts of his case. He seemed to sense a certain friendliness in me, born no doubt of the interest I could not conceal, and the gentle manner in which I questioned him. Not that he ever recognized me during his attacks, when I hung breathlessly upon his chaotic but cosmic word-pictures; but he knew me in his quiet hours when he would sit by his barred window weaving baskets of straw and willow, and perhaps pining for the mountain freedom he could never again enjoy. His family never called to see him; probably it had found another temporary head, after the manner of decadent mountain folk.

By degrees, I commenced to feel an overwhelming wonder at the mad and fantastic conceptions of Joe Slater. The man himself was pitiably inferior in mentality and language alike; but his glowing, titanic visions, though described in a barbarous disjointed jargon, were assuredly things which only a superior or even exceptional brain could conceive How, I often asked myself, could the stolid imagination of a Catskill degenerate conjure up sights whose very possession argued a lurking spark of genius? How could any backwoods dullard have gained so much as an idea of those glittering realms of supernal radiance and space about which Slater ranted in his furious delirium? More and more, I inclined to the belief that in the pitiful personality who cringed before me lay the disordered nucleus of something beyond my comprehension; something infinitely beyond the comprehension of my more experienced but less imaginative medical and scientific colleagues.

And yet I could extract nothing definite from the man. The sum of all my investigation was, that in a kind of semi-corporeal dream-life Slater wandered or floated through resplendent and prodigious valleys, meadows, gardens, cities, and palaces of light, in a region unbounded and unknown to man; that there he was no peasant or degenerate, but a creature of importance and vivid life, moving proudly and dominantly and checked only by a certain deadly enemy, who seemed to be a being of visible yet ethereal structure, and who did not appear to be of human shape, since Slater never referred to it as a man, or as aught save a thing. This thing had done Slater some hideous but unnamed wrong, which the maniac (if maniac he were) yearned to avenge.

From the manner in which Slater alluded to their dealings, I judged that he and the luminous thing had met on equal terms; that in his dream existence, the man was himself a luminous thing of the same race as his enemy. This impression was sustained by his frequent references to flying through space and burning all that impeded his progress. Yet these conceptions were formulated in rustic words wholly inadequate to convey them, a circumstance which drove me to the conclusion that if a dream world indeed existed, oral language was not its medium for the transmission of thought. Could it be that the dream soul inhabiting this inferior body was desperately struggling to speak things which the simple and halting tongue of dullness could not utter? Could it be that I was face to face with intellectual emanations, which would explain the mystery if I could but learn to discover and read them? I did not tell the older physicians of these things, for middle age is skeptical, cynical, and disinclined to accept new ideas. Besides, the head of the institution had but lately warned me in his paternal way that I was overworking, that my mind needed a rest.

It had long been my belief that human thought consists basically of atomic or molecular motion, convertible into ether waves or radiant energy like heat, light, and electricity. This belief had early led me to contemplate the possibility of telepathy or mental communication by means of suitable apparatus, and I had in my college days prepared a set of transmitting and receiving instruments somewhat similar to the cumbrous devices employed in wireless telegraphy at that crude, pre-radio period. These I had tested with a fellow-student, but achieving no result had soon packed them away with other scientific odds and ends for possible future use.

Now, in my intense desire to probe into the dream-life of Joe Slater, I sought these instruments again and spent several days in repairing them for action. When they were complete once more, I missed no opportunity for their trial. At each outburst of Slater's violence, I would fit the transmitter to his forehead and the receiver to my own, constantly making delicate adjustments for various hypothetical wave-lengths of intellectual energy. I had but little notion of how the thought-impressions would, if successfully conveyed, arouse an intelligent response in my brain, but I felt certain that I could detect and interpret them. Accordingly, I continued my experiments, though informing no one of their nature.

It was on the twenty-first of February, 1901, that the thing occurred. As I look back across the years, I realize how unreal it seems and sometimes wonder if old Doctor Fenton was not right when he charged it all to my excited imagination. I recall that he listened with great kindness and patience when I told him, but afterward gave me a nerve-powder and arranged for the half-year's vacation on which I departed the next week.

That fateful night I was wildly agitated and perturbed, for despite the excellent care he had received, Joe Slater was unmistakably dying. Perhaps it was his mountain freedom that he missed, or perhaps the turmoil in his brain had grown too acute for his rather sluggish physique, but at all events, the flame of vitality flickered low in the decadent body. He was drowsy near the end, and as darkness fell, he dropped off into a troubled sleep.

I did not strap on the straightjacket as was customary when he slept since I saw that he was too feeble to be dangerous, even if he woke in mental disorder once more before passing away. But I did place upon his head and mine the two ends of my cosmic "radio," hoping against hope for a first and last message from the dream world in the brief time remaining. In the cell with us was one nurse, a mediocre fellow who did not understand the purpose of the apparatus, or think to inquire into my course. As the hours wore on, I saw his head droop awkwardly in sleep, but I did not disturb him. I myself, lulled by the rhythmical breathing of the healthy and the dying man, must have nodded a little later.

The sound of a weird lyric melody was what aroused me. Chords, vibrations, and harmonic ecstasies echoed passionately on every hand, while on my ravished sight burst the stupendous spectacle ultimate beauty. Walls, columns, and architraves of living fire blazed effulgently around the spot where I seemed to float in the air, extending upward to an infinitely high vaulted dome of indescribable splendor. Blending with this display of palatial magnificence, or rather, supplanting it at times in kaleidoscopic rotation, were glimpses of wide plains and graceful valleys, high mountains and inviting grottoes, covered with every lovely attribute of scenery which my delighted eyes could conceive of, yet formed wholly of some glowing, ethereal plastic entity, which in consistency partook as much of spirit as of matter. As I gazed, I perceived that my own brain held the key to these enchanting metamorphoses; for each vista that appeared to me was the one my changing mind most wished to behold. Amidst this elysian realm, I dwelt not as a stranger, for each sight and sound was familiar to me, just as it had been for uncounted eons of eternity before and would be for like eternities to come.

Then the resplendent aura of my brother of light drew near and held colloquy with me, soul to soul, with a silent and perfect interchange of thought. The hour was one of approaching triumph, for was not my fellow-being escaping at last from a degrading periodic bondage; escaping forever, and preparing to follow the accursed oppressor even unto the uttermost fields of ether, that upon it might be wrought a flaming cosmic vengeance which would shake the spheres? We floated thus for a little time, when I perceived a slight blurring and fading of the objects around us, as though some force were recalling me to earth—where I least wished to go. The form near me seemed to feel a change also, for it gradually brought its discourse toward a conclusion, and itself prepared to quit the scene, fading from my sight at a rate somewhat less rapid than that of the other objects. A few more thoughts were exchanged, and I knew that the luminous one and I were being recalled to bondage, though for my brother of light, it would be the last time. The sorry planet shell being well-nigh spent, in less than an hour, my fellow would be free to pursue the oppressor along the Milky Way and past the hither stars to the very confines of infinity.

A well-defined shock separates my final impression of the fading scene of light from my sudden and somewhat shamefaced awakening and straightening up in my chair as I saw the dying figure on the couch move hesitantly. Joe Slater was indeed awaking, though probably for the last time. As I looked more closely, I saw that in the sallow cheeks shone spots of color, which had never before been present. The lips, too, seemed unusual, being tightly compressed, as if by the force of a stronger character than had been Slater's. The whole face finally began to grow tense, and the head turned restlessly with closed eyes.

I did not rouse the sleeping nurse but readjusted the slightly disarranged headband of my telepathic "radio," intent to catch any parting message the dreamer might have to deliver. All at once, the head turned sharply in my direction, and the eyes fell open, causing me to stare in blank amazement at what I beheld. The man who had been Joe Slater, the Catskill decadent, was gazing at me with a pair of luminous, expanding eyes whose blue seemed subtly to have deepened. Neither mania nor degeneracy was visible in that gaze, and I felt beyond a doubt that I was viewing a face behind which lay an active mind of high order.

At this juncture, my brain became aware of a steady external influence operating upon it. I closed my eyes to concentrate my thoughts more profoundly and was rewarded by the positive knowledge that my long-sought mental message had come at last. Each transmitted idea formed rapidly in my mind, and though no actual language was employed, my habitual association of conception and expression was so great that I seemed to be receiving the message in ordinary English.

"Joe Slater is dead," came the soul-petrifying voice of an agency from beyond the wall of sleep. My opened eyes sought the couch of pain in curious horror, but the blue eyes were still calmly gazing, and the countenance was still intelligently animated. "He is better dead, for he was unfit to bear the active intellect of cosmic entity. His gross body could not undergo the needed adjustments between ethereal life and planet life. He was too much an animal, too little a man; yet it is through his deficiency that you have come to discover me, for the cosmic and planet souls rightly should never meet. He has been in my torment and diurnal prison for forty-two of your terrestrial years.

"I am an entity like that which you yourself become in the freedom of dreamless sleep. I am your brother of light and have floated with you in the effulgent valleys. It is not permitted me to tell your waking earth-self of your real self, but we are all roamers of vast spaces and travelers in many ages. Next year I may be dwelling in Egypt, which you call ancient, or in the cruel empire of Tsan Chan, which is to come three thousand years hence. You and I have drifted to the worlds that reel about the red Arcturus and dwelt in the bodies of the insect-philosophers that crawl proudly over the fourth moon of Jupiter. How little does the earth self know life and its extent! How little, indeed, ought it to know for its own tranquility!

"Of the oppressor, I cannot speak. You on earth have unwittingly felt its distant presence—you who without knowing idly gave the blinking beacon the name of Algol, the Demon-Star It is to meet and conquer the oppressor that I have vainly striven for eons, held back by bodily encumbrances. Tonight I go as a Nemesis bearing just and blazingly cataclysmic vengeance. Watch me in the sky close by the Demon-Star.

"I cannot speak longer, for the body of Joe Slater grows cold and rigid, and the coarse brains are ceasing to vibrate as I wish. You have been my only friend on this planet—the only soul to sense and seek for me within the repellent form which lies on this couch. We shall meet again—perhaps in the shining mists of Orion's Sword, perhaps on a bleak plateau in prehistoric Asia, perhaps in unremembered dreams tonight, perhaps in some other form an eon hence, when the solar system shall have been swept away."

At this point, the thought-waves abruptly ceased, the pale eyes of the dreamer—or can I say, dead man?—commenced glazing fishily. In a half-stupor, I crossed over to the couch and felt of his wrist but found it cold, stiff, and pulseless. The sallow cheeks paled again, and the thick lips fell open, disclosing the repulsively rotten fangs of the degenerate Joe Slater. I shivered, pulled a blanket over the hideous face, and awakened the nurse. Then I left the cell and went silently to my room. I had an instant and unaccountable craving for a sleep whose dreams I should not remember.

The climax? What plain tale of science can boast of such a rhetorical effect? I have merely set down certain things appealing to me as facts, allowing you to construe them as you will. As I have already admitted, my superior, old Doctor Fenton, denies the reality of everything I have related. He vows that I was broken down with nervous strain and badly in need of a long vacation on full pay, which he so generously gave me. He assures me on his professional honor that Joe Slater was but a low-grade paranoiac, whose fantastic notions must have come from the crude hereditary folk-tales which circulated in even the most decadent of communities. All this he tells me—yet I cannot forget what I saw in the sky on the night after Slater died. Lest you think me a biased witness, another pen must add this final testimony, which may perhaps supply the climax you expect. I will quote the following account of the star Nova Persei verbatim from the pages of that eminent astronomical authority, Professor Garrett P. Serviss:

> "On February 22, 1901, a marvelous new star was discovered by Doctor Anderson of Edinburgh, not very far from Algol. No star had been visible at that point before. Within twenty-four hours, the stranger had become so bright that it outshone Capella. In a week or two, it had visibly faded, and in the course of a few months, it was hardly discernible with the naked eye."

A LOVE BEST SERVED COLD

By Thomas M. Malafarina

The solitary young man sat silently in the shadowed blackness of his living room. The sole illumination came from the faint glow of light filtering through the open doorway of the adjacent bedroom, the source of which was a single candle burning on a nearby dresser. He always kept one burning. The blood-red candle stood anchored in a puddle of hardened wax inside the inverted lid of a jar that had formerly contained his last helping of applesauce. It was his favorite kind, not the health-conscious stuff, but the type made with real sugar; lots and lots of sugar. He had no idea when he might be fortunate enough to find another jar, so he savored the delectable memory for as long as he could.

Oswald liked the dark. In fact, he loved it and always had for as long as he could remember. While most small children would scream in terror at the idea of being left alone in a dark bedroom at night, Oswald welcomed it and always longed for more. As a child, he cherished the darkness like a best friend, and now, as an adult, he embraced it like a long lost lover. And he was pleased there was now so much darkness to enjoy; now that the world had finally changed for the better.

The inhabitants of the earth as it had once been, always seemed to worship illumination and would often shun those like Oswald, who thrived in darkness. He recalled how, in the old days, every summer, scores of individuals would spend a substantial amount of their hard-earned incomes on traveling long distances and paying exorbitant fees simply to bake in the sweltering, blazing sun, like raw meat on a skillet. They thought nothing of risking the threat of skin cancer by lounging on some scalding oceanfront beach. All of that expense and aggravation just to soak in sunlight was something he could never understand, especially when there was so much more to enjoy in the dark.

He suspected light represented life to most people, while darkness symbolized death. "So, what was wrong with death?" Oswald thought to himself. After all, no one gets out of this world alive. So why not simply accept darkness and accept death and then learn to treasure it as simply another part of living?

Oswald J. Gorn wasn't what anyone would consider typical, nor had he ever been. During his high school days, he had been labeled with such disparaging terms as "creepy," "weirdo," "Oddwald," "freaky," and even "scary." He didn't mind the insults and in many ways liked the attention his perceived oddness brought to him. Oswald realized if he had been able to fit in, if he were just like everyone else, it was likely no one would have ever even taken notice of him at all. It wasn't that he needed or wanted their attention, but he found it fascinating how the other students would go out of their way to look and act like everyone else so they could fit in and to get noticed by the so-called cool kids. He managed to accomplish the exact same thing, albeit it in a negative way, by not trying to fit in but simply by being himself.

During and even after high school, Oswald didn't date, so to speak. He had absolutely no interest in building any type of relationship with any female. Some of the jocks in high school had insinuated Oswald might be gay, although he was quite certain he was not. He had nothing against people who were gay, but it was simply not the way he rolled. He did, however, realize there was something out of the ordinary about his sexual desires, and he didn't know exactly what that might be, but he knew it was not homosexuality. But he did suspect and was quite certain that many of those same overly-macho, locker-room-towel-snapping jock types might have some of their own homosexual issues to work out.

Most of his classmates would have been surprised to learn Oswald wasn't a virgin and hadn't been since the age of sixteen. He found there were quite a few girls in the school who were attracted to his idiosyncrasies, to his dark black clothing, his long wild hair, and the sinister-looking jewelry consisting primarily of ornamental skulls and bones.

He never even had to leave his house to score with several different girls any time he wanted to; they simply came to him. But oddly, he wasn't very interested in any of those girls. They seemed to be lacking something, but he couldn't quite figure out what it might be.

He didn't consider himself what the other students referred to as "Goths" or "vampires," and if asked, Oswald would have stated categorically that he had no desire to be lumped into any group. He preferred to stay to himself and to do what he wanted when he wanted.

After graduation, he chose not to attend college, much to his parents' chagrin. But Oswald knew college wasn't the route he wanted to take in life. He wanted to spend a few years trying to discover what his true calling might be. He wanted to experiment with a number of different occupations until he hopefully found one he liked. Perhaps then he might decide to return to school to focus on furthering his education in that chosen field, but at eighteen years old, he had no idea what he wanted to do with his life.

Now looking back after several years, he realized he had made the right decision, especially considering how useless all of those thousands of college degrees were now that the steaming defecation had finally hit the proverbial oscillating ventilation. Now that the world was a stinking living graveyard, a good working knowledge of carpentry and plumbing, as well as familiarity with guns, knives, self-defense, or hunting, were all more valuable skills than an MBA ever would be.

Oswald peered through the darkness into the adjacent bedroom and considered going in to do what he needed and wanted to do, but decided to wait a bit and savor the anticipation just a little bit longer. He could see the sheets on the bed ripple from the movement of its occupant and heard a slow moaning sound like that of someone in pain.

He smiled knowingly and looked at the battery-powered digital clock on the nightstand next to the bed and saw it was ten-fifteen. He decided to wait until ten-thirty if for no other reason than simply because he could. He often played these sorts of games with himself; he felt it helped keep his life interesting.

Oswald thought back to the various part-time, full-time, permanent, and temporary jobs he had tried after high school and how he never seemed to fit in well with any of them. It was not like he really cared as these were all experimental jobs, but he quickly learned that the people hiring him, those paying his salary, were not quite as accepting of his peculiarities as he thought they might be.

Although Oswald had quit many of his jobs, he was, more often than not, fired most of the time. Yet he had always managed to find employment in one form or another and was able to afford to live on his own in his apartment, although it was a far cry from luxurious by any stretch of the imagination.

After three years of hopping from one job to the next, he began to think he might never find his true calling. That was until he answered a want ad in the local newspaper for a mortuary in his town that was looking for a general laborer/helper. Oswald had no idea what the job was or what it might pay, but for some unknown reason, the idea seemed to appeal to him. After one quick interview, he was immediately hired.

And much to his surprise, he found it to be the perfect job. He did virtually anything and everything the funeral director, Mr. Wilcox, needed from parking cars, to setting up chairs for the services, to preparing the funeral parlor. After several weeks he was surprised when Mr. Wilcox asked him to help assist in the preparation of a body for burial.

He had no idea what to expect. Up until that point, he had never been allowed to go into the embalming room and was thrilled at the chance to be part of the action. His first assignment was simply to watch Mr. Wilcox prepare the body and hand him whatever tools he might need to complete his work.

Oswald was shocked and pleasantly surprised to discover the body lying naked on the slab in the center of the laboratory was that of a young woman, perhaps twenty-five years old, just a few years older than he was. Her face was distorted, and her body badly cut and bruised as if she had been in an accident or had been beaten or perhaps had even been murdered.

As his eyes traced the contours of her naked body, Oswald felt something incredible stir inside of him. A sensation of sexual arousal, the likes of which he had never experienced with any living girl before. He realized it had nothing to do with the corpse's voluptuous shape, full breasts, or lovely legs, but it was her pale color and the chalky mottled condition of her dead flesh. At first, the strange sensation frightened him, but then he realized this was what he had been missing all of those years. This was the one thing which none of his past lovers could provide; this was a reality; this was death.

Over the course of the next several months, when Mr. Wilcox was not around, Oswald would sneak into the lab and check out what special treat awaited him on the slab. Most of the time, he was disappointed to discover shriveled old men or wrinkled old women. But every so often, he would be rewarded with a young or middle-aged woman laid out on the table. And if the occupant happened to tickle his fancy, he would simply drop his drawers and have his way with the chilly cadavers. He figured what the hell, they were already dead; no harm, no foul.

Oswald did, however, understand right from wrong as dictated by the mores of the civilized world and knew he would be chastised by society and prosecuted by the law if caught. However, he also knew what he liked, and those dead bodies, rigid with rigor, cold with death, having the slight scent of impending putrefaction were exactly what he desired. He had never experienced lovemaking with any living girl that could compare with even one of these wonderful ice princesses.

Then as he had feared, his good times soon came to an abrupt and tragic end. One night he was enjoying the pleasure of an attractive thirty-something young lady who had passed away from an aneurysm or something of that nature when the funeral director walked in and caught him in the act. Wilcox was outraged, and in his fury, he grabbed one of the implements of his trade, a long drainage tube of some sort, and proceeded to whip and beat Oswald with it.

Unable to defend himself with his pants down around his ankles, the young man tripped and fell to the ground, trying to ward off the attack with flailing arms. Eventually, he managed to free one of his legs and kicked out wildly and accidentally struck the mortician in the chin hard with the heel of his foot. The blow was a wild gesture of self-defense, completely unplanned, but somehow it managed to knock the man backward. He lost his balance, fell to the floor, cracked his head against the marble tile, and died instantly.

Unsure of what to do next, Oswald panicked, realizing his life was essentially over. Self-defense or not, there wasn't a jury in the world that would accept his story. After all, Wilcox was a well-known, well-respected local businessman, and he was . . . well, a freak in the eyes of many. And if the knowledge of his illicit activities with the dearly departed ever surfaced, they would lock him up and throw away the key.

Oswald hid the man's body in a closet. Then he did his best to wipe away any trace of his ever being in the building and fled home to his apartment, unsure of what he would do to next. Then to his dismay, something happened which he had never believed could have happened; something, which made his problem pale in comparison.

The press called it the plague, Internet bloggers called it the long-awaited Zombie Apocalypse, but Oswald thought of it as his salvation. Whatever it was and whatever had caused it to occur, no one knew for certain, but for some reason, the dead had begun to leave their graves, rise up, and feast on the flesh of the living.

It didn't take long for local society to break down completely; just a matter of weeks, and then the entire world was thrust into chaos and anarchy. For most people, it meant the end of the world, the end of mankind's reign at the top of the food chain. But this was not necessarily the case for Oswald.

He understood survival would be a challenge, and at some point in time, he would likely end up being killed or simply dying only to arise once again to join the ranks of the undead. But this thought did not trouble him. Oswald always felt death was simply a part of life, and that was true now more than ever. He could only do what he could to get by until that day came, and in the meantime, he planned on enjoying himself as best as he could.

He soon learned that this brave new world of walking corpses was exactly the type of world he wanted to live in. He did not flee for his life but adapted and learned quickly how not only to survive in such a world but how to truly enjoy life for the first time and to partake in the many benefits such a world had to offer.

As Oswald sat in his dark living room looking out into the partially lighted bedroom, he glanced once again at the clock and noticed that an hour had passed. It was now close to eleven o'clock. He was amazed at how much time had passed so quickly. From the adjacent room, Oswald heard the bed squeaking once again, followed by the faint moaning sound.

"Well, no time like the present," he said to no one in particular. Then he stood and walked slowly into the dimly lit bedroom.

Lying on top of the sheets was the writhing body of a naked woman. Her wrists and ankles were each secured with heavy rope to one of the four bedposts. There was a gag over her mouth. He was not concerned about her screaming, as he was quite certain no one would hear her, but he did worry about her possibly biting him. He knew that would not be good at all.

She looked at Oswald through one filmy dead eye sunken deep in a bony dark ringed socket, not with fear or hatred but with an insatiable hunger. The other eye was missing, leaving a hollow pit crawling with worms. All that was left of her once beautiful tresses were a few patches, wispy strands of wild straw-like hair.

Her mottled gray flesh was covered with the filth and grime typical of her kind, and dozens of flies swarmed about her. Some of them stopped to deposit their eggs in the puss-filled weeping sores, which covered her spasmodically gyrating corpse. Maggots from earlier deposits crawled from boreholes and dropped onto the bedsheets.

The single candle, although scented, did little to mask the vile stench of decomposition, which permeated the room. To most, the aroma would be considered repulsive, but to Oswald, it was the scent of love. As he made his way toward the bed, he began to undress slowly, knowing once again, he would have the opportunity to enjoy the fruits of the new world; a love best served cold.

HOMECOMING

BY THOMAS M. MALAFARINA

"Home is a place you grow up wanting to leave, and grow old wanting to get back to" —John Ed Pearce

"When you finally go back to your old hometown, you find it wasn't the old home you missed but your childhood"
—Sam Ewing

"Nothing but the dead and dying, back in my little town"
—Paul Simon and Art Garfunkel

"You can't go home again." —Thomas Wolfe

Mason always believed someday he would return. There was something about his hometown and the many memories of his happy childhood there, which seemed to beckon to him. Ashton, Pennsylvania, was somewhere in his mind and close to his heart throughout his entire life. It was odd how no matter how long he was away or where he happened to live, Ashton was the only place he truly considered home. There were times when he believed he could actually feel it pulling him, almost calling to him in a sad and mournful voice like the heartbroken cries of a jilted lover. "Come home . . . come home . . . come home."

However, life had to be lived, and there were things Mason Fredericks wanted to accomplish in his life, which he just couldn't find in his simple little town. As a result, after graduation, he had said goodbye to his hometown to attend college in another state and had never returned, not for any reason. He had missed all of his high school class reunions and all of his cousins' weddings. In fact, he didn't even return to attend family funerals, including those of his parents and his older brother.

During quiet moments at night or when he was traveling alone on long business trips, Mason often had pleasant memories of his youth in Ashton. He often thought about the parks, the local stores, and of his childhood friends. He had been a paperboy and as such, had known just about everyone in town.

At different times in his life, he had considered stopping back to see what had become of his precious Ashton, but he never did. He knew about the adage "You can never go home again," which was a take on an original quote by Thomas Wolfe, and he believed he understood what that meant. He knew if he were to go home, all that would await him, there would be change and disappointment. He loved his hometown but knew he would have trouble dealing with the changes.

The playgrounds, the schools, the stores, the houses, the people all would be different now. The world is constantly moving forward, and as it did, it left the happy memories of young boys like Mason in its wake, replacing them with whatever was to follow. He often imagined the Ashton of his youth as a series of plastic railroad models laid out on a card table. Then while enjoying his fantasy, he imagined life coming along in the form of a rowdy child, who with a beefy arm would simply sweep his memories onto the floor where they would shatter into pieces.

Now, after more than forty years, he had done it. He had finally returned home. Mason stood on the sidewalk staring in amazement at what he saw. He had prepared himself to see many changes. So many that he assumed he would barely recognize his hometown. But that hadn't been the case at all. To his shock, the town looked exactly as it had looked when he was a boy. Over there was Leon's Barber Shop, and there was Marco's Shoe Repair. He turned and saw Woodman's Restaurant and Gerhard's Dress Shop. It was incredible! The town looked exactly as he had remembered it from his childhood . . . exactly.

Then he realized something was wrong. What he was seeing wasn't possible. He recalled when he had left for college at age eighteen, Woodman's Restaurant had no longer been in business. The owner Stan Woodman had passed away, and his children had no interest in the business. As a result, his widow had chosen to shut the place down. And hadn't Marco the shoemaker retired, closed down the shoe repair shop, and moved to Florida back when Mason was still in high school? Yet here they all seemed to be. None of this made any sense.

"Hey, Perry Mason!" A voice called from a distance. He hadn't heard the voice or that name in almost fifty years, but he recognized both immediately. It was Jimmy "Duke" Wellington, a well-known local troublemaker who had been two years older than Mason. Duke had always call Mason "Perry Mason" because of the popular TV Show from his childhood.

Then an icy chill crept down the back of Mason's neck when he realized it couldn't possibly be Jimmy Wellington because he knew Jimmy died in an automobile accident on his way home from high school graduation over forty years earlier. Mason looked in the direction of the voice, and sure enough, it was a twelve-year-old version of Duke Wellington, and he was approaching a skinny young boy of about ten with a newspaper sack over his shoulder.

Mason felt his breath catch in his throat. He knew that boy. Somehow, impossibly, that boy was him, a young version of Mason Fredericks. Mason suddenly felt weak, his legs became wobbly, his hands trembled, and a buzzing noise began to rise inside his head. Then everything around him went black.

———•—

Mason awoke, confused. The last thing he remembered was standing downtown. Then something . . . something happened. In his confusion, Mason had the strange detached feeling he often experienced after waking from a dream. Maybe that was what had happened. Perhaps he had been dreaming about something. He wished he could recall what it had been.

He looked around and discovered he was in the middle of a cemetery. He had no idea how he had gotten there. He recognized it as Brockman's Cemetery, which he recalled was located near the western end of Ashton; an area locals referred to as the top of town. He remembered that his parents, as well as his older brother, were buried in this graveyard.

Mason looked down at the tombstones laid out in front of him and discovered he was standing at the exact location of his family's burial plots. He suddenly felt a pang of guilt for having not attended their funerals. There had been no good reason for his absence, no justifiable excuse. Although at the time, his justifications did seem legitimate enough, at least to him. When his parents passed, he had been working in China as a representative for his company seeking new business opportunities. When his brother called with the news that his parents had both been killed in an automobile accident, Mason explained that he simply couldn't get back to the states for the funerals. The deal he had been brokering was too big and far too critical for him to leave at this jointure.

Mason's brother had been furious with him, but Mason insisted there was nothing he could do about the situation. Then after a heated argument, just before his brother disconnected, he told Mason, he never wanted to speak to him again and that he should ever bother to return home. Mason knew he was wrong, and his older brother had every right to feel the way he did.

Now standing in this place of the dead, Mason was suddenly filled with sadness at the realization of how he had disrespected his parents and had let down his brother. They were all dead now, and it was much too late to do anything about it. The melancholy inside him seemed to grow more intense as it finally sunk in that they were gone for good, and he would never see them again.

Of course, he had known this reality for many years, but there seemed to be something so final about seeing their headstones carved with their birth and death dates that made it all so real to him, perhaps for the first time. Mason supposed this was what people meant when they spoke of closure. For the first time in his life, he realized he was all alone in the world. This realization troubled him more than he could have imagined.

In the distance, Mason saw a long black hearse followed by a similarly dark sedan coming along the gravel lane toward him. They stopped close to where he stood separated from each other by about ten feet. Two tall bleak-looking men in dark suits exited the hearse and walked to the rear, where one of them opened the rear tailgate. Mason instantly recognized the one opening the gate. It was Jim Kulp, a member of his graduating class and son of the funeral company's original founder, Bradford Kulp. Jim had apparently taken over the family business as Mason, and most townspeople assumed he would.

Mason wondered who the poor soul in the back of the hearse might be. Then the doors to the black sedan opened and four strangers in similar dark suits got out and joined the other two behind the hearse. Looking like sentinels, they lined up in formation, three on each side, and slowly began sliding the casket from the hearse as its handles passed along the line.

Then Mason saw a weeping woman exiting the back of the sedan wearing a dark dress and black scarf over her head. To his shock, he realized it was his cousin Marylyn. Even though he hadn't seen her in close to forty years, she looked every bit as pretty as he had remembered her, much older but nonetheless beautiful. His heart went out to his cousin. He recalled she had married her high school sweetheart Bernie Walters and they had been together all these years. Surely, it must be devastating for her to lose him after so long. Then Mason wondered why their kids weren't here, not to mention Bernie's many friends and relatives. Mason assumed having lived in the area all of his life. Bernie should have had a great precession of cars, not just these two pathetic funeral vehicles. He suddenly felt great compassion for his poor cousin.

Mason decided he would approach her and offer his condolences for her loss. He realized he would likely have to introduce himself as she hadn't seen him in so long, and she would likely not recognize him. He walked up and stood beside her as the pallbearers slowly walked the casket over toward the graveyard.

He said, "Marylyn? It's me . . . I'm sorry . . . about Bernie . . . I guess . . . Geeze . . . I just don't know what to say." He raised his hand to place it consolingly on her shoulder but stopped short when he heard her speak his name.

"Oh, Mason," Marylyn said with a sigh.

Mason was surprised. "Why . . . um . . . Marylyn . . . I'm surprised that you recognized me . . . you know . . . after all these years."

Marylyn sniffled and dabbed her eyes, "Mason, why did you stay away so long? I remember how we were so close when we were children. You were like a brother to me, and I really missed you so much over the years. And now to have to see you . . . like this." She began to cry again.

"I . . . I understand, Marylyn," Mason said, sounding contrite, "I missed you as well. I . . . I often thought about coming home . . . but I never seemed to get around to it. I'm so terribly sorry."

She blubbered, "I had so hoped you would have been able to meet my daughter, Sarah. I often told her stories about you. We followed your career and cut out articles whenever one appeared in the business section of the newspaper. Sarah's all grown up now and has a daughter of her own. I'm a grandmother. Can you believe it? Me, a grandmother?"

"That's . . . that is very hard to believe, Marylyn," Mason replied, "I, myself . . . I never married or had any children. I guess I could never find the time. But I'm home now, Marylyn. Maybe I can find some way to make up for lost time."

"So . . . well . . . I guess this is our final goodbye Mason," she said with tears now running down her cheeks.

Mason was confused and replied, "No, Marylyn. You don't understand. I'm home now. And I retired last year, so if I want, I can be home for good."

Just then, Jim Kulp walked up to Marylyn and said. "Are you going to be alright now, Mrs. Walters? Is there anything I can get for you before we proceed?"

"Hey, Jim," Mason said, "It's me, Mason Fredericks. You probably didn't recognize me. I haven't seen you since graduation."

Marylyn said, "No. But thank you, Jim. I'll be all right. You can proceed with what you have to do."

Mason was even more perplexed than previously. "Jim. It's me, Mason. From high school? There's no need for you to be so antisocial."

"I feel sort of strange not having a ceremony or minister for you today, Marylyn," Jim said, blatantly ignoring Mason. "Are you sure that is what he would have wanted?"

"To be honest, Jim. I have no idea what he would have wanted." Marylyn explained. He had no living relatives and left no will. I just want to get this over with and head home."

Mason said, "What do you mean, Marylyn? Bernie had tons of relatives in the area and probably just as many friends. Where are they all?"

Jim said to Marylyn, "Ok. This won't take but a few minutes. You can wait in the car if you'd like."

Marylyn turned and went into the sedan, closing the door behind her. Mason watched the team of dark-suited men standing next to the casket, which now sat next to a recently dug grave he hadn't noticed before. It was located right next to his older brother's plot.

"Well, Mason," Jim said, looking down into the hole as the casket was lowered, "You did your best to stay away all these years, and now you're back for good. Who said you can never come home again?"

BREATHE

BY THOMAS M. MALAFARINA

The claustrophobic sensation of suffocation was more than Ron could stand. Someone had gagged him, and although his nose was clear, he still couldn't seem to get enough air. Ron could see nothing; he was in a world of complete blackness. He was certain he was going to die the agonizingly slow death of oxygen deprivation. This had been his life-long fear. He didn't know who had done this to him or why, but one thing he did know was if he didn't find some way out of this situation, he would likely go insane long before he finally did die. Although he technically might be able to get enough oxygen through his nose to keep himself alive, it would do nothing to satisfy his need for a deep cleansing lung full of air. He could do nothing to keep his ever-increasing panic attack at bay.

Ron needed to breathe. He had to find some way to get free, so he could breathe; that's all he needed was to breathe. His hands and feet were bound, so he tried wiggling his mouth to try to loosen the bandana holding the gag in place but to no avail. The more he struggled, the more air he seemed to need, and the more he realized how little air he was actually getting. It was maddening. His panic was rising. He could no longer think rationally. He was drenched in an icy sweat and could smell the stench of his own rising fear. He knew in just a few more seconds if he didn't get free, he would go completely insane. He struggled uselessly as his air supply seemed to dwindle further.

Then he suddenly awoke to darkness. He felt the comfort of a pillow under his head and knew it had all been a horrible dream. He was at home in his bed, and it must have all been a horrible nightmare. Ron really did have sinus issues as well as chronic lung issues and, as such, was a mouth-breather. He could never seem to get enough air, especially during allergy season, even when he used his Albuterol inhaler. As a result, he was also extremely claustrophobic, and some of his worst nightmares revolved around his not being able to get enough air. Thank God, this one was finally over.

Unconsciously, Ron reached up to verify his mouth was clear of any obstructions even though he understood he had been dreaming. However, when he did, his knuckles scraped along some sort of rough wooden surface just a few inches away from his face, and then the horrifying reality came rushing back to him. It was strange how his mind tricked him. Maybe insanity was better. Because he now remembered, he was not resting comfortably in his bed. Someone had buried him alive.

THE PREMATURE BURIAL

BY EDGAR ALLAN POE 1850

THERE are certain themes of which the interest is all-absorbing, but which are too entirely horrible for the purposes of legitimate fiction. These the mere romanticist must eschew if he does not wish to offend or to disgust. They are with propriety handled only when the severity and majesty of Truth sanctify and sustain them. We thrill, for example, with the most intense of "pleasurable pain" over the accounts of the Passage of the Beresina, of the Earthquake at Lisbon, of the Plague at London, of the Massacre of St. Bartholomew, or of the stifling of the hundred and twenty-three prisoners in the Black Hole at Calcutta. But in these accounts it is the fact—it is the reality—it is the history which excites. As inventions, we should regard them with simple abhorrence.

I have mentioned some few of the more prominent and august calamities on record, but in these, it is the extent, not less than the character of the calamity, which so vividly impresses the fancy. I need not remind the reader that, from the long and weird catalog of human miseries, I might have selected many individual instances more replete with essential suffering than any of these vast generalities of disaster. The true wretchedness, indeed—the ultimate woe—is particular, not diffuse. That the ghastly extremes of agony are endured by man the unit, and never by man the mass—for this, let us thank a merciful God!

To be buried while alive is, beyond question, the most terrific of these extremes, which have ever fallen to the lot of mere mortality.

That it has frequently, very frequently, so fallen will scarcely be denied by those who think. The boundaries which divide Life from Death are at best shadowy and vague. Who shall say where the one ends, and where the other begins? We know that there are diseases in which occur total cessations of all the apparent functions of vitality, and yet in which these cessations are merely suspensions, properly so-called.

They are only temporary pauses in the incomprehensible mechanism. A certain period elapses, and some unseen mysterious principle again sets in motion the magic pinions and the wizard wheels. The silver cord was not for ever loosed, nor the golden bowl irreparably broken. But where, meantime, was the soul?

Apart, however, from the inevitable conclusion, a priori that such causes must produce such effects—that the well-known occurrence of such cases of suspended animation must naturally give rise, now and then, to premature interments—apart from this consideration, we have the direct testimony of medical and ordinary experience to prove that a vast number of such interments have actually taken place.

I might refer at once, if necessary, to a hundred well-authenticated instances. One of very remarkable character, and of which the circumstances may be fresh in the memory of some of my readers, occurred, not very long ago, in the neighboring city of Baltimore, where it occasioned a painful, intense, and widely-extended excitement. The wife of one of the most respectable citizens-a lawyer of eminence and a member of Congress—was seized with a sudden and unaccountable illness, which completely baffled the skill of her physicians. After much suffering, she died or was supposed to die. No one suspected, indeed, or had reason to suspect that she was not actually dead. She presented all the ordinary appearances of death. The face assumed the usual pinched and sunken outline. The lips were of the usual marble pallor. The eyes were lustreless. There was no warmth. Pulsation had ceased. For three days, the body was preserved unburied, during which it had acquired a stony rigidity. The funeral, in short, was hastened, on account of the rapid advance of what was supposed to be decomposition.

The lady was deposited in her family vault, which, for three subsequent years, was undisturbed. At the expiration of this term, it was opened for the reception of a sarcophagus;—but, alas! how fearful a shock awaited the husband, who, personally, threw open the door!

As its portals swung outwardly back, some white-apparelled object fell rattling within his arms. It was the skeleton of his wife in her yet unmoulded shroud.

A careful investigation rendered it evident that she had revived within two days after her entombment; that her struggles within the coffin had caused it to fall from a ledge or shelf to the floor, where it was so broken as to permit her to escape. A lamp that had been accidentally left, full of oil, within the tomb, was found empty; it might have been exhausted, however, by evaporation. On the uttermost of the steps which led down into the dread chamber was a large fragment of the coffin, with which, it seemed, that she had endeavored to arrest attention by striking the iron door. While thus occupied, she probably swooned, or possibly died, through sheer terror; and, in failing, her shroud became entangled in some iron-work which projected interiorly. Thus she remained, and thus she rotted, erect.

In the year 1810, a case of living inhumation happened in France, attended with circumstances which go far to warrant the assertion that the truth is, indeed, stranger than fiction. The heroine of the story was a Mademoiselle Victorine Lafourcade, a young girl of an illustrious family, of wealth, and of great personal beauty. Among her numerous suitors was Julien Bossuet, a poor litterateur, or journalist of Paris. His talents and general amiability had recommended him to the notice of the heiress, by whom he seems to have been truly beloved; but her pride of birth decided her, finally, to reject him, and to wed a Monsieur Renelle, a banker and a diplomatist of some eminence. After marriage, however, this gentleman neglected, and, perhaps, even more positively ill-treated her. Having passed with him some wretched years, she died—at least her condition so closely resembled death as to deceive every one who saw her. She was buried—not in a vault, but in an ordinary grave in the village of her nativity. Filled with despair, and still inflamed by the memory of a profound attachment, the lover journeys from the capital to the remote province in which the village lies, with the romantic purpose of disinterring the corpse, and possessing himself of its luxuriant tresses. He reaches the grave. At midnight he unearths the coffin, opens it, and is in the act of detaching the hair when he is arrested by the unclosing of the beloved eyes. In fact, the lady had been buried alive. Vitality had not altogether departed, and she was aroused by the caresses of her lover from the lethargy which had been mistaken for death. He bore her frantically to his lodgings in the village. He employed certain powerful restoratives suggested by no little medical learning. In fine, she revived. She recognized her preserver. She remained with him until, by slow degrees, she fully recovered her original health.

Her woman's heart was not adamant, and this last lesson of love sufficed to soften it. She bestowed it upon Bossuet. She returned no more to her husband, but, concealing from him her resurrection, fled with her lover to America. Twenty years afterward, the two returned to France, in the persuasion that time had so greatly altered the lady's appearance that her friends would be unable to recognize her.

They were mistaken, however, for, at the first meeting, Monsieur Renelle did actually recognize and make claim to his wife. This claim she resisted and a judicial tribunal sustained her in her resistance, deciding that the peculiar circumstances, with the long lapse of years, had extinguished, not only equitably, but legally, the authority of the husband.

The "Chirurgical Journal" of Leipsic—a periodical of high authority and merit, which some American bookseller would do well to translate and republish, records in a late number a very distressing event of the character in question.

An officer of the artillery, a man of gigantic stature and of robust health, being thrown from an unmanageable horse, received a very severe contusion upon the head, which rendered him insensible at once; the skull was slightly fractured, but no immediate danger was apprehended. Trepanning was accomplished successfully. He was bled, and many other of the ordinary means of relief were adopted.

Gradually, however, he fell into a more and more hopeless state of stupor, and, finally, it was thought that he died.

The weather was warm, and he was buried with indecent haste in one of the public cemeteries. His funeral took place on Thursday. On the Sunday following, the grounds of the cemetery were, as usual, much thronged with visitors, and about noon an intense excitement was created by the declaration of a peasant that, while sitting upon the grave of the officer, he had distinctly felt a commotion of the earth, as if occasioned by someone struggling beneath. At first little attention was paid to the man's asseveration, but his evident terror and the dogged obstinacy with which he persisted in his story had at length their natural effect upon the crowd. Spades were hurriedly procured, and the grave, which was shamefully shallow, was in a few minutes so far thrown open that the head of its occupant appeared. He was then seemingly dead, but he sat nearly erect within his coffin, the lid of which, in his furious struggles, he had partially uplifted.

He was forthwith conveyed to the nearest hospital, and there pronounced to be still living, although in an asphytic condition.

After some hours, he revived, recognized individuals of his acquaintance, and, in broken sentences, spoke of his agonies in the grave.

From what he related, it was clear that he must have been conscious of life for more than an hour, while inhumed, before lapsing into insensibility. The grave was carelessly and loosely filled with exceedingly porous soil, and thus, some air was necessarily admitted. He heard the footsteps of the crowd overhead and endeavored to make himself heard in turn. It was the tumult within the grounds of the cemetery, he said, which appeared to awaken him from a deep sleep, but no sooner was he awake than he became fully aware of the awful horrors of his position.

This patient, it is recorded, was doing well and seemed to be in a fair way of ultimate recovery, but fell victim to the quackeries of medical experiment. The galvanic battery was applied, and he suddenly expired in one of those ecstatic paroxysms, which, occasionally, it superinduces.

The mention of the galvanic battery, nevertheless, recalls to my memory a well known and very extraordinary case in point, where its action proved the means of restoring to animation a young attorney of London, who had been interred for two days. This occurred in 1831, and created, at the time, a very profound sensation wherever it was made the subject of converse.

The patient, Mr. Edward Stapleton, had died, apparently of typhus fever, accompanied with some anomalous symptoms which had excited the curiosity of his medical attendants. Upon his seeming decease, his friends were requested to sanction a post-mortem examination but declined to permit it. As often happens, when such refusals are made, the practitioners resolved to disinter the body and dissect it at leisure, in private. Arrangements were easily effected with some of the numerous corps of body-snatchers, with which London abounds, and, upon the third night after the funeral, the supposed corpse was unearthed from a grave eight feet deep, and deposited in the opening chamber of one of the private hospitals.

An incision of some extent had been actually made in the abdomen when the fresh and undecayed appearance of the subject suggested an application of the battery. One experiment succeeded another, and the customary effects supervened, with nothing to characterize them in any respect, except, upon one or two occasions, a more than ordinary degree of life-likeness in the convulsive action.

It grew late. The day was about to dawn, and it was thought expedient, at length, to proceed at once to the dissection. A student, however, was especially desirous of testing a theory of his own and insisted upon applying the battery to one of the pectoral muscles. A rough gash was made, and a wire hastily brought in contact, when the patient, with a hurried but quite nonconvulsive movement, arose from the table, stepped into the middle of the floor, gazed about him uneasily for a few seconds, and then—spoke. What he said was unintelligible, but words were uttered; the syllabification was distinct. Having spoken, he fell heavily to the floor.

For some moments, all were paralyzed with awe—but the urgency of the case soon restored them their presence of mind. It was seen that Mr. Stapleton was alive, although in a swoon. Upon exhibition of ether, he revived and was rapidly restored to health and to the society of his friends—from whom, how-ever, all knowledge of his resuscitation was withheld until a relapse was no longer to be apprehended. Their wonder—their rapturous astonishment—may be conceived.

The most thrilling peculiarity of this incident, nevertheless, is involved in what Mr. S. himself asserts. He declares that at no period was he altogether insensible—that, dully and confusedly, he was aware of everything which hap-pened to him, from the moment in which he was pronounced dead by his physicians, to that in which he fell swooning to the floor of the hospital. "I am alive," were the uncomprehended words which, upon recognizing the locality of the dissecting-room, he had endeavored, in his extremity, to utter.

It was an easy matter to multiply such histories as these—but I forbear—for, indeed, we have no need of such to establish the fact that premature interments occur. When we reflect on how very rarely, from the nature of the case, we have it in our power to detect them, we must admit that they may frequently occur without our cognizance.

Scarcely, in truth, is a graveyard ever encroached upon, for any purpose, to any great extent, that skeletons are not found in postures which suggest the most fearful of suspicions.

Fearful indeed the suspicion—but more fearful the doom! It may be asserted, without hesitation, that no event is so terribly well adapted to inspire the supremeness of bodily and of mental distress, as is burial before death. The unendurable oppression of the lungs—the stifling fumes from the damp earth—the clinging to the death garments—the rigid embrace of the narrow house—the blackness of the absolute Night—the silence like a sea that overwhelms—the unseen but palpable presence of the Conqueror Worm—these things, with the thoughts of the air and grass above, with memory of dear friends who would fly to save us if but informed of our fate, and with consciousness that of this fate they can never be informed—that our hopeless portion is that of the really dead—these considerations, I say, carry into the heart, which still palpitates, a degree of appalling and intolerable horror from which the most daring imagination must recoil. We know of nothing so agonizing upon Earth—we can dream of nothing half so hideous in the realms of the nethermost Hell. And thus all narratives upon this topic have an interest profound; an interest, nevertheless, which, through the sacred awe of the topic itself, very properly and very peculiarly depends upon our conviction of the truth of the matter narrated.

What I have now to tell is of my own actual knowledge—of my own positive and personal experience.

For several years I had been subject to attacks of the singular disorder which physicians have agreed to term catalepsy, in default of a more definitive title. Although both the immediate and the predisposing causes, and even the actual diagnosis, of this disease are still mysterious, its obvious and apparent character is sufficiently well understood. Its variations seem to be chiefly of degree. Sometimes the patient lies, for a day only, or even for a shorter period, in a species of exaggerated lethargy. He is senseless and externally motionless, but the pulsation of the heart is still faintly perceptible; some traces of warmth remain; a slight color lingers within the center of the cheek; and, upon application of a mirror to the lips, we can detect a torpid, unequal, and vacillating action of the lungs. Then again, the duration of the trance is for weeks—even for months, while the closest scrutiny and the most rigorous medical tests fail to establish any material distinction between the state of the sufferer and what we conceive of absolute death. Very usually, he is saved from premature interment solely by the knowledge of his friends that he has been previously subject to catalepsy, by the consequent suspicion excited, and, above all, by the non-appearance of decay. The advances of the malady are, luckily, gradual. The first manifestations, although marked, are unequivocal.

The fits grow successively more and more distinctive and endure each for a longer term than the preceding. In this lies the principal security from inhumation. The unfortunate whose first attack should be of the extreme character, which is occasionally seen, would almost inevitably be consigned alive to the tomb.

My own case differed in no important particular from those mentioned in medical books. Sometimes, without any apparent cause, I sank, little by little, into a condition of hemi-syncope, or half swoon; and, in this condition, without pain, without ability to stir, or, strictly speaking, to think, but with a dull, lethargic consciousness of life and of the presence of those who surrounded my bed, I remained, until the crisis of the disease restored me, suddenly, to perfect sensation. At other times I was quickly and impetuously smitten. I grew sick, and numb, and chilly, and dizzy, and so fell prostrate at once. Then, for weeks, all was void, and black, and silent, and Nothing became the universe. Total annihilation could be no more. From these latter attacks, I awoke, however, with a gradation slow in proportion to the suddenness of the seizure. Just as the day dawns to the friendless and houseless beggar who roams the streets throughout the long desolate winter night—just so tardily—just so wearily—just so cheerily came back the light of the Soul to me.

Apart from the tendency to trance, however, my general health appeared to be good; nor could I perceive that it was at all affected by the one prevalent malady—unless, indeed, an idiosyncrasy in my ordinary sleep may be looked upon as superinduced. Upon awaking from slumber, I could never gain, at once, thorough possession of my senses, and always remained, for many minutes, in much bewilderment and perplexity;—the mental faculties in general, but the memory in especial, being in a condition of absolute abeyance.

In all that I endured, there was no physical suffering but of moral distress an infinitude. My fancy grew charnel. I talked "of worms, of tombs, and epitaphs." I was lost in reveries of death, and the idea of premature burial held continual possession of my brain. The ghastly Danger to which I was subjected haunted me day and night. In the former, the torture of meditation was excessive—in the latter, supreme. When the grim Darkness overspread the Earth, then, with every horror of thought, I shook—shook as the quivering plumes upon the hearse. When Nature could endure wakefulness no longer, it was with a struggle that I consented to sleep—for I shuddered to reflect that, upon awaking, I might find myself the tenant of a grave. And when, finally, I sank into slumber, it was only to rush at once into a world of phantasms, above which, with vast, sable, overshadowing wing, hovered, predominant, the one sepulchral Idea.

From the innumerable images of gloom, which thus oppressed me in dreams, I select for record but a solitary vision. Methought I was immersed in a cataleptic trance of more than usual duration and profundity. Suddenly there came an icy hand upon my forehead, and an impatient, gibbering voice whispered the word "Arise!" within my ear.

I sat erect. The darkness was total. I could not see the figure of him who had aroused me. I could call to mind neither the period at which I had fallen into a trance nor the locality in which I then lay. While I remained motionless, and busied in endeavors to collect my thought, the cold hand grasped me fiercely by the wrist, shaking it petulantly, while the gibbering voice said again:

"Arise! did I not bid thee arise?"

"And who," I demanded, "art thou?"

"I have no name in the regions which I inhabit," replied the voice, mournfully; "I was mortal, but am fiend. I was merciless, but am pitiful. Thou dost feel that I shudder.—My teeth chatter as I speak, yet it is not with the chilliness of the night—of the night without end. But this hideousness is insufferable. How canst thou tranquilly sleep? I cannot rest for the cry of these great agonies.

These sights are more than I can bear. Get thee up! Come with me into the outer Night, and let me unfold to thee the graves. Is not this a spectacle of woe?—Behold!"

I looked; and the unseen figure, which still grasped me by the wrist, had caused to be thrown open the graves of all mankind, and from each issued the faint phosphoric radiance of decay, so that I could see into the innermost recesses, and there view the shrouded bodies in their sad and solemn slumbers with the worm. But alas! The real sleepers were fewer, by many millions, than those who slumbered not at all, and there was a feeble struggling, and there was a general sad unrest, and from out the depths of the countless pits there came a melancholy rustling from the garments of the buried. And of those who seemed tranquilly to repose, I saw that a vast number had changed, in a greater or less degree, the rigid and uneasy position in which they had originally been entombed. And the voice again said to me as I gazed:

"Is it not—oh! is it not a pitiful sight?"—but, before I could find words to reply, the figure had ceased to grasp my wrist, the phosphoric lights expired, and the graves were closed with a sudden violence, while from out them arose a tumult of despairing cries, saying again: "Is it not—O, God, is it not a very pitiful sight?"

Phantasies such as these, presenting themselves at night, extended their terrific influence far into my waking hours. My nerves became thoroughly unstrung, and I fell prey to perpetual horror. I hesitated to ride, or to walk, or to indulge in any exercise that would carry me from home. In fact, I no longer dared trust myself out of the immediate presence of those who were aware of my proneness to catalepsy, lest, falling into one of my usual fits, I should be buried before my real condition could be ascertained. I doubted the care, the fidelity of my dearest friends. I dreaded that, in some trance of more than customary duration, they might be prevailed upon to regard me as irrecoverable. I even went so far as to fear that, as I occasioned much trouble, they might be glad to consider any very protracted attack as sufficient excuse for getting rid of me altogether. It was in vain they endeavored to reassure me by the most solemn promises. I exacted the most sacred oaths that under no circumstances they would bury me until decomposition had so materially advanced as to render farther preservation impossible. And, even then, my mortal terrors would listen to no reason—would accept no consolation. I entered into a series of elaborate precautions.

Among other things, I had the family vault so remodeled as to admit of being readily opened from within. The slightest pressure upon a long lever that extended far into the tomb would cause the iron portal to fly back. There were arrangements also for the free admission of air and light, and convenient receptacles for food and water, within immediate reach of the coffin intended for my reception. This coffin was warmly and softly padded and was provided with a lid, fashioned upon the principle of the vault-door, with the addition of springs so contrived that the feeblest movement of the body would be sufficient to set it at liberty. Besides all this, there was suspended from the roof of the tomb, a large bell, the rope of which, it was designed, should extend through a hole in the coffin, and so be fastened to one of the hands of the corpse. But, alas? what avails the vigilance against the Destiny of man? Not even these well-contrived securities sufficed to save from the uttermost agonies of living inhumation, a wretch to these agonies foredoomed!

There arrived an epoch—as often before there had arrived—in which I found myself emerging from total unconsciousness into the first feeble and indefinite sense of existence. Slowly—with a tortoise gradation—approached the faint gray dawn of the psychal day.

A torpid uneasiness. An apathetic endurance of dull pain. No care—no hope—no effort. Then, after a long interval, a ringing in the ears; then, after a lapse still longer, a prickling or tingling sensation in the extremities; then a seemingly eternal period of pleasurable quiescence, during which the awakening feelings are struggling into thought; then a brief re-sinking into non-entity; then a sudden recovery. At length, the slight quivering of an eyelid, and immediately thereupon, an electric shock of a terror, deadly and indefinite, which sends the blood in torrents from the temples to the heart. And now the first positive effort to think. And now the first endeavor to remember. And now a partial and evanescent success. And now the memory has so far regained its dominion, that, in some measure, I am cognizant of my state. I feel that I am not awaking from ordinary sleep. I recollect that I have been subject to catalepsy. And now, at last, as if by the rush of an ocean, my shuddering spirit is overwhelmed by the one grim Danger—by the one spectral and ever-prevalent idea.

For some minutes after this fancy possessed me, I remained without motion. And why? I could not summon the courage to move. I dared not make the effort which was to satisfy me of my fate—and yet there was something at my heart which whispered to me it was sure. Despair—such as no other species of wretchedness ever calls into being—despair alone urged me, after long irresolution, to uplift the heavy lids of my eyes. I uplifted them. It was dark—all dark. I knew that the fit was over. I knew that the crisis of my disorder had long passed. I knew that I had now fully recovered the use of my visual faculties—and yet it was dark—all dark—the intense and utter raylessness of the Night that endureth forevermore.

I endeavored to shriek-, and my lips and my parched tongue moved convulsively together in the attempt—but no voice issued from the cavernous lungs, which oppressed as if by the weight of some incumbent mountain, gasped and palpitated, with the heart, at every elaborate and struggling inspiration.

The movement of the jaws, in this effort to cry aloud, showed me that they were bound up, as is usual with the dead. I felt, too, that I lay upon some hard substance, and by something similar, my sides were, also, closely compressed. So far, I had not ventured to stir any of my limbs—but now I violently threw up my arms, which had been lying at length, with the wrists crossed. They struck a solid wooden substance, which extended above my person at an elevation of not more than six inches from my face. I could no longer doubt that I reposed within a coffin at last.

And now, amid all my infinite miseries, came the cherub Hope sweetly—for I thought of my precautions. I writhed and made spasmodic exertions to force open the lid: it would not move. I felt my wrists for the bell-rope: it was not to be found. And now the Comforter fled for ever, and a still sterner Despair reigned triumphant; for I could not help perceiving the absence of the paddings which I had so carefully prepared—and then, too, there came suddenly to my nostrils the strong peculiar odor of moist earth. The conclusion was irresistible.

I was not within the vault. I had fallen into a trance while absent from home-while among strangers—when, or how, I could not remember—and it was they who had buried me as a dog—nailed up in some common coffin—and thrust deep, deep, and for ever, into some ordinary and nameless grave.

As this awful conviction forced itself, thus, into the innermost chambers of my soul, I once again struggled to cry aloud. And in this second endeavor, I succeeded. A long, wild, and continuous shriek, or yell of agony, resounded through the realms of the subterranean Night.

"Hillo! hillo, there!" said a gruff voice in reply.

"What the devil's the matter now!" said a second.

"Get out o' that!" said a third.

"What do you mean by yowling in that ere kind of style, like a cattymount?" said a fourth; and hereupon I was seized and shaken without ceremony, for several minutes, by a junto of very rough-looking individuals. They did not arouse me from my slumber—for I was wide awake when I screamed—but they restored me to the full possession of my memory.

This adventure occurred near Richmond, in Virginia. Accompanied by a friend, I had proceeded, upon a gunning expedition, some miles down the banks of the James River. Night approached, and we were overtaken by a storm. The cabin of a small sloop lying at anchor in the stream, and laden with garden mold, afforded us the only available shelter. We made the best of it and passed the night on board. I slept in one of the only two berths in the vessel—and the berths of a sloop of sixty or twenty tons need scarcely be described. That which I occupied had no bedding of any kind. Its extreme width was eighteen inches. The distance of its bottom from the deck overhead was precisely the same. I found it a matter of exceeding difficulty to squeeze myself in. Nevertheless, I slept soundly, and the whole of my vision—for it was no dream, and no nightmare—arose naturally from the circumstances of my position—from my ordinary bias of thought—and from the difficulty, to which I have alluded, of collecting my senses, and especially of regaining my memory, for a long time after awaking from slumber. The men who shook me were the crew of the sloop, and some laborers engaged in unloading it. From the load itself came the earthy smell. The bandage about the jaws was a silk handkerchief in which I had bound up my head, in default of my customary nightcap.

The tortures endured, however, were indubitably quite equal for the time, to those of actual sepulture. They were fearfully—they were inconceivably hideous, but out of Evil proceeded Good, for their very excess wrought in my spirit an inevitable revulsion. My soul acquired tone—acquired temper. I went abroad. I took vigorous exercise. I breathed the free air of Heaven. I thought upon other subjects than Death. I discarded my medical books. "Buchan," I burned. I read no "Night Thoughts"—no fustian about churchyards—no bugaboo tales—such as this. In short, I became a new man and lived a man's life. From that memorable night, I dismissed my charnel apprehensions forever, and with them vanished the cataleptic disorder, of which, perhaps, they had been less the consequence than the cause.

There are moments when, even to the sober eye of Reason, the world of our sad Humanity may assume the semblance of a Hell—but the imagination of man is no Carathis, to explore with impunity its every cavern. Alas! the grim legion of sepulchral terrors cannot be regarded as altogether fanciful—but, like the Demons in whose company Afrasiab made his voyage down the Oxus, they must sleep, or they will devour us—they must be suffered to slumber, or we perish.

WHENCE COMETH THE WOLF?

BY THOMAS M. MALAFARINA

Morning brought a new day complete with the bright sun rising over the eastern hillside casting its warm glow across the acres of corn as the cool, moist evening dew clung desperately to the tall blades of grass along the sloping ridge. Birds chirped their good morning songs while in the distance, you could hear the sounds of people waking to greet another day from the nearby housing subdivision.

In the tall grass atop the hill, a man rustled groggily awakening from his night's sleep. One eye fluttered open, and he saw the sunlit morning through long bunches of weedy grass growing wild around his face. On the side of one particular long weed, a young grasshopper clung, seeming to stare curiously at the man.

A chill ran through his body, and he became aware he was lying in the wet dewy grass completely naked. Remaining perfectly still not daring to get up from his prone position, Lonnie Talbert tried to analyze the situation and determine where he might be and just how bad things were this time.

As he lay quietly, he heard the cawing of several birds, and listening more intently, he could hear the buzzing of insects, perhaps bees, no, it seemed to be flies; hundreds of them. His stomach lurched with the realization of the implications of what he was hearing. Slowly he lifted his head ever so slightly, and over the tops of the tall weeds, he could see several large black birds perhaps ten of them all busy picking and pulling at something in the grass a few feet away.

His heart skipped a beat at the comprehension of what had likely happened yet again as it had happened for the first time a month ago.

Rising up on two hands supporting himself with his arms, he looked uncertainly across the top of the tall grass and saw what he feared most. Two of the blackbirds were fighting over a long stringy morsel of pinkish-gray food. They each had their beaks clamped on a piece of intestine and were having a ghastly tug-of-war with it.

Within one second, Lonnie saw the complete picture. On a blanket not five feet from him, lay the body of a naked woman, her stomach ripped open; her entrails spilled onto the blanket, blood splattered everywhere. Her body was a brutal landscape of gashes and rips, leaving her scarcely recognizable as human.

Her mouth hung agape, her dark blue tongue hanging loosely from an opening enlarged by a long deep red gouge leading down to her neck where muscle hung loosely like strands of thick spaghetti. Flies swarmed around her face, and several could be seen crawling along her lolling tongue. One of her eyes stared sightlessly upward through a film of death while the other dangled by thin bloody filaments down along the side of her cheek. One of the blackbirds had perched on her forehead and started pecking at the filaments with the hopes of snagging the soft juicy prize.

Large clumps of the woman's hair with pieces of scalp still attached lay strewn about the blanket her skull nothing more than a revolting patchwork of blood-covered white spaces where the scalp had once resided. Scores of blue and green flies walked freely along the bloody areas drinking, laying eggs, and doing whatever else the vile insects did in such a situation.

Her right arm lay stretched back alongside her battered head, the left arm was ripped off at the shoulder and lay in the grass perhaps ten or twenty feet away from the body. Another cluster of birds was pecking and feasting on it off in the distance. From the torn flesh of the place where the arm was formerly located, white bone jutted obtrusively.

Above the mangled abdominal area was a flat patch of blood and muscles where her breasts should have been. Lonnie didn't even want to venture a guess what might have happened to them. Oddly, her legs remained intact and strangely still quite beautiful. The contrast between her legs and the horrifically bloody remains was startling.

"What was her name?" he thought to himself, unable to recall.

Lonnie looked down at his own body and saw blood covered him; what seemed like gallons of gore.

"Not again!" Lonnie cried. "Not again! Why does this keep happening to me?"

Staying as low to the ground as possible, he searched through the tall grass for his clothing and found them on a pile mixed up with the girl's all damp from the cool evening but at least still intact. He took the girl's white printed dress and with the wetness still lingering on the grass, washed as much of the blood off his body as possible then tossed the garment aside. Still incredibly chilled from the cold, he put on his damp clothing and ran stooped over toward the nearby road where he saw a car parked.

He recalled it was the girl's car. "Thank goodness." Lonnie thought. He was lucky no one had driven by and checked on the car or had seen him lying there naked as the day he was born covered in blood. He climbed into the car seeing she had left the keys in the ignition. He started the engine and turned on the heater. Cold air came flooding from the vents, chilling him further. He turned down the fan giving the heater a chance to warm up. Looking back toward the place where the body lay, he was satisfied to see from the road nothing looked out of the ordinary the body well hidden in the tall grass. It might be a number of days or weeks until someone actually discovered her, and by then, he would be long gone, again.

As he drove away, he tried to remember the events of the previous evening before he had blacked out. He recalled his cousin Ron dropping him off at a local bar on his way to work. Ron worked third shift at a local factory. His cousin's schedule actually worked out well for Lonnie since he was a night owl by nature. Lonnie said he'd take a cab home. He'd met the girl (What was her name, Sarah? Sally? Sandy?), and they had hit it off immediately. Then after a few drinks and a little slow dancing, they headed out to her car.

She had brought him out to the rural hilltop site pulled over and had taken a thick blanket from the trunk. Walking down into the tall grass overlooking the cornfield, they had lain down on the blanket and gotten to know each other much better. The last thing he recalled was lying on his back in the grass afterward and looking up at the beautiful full moon. Then he must have blacked out just like had happened the previous month. That led him to think about the events of the previous month.

Although that had been a completely different situation, the results were no less horrific. He remembered how he had been walking home to his apartment after another late night at a local New York City bar. He had been laid off from his job several months earlier and didn't really have a set schedule or any reason to get up in the morning, so he tended to stay out late and then slept most of the day.

As he turned a corner to take a short cut down an alley, several thugs dressed in gang colors stopped him encircling him. Once they had surrounded him, each of them brandishing knives, they told him to give them his wallet, or they would cut him and cut him good. He saw their deadly blades gleaming in the light of the full moon. Then the first blackout came.

When he awoke the next morning, he was in the same alley with his clothing shredded soaked in blood and with barely enough material remaining to keep the clothes on his body. At first, based on the condition of his clothing, he thought perhaps the gang had actually cut him, and somehow, he had survived. Yet he felt no pain, and none of the blood appeared to be his. Standing and looking around as the sun slowly climbed in the sky, its beams entering the alley from between the tall city buildings; he saw the carnage laid out before him.

The alley looked as though it had been the scene of a jet airliner crash. Severed limbs and body parts were scattered around the blood-soaked street. Lonnie saw several headless torsos with their slick entrails piled next to them. Not four feet from where he stood, the head of the gang member who had threatened him stared lifelessly at him through gray-filmed eyes. Sewer rats the size of small cats wandered from body to body, sampling bits of flesh and innards. Some were eating the eyes from other severed heads. Lonnie turned his head bent and vomited onto the street. He looked at the regurgitated mess and saw it was blood-red in color. Upon closer inspection, he thought he saw a piece of a human ear floating among the filth.

He staggered down the alley, making it back to his apartment just a few blocks away without being seen. Once there, he showered and disposed of the bloody rags that were once his clothing then took another long hot shower. Afterward, he realized just how exhausted he was and collapsed in bed, where he fell fast asleep. Horrible images he couldn't begin to explain riddled his dreams. He saw the gang members screaming and being torn to pieces, seeing all of this as if through his own eyes. Throughout the scattered flashing images, he heard the growling of a wild animal. He woke up later that morning, hearing police sirens approaching. Staggering to the window, he saw a number of patrol cars converging on the alley several blocks away. He knew what they had found.

The only thing he could think to do was to get out of the city for a while. He got dressed and packed a duffle bag with essentials. He had no idea what had happened or why he had blacked out, but after seeing what he had vomited, he knew somehow the carnage he saw was of his own making.

He called his cousin Ron in Pennsylvania and asked if he could come to visit for a few weeks. Ron lived in an apartment a few miles west of the city of Reading. Ron knew Lonnie was a night owl, and they would both be sleeping during the day, which wouldn't cause any interruption of his third-shift lifestyle. So he agreed for Lonnie to visit for a short while.

Lonnie caught the next Amtrak train to Philadelphia, then he took a bus to Reading and finally took a cab to Ron's apartment. After the first two weeks, Ron agreed Lonnie could stay for a few extra weeks longer since things had been going so smoothly. That was until the previous evening.

Now Lonnie was back where he started a month earlier confused, frustrated, and suffering from guilt over yet another death, and this time, it wasn't a group of thugs bent on hurting him but a defenseless woman. He drove away in the dead girl's car from the latest unspeakable scene and contemplated what he should do next. He had to figure out what was wrong with him, and there was definitely something very wrong. Up until two months earlier, his life had been typical and normal; that was obviously no longer the case. Because if he truly was responsible for the savagery he had witnessed at each of those horrible events, Lonnie would have to do something.

He turned up the fan on the car heater enjoying the warm air surrounding him taking away the chill and helping to dry his clothing. When he got to Ron's apartment, he crept inside, being careful not to wake him and gathered up all of his belongings. Then he wrote a note thanking Ron but saying he needed to get back to the city, start looking for another job and get his life back on track.

Then Lonnie took his meager belongings and climbed back into the girl's car, pointing it in the direction of New York City. As he drove, he thought more about when all the strangeness had started trying to pinpoint an incident, which might have served as a catalyst to trigger the horrid events. The only weird thing he could recall was the incident, which happened three months earlier with that weird Goth chick at the nightclub.

Lonnie had stopped by one of the city's slightly freaky nightclubs after hearing a number of his buddies bragging about the quality of the girls frequenting the place. He hadn't been disappointed. The place was crawling with some of the hottest women he had seen in a long time. Lonnie was standing by the bar waiting for his drink when an incredibly attractive Goth-looking girl approached him and without preamble kissed him smack on the lips prying his lips open with her tongue then sending said tongue halfway down his throat.

He stood looking at her in shock for a moment, then introduced himself and offered to buy her a drink learning her name was Cassandra. Next thing he knew, they were in an alley behind the bar up, and he had her pressed against a brick wall. He recalled she was like a wild animal, and things were going great until she bit him hard on the shoulder—not a love bite or anything of that nature but a full-on-sink-your-teeth-in-and-draw-blood type of bite.

That act alone put a damper on what might have proven to be a pleasant event. Lonnie had pushed her away, fighting back the urge to haul off and punch her in the face. However, his mother had raised him never to hit a woman, even a psycho bitch like that one. He recalled she had backed down the alley laughing at him.

As she walked away, she said something like, "I'll be seeing you again, Lonnie. I chose you. You're one of us now."

He had no idea what she meant by the remark and at the time, passed it off as a wacky comment from a crazy chick.

Now, driving up I-95 toward New York, Lonnie started to wonder what she had meant. He certainly had changed since that event.

"I chose you. You're one of us now." he heard the strange girl say in his mind again.

He looked over at the passenger's seat, and for a second, he saw the Goth chick sitting there smiling at him with blood running down her chin and her eyes glowing yellow-red like a wild animal's. For a moment, he almost lost control of the car but managed to regain his composure. Then the girl was gone. The last thing he needed was to be pulled over by a cop in a dead girl's car.

Speaking of the car, Lonnie had formulated a plan to take the car to any one of several choice neighborhoods in the city. He was going to wipe off all of his fingerprints and then leave it there with the windows open and the keys in the ignition. He then planned to take the subway back to his hotel. He figured it might take all of a half-hour for the thing to disappear never to be seen again

Lonnie arrived back in the Big Apple shortly after noon. Then after dumping the car, he returned home, walking up the stairs to his apartment exhausted. As he entered the apartment, he noticed something strange. He couldn't explain it, but the hair seemed to rise on the back of his neck, and his senses tingled; he somehow knew he wasn't alone. He walked into his living room and found the Goth chick, Cassandra, from three months earlier, relaxing in his favorite chair.

"Hi, Lonnie," she said with a comfortable attitude suggesting they were old friends, and her being in his apartment was normal.

"What are you doing here?" he asked, still a bit shocked to see her.

"Why, silly, I've been waiting for you to come home." She slowly rose from the chair and walked toward him. She ran her fingers along the buttons of his shirt sensually. "I was starting to think you might never come back to me."

Lonnie pushed her hands down and said sternly, "Look, Cassandra. I don't know what you think you're doing here, but this isn't your home, and you've got no business being here."

"Oh, Lonnie," she said with a smile, "you just don't seem to understand. I like you. I mean, I really like you a lot. That's why I chose you, and why we'll be together from now on."

Lonnie thought aloud, "That's what you said the night we met. You said you'd chosen me. What did it mean? What are you talking about?"

Cassandra asked with a quizzical expression, "Tell me, Lonnie. Has anything strange happened to you lately you can't seem to explain? Maybe something you did or think you might have done, which might be considered out of character for you."

Lonnie saw the dead gang members and the dead girl flash across his mind. Then he saw Cassandra looking at him with recognition as if she could read his thoughts.

She said coyly, "Oh my, Lonnie. Have you been a bad boy? Did you maybe have a nasty run in a month or so ago with some bad gang members?"

"How did you know about . . ." Lonnie stopped himself before saying more than he wanted to.

Cassandra continued, "How did I know about that, you wanted to ask? Well, I knew about it because I was there. Yes, I was right there with you."

"Y . . . y . . . you . . . w . . . w . . . were . . . th . . . th . . . there?" he stammered.

"Yes, sir-ee! I was right there by your side," she informed him, "and I planned on being with you last night as well, but for some reason, you weren't around. Which means you likely got yourself into some trouble all by our lonesome, I suppose."

Lonnie's head was spinning, "What's going on, Casandra? What's wrong with me? Why is all this happening to me?" He wanted to bolt from the room and leave this strange woman behind, but he had to get to the bottom of this.

"I'd better explain this all to you, Lonnie," she replied. "You see that night at the club in the alley, remember? Well it was time for me to choose a mate, and there was something about you, I found so irresistible I couldn't help myself. So I decided right then and there to choose you to be my mate."

"Choose a mate?" Lonnie said, questioning. "You bit me on the shoulder, and you, you drew blood."

"Oh, I did a lot more than, Lonnie, my sweet," she said. "Do you know what a lycanthrope is?"

Lonnie thought for a moment then replied, "A lycanthrope? No, is it some sort of plant or something?"

Cassandra chuckled, "No, Lonnie. A lycanthrope is a shapeshifter, what you know as a werewolf. I'm a werewolf, and now thanks to me, you're one too."

"That's ridiculous!" Lonnie argued. "It's all nonsense and old wives' tales. You know, it's nothing but a legend. It isn't real."

"Lonnie. I want you to think real hard about what happened in the alley last month and what probably happened to you last night. Those were both nights of full moons. That's why you changed. You changed so you could hunt. I was there for your first kill in the alley. I was there to help you, although to be honest, you really didn't need much help. I just had to take care of one or two of them who almost got away. But you were a natural."

Lonnie stood staring in shock, "But I don't recall much of any of what happened."

"That's typical. But soon you'll become more aware, and then you'll look forward to the change with great anticipation. Eventually, when you become more experienced, you'll be able to change at will and won't need the help of the full moon. Then you'll know you've become complete."

Lonnie contemplated, "And I'm supposed to be your mate?"

"Yes. I've marked you, so none of the others will try to claim you. "

"Others?" He questioned.

Cassandra explained, "Yes, others. We're a pack. We live together, hunt together, and take care of each other. You won't need to worry about your old life any longer: your job, your friends, your family, or this apartment. You'll come to live with the pack, and we'll show you the way of the wolf. We'll teach you to use your new powers. We'll turn you into a great hunter, and perhaps someday you might be king of the pack, and when that happens, I'll be your queen."

"But I don't want to hunt and kill people. It's not who I am."

"It may not be who you were," she said, "but it's who you are now. Here, let me prove it to you."

Cassandra walked to the door leading to Lonnie's bedroom. She slowly opened the door, and Lonnie was shocked to see a beautiful young woman tied and gagged spread out naked on his bed, her arms and legs bound to the four posts. The bound woman looked at him with fear of anticipation at what was to come. There were cuts at various locations along her body, and blood stained the bedsheets.

"Now, Lonnie," Cassandra said, "you need to accept who you are. You need to embrace the wolf within you. You need to hunt. You need to kill."

Lonnie's sense of smell reached a level he never believed possible. He could smell the girl's blood. He could smell her sweat. He could smell her fear. His sight could see beyond her physical presence seeing a type of reddish-orange glow surround her obviously brought on by her fear. He could hear her heart thumping hard inside her chest and could feel his own heart begin to thump harder in anticipation.

"That's it, Lonnie," Cassandra prodded. "Smell her blood, Lonnie. Let the fever grow inside you. You want to feast on her flesh, Lonnie. Change, Lonnie, change!" Cassandra's voice grew louder with each shout of encouragement.

Lonnie could feel the change starting. He looked down at his hands and saw his fingers lengthening, darkening in color, and becoming leathery in appearance as his nails grew out into long yellowed razor-sharp claws. Turning his hands over, he saw coarse animal-hair sprouting from the backs of them. He felt his canine teeth getting longer the bottom ones protruding upward from his salivating lower jaw. He kicked off his shoes to stop the pain he was feeling in his feet as they enlarged in size their nails growing to mirror the claws on his hands. He felt the urge to kill, to rip apart, to savage the helpless girl now tied to his bed. The smell of her blood was driving him into an uncontrollable frenzy.

With the roar of a wild beast he had become, Lonnie jumped up onto the bed eager to begin feasting on the entrails of the powerless victim. He stood over her body, looking down into her pleading eyes. Then in an instant, the night before came back to him, and in his mind's eye, he saw what he had done to the woman in Pennsylvania and was sickened by what he recalled. He understood this is what he had become. This is what Cassandra had turned him into; a savage grunting slobbering beast bent on slaughtering anyone and anything in his path. Standing over the naked woman, he raised his clawed hand high above his head, bringing it down quickly and slicing through the bonds, securing her to the bed.

Then in one rapid motion, he turned and lunged at Cassandra slashing and tearing at her with a fury he had never known before. He savagely gouged and cut her as blood and flaps of skin flew in every direction. He noticed she had begun to transform into her wolf form. As she changed, the wounds he had inflicted began to close up and miraculously heal right before his eyes. Lonnie understood if he didn't act quickly before the transformation was complete, she would likely kill him, as she was much more experienced at being a werewolf than he was.

Lonnie did the only thing he could think of. He buried his claws deep into her still human chest shattering her ribs into fragments, then he ripped her heart from its cavity, brought it to his mouth, and devoured it before her dying eyes. Cassandra collapsed to the floor in a heap as the transformation reversed itself, and she returned to her human appearance blood pooling on the floor next to her tattered remains.

Lonnie was suddenly aware of the other woman screaming. He turned to see her cowering in the corner in shock with tears streaming down her face. The urge to fall on her and rip her to shreds was almost more than Lonnie could suppress, but he was determined to keep hold of this remaining bit of his humanity. He began slowly transforming back to his human self as he gathered shoes and clothing and raced from the apartment.

Lonnie understood the life he once enjoyed was over forever. When the police found Cassandra's body in his apartment, the authorities would be after him. When the "pack" of werewolves found out what he had done to Cassandra, they too would likely try to hunt him down. He'd have to get out of town and away from any friends, relatives, or ties to his previous life. He'd be on the run, "a lone wolf," he thought to himself with a self-deprecating laugh. He had no idea what his life would be like from then on, but he was determined to find a way to keep the wolf inside him at bay and never hurt another human again. He could only hope he would be successful.

THE BEAST UNSEEN

By Thomas M. Malafarina

"**O**h sweet mother of God!" the police officer exclaimed as the ceiling light was switched on showering the room with an effervescent glow, providing a much too perfect view of the unimaginable carnage neither he nor any of his fellow officers would ever be able to forget. In fact, the horrifying sight would haunt all of their nightmares for many years to come.

"Oh, Good Christ in Heaven," another officer shouted, followed by cries of anguish and revulsion coming from the other officers in the room.

They were standing, mouths agape, staring in disbelief at the butchery surrounding them. The place was a slaughterhouse. Blood, entrails, body parts, and other unrecognizable fleshy fragments were strewn all about the room. The walls were streaked with gore. There was barely a surface anywhere in the room that didn't show signs of the abhorrent violence, which had taken place there. It looked as if someone had taken gallons of red paint, added several pounds of boiled noodles then tossed the entire mess into a large industrial fan.

Jim Fredrickson, the youngest member of the police squad and fortunately the one closest to the front door, turned quickly and staggered outside, his hand covering his mouth as a volcanic eruption of hot vomit forced its way out between his fingers. Once clear of the crime scene, he bent over the porch rail and let the contents of his stomach spew all over a clump of shrubbery. He was certain he would hear about it from Police Chief Matt Sinclair, but at least for the moment, he didn't care.

Bobby O'Neil, another officer, still inside, was far too shocked to react; he looked around in astonishment as if he had inadvertently found himself immersed in some sort of hellish nightmare landscape, which in fact he had. It was unlike anything he had ever seen in his life, and he hoped to God, he would never have to see anything like it again.

"What the hell could have possibly done this?" Police Chief Sinclair said aloud in a stunned raspy voice. He was standing at the front of the group and was equally as shocked as they were. Matthew Sinclair had seen many horrors in his twenty-seven years on the force, including victims of automobile fatalities and even small passenger plane crashes, but he had never seen anything like the sight he now was witnessing. "This place is a charnel house! What kind of savage would even think to do such a thing?"

It looked like a thousand spinning blades had flown into the room and puréed the victims like a giant blender chewing them into tiny crimson pieces. Sinclair wasn't even sure at this point how many victims he had. What was worse, he had no idea where to begin the identification process. He suspected this would be one for the lab boys to sort through, and he was very grateful for that fact. Because right now, all he wanted to do was be as far away from this horror as possible.

Taking a deep swallow trying to keep his own upset stomach from turning over, he asked, "What do we know about this place? Who's supposed to live here?"

O'Neill stepped up with a note pad, which trembled in his quivering hand and said in an equally shaky voice, "The 911 dispatcher said the house is owned by a John and Maria Stinson. They live, I mean, lived here with . . . Oh, Christ!"

"Come on, man," Sinclair demanded, "spit it out."

"They lived here with their five children, all under twelve," O'Neil said, then looked around the gut-wrenching spectacle in the room, realizing that somewhere among the tatters of what were once human beings were likely bits and pieces of this precious family. He swallowed hard and continued, "Two boys and three, three little girls."

"Sweet Jesus!" Sinclair said, "What sort of maniac are we dealing with here?"

O'Neil hesitated for a moment then said: "Chief, I don't think this was done by any man; any human."

Sinclair looked at him curiously and said, "What are you saying, Bob? Do you think an animal of some kind did this?"

"Well," O'Neil said, "look at this place Chief. I doubt anything but some sort of animal or may a bunch of animals, could have done this."

The Chief looked around the room reluctantly, knowing he had to study every aspect of the crime scene but wanting desperately not to have these images burned into his memory, yet knowing they would be. Maybe O'Neill had something there. In all of his years on the job, Sinclair had never seen any human inflict this sort of atrocity, even the craziest of the crazy.

He noticed a large framed blood-splattered family portrait hanging askew on the wall to his right. It was of the Stinson family; father, mother, and the five young children. Each of the kids was fair-haired with blue eyes, as were the parents. Large ruby-stained clumps of that same hair attached to shredded sections of scalp were scattered all about the horrifying scene.

It was becoming more difficult by the minute for the Chief to keep his focus. Suddenly, all he could think about were his own beautiful grandkids. He couldn't imagine such a fate befalling them. His emotions were heading in a variety of directions simultaneously. He wanted to run to his daughter's house and hug his grandkids, while at the same time, he wanted to find whoever had wiped out this family and put a bullet between their accursed eyes.

Then he noticed something he had missed during his initial glance around the room. On the far wall amid the stipples of crimson was a series of small blood-smeared handprints, looking as if a young child had walked along the wall using it for support. Sinclair carefully walked among the carnage doing his best not to disturb anything, and when he got closer to the wall, he noticed small bloody footprints on the tile floor, not shoeprints but bare footprints. The prints led down a hall and stopped outside of a hall closet.

"O'Neil!" Sinclair called, trying not to sound too excited. As Bobby O'Neil approached, Sinclair said nothing but pointed first to the handprints on the wall, then to the tiny footprints then to the door of the hall closet. He signaled for O'Neil to walk with him down the hall. Once outside of the closet, O'Neil drew his service revolver and pointed it along with his flashlight at the closet as Sinclair, using a handkerchief, grabbed the handle, twisted, and threw open the door.

At first, the closet appeared empty. Then O'Neil shouted. "Chief. There's a little girl in there! She's huddled near the back of the closet."

Sinclair looked around the door and peered inside. O'Neil was right. On the floor near the back of the closet a little girl of about six years old was sitting tightly against the wall with her bloody hands wrapped around her knees which she used to hide her face; as if in doing so she could protect herself from who or whatever had murdered the family outside. She was also barefoot, and Sinclair could see dried blood covered the bottoms of her feet as well.

O'Neil looked expectedly at Sinclair as if waiting for him to provide some guidance as to what he should do next. Sinclair looked at him sternly and jerked his head in the direction of the child, suggesting that O'Neil take the lead. O'Neil had young kids of his own and didn't project as large or intimidating a figure as Sinclair did. He placed his gun back into his holster, put away his flashlight, and got down on his hands and knees, crawling into the closet to speak to the girl.

After a few minutes, O'Neil backed out of the closet with the small girl in tow. Sinclair immediately noticed the girl was dark-haired and likely not one of the Stinson kids. Perhaps she was a cousin or a friend visiting or sleeping over for the night. Sinclair called out to Officer Mary Mortenson, the only female officer on the squad.

When Mortenson approached, Sinclair whispered, "This kid was hiding in the closet, she's likely traumatized. From what I can tell, she isn't one of the Stinson kids. They were all towheads. Maybe she's a friend or relative. We need to get her to talk. Take her outside away from all of this mess and see if you can get her to tell you anything. The ambulance should be here soon. Have them check her out as well. Mary, she may be the closest thing we have to a witness."

Mary nodded, then bent down and looked at the child's downcast face saying, "Honey? Don't be afraid. My name is Mary, and I'm here to take care of you. What's your name?" The young girl looked up with eyes that were void of all emotion, saying nothing. Mary sensed this girl was going to need a lot more help than she or any paramedics would be capable of providing. It would likely take years of psychological therapy to get over an ordeal as horrible as the one she must have witnessed. Mary could only hope the child had made it safely to the closet before the worst of the bloody carnage had taken place.

To Mary's surprise, the little girl let go of O'Neil's hand and raised both of her arms to go with Mary, who bent down and lifted the girl up, burying the child's head in the crook of her neck before heading down the hall. There was no reason for the poor darling to have to see the horror waiting in the main living room again. Once had most certainly been too much.

As Mary carefully made her way toward the front door, across what seemed like the vast expanse of the gruesome living room turned slaughterhouse Mary could see young Jim Fredrickson staggering back into the house, looking pale and worse for wear. She hated to leave her fellow officers in here, but the Chief had asked her to take care of the girl, so that was what she knew she had to do.

Sinclair and O'Neil reentered the living room seeing two officers, Jones and Farley, still standing in stunned silence. Sinclair also noticed that young Jim Frederickson had made it back inside. He didn't blame Jim for not being able to keep from puking his guts out. Sinclair was barely able to keep his own lunch in his stomach.

"Farley!" Sinclair called, "If you haven't already done so, call the forensic team and tell them we need them pronto!"

Sinclair was fairly certain that neither of the two officers had thought to call anyone and had probably been standing there like two slack-jawed morons since entering the terrible room of death.

"Uh, um," Farley stammered, "will do Chief." Then he got on his radio and passed the necessary information on to the dispatcher.

Sinclair said, "Jonesie and Fredrickson. Watch the front door and make sure no one but the forensic crew comes in here without clearing it with me." They both looked relieved to have a chance to turn their backs on this horror.

"Affirmative Chief!" Jones said as the two officers turned to head toward the door. But after only a few steps, they stopped dead in their tracks.

Mary Mortenson, who had been carrying the little girl to safety, was standing at the front door and seemed to be shaking almost uncontrollably. She still held the little girl in her arms. But the two officers could see something was very, very wrong, not just with Mary, but with the little girl as well.

The child was impossibly changing somehow. When they had last seen her, the girl's face had still been buried in the crook of Mary's neck, where she was apparently shielding her eyes from the horrors of the room but now . . .

"What the hell!" Jones shouted as Mary began to spasm even more violently. The little girl raised her head slightly, her eyes now peering out at the police officers. But they were no longer the eyes of a child, the eyes they had expected to see. The girl's head had tripled in size and two huge segmented insect eyes the size of softballs bugged out from under a bulbous wrinkled, leathery forehead. Her mouth, its mouth—they could no longer think of this creature as a little girl—had also become inhumanly large with massive lips and what seemed like hundreds of blood-stained long needle-like teeth, most of which were sunk several inches into Mary's neck.

As Mary's body twitched horribly, the stunned officers saw five long sharp claws exploding from inside her and out through her back, rapidly tearing upward until they reached her neck. At that point, the body split in half, and the now-dead woman's head flew across the room, striking an unsuspecting officer Jones directly between the eyes, killing him instantly. In a few seconds, the remaining officers would wish they had been as lucky as Jones had just been.

The creature now standing over Mary Mortenson's shattered corpse looked unlike anything Officer Farley, or young Officer Frederickson had ever seen in their soon to be terminated lives. Farley reached to grab for his gun, but at a speed, he had never anticipated, the creature shot across the room, simultaneously slicing off his right arm and raking its razor-sharp talons across Jim Frederickson's throat; severing his head from his shoulders. Then it buried its talons deep into Farley's stomach, ripping out his entrails and flinging them haphazardly across the room where that splattered against a wall, clinging momentarily until they slid down and oozed onto the floor.

Bob O'Neil rushed across the room toward the beast, his gun drawn and firing blindly, unfortunately not even hitting the creature once. Then just before the thing attacked him, O'Neil had a brief second of clarity before his life was ended, where he saw the creature in its entirety.

In its current hunkered position, the thing stood about four feet tall, its head a huge light bulb shaped thing with a high, bald forehead leading back to a horse's mane of long black hair. Between its two widely spaced segmented insectile eyes was a pig-like snout with two flaring nostrils, glistening with snot. The mouth from top to bottom had to be eight or ten inches containing its hideously long, sharp fangs. O'Neill could see pieces of Mary's flesh still clinging to the bloody needle-like teeth.

Its arms seemed to start near the top of its head and hung down ape-like dragging on the floor. The hands were huge, at least a foot or more long, and were tipped with long talon-like claws. Its torso was small in comparison to its head and long arms but was still very muscular and covered with long matted hair or fur. Its legs were equally long and currently bent in the squatted position. O'Neil could tell in his momentary glance that if it were standing up to its full height, the beast would be well over nine feet tall. Its feet were huge and had similar claws to those on its hands.

Before this brief observation had a chance to register, the creature sprang forward from its squatted location. In the matter of a millisecond, it was using those claws to slash and shred O'Neil to pieces. Although he died almost instantaneously, those few remaining seconds were the most agonizing he had ever experienced.

Then the thing turned and looked across the room at Chief Of Police Matt Sinclair. He was the only remaining human still alive in the slaughterhouse. He already had his gun drawn and pointed directly at the hideous creature. Before the thing even and a chance to think about attacking it heard the thunderous boom of Sinclair's weapon at the same instant, the back of its skull exploded in a shower of blood, bone, and grey matter. It collapsed on its back, dead on the floor.

By the time Sinclair walked over to examine the corpse, he was horrified to see it had returned to its human form; that of an innocent-looking six-year-old girl. She lay sprawled on the floor with a large caliber bullet hole in her forehead and the back of her skull blown out.

"What in the name of God have you done?" A frightened voice called out from the front door. Sinclair turned to see several people looking at him with horrified expressions of both disbelief and revulsion on their shocked faces.

Seeing their confusion, Sinclair stammered, "No, no, you don't, you don't understand. It, it wasn't . . ."

———•—•———

The official report of the incident from the local district attorney, which came out a few weeks after the incident, called the event "a tragedy" and Chief Sinclair's actions "unintentional and accidental." The official take on the event was that a collection of unknown wild animals had somehow found their way into the Stinson home, killing and partially devouring the unfortunate family. When the police came onto the scene, the home had been cleared, and the threat no longer deemed present.

Unfortunately, at some point during the investigation, the wild animals must have returned and caught the police by surprise and slaughtering most of them. It was assumed that in the chaos, Chief Sinclair must have tried to shoot one of the creatures, which apparently had been attacking a young girl, but he had inadvertently shot and killed the girl by mistake. Attempts to identify the girl or her next of kin were futile, and the girl remains a Jane Doe.

The report stated that Chief Sinclair had been relieved of duty and voluntarily agreed to retire from the police force. At the time the report was written, there were no plans to file criminal charges against Sinclair, and since the girl remains unidentified, no civil suit would likely follow either.

What the official report failed to mention was that former Police Chief Matthew Sinclair was committed to a psychiatric facility where he remains to this day sedated, lying in a hospital bed in an eight by ten padded room on twenty-four-hour suicide watch. He is completely non-communicative and spends his days staring into space, drooling, and repeating the phrase, "The beast unseen. The beast unseen."

REMEMBER WHEN

By Thomas M. Malafarina

"There is something haunting in the light of the moon; it has all the dispassionateness of a disembodied soul, and something of its inconceivable mystery." —Joseph Conrad

"The leaves of memory seemed to make a mournful rustling in the dark." —Henry Wadsworth Longfellow

Emily stood slightly bent forward in the cold night air, deep in concentration, resting the palms of her tightly clenched hands firmly against the dark rod iron railing, which surrounded the flagstone veranda, extending out from her second-floor bedroom. She looked out into the expanse of empty woodlands behind her home, with eyes accustomed to the night, as the engulfing blackness swirled around her like a shroud of death, embracing her like a dark, mysterious lover.

She was completely naked. The pale milky white skin of her back glistened with perspiration in the moonlight; her long blonde hair flowed ethereally in the soft night breeze. She didn't mind the chill in the air, and in fact, she seemed to desire it. Behind her, a set of double French doors stood open wide, the evening breeze rippling the sheer translucent gossamer-like curtains, creating a macabre ghostly dance as the sounds of the darkness surrounded her; crickets chirping, owls hooting and bullfrogs calling from the nearby creek.

The house where she stood wasn't exactly her home, but it was her present home, located in a rural section of western Berks County, Pennsylvania. She had no real home to speak of, and could scarcely recall anymore, that one particular place she had once thought of as home. She no longer had or desired to have any sort of permanent place to "put down roots" so to speak. Instead, out of necessity, she opted to move often, from place to place, from town to town, from country to country; it was always better that way.

She appeared to be only about twenty-five years old to those very few of her neighbors who had managed to get a glimpse her in the evenings, as was never seen during the day, which they all found quite odd. These local women, who liked to gossip with each other regularly, were all quite leery of her, not just because of her peculiar nocturnal lifestyle, but because she was a newcomer to the area, having relocated from places unknown.

The particular place where Emily had most recently chosen to reside was a tightly knit community of people who had all known each other for many years. They were slow to accept strangers from even just a few miles away, not to mention someone from possibly some distant land.

Most of those same women tended to keep to themselves in their isolated local cliques, having little interest in outsiders. This was especially true when it came to a single woman who was so young, so beautiful, and so potentially tempting to their less than trustworthy husbands.

Emily often laughed to herself when she thought of how the older women would be shocked beyond comprehension to know her real age. But then again, if they were ever to discover that closely guarded secret, then she supposed a little surprise would be the least of their problems. No sir, if they were to learn the truth, their days of sitting around their pools sipping margaritas and gossiping would be all over.

She slowly turned to face the open double doorway, and looking through the wide expanse to the inside of the bedroom, saw the man lying sprawled on his back across the king-size bed. He was likewise naked, but his arms and legs were thrown outward appearing to hang limply, the once-crisp white sheets now a disheveled mess, stained crimson.

The brightly painted white walls of the formerly immaculate bedroom were now splattered with rose-colored stippling, and the man's entrails lay spilled in a gelatinous heap between the legs of his rapidly cooling corpse; all bloody remnants from the carnage of her animal-like frenzy.

She now leaned her bare buttocks against the cold iron railing and stretched her arms far into the air forming an extended V-shape. The moonlight reflected off her firm, ample breasts, coated with shining cherry red blood splotches, as was her tight stomach. The still un-coagulated bloody fluid trickled slowly down the insides of her legs as well, forming a puddle on the patio floor beneath her.

The flagstone stretching out before her was a path of gruesome scarlet footprints, her footprints leading from the bedroom to the railing where she now stood. She stretched out all of her muscles and opened her mouth to an incredibly wide degree releasing an ear-piercing howl, which reverberated and echoed far into the distance, sounding like the cry of some wild woodland creature.

As she did so, two long, razor-sharp incisors extended downward from the top of her mouth as well as two slightly shorter yet equally fearsome oversized canines from her lower jaw glimmered in the moonlight. The pairs formed two sets of formidable weapons designed for carnivorous flesh-ripping, which she knew they did quite proficiently.

As she released her ear-piercing banshee's cry, several thick droplets of blood fell from her fangs and landed on her heaving breasts, trickling down along their swell to the sides where they hung precariously for a few seconds, before falling to the ground. Her eyes glowed with white-hot luminescent fire, and the front side of her face and hair glistened with a combination of perspiration, blood, and gore. The fury slowly began to leave her eyes, as she gradually was able to relax, allowing her to return from the realm of savage mayhem to a more rational and reasonable place of calm serenity.

It was over, at last, she thought, over once again. She had done what she had needed to do to try to quell the insatiable hunger growing inside of her as she had done countless times before. However, each time it became harder to control, and of late, the cravings seemed to come more frequently. For now, she could rest, having satisfied both her physical hunger as well as this new emerging feral desire.

She tried to recall the name of the dead man whose prone, eviscerated body now occupied her bed, but she couldn't. Had it been Brian, or William or maybe Charles? She couldn't recall and supposed it didn't really matter anyway. He was nothing more than a mere human, and he had served the purpose for which she had brought him here.

Emily followed the path of bloody footprints slowly back to the bedroom and examined the carnage she had created. As she walked, she looked more like a beautiful goddess than a bloodthirsty creature of the damned. Suddenly, quick images and brief glimpses of memory flashed through her mind.

She recalled the man's dying screams bubbling within his throat as she had bitten deep into his neck, severing his carotid artery, then systematically ripping and peeling back his flesh, exposing his musculature and spinal column. Looking at him now, dead in her bed, she was surprised that she hadn't completely decapitated him in her blind animal rage. She remembered how she had done something similar to several other victims of late. She understood something about her was changing, becoming more aggressive, more savage, something she knew she couldn't hope to control for very much longer.

She recalled how the man's eyes had looked pleadingly at her as his lifeblood rapidly drained away, and he had finally given in to the creeping black grip of death. The memory of the blood pumping in gushes from his shredded throat began to excite her anew, and for a moment, she felt a hot flush growing from deep within her signaling the animal rage was trying once again to take over.

"No," she screamed inside of her mind, knowing she had to suppress the growing sensations, believing if she gave in to the beast this time it would take over completely and she'd remain a mad, savage frothing animal incapable of any rational thought whatsoever. And if that happened, she'd be as good as dead. She would no longer be able to hide or protect her secret.

Trying to remain in control while looking at the man, she was astonished once again to see how savagely she had disemboweled him and spilled his steaming insides onto the sheets. She couldn't recall ever doing such a thing before, had no idea why she would have done so this time, and had absolutely no memory of doing it either. Something had apparently triggered a fury within her the likes of which she had previously been unaware. She believed she knew what was happening to her, and if what she thought was true, it was likely the same illness that had struck Bartholomew so long ago; the sickness, which had eventually destroyed her lover and mentor.

She decided she'd think about all of this later as she had important business to attend to and couldn't dwell on such things. She lifted the sheets and checked the stainless steel troughs positioned along the sides of the bed, which were there specifically to collect the blood running down over the sides of the bed. These troughs led to a series of glass containers connected to plastic tubing and were positioned underneath the bed. Despite the splatter on the walls and the wasted blood, which had soaked into the satin sheets, she had managed to collect a significant amount of fluid from this man.

Directly below the blood-soaked silky sheets were rubber mattress covers, which allowed the majority of the blood to flow into the troughs. She had to accept a small degree of waste, as it was what she thought of as a cost of doing business, an acceptable loss in order for her to lure the man to her bed with the promise of sexual favors. Yes, she could have hunted him down and killed him in the street, but this was much more efficient. She mentally scolded herself for losing control and for ravaging the man so severely. She was certain this time her actions had caused her to waste much more of his precious fluid than she had wanted to.

Nonetheless, with the new blood from this evening's kill combined with the supply she already had from a large variety of forest animals and some local cattle, she assumed there was enough to feed her for several weeks to come. At least the blood would help to take care of her physical needs. However, the more profound craving, the new bloodlust, which came from deeper inside, the desire to hunt, the longing to ravage and kill, was something which she had fought almost constantly these days. She had known it had been there, lurking in the background to a lesser degree for the past two hundred or more years, but it had always been easy for her to control until recently.

As she stood staring at the eviscerated corpse, she found herself thinking back to how it all began. Although she didn't enjoy reminiscing about the long-ago times, she found herself doing so more often of late, as if to suggest these memories were all she had. She understood she was completely alone and had been for far too many years and believed she would be for as long as she could endure.

She thought of these sometimes melancholy moments as her time to "Remember When." During these quiet, reflective moments after a kill, she often found herself recounting her rebirth from the human she had once been into whatever manner of creature she had become, and tonight was apparently to be no exception.

She recalled how, as a young woman living in the coal regions of Pennsylvania during the early 1800s, she had been practically starving, penniless, forced to work as a prostitute just to try to survive. As a young adult, Emily had moved from small mining town to mining town frequenting bars with the hopes of finding some drunken miner who might be willing to part with some of his meager wages in exchange for her companionship.

Emily Flannery, as she had been called during that time, had been brought to the United States in her mother's womb from Ireland and was born shortly after their arrival in Pennsylvania. Her mother had also been a prostitute, and Emily had never known her father. She doubted her mother ever had any idea which of her many clients the father might have been either.

When her mother died some fourteen years later, Emily found herself alone, with no home and no means of support, in an area where jobs for young girls were few and far between. Some of her mother's prostitute friends had taken Emily in, partly out of pity and partly out of greed for the moneymaking potential they saw in the beautiful young girl. The women immediately began teaching her the trade, so to speak, and she began working the streets in earnest just before the age of fifteen. She was quite developed for such a young girl, and with the right clothing and makeup, she could pass for much older, although many of the men preferred thinking of her at her real age. Most of the other prostitutes believed Emily was a natural and was born for the profession, which in a way she literally had been.

She practiced her craft, as it were for about ten years until, at the age of twenty-five, she met someone who changed her life forever. She recalled how she had been entertaining one particularly odd young gentleman of about thirty years old who seemed much different from anyone she had ever met before. He had a dark, brooding sort of personality, was something of an expensive dresser, apparently wealthy, and was someone who seemed much more refined than most of her regular working-class clients. He only sought her favors in the late evening hours and would always leave before dawn. Because of his wealth, and because of the special attention he always paid to Emily, he soon became her highest paying and most preferred customer. After a time, she was permitted to call on him at his own luxurious home.

Unlike most of the men she encountered, he seemed genuinely interested in Emily and spent many hours talking with her and asking her many intimate and personal questions about her life. She told him of her tragic past, the death of her mother, her introduction to prostitution at such a very young age, and how, although she longed for a different kind of life, she was forced to do what she did simply to survive. When he offered her a chance to take control of her life, of her future, and to break free of her current situation, she was extremely interested, although she assumed he was simply stringing her along as other men had done in the past.

The man, whose name was Bartholomew, spent so much time with her, that at his request, he soon became her sole patron and she began to trust him completely. Although she knew little of real love and was uncertain if she could love any man, she realized by his actions that Bartholomew had truly fallen in love with her, and she believed she might someday be able to learn to love him in return.

Perhaps it was simply a fantasy, or maybe she was lying to herself, she didn't know. But she did know it was something she needed, something she longed for more than anything else in the world.

One night while they were together and she was genuinely making love to him, not just doing the job he paid her to do, he began to change right before her eyes. The scene came back to her brief in horrifying fleeting visions, never really forming or becoming cohesive images. She recalled hearing him making animal-like grunting noises, which, although this was nothing new to the often-vocal Bartholomew, it somehow seemed more savage than what was typical. She noticed the muscles in his arms and chest tighten and saw his back and shoulders appearing to grow, perhaps double in size.

His face seemed to change as well; his eyes became white-hot glowing orbs as four large fangs began to protrude from his impossibly wide-open mouth. Even the rest of his face seemed to take on an animal-like appearance as his ears grew large and pointed, sliding back along the side of his skull as his nose seemed to become more of a snout, like that of a pig or a bat. His skin took on a grayish tint and was covered with slick perspiration. She could smell a foul stench all around her as if she was trapped inside a cave filled with wild animals.

Next, she recalled a sharp pain across the front of her neck as he apparently had savagely ripped at the flesh of her throat. She remembered seeing his wildly insane eyes, crimson covered fangs, and blood-splattered animal face fading as everything in her field of vision suddenly went black.

Emily didn't know how long she had been unconscious, but when she awoke, she was in the basement of Bartholomew's home in the pitch darkness illuminated by a single candle. She was lying on the floor on a blood-soaked mattress, chained to a nearby water pipe as Bartholomew sat quietly across the room from her on a rocking chair. He was naked as was she, and she felt a cold, damp chill racing through her body, colder than any she had ever felt before.

Of all the scattered images, she recalled from that fateful evening, that one particular image was by far the most vivid. She remembered the sight of Bartholomew sitting in the rocker and recalled looking into his familiar, loving eyes filled with such great despair; she realized something must have gone horribly wrong.

Bartholomew came to the side of her blood-soaked mattress in tears and fell to his knees, pleading for her forgiveness. She tugged at the chains, which held her and was suddenly terrified of the man whom only a short while ago she was sure she was beginning to love. He explained the chains were just a temporary measure for her protection until he could make the entire situation clearer for her.

He told her how he loved her more than life itself. However, because of what had happened, he feared she'd never be able to return his love and might even grow to despise him. Disoriented, Emily didn't understand what he was saying, as the fear within her steadily grew, but she nonetheless forced herself to remain calm and to listen to what he had to say.

Bartholomew said he had once been human like her a long time ago but was human no longer. He explained how he was actually not really thirty years old but was, in fact, over three hundred. He said he was some sort of demon, a beast, through a curse placed upon him by an old village witch. Although it was true he was wealthy and loved her with all of his heart, he was no longer a man but a vile creature, one whose nature he, himself, still didn't completely understand.

Then Bartholomew told of how he noticed during the past year or so, changes were beginning to occur in him, which caused him to lose control over what he referred to as "the beast" within him.

He said while they were making love, he was thinking about of how much he adored her and could tell by the look in her eyes that she too loved him. That single realization had made his emotions surge to the point where he thought he could stand it no longer. Then, with his guard down, he hadn't felt the beast come forward, and as a result, he must have lost control because he blacked out and could remember nothing.

When he returned to awareness, he had seen he had ripped Emily's throat out, and he was certain he had killed her. He had become so distraught at the thought of his taking the life of the only woman he had ever loved, that he brought her body down into his cellar to be with her alone for one last night. He told Emily he planned on sitting by her side all night, with the intention of killing himself in the morning. He told her the sun was deadly for him and planned on ending his life by walking out into the morning sunlight and allowing it to burn the flesh from his body.

Emily didn't quite understand everything Bartholomew was saying and knew nothing of the creature he claimed to be. So much of what he said made little sense to her, but she still trusted Bartholomew and listened intently so she might learn. She could see the genuine love and sorrow in his expression, and instead of feeling anger toward him, she only felt sadness and pity.

He looked up at Emily from bended knee with pleading eyes and begged her to stay with him. He said he would explain everything to her if she would just give him a chance. Despite everything, she realized she still loved and trusted him, and understood she had no life without him, so she agreed. Then she soon learned she too had become the same type of being as Bartholomew. The witch's curse had spread like a disease from his blood to hers.

She lived with Bartholomew for the next several years as he did his best to school her in the ways of the creature he was and which he had unknowingly made her. He didn't have an actual name to refer to what manner of beings they were; he simply knew they were different from the humans. He understood they were neither alive nor dead, they didn't appear to age, and he had no idea how long their life span might actually be.

Some of the local townspeople told tales of creatures that were somewhat similar to her and Bartholomew, beings they referred to by many different names. Some of the Greek immigrants call them vrykolakas, while the Romanians called them strigoi. Some other Eastern European miners called spoke of vampires. Still, others told tales of werewolves and shape-shifting lycanthropes. Still, none of these tales corresponded exactly with what manner of creatures they were. Emily was unsure how to describe them, and Bartholomew never cared enough to embrace any of the many possible descriptions.

He explained she had been the first in his long life, who had transformed into a creature such as he was. He knew of no other beings like them anywhere in the world. He always assumed there must be similar beings somewhere, but he had never encountered any. To the best of his knowledge, they were alone together.

Bartholomew preferred to live in the present rather than dwell on the past, and taught Emily whatever she needed to learn to survive in her new condition. He showed her how to hunt and feed on the blood of others and how best to avoid detection from the local population. He explained her strengths as well as her weaknesses. Bartholomew warned her about how the sunlight could burn her flesh and would destroy her. He explained she could quite possibly live forever if she chose to, but she die if she was not careful and fell into the hands of the humans.

Whenever she recalled this particular instruction, she couldn't help but appreciate its irony. I was a band of such self-proclaimed demon hunters who had captured Bartholomew and driven a wooden stake through his heart then impaled him high on a pole, as the morning sun rose brightly and burned his body to a crisp. The crucifix and garlic which the superstitious fools had hung around his neck and the holy water they had sprinkled on his forehead as well as the wooden steak they had driven through his heart did nothing to harm him whatsoever; nor did the silver daggers they plunged into him time and time again. However, once they had managed to overpower and immobilize him, they were able to allow the sun to wreak its havoc upon him.

Emily recalled how, toward the end of his life, Bartholomew hadn't really been himself for quite some time. He had started to change shortly after their first decade or two together in a way very similar to how she was now finding herself changing. He had become more savage, more animal-like, caring less about his physical appearance and well-being, and more about satisfying the ever-increasing bloodlust. Emily believed it was this; Bartholomew's giving in to his growing savage nature, which caused him to drop his guard, allowing the human hunters to capture and destroy him.

When she had spoken to him about this phenomenon during one of his more lucid moments, he explained how, over the years, the physical need for nourishment began to diminish, but a much deeper, a much more feral need arose. He warned her it might not show up for two hundred years or more, but she should watch for signs of its coming and try to learn to control it.

He described the feeling as something akin to what humans of their day called senility. Yes, it might have been true they were immune to virtually all of the diseases, which plagued humanity, giving them the potential for very long lives. However, perhaps it was the fact they had both started out as humans themselves, with human brains, which may have been a major contributing factor to the onset of the mental disorder. Neither of them knew for sure, and since there were no others of their kind to provide the answers to their many questions, they could only speculate.

Sometimes it seemed these events had happened such a long time ago to Emily, yet when she was playing "Remember When," it was as if it had just occurred yesterday. Now it appeared that after more than two hundred years, the same horrible affliction, which had taken her beloved Bartholomew, was wrapping its tentacles of insanity around her brain as well. And for the first time in a very long time, she was genuinely terrified.

She imagined herself transformed into a raving drooling beast unable to stop herself from rampaging and killing without purpose until she too was captured and killed. She didn't like the idea of someone else deciding when it was her time to die. There was something so horribly undignified about the idea; it sent pangs of revulsion to the very pit of her stomach.

She knew she was alone in the world, the only one of her kind; she too had never found another like her. She had been able to travel all over the world during the past more than two hundred years thanks to the fortune, Bartholomew had left for her.

She understood he had, in fact, "created" her quite accidentally. Bartholomew had fallen in love with Emily and had been heartsick when his savage side took over, and he had thought he had destroyed her. Until she had awoken from her slumber of death and discovered she shared the same condition as he, Bartholomew had never known such a thing had been possible.

For a time, he had considered trying to create others of their kind, perhaps produce an army of beings just like he and Emily but decided it might be more prudent to wait a bit to observe her and see what effect the change might have on her. However, as his mind slowly began to deteriorate, and he slipped further into the belly of the beast, he never had the opportunity to do so.

Emily looked around the bloody bedroom, having returned from her mental journey to the land of "Remember When," back to the present. She felt strange as if she were walking a tightrope high above a crowd, trying not to lose her balance and fall to the ground below. She felt like she was losing a tug-of-war with her animal side and soon would slide into the world of the beast, knowing if she did, she might never return. She felt she was hanging onto what little still remained of Emily but would soon be lost forever.

While she still was able to think rationally, Emily made her decision. She looked at the blood-splattered digital clock on the dresser next to the bed. It was five thirty-two in the morning. Sunrise was less than a half-hour away.

She walked purposefully down the stairs to the first floor of the large house and out into the kitchen, where she searched through a utility drawer and found several disposable lighters as well as a metal canister of lighter fluid. She systematically walked from room to room, setting fire to all of the drapes, curtains, and virtually anything that would burn.

Next, she returned to the second floor and repeated the process throughout that level, ending in her bedroom. She could smell the acrid odor of smoke wafting up from the lower level as the fire spread. She looked out through the open French doors with their curtains ablaze and could see the sun beginning to rise over the eastern horizon. How long had it been since she had seen a sunrise? She had forgotten just how beautiful it could be.

Emily started to walk slowly out once again onto the flagstone veranda, feeling the pull of the beast within her trying to force her to flee to safety, but she knew what she must do. This would be her last sunrise, and she planned on spending what time she had remaining playing "Remember When" and thinking about her long lost lover, Bartholomew.

Still naked, she approached the railing of patio and reached her arms high into the air, giving one final mournful cry for her lost love as her skin began to steam under the growing light of the sun. Soon her flesh bubbled into large puss-filled blisters, which quickly popped open and subsequently burst into flames. Now her cries were those of an animal in pain as the flesh began to slough from her bones, which in turn crumpled onto a pile before catching afire and burning quickly to dust, blowing away in the morning breeze. As Emily's conciseness faded to nothingness among the searing pain, she was able to "Remember When" one final time and thought only of Bartholomew.

THE MORTAL IMMORTAL

BY MARY SHELLEY

July 16, 1833.—This is a memorable anniversary for me; on it, I complete my three hundred and twenty-third year! The Wandering Jew?—certainly not. More than eighteen centuries have passed over his head. In comparison with him, I am a very young Immortal.

Am I, then, immortal? This is a question which I have asked myself, by day and night, for now, three hundred and three years, and yet cannot answer it. I detected a grey hair amidst my brown locks this very day—that surely signifies decay. Yet it may have remained concealed there for three hundred years—for some persons have become entirely white-headed before twenty years of age.

I will tell my story, and my reader shall judge for me. I will tell my story, and so contrive to pass some few hours of a long eternity, become so wearisome to me. Forever! Can it be? To live forever! I have heard of enchantments, in which the victims were plunged into a deep sleep, to wake, after a hundred years, as fresh as ever: I have heard of the Seven Sleepers—thus, to be immortal would not be so burdensome: but, oh! the weight of never-ending time—the tedious passage of the still-succeeding hours! How happy was the fabled Nourjahad!— But to my task. All the world has heard of Cornelius Agrippa. His memory is as immortal as his arts have made me. All the world has also heard of his scholar, who, unawares, raised the foul fiend during his master's absence, and was destroyed by him. The report, true or false, of this accident, was attended with many inconveniences to the renowned philosopher. All his scholars at once deserted him—his servants disappeared. He had no one near him to put coals on his ever-burning fires while he slept, or to attend to the changeful colors of his medicines while he studied. Experiment after experiment failed, because one pair of hands was insufficient to complete them: the dark spirits laughed at him for not being able to retain a single mortal in his service.

I was then very young—very poor—and very much in love. I had been for about a year the pupil of Cornelius, though I was absent when this accident took place. On my return, my friends implored me not to return to the alchymist's abode. I trembled as I listened to the dire tale they told; I required no second warning, and when Cornelius came and offered me a purse of gold if I would remain under his roof, I felt as if Satan himself tempted me. My teeth chattered—my hair stood on end;—I ran off as fast as my trembling knees would permit. My failing steps were directed whither for two years they had every evening been attracted,—a gently bubbling spring of pure living water, beside which lingered a dark-haired girl, whose beaming eyes were fixed on the path I was accustomed each night to tread. I cannot remember the hour when I did not love Bertha; we had been neighbors and playmates from infancy,—her parents, like mine, were of humble life, yet respectable,—our attachment had been a source of pleasure to them. In an evil hour, a malignant fever carried off both her father and mother, and Bertha became an orphan. She would have found a home beneath my paternal roof, but, unfortunately, the old lady of the near castle, rich, childless, and solitary, declared her intention to adopt her. Henceforth Bertha was clad in silk—inhabited a marble palace—and was looked on as being highly favored by fortune. But in her new situation among her new associates, Bertha remained true to the friend of her humbler days; she often visited the cottage of my father, and when forbidden to go thither, she would stray towards the neighboring wood, and meet me beside its shady fountain.

She often declared that she owed no duty to her new protectress equal in sanctity to that which bound us. Yet still, I was too poor to marry, and she grew weary of being tormented on my account. She had a haughty but an impatient spirit and grew angry at the obstacle that prevented our union. We met now after an absence, and she had been sorely beset while I was away; she complained bitterly, and almost reproached me for being poor. I replied hastily—"I am honest if I am poor!—were I not, I might soon become rich!"

This exclamation produced a thousand questions. I feared to shock her by owning the truth, but she drew it from me, and then, casting a look of disdain on me, she said,—"You pretend to love, and you fear to face the Devil for my sake!"

I protested that I had only dreaded to offend her;—while she dwelt on the magnitude of the reward that I should receive. Thus encouraged—shamed by her—led on by love and hope, laughing at my later fears, with quick steps and a light heart, I returned to accept the offers of the alchemist and was instantly installed in my office. A year passed away. I became possessed of no insignificant sum of money. Custom had banished my fears. In spite of the most painful vigilance, I had never detected the trace of a cloven foot, nor was the studious silence of our abode ever disturbed by demoniac howls. I still continued my stolen interviews with Bertha, and Hope dawned on me— Hope—but not perfect joy: for Bertha fancied that love and security were enemies, and her pleasure was to divide them in my bosom. Though true of heart, she was something of a coquette in manner; I was jealous as a Turk. She slighted me in a thousand ways, yet would never acknowledge herself to be in the wrong. She would drive me mad with anger and then force me to beg her pardon. Sometimes she fancied that I was not sufficiently submissive, and then she had some story of a rival, favored by her protectress. She was surrounded by silk-clad youths—the rich and gay. What chance had the sad-robed scholar of Cornelius compared with these?

On one occasion, the philosopher made such large demands upon my time, that I was unable to meet her as I was wont. He was engaged in some mighty work, and I was forced to remain, day and night, feeding his furnaces and watching his chemical preparations. Bertha waited for me in vain at the fountain. Her haughty spirit fired at this neglect; and when at last I stole out during a few short minutes allotted to me for slumber and hoped to be consoled by her, she received me with disdain, dismissed me in scorn, and vowed that any man should possess her hand rather than he who could not be in two places at once for her sake. She would be revenged! And truly, she was. In my dingy retreat, I heard that she had been hunting, attended by Albert Hoffer. Albert Hoffer was favored by her protectress, and the three passed in cavalcade before my smoky window. Methought that they mentioned my name; it was followed by a laugh of derision, as her dark eyes glanced contemptuously towards my abode.

Jealousy, with all its venom and all its misery, entered my breast. Now I shed a torrent of tears, to think that I should never call her mine; and, anon, I imprecated a thousand curses on her inconstancy. Yet, still, I must stir the fires of the alchymist, still attend on the changes of his unintelligible medicines.

Cornelius had watched for three days and nights, nor closed his eyes. The progress of his alembics was slower than he expected: in spite of his anxiety, sleep weighed upon his eyelids. Again and again, he threw off drowsiness with more than human energy; again and again, it stole away his senses. He eyed his crucibles wistfully. "Not ready yet," he murmured; "will another night pass before the work is accomplished? Winzy, you are vigilant—you are faithful— you have slept, my boy—you slept last night. Look at that glass vessel. The liquid it contains is of a soft rose-color: the moment it begins to change hue, awaken me—till then, I may close my eyes. First, it will turn white, and then emit golden flashes; but wait not till then; when the rose-color fades, rouse me." I scarcely heard the last words, muttered, as they were, in sleep. Even then, he did not quite yield to nature. "Winzy, my boy," he again said, "do not touch the vessel—do not put it to your lips; it is a philter—a philter to cure love; you would not cease to love your Bertha—beware to drink!"

And he slept. His venerable head sunk on his breast, and I scarce heard his regular breathing. For a few minutes, I watched the vessel—the rosy hue of the liquid remained unchanged. Then my thoughts wandered—they visited the fountain, and dwelt on a thousand charming scenes never to be renewed— never! Serpents and adders were in my heart as the word "Never!" half formed itself on my lips. False girl!—false and cruel! Nevermore would she smile on me as that evening she smiled at Albert. Worthless, detested woman! I would not remain unrevenged—she should see Albert expire at her feet—she should die beneath my vengeance. She had smiled in disdain and triumph—she knew my wretchedness and her power. Yet what power had she?—the power of excit- ing my hate—my utter scorn—my—oh, all but indifference! Could I attain that—could I regard her with careless eyes, transferring my rejected love to one fairer and truer, that was indeed a victory!

A bright flash darted before my eyes. I had forgotten the medicine of the adept; I gazed on it with wonder: flashes of admirable beauty, more bright than those which the diamond emits when the sun's rays are on it, glanced from the surface of the liquid; and odor the most fragrant and grateful stole over my sense; the vessel seemed one globe of living radiance, lovely to the eye, and most inviting to the taste. The first thought, instinctively inspired by the grosser sense, was, I will—I must drink. I raised the vessel to my lips. "It will cure me of love—of torture!" Already I had quaffed half of the most delicious liquor ever tasted by the palate of man when the philosopher stirred. I started—I dropped the glass—the fluid flamed and glanced along the floor, while I felt Cornelius's gripe at my throat, as he shrieked aloud, "Wretch! you have destroyed the labor of my life!"

The philosopher was totally unaware that I had drunk any portion of his drug. His idea was, and I gave a tacit assent to it, that I had raised the vessel from curiosity, and that, frightened at its brightness, and the flashes of intense light it gave forth, I had let it fall. I never undeceived him. The fire of the medicine was quenched—the fragrance died away—he grew calm, as a philosopher should under the heaviest trials, and dismissed me to rest.

I will not attempt to describe the sleep of glory and bliss, which bathed my soul in paradise during the remaining hours of that memorable night. Words would be faint and shallow types of my enjoyment, or of the gladness that possessed my bosom when I woke. I trod air—my thoughts were in heaven. Earth appeared heaven, and my inheritance upon it was to be one trance of delight. "This it is to be cured of love," I thought; "I will see Bertha this day, and she will find her lover cold and regardless; too happy to be disdainful, yet how utterly indifferent to her!" The hours danced away. The philosopher, secure that he had once succeeded, and believing that he might again, began to concoct the same medicine once more. He was shut up with his books and drugs, and I had a holiday. I dressed with care; I looked in an old but polished shield that served me for a mirror; I thought my good looks had wonderfully improved. I hurried beyond the precincts of the town, joy in my soul, the beauty of heaven and earth around me. I turned my steps toward the castle—I could look on its lofty turrets with a lightness of heart, for I was cured of love. My Bertha saw me afar off, as I came up the avenue. I know not what sudden impulse animated her bosom, but at the sight, she sprung with a light fawn-like bound down the marble steps and was hastening towards me. But I had been perceived by another person. The high-born old hag, who called herself her protectress, and was her tyrant, had seen me also; she hobbled, panting, up the terrace; a page, as ugly as herself, held up her train, and fanned her as she hurried along, and stopped my fair girl with a "How, now, my bold mistress? whither so fast? Back to your cage—hawks are abroad!"

Bertha clasped her hands—her eyes were still bent on my approaching figure. I saw the contest. How I abhorred the old crone who checked the kind impulses of my Bertha's softening heart. Hitherto, respect for her rank had caused me to avoid the lady of the castle; now, I disdained such trivial considerations. I was cured of love, and lifted above all human fears; I hastened forwards, and soon reached the terrace. How lovely Bertha looked! Her eyes flashing fire, her cheeks glowing with impatience and anger; she was a thousand times more graceful and charming than ever. I no longer loved—oh, no! I adored—worshipped—idolized her!

She had that morning been persecuted, with more than usual vehemence, to consent to an immediate marriage with my rival. She was reproached with the encouragement that she had shown him—she was threatened with being turned out of doors with disgrace and shame. Her proud spirit rose in arms at the threat; but when she remembered the scorn that she had heaped upon me, and how, perhaps, she had thus lost one whom she now regarded as her only friend, she wept with remorse and rage. At that moment, I appeared. "Oh, Winzy!" she exclaimed, "take me to your mother's cot; swiftly let me leave the detested luxuries and wretchedness of this noble dwelling—take me to poverty and happiness."

I clasped her in my arms with transport. The old dame was speechless with fury and broke forth into invective only when we were far on the road to my natal cottage. My mother received the fair fugitive, escaped from a gilt cage to nature and liberty, with tenderness and joy; my father, who loved her, welcomed her heartily; it was a day of rejoicing, which did not need the addition of the celestial potion of the alchymist to steep me in delight. Soon after this eventful day, I became the husband of Bertha. I ceased to be the scholar of Cornelius, but I continued his friend. I always felt grateful to him for having, unaware, procured me that delicious draught of a divine elixir, which, instead of curing me of love (sad cure! solitary and joyless remedy for evils which seem blessings to the memory), had inspired me with courage and resolution, thus winning for me an inestimable treasure in my Bertha. I often called to mind that period of trance-like inebriation with wonder. The drink of Cornelius had not fulfilled the task for which he affirmed that it had been prepared, but its effects were more potent and blissful than words can express. They had faded by degrees, yet they lingered long—and painted life in hues of splendor. Bertha often wondered at my lightness of heart and unaccustomed gaiety, for, before, I had been rather serious, or even sad, in my disposition. She loved me the better for my cheerful temper, and our days were winged by joy. Five years afterward, I was suddenly summoned to the bedside of the dying Cornelius. He had sent for me in haste, conjuring my instant presence. I found him stretched on his pallet, enfeebled even to death; all of life that yet remained animated his piercing eyes, and they were fixed on a glass vessel, full of roseate liquid. "Behold," he said, in a broken and inward voice, "the vanity of human wishes! a second time my hopes are about to be crowned, a second time they are destroyed. Look at that liquor—you may remember five years ago I had prepared the same, with the same success;—then, as now, my thirsting lips expected to taste the immortal elixir—you dashed it from me! and at present, it is too late."

He spoke with difficulty and fell back on his pillow. I could not help saying,—"How, revered master, can a cure for love restore you to life?"

A faint smile gleamed across his face as I listened earnestly to his scarcely intelligible answer. "A cure for love and for all things—the Elixir of Immortality. Ah! if now I might drink, I should live forever!" As he spoke, a golden flash gleamed from the fluid; a well-remembered fragrance stole over the air; he raised himself, all weak as he was—strength seemed miraculously to re-enter his frame—he stretched forth his hand—a loud explosion startled me—a ray of fire shot up from the elixir, and the glass vessel which contained it shivered to atoms! I turned my eyes towards the philosopher; he had fallen back—his eyes were glassy—his features rigid—he was dead!

But I lived, and was to live forever! So said the unfortunate alchymist, and for a few days, I believed his words. I remembered the glorious intoxication that had followed my stolen draught. I reflected on the change I had felt in my frame—in my soul—the bounding elasticity of the one—the buoyant lightness of the other. I surveyed myself in a mirror and could perceive no change in my features during the space of the five years, which had elapsed. I remembered the radiant hues and grateful scent of that delicious beverage—worthy the gift it was capable of bestowing—I was, then, IMMORTAL!

A few days after, I laughed at my credulity. The old proverb, that "a prophet is least regarded in his own country," was true with respect to me and my defunct master. I loved him as a man—I respected him as a sage—but I derided the notion that he could command the powers of darkness, and laughed at the superstitious fears with which he was regarded by the vulgar. He was a wise philosopher but had no acquaintance with any spirits but those clad in flesh and blood. His science was simply human, and human science, I soon persuaded myself, could never conquer nature's laws so far as to imprison the soul forever within its carnal habitation. Cornelius had brewed a soul-refreshing drink— more inebriating than wine—sweeter and more fragrant than any fruit: it pos- sessed probably strong medicinal powers, imparting gladness to the heart and vigor to the limbs; but its effects would wear out; already they were diminished in my frame. I was a lucky fellow to have quaffed health and joyous spirits, and perhaps a long life, at my master's hands, but my good fortune ended there: longevity was far different from immortality.

I continued to entertain this belief for many years. Sometimes a thought stole across me—Was the alchymist indeed deceived? But my habitual credence was that I should meet the fate of all the children of Adam at my appointed time—a little late, but still at a natural age. Yet it was certain that I retained a wonderfully youthful look. I was laughed at for my vanity in consulting the mirror so often, but I consulted it in vain—my brow was untrenched—my cheeks—my eyes—my whole person continued as untarnished as in my twentieth year.

I was troubled. I looked at the faded beauty of Bertha—I seemed more like her son. By degrees, our neighbors began to make similar observations, and I found at last that I went by the name of the Scholar bewitched. Bertha herself grew uneasy. She became jealous and peevish, and at length, she began to question me. We had no children; we were all in all to each other; and though, as she grew older, her vivacious spirit became a little allied to ill-temper, and her beauty sadly diminished, I cherished her in my heart as the mistress I idolized, the wife I had sought and won with such perfect love.

At last, our situation became intolerable: Bertha was fifty—I twenty years of age. I had, in very shame, in some measure adopted the habits of advanced age; I no longer mingled in the dance among the young and gay, but my heart bounded along with them while I restrained my feet, and a sorry figure I cut among the Nestors of our village. But before the time I mention, things were altered—we were universally shunned; we were—at least, I was—reported to have kept up an iniquitous acquaintance with some of my former master's supposed friends. Poor Bertha was pitied but deserted. I was regarded with horror and detestation.

What was to be done? we sat by our winter fire—poverty had made itself felt, for none would buy the produce of my farm, and often I had been forced to journey twenty miles to someplace where I was not known, to dispose of our property. It is true. We had saved something for an evil day—that day had come.

We sat by our lone fireside—the old-hearted youth and his antiquated wife. Again Bertha insisted on knowing the truth; she recapitulated all she had ever heard said about me and added her own observations. She conjured me to cast off the spell; she described how much more comely grey hairs were than my chestnut locks; she descanted on the reverence and respect due to age—how preferable to the slight regard paid to mere children: could I imagine that the despicable gifts of youth and good looks outweighed disgrace, hatred, and scorn? Nay, in the end, I should be burnt as a dealer in the black art, while she, to whom I had not deigned to communicate any portion of my good fortune, might be stoned as my accomplice. At length, she insinuated that I must share my secret with her and bestow on her like benefits to those I myself enjoyed, or she would denounce me—and then she burst into tears. Thus beset, methought it was the best way, to tell the truth. I reveled it as tenderly as I could and spoke only of a very long life, not of immortality—which representation, indeed, coincided best with my own ideas. When I ended, I rose and said,—"And now, my Bertha, will you denounce the lover of your youth?—You will not, I know. But it is too hard, my poor wife, that you should suffer for my ill-luck and the accursed arts of Cornelius. I will leave you—you have wealth enough, and friends will return in my absence. I will go; young as I seem and strong as I am, I can work and gain my bread among strangers, unsuspected and unknown. I loved you in youth; God is my witness that I would not desert you in age, but that your safety and happiness require it."

I took my cap and moved toward the door; in a moment, Bertha's arms were around my neck, and her lips were pressed to mine. "No, my husband, my Winzy," she said, "you shall not go alone—take me with you; we will remove from this place, and, as you say, among strangers, we shall be unsuspected and safe. I am not so old as quite to shame you, my Winzy, and I daresay the charm will soon wear off, and, with the blessing of God, you will become more elderly-looking, as is fitting; you shall not leave me."

I returned the good soul's embrace heartily. "I will not, my Bertha, but for your sake, I had not thought of such a thing. I will be your true, faithful husband while you are spared to me, and do my duty by you to the last." The next day we prepared secretly for our emigration. We were obliged to make great pecuniary sacrifices—it could not be helped. We realized a sum sufficient, at least, to maintain us while Bertha lived, and, without saying adieu to any one, quitted our native country to take refuge in a remote part of western France.

It was a cruel thing to transport poor Bertha from her native village, and the friends of her youth, to a new country, new language, new customs. The strange secret of my destiny rendered this removal immaterial to me, but I compassion-ated her deeply and was glad to perceive that she found compensation for her misfortunes in a variety of little ridiculous circumstances. Away from all tell-tale chroniclers, she sought to decrease the apparent disparity of our ages by a thousand feminine arts—rouge, youthful dress, and assumed juvenility of manner. I could not be angry. Did I not myself wear a mask? Why quarrel with hers, because it was less successful? I grieved deeply when I remembered that this was my Bertha, whom I had loved so fondly and won with such transport—the dark-eyed, dark-haired girl, with smiles of enchanting archness and a step like a fawn—this mincing, simpering, jealous old woman. I should have revered her grey locks and withered cheeks, but thus!—It was my work, I knew, but I did not, the less deplore this type of human weakness.

Her jealousy never slept. Her chief occupation was to discover that, in spite of outward appearances, I was myself growing old. I verily believe that the poor soul loved me truly in her heart, but never had a woman so tormenting a mode of displaying fondness. She would discern wrinkles in my face and decrepitude in my walk, while I bounded along in youthful vigor, the youngest looking of twenty youths. I never dared address another woman. On one occasion, fancying that the belle of the village regarded me with favoring eyes, she brought me a grey wig. Her constant discourse among her acquaintances was that though I looked so young, there was ruin at work within my frame, and she affirmed that the worst symptom about me was my apparent health. My youth was a disease, she said, and I ought at all times to prepare, if not for a sudden and awful death, at least to awake some morning white-headed and bowed down with all the marks of advanced years. I let her talk—I often joined in her conjectures. Her warnings chimed in with my never-ceasing speculations concerning my state, and I took an earnest, though painful, interest in listening to all that her quick wit and excited imagination could say on the subject.

Why dwell on these minute circumstances? We lived on for many long years. Bertha became bedrid and paralytic; I nursed her as a mother might a child. She grew peevish and still harped upon one string—of how long I should survive her. It has ever been a source of consolation to me that I performed my duty scrupulously towards her. She had been mine in youth; she was mine in age, and at last, when I heaped the sod over her corpse, I wept to feel that I had lost all that really bound me to humanity.

Since then, how many have been my cares and woes, how few and empty my enjoyments! I pause here in my history—I will pursue it no further. A sailor without rudder or compass, tossed on a stormy sea—a traveler lost on a widespread heath, without landmark or stone to guide him—such I have been: more lost, more hopeless than either. A nearing ship, a gleam from some far cot, may save them; but I have no beacon except the hope of death. Death! mysterious, ill-visaged friend of weak humanity! Why alone of all mortals have you cast me from your sheltering fold? Oh, for the peace of the grave! the deep silence of the iron-bound tomb! that thought would cease to work in my brain, and my heart beat no more with emotions varied only by new forms of sadness!

Am I immortal? I return to my first question. In the first place, is it not more probably that the beverage of the alchymist was fraught rather with longevity than eternal life? Such is my hope. And then be it remembered that I only drank half of the potion prepared by him. Was not the whole necessary to complete the charm? To have drained half the Elixir of Immortality is but to be half-immortal—my For-ever is thus truncated and null.

But again, who shall number the years of the half of eternity? I often try to imagine by what rule the infinite may be divided. Sometimes I fancy age advancing upon me. One grey hair I have found. Fool! do I lament? Yes, the fear of age and death often creeps coldly into my heart, and the more I live, the more I dread death, even while I abhor life. Such an enigma is man—born to perish—when he wars, as I do, against the established laws of his nature.

But for this anomaly of feeling surely I might die: the medicine of the alchymist would not be proof against fire—sword—and the strangling waters. I have gazed upon the blue depths of many a placid lake, and the tumultuous rushing of many a mighty river, and have said, peace inhabits those waters; yet I have turned my steps away, to live yet another day. I have asked myself whether suicide would be a crime in one to whom thus only the portals of the other world could be opened. I have done all, except presenting myself as a soldier or duelist, an objection of destruction to my—no, not my fellow mortals, and therefore I have shrunk away. They are not my fellows. The inextinguishable power of life in my frame and their ephemeral existence places us wide as the poles asunder. I could not raise a hand against the meanest or the most powerful among them.

Thus have I lived on for many a year—alone, and weary of myself—desirous of death, yet never dying—a mortal immortal. Neither ambition nor avarice can enter my mind, and the ardent love that gnaws at my heart, never to be returned—never to find an equal on which to expend itself—lives there only to torment me.

This very day I conceived a design by which I may end all—without self-slaughter, without making another man a Cain—an expedition, which mortal frame can never survive, even endued with the youth and strength that inhabits mine. Thus I shall put my immortality to the test and rest forever—or return, the wonder and benefactor of the human species.

Before I go, a miserable vanity has caused me to pen these pages. I would not die and leave no name behind. Three centuries have passed since I quaffed the fatal beverage; another year shall not elapse before, encountering gigantic dangers—warring with the powers of frost in their home—beset by famine, toil, and tempest—I yield this body, too tenacious a cage for a soul which thirsts for freedom, to the destructive elements of air and water; or, if I survive, my name shall be recorded as one of the most famous among the sons of men; and, my task achieved, I shall adopt more resolute means, and, by scattering and annihilating the atoms that compose my frame, set at liberty the life imprisoned within, and so cruelly prevented from soaring from this dim earth to a sphere more congenial to its immortal essence.

www.ingramcontent.com/pod-product-compliance
Lightning Source LLC
Chambersburg PA
CBHW030514020726
47494CB00004B/1093